THE GIRLS FROM THE BEACH

ALSO BY ANDIE NEWTON

The Girl I Left Behind
The Girl from Vichy

THE GIRLS FROM THE BEACH

Andie Newton

An Aria Book

This edition first published in United Kingdom in 2021 by Aria,
an imprint of Head of Zeus

A CIP catalogue record for this book is available from the
British Library.

9 7 5 3 1 2 4 6 8

ISBN (PB): 9781800246249
ISBN (E): 9781789546699

Cover design © Leah Jacobs-Gordon

Typeset by Siliconchips Services Ltd UK

Printed and bound in Great Britain by
CPI Group (UK) Ltd, Croydon cr0 4yy

Aria
c/o Head of Zeus
First Floor East
5–8 Hardwick Street
London EC1R 4RG

www.ariafiction.com

To Matt, Zane, and Drew

Prologue

The delivery arrived just after lunch: a bulky cardboard box wheeled in on a dolly by a man dressed in a brown uniform. The reporter sent for it that morning from the storage unit where it had sat for over five years, paying extra to have it messengered express.

He jumped up from his chair where he'd been anxiously waiting, and peeked through his office blinds, watching the delivery man weave his way through the second-floor newsroom, past the drum of electric typewriters and correspondents on phones.

He tipped the messenger well; it wasn't every day a reporter was hand-delivered the story of a lifetime—the kind that made you wonder, the kind that made the little hairs on the back of your neck stand up—the kind that made you question what you knew about the war and its heroine nurses.

The box belonged to his mother, and he felt a pang of remembrance when he saw her handwriting next to the curling postage stamps. He didn't think much of the box at the time she'd sent it to him; it was something to go through later. But when his boss asked him to work on a series of stories about WWII nurses, he remembered what his mom told him about the women who disappeared.

He used his scissors like box cutters to cut through the tape, knowing curious reporters on the other side of the door were listening, and probably drooling. He stood back after looking inside, hand over mouth; there was more than he expected. He dug in with both hands, sifting through old photographs of his mother's field hospital and women of the 45th, letters, and medals, and notes.

And a single diary entry dated 1945.

We'd heard stories about the nurses in tent seven. A secret mission, stolen money, and spies, some of them posing as soldiers. One thing I know for certain: Kit was involved. She might be the only person who can shed light on those five days in September and tell the world what happened when the women went missing.

I

KIT

Lorraine, France

September 1944

A man burst into our clearing station unannounced, scanning the lot of us—three nurses and one surgeon caring for the Third Army. After standing in the open tent flaps and letting the rain and cold push in, he stomped over to the operating table where the doctor and our chief nurse were up to their elbows in a private's abdomen. A heated exchange followed.

"But I'm two nurses down from yesterday!" the doctor spouted, thrusting a pointed finger in the air, when the man leaned into his ear. I watched them from afar, trying to hear, trying to listen, but they were whispering.

The doctor moved his pointed finger to me.

"Mother of God," I said, looking away, and my patient struggled under his bandages, reaching for his face like so many of the wounded did, wanting to know how deep the gashes went, but had lost the ability to tell.

"Nurse?" my patient said.

"Just saying a prayer, private. Wrapping you up now. Not to worry." I squeezed his hand when evac took him away, wishing him well, before my gaze trailed back up to the man.

His eyes looked dark and burdened with thought—not the kind of look I expected if he had come to confront me about the cigarettes I'd lifted from ration packs, and what nerve if he had, coming into our tent when our boys are in such miserable condition. Was he even American? It was hard to tell with the fatigues he wore, which looked unpatched and black at my angle.

Roxy, the other nurse on shift in our cramped little clearing station, looked up from the bedside of some poor fella who bought a heap of shrapnel in his face. "You get yourself in trouble again, doll?" She looped gauze around her patient's head, glancing up and chewing her gum. "Kit, you do something?"

"No," I said, followed by a cringe. We'd been at this clearing station for three days, having just bivouacked to our new field hospital after the battle for Arracourt started; I hadn't had time to get in serious trouble. The spare time I did have I spent sleeping, sometimes on our medical cots in between patients—definitely not something I remember Nurse Blanchfield mentioning in the War Department film on what to expect.

"You write another complaint letter?" Roxy asked, and I rolled my eyes.

Letters. "No," I said. Roxy didn't like the letters, said

it put a target on her and our chief nurse's backs since we bunked and nursed together. Not that I complained about anything that important; better toiletries, and a share of the command staff's wine was about all I had requested.

"Maybe you stayed out too late?" Roxy said, and I shook my head. "Oh, I know!" Her eyebrows rose into her forehead, fanning her thick lashes. "Maybe you forgot a shift? They don't like shift dodgers, ya know…"

"That's not it," I said.

"Maybe you—"

"Roxy," I said, but she leaned over her patient and projected her whisper with a cupped hand.

"Boy, the doctor looks mad," she said, followed by a whistle.

I glared. "Would you—jeez!" I said, and she finally clammed up.

As much as I didn't want to admit it, he looked mad all right, shaking that pointed finger. I certainly didn't have to come all the way to France to get a finger pointed at me. I could have stayed on the dairy farm in Washington where I was doing a fine job upsetting my father regularly by smoking in the barn, and everyone knows you shouldn't smoke in a barn with all that hay, but I was trying to hide my ugly little habit from my mother.

The doctor shook his head as he continued to operate, and the man left in a rush, throwing back the tent flaps.

"Well think," Roxy said. "You must have done something."

Headlamps from his parked vehicle shined onto our tent. He was waiting for the doctor to finish. *It's not the cigarettes, and it's not the letters…* I gasped, hand to my mouth. *Ah hell, what if he knows?* My stomach sank, thinking someone had found me out.

Roxy waved me over to help her, and I composed myself as best I could, holding her patient's head steady between my hands.

"No sense in getting upset yet. Right?" Roxy said, but even she glanced up at the illuminated tent flaps. "I guess you'll know when the doctor's done."

I nodded, and her patient squirmed. "Hold still, soldier," I said, tightening my grip on his head. His cheek had been a pile of mush before Roxy got a hold of it, and she stitched him up as clean as she could before evac and reconstruction, but there was little she could do. The scar that would form would be his reminder, a souvenir from this damn war.

He caught me looking into his eyes and mumbled some words. "Don't worry," I said. "Roxy here knows what she's doing. Don't you, Rox?"

"Sure do." Roxy pulled scissors from my waistband to cut the gauze. The soldier whimpered a bit, then asked the question we knew we couldn't answer truthfully.

"Are the girls gonna wanna kiss me back home?" Suddenly his voice sounded like all the other boys before landing on the beaches, naïve and sweet, and oh so pure, not yet sullied by the harsh reality of war.

Roxy stopped chewing her gum and batted those big brown eyes of hers. "Hey, now, big fella." Roxy grabbed the soldier's hand and pressed it against her right breast, which was covered only by the thin twill of her olive drab nursing fatigues. "Who cares about kissing when you've got these big hands?" Only Roxy could do these things and get away with it. She gave me a wink. "Right, Kit?"

"Roxy doesn't lie," I said, and that really was the truth. "She's from New Jersey."

Roxy smiled with that famous Roxy smile of hers. "That's right, I'm from Jersey and ask anyone out here. Nobody from Jersey will lie to you." She leaned over the soldier and kissed him right on the mouth. "If anyone gives you crap back home, you tell 'em you had the greatest dame in all the Nurse Corps. You got me?"

She kissed him again before the medics moved him to evac, only he smooched back a second too late while staring at the tent ceiling. And he was gone; only the faint scent of Roxy's hair soap to remember her by.

We rushed to prepare her vacant bed, and soon enough we each had another patient. Spitting rain turned into a pour, knocking on the tent like big, fat knuckles, channeling a muddy soup of water around our floorboards.

The doctor took off his gloves, and I immediately sat down when I heard the latex peel and snap from his fingers. He rushed toward me, and I had a terrible sinking feeling that this had nothing to do with my secret, but had everything to do with my brother, who'd been captured by the Germans not long ago. Red, our chief nurse, walked up behind him and my whole body tightened, bracing for the terrible news he was about to deliver.

"Doctor Burk—"

"Kit," he said, and I stopped breathing, waiting for those inevitable words of doom. *Your brother's dead.* My heart lobbed in my chest and pumped in my ears. "Is it my brother?"

He shook his head, and the breath I'd been holding blew from my mouth, but I still wasn't completely relieved. He motioned for Red to sit next to us. "Some men are waiting for you outside this tent—a sergeant and one other—you'll need to go with them and do whatever they say."

"From the Nurse Corps?" I asked.

"Sergeant Meyer is his name." He swallowed, appearing conflicted, which did little to ease my nerves. "He'll tell you everything you need to know."

I pointed to my wounded soldier, waiting to be bandaged. "But I have a patient," I said.

"Roxy and I will manage," he said, and Roxy looked up from the suture needle she was threading. Red looked concerned, taking off her hair cap and holding it between her hands.

"But Doctor Burk…" Red said.

"It's an order, Red," he said, and that was enough for her. "Do what they ask."

The tent flaps flew open and the sergeant stepped inside. He pointed at me and then to Red. "You two," he said, hiking a thumb over his shoulder, "this way."

The doctor patted the top of my head as if he was sending me off to an unknown place, never to see me again. "I don't understand." I looked to Red for help, but she'd made way to leave.

"Kit," Red said. "It's an order." She fit her helmet over her head, hastily tucking in her ginger curls, and left out the open tent flaps. The doctor put his head in his hands, which only made me feel more uneasy than before.

"Where are we going?" I said.

The sergeant hiked his thumb over his shoulder again. "You're wasting time."

Roxy pretended not to know anything strange was going

on, refitting her pink headscarf and tying it just so over her dark hair, but she was a lousy pretender. She reached for my hand. "I'll keep things going here," she said.

The doctor handed me my helmet.

And I walked out of our clearing tent and into the rain.

I climbed into the back of a covered army lorry, taking a seat across from Red on a metal bench. A soldier sat with us, helmet down low, holding a gun by his side. I wasn't sure if he was guarding or protecting us. The engine started up and we lurched forward, driving down a dirt road with our lights off. I held on to the bench.

The soldier didn't move, and I looked him up and down, studying him, black duty boots, and worn fatigues but no patches. "You got a name?"

He moved slightly so he could see me, and shook his head.

"Well, can you at least tell us where we're going?" I said, and he shook his head again.

"We'll find out soon enough," Red said, but my stomach swirled from not knowing.

German screamers dropped in the horizon, lighting up the sky in quick bursts while we jostled and swayed in the back from the uneven road. The lorry turned sharply, and the body-shaking zing of German 88s spewed into the air.

"Red," I called out, and she placed her hand on my knee. "We're driving into it."

"Like old times, Kit. Me and you," she said. "Utah Beach."

A blast on the road threw me from the bench into the tailgate. My ears rang, spits of mud flew up from the back

ANDIE NEWTON

tires, and my helmet slipped off my head, dangling from my neck.

Utah. D-Day+4

Red and I waited in line for the ladder ropes off the SS Pendleton, *the sea washing up against the ship in swift waves, causing the landing craft to whack against the starboard side. A boom from a German shell on the beach, and I grabbed Red's arm, looking over the bow of the ship into the swirling water and at a mine that had yet to be swept.*

"Don't look at it," Red said. "Mind your feet and get in that landing craft. You hear? Be glad we have ladder ropes." She looked at me. "It was worse in North Africa."

"Worse?" A shell exploded in the water, spraying us like a typhoon, very close to the mine, which could explode from troubled waters. "We're gonna die, Red!" Dead soldiers bobbed in the water, sinking and then reappearing moments later, bloated as whales.

Red turned me by the shoulders. "We're not going to die. Got it?" She nudged me toward the rope ladder. "Now go. Eyes on your boots, Kit!"

GIs already in the landing craft shouted at us to hurry as we climbed down the rope, canteens hanging from our belts, medical kits tied around our waists, and wearing men's uniforms that were two sizes too big. Only I fell feet above the craft and landed mighty hard from a shift in the water. Red grabbed me by the sleeve and pulled me in close next to her in the rear of the craft. "Stick close to me," she said, and that was exactly what I'd been doing since we met in England, waiting for orders at the evacuation hospital at Tortworth Castle. She'd just arrived from North Africa, having already seen her fair share of horrors, and took me under her wing.

Our craft motored toward the shore after a listing start. The nurse next to me vomited into her helmet. "Helmets on!" Red barked, and the nurse burst into tears, holding her helmet like a bucket between her legs. Red dumped the helmet out in the water collecting around our boots and told her to put it back on her head.

The bow ramp lowered, and we marched right into the water, which looked to be about waist-deep. "The swells come in fast," someone shouted. "Get off the beach!"

I stepped into the cold ocean water as a German aircraft fired on the beach, punching holes into the sand. Zap, zap, zap. Nurses fell into the surf like dominoes, screaming along with the sharp zips of returning fire. Ships still looking for sea-lanes erupted into flames. A swell took me under, and I sank to the seafloor under the weight of my pack. Red's searching hand grabbed a hold of my collar and lifted my nose above the churning water, dragging me to the beach.

"Kick," was all I heard between the pulses of water splashing into my ears. "Kick!"

Somehow, someway, I was able to turn upright by digging my water-filled boots into the soft sand. I gasped for air and got a load of saltwater instead. The enemy aircraft flew off inland, smoke billowing from one of its engines and droning from being hit, while we washed up onto the shore, coughing and yakking up the sea.

I clawed my way up the beach, one hand after the other. Red spat out some sand, coughing and mumbling, before *swiping seaweed from her eyes. Her chinstrap dangled from her helmet, then a rolling wave took it from her head. "Damn, Kit, you're heavy for being so small."*

I spat once in the surf, lifting my face from the sand, and she tugged a lock of my hair where the seawater had turned it dishwater brown.

"You okay?" she said. "I thought I'd lost you there."

"Yeah." I patted the sodden pockets of my uniform, feeling my army knife and the morphine syrettes I'd packed earlier, taking a big sigh.

Two more enemy aircraft flew out of the clouds like angry bees, engines revving. Zap, zap, zap... Patrolling MPs shouted at us to run, and Red took me by the hand, and together we ran up the beach and into the war.

The lorry's gears shifted into a low groan. We turned away from the fighting, and the noises of the war fell behind darkened hills. I could tell we'd driven into the country from the smell alone, with the reek of rotten grapes thick in the air from vineyards left to the crows. And the soil. French dirt smelled like spoiled milk when wet—and boy was it wet. I'd never seen rain like I'd seen in France.

We crept up a mound of dirt that resembled a trail, gears grinding, engine chugging, and drove right through a spot of tall trees with low-hanging branches. An occasional explosion in the distance sparkled through the leaves and shimmered like fairy lights dancing on the ground.

"Where are we?" I said.

Red looked out the back of the lorry, shrugging. "I don't know…"

I addressed the soldier. "Will you tell us now?" I asked, but he only looked straight, hand on his gun barrel beside him. Sergeant Meyer cut the engine, and I held on to the seat as we rolled to a slow stop into some thorny bushes. Gooseflesh erupted up and down my arms from a pocket of static air. I heard the sergeant's door open and close, and I saw a cottage in the distance, darker than the night, with a roof that had toppled inward from a bomb. He came around the side of the lorry and unlatched the back, whispering for us to follow him. The air felt cleaner here, cold, and less wet from the sheltering trees. Quiet.

The sergeant talked to Red, leaving me lagging behind, as we walked toward a barn several yards away made of wood and rock. "Are we clear?" he said to Red, and she nodded.

The sergeant shoved a medic's bag into my hands and rolled open the squealing barn door. It was bright inside, lit up by lanterns. I saw firewood stacked in the corner next to a cold, black stove. And a farm boy, which surprised me. Too young to be the owner of the farm and still too young to fight in the war. He stood against the wall with a rifle at ease by his side, but when he saw the sergeant, he disappeared into the dark back where the rafters had fallen and split.

"Well, go on," he said, and the soldier who'd ridden with us stayed behind to guard the door while I walked inside.

A soldier lay on a makeshift cot made of blankets and hay, groaning, with shaggy blond hair that hadn't been washed in days. Dirt covered his uniform as if he'd been lying outside on the ground for some time. One arm thrashed about at his side from shock, his eyes glassy and swiveling like a compass with nowhere to go. When the barn doors closed behind us, I smelled him, irony and warm from wounds left unattended for too long.

Then he spoke and the gasp that came from my mouth sounded more like a last breath.

"Fräulein," he said, reaching for me. "*Hilfe*."

"He's German?" I said, and the sergeant huddled me and Red into the corner.

"He's an SS officer, dressed up as one of ours," he said. "He's important. And he knows it. I need you to make sure he doesn't die. Get him coherent. Then I need you to talk to him."

"Me?" I put a hand on my chest. "But I'm a nurse!"

"Who speaks German," he said, and there was a pause.

A long, awkward pause.

My mouth gaped open as if it was such an outlandish idea—me speaking German.

"Are you denying it?" he said.

I looked at the ground, searching for words that weren't the truth. After all these months, my secret was out.

Red reached for my arm. "You speak German?" she said, but I wasn't prepared to answer and blathered some words, which nobody could hear.

"Kit—"

"Yeah, all right," I finally said. "I know it."

"How come you didn't tell me?" she said.

I took a long jittering breath from having said it out loud; there was no going back. "Because if anyone knew they'd send me to a POW hospital." I swallowed. "I didn't come here to fix up Germans."

She squeezed my shoulder, and my eyes lifted to hers. There were no words between us, but I knew she understood and respected how I felt even though she wouldn't have any qualms about serving in a POW hospital—a patient was a patient.

"How did you find out?" I looked at Meyer.

"I'm OSS."

I covered my mouth. *OSS—Office of Strategic Services.*

"You can hide that sort of thing from the Nurse Corps—" he shook his head "—but not from us. Don't worry, I won't tell anyone your little secret if you do this. You help me, and I'll help you. Understand?"

Red tore off the German's jacket and clothes, ripping his shirt in half to assess his wounds. A bullet had pierced his upper chest, and the blood that had once pulsed from the hole was now crusty and brown. When Red pressed a few sheets of gauze to it he cried out with nail-scratching pain.

"But it's illegal, Sergeant," I whispered. "There's rules— the Geneva Conventions. He needs to be brought to a field hospital."

"This is war. Not everything is legal out here."

Red rolled him over to see the bullet's exit wound, but there wasn't one. She felt his tender flesh above his shoulder blade, nodding to me that she'd found the bullet that was still lodged in his body. This man could live if we let him, but we'd have to hurry, and I knew that each second I spent staring at him was a second wasted. The German waved in and out of consciousness, his head flopping and jerking.

"But I could get in trouble for this," I said in a breathy whisper. "Big trouble."

I wanted to ask why us—why me and Red specifically— but as I watched Red preparing for surgery, I thought maybe I knew. Red was a seasoned army nurse, having served in two campaigns; she was the most qualified to do the things he asked, except for our surgeon, and nobody would have put Doctor Burk in that kind of situation. As for me, well, that was an easy one. Surely there were other medics and nurses who spoke German, but probably none who got in trouble as much as me. Petty rules I'd broken, sure, but a troublemaker nonetheless, and one who kept secrets.

"Kit…" Red looked over her shoulder, motioning with her fingers. "Morphine."

I took a step back, gripping the medic bag a little tighter. "Kit," the sergeant said, and I was surprised to hear him call me by my nickname, "what do you think they're doing to our boys over there, the ones they capture and imprison?"

The sergeant let me soak in that thought for a moment before he brought out his big gun, which was more like a bird that had crawled into my heart and ruffled sharp feathers. "Your brother was part of the Eighth—the airmen captured not long ago by the Germans. Is that right?" he said, and I whipped my head up, meeting his eyes. "If this Kraut dies, we get nothing. If you save him it could lead to information that would end the war, bring all our POWs home. Is that worth violating the rules of war?"

Maybe a second passed, I don't know. I wasn't thinking anymore about what was legal and what wasn't. I was only thinking of my brother and the day he left for basic. How he swept his hair from his eyes and told me to remember his face, not him walking away. But I'd watched him leave anyway, slinging his duffel bag over his shoulder and walking down the long gravel road away from our farm until I couldn't see him anymore.

"Do you know my brother?"

"I know men like him—brave."

It was true. All our men were brave, walking into the war and into the fire.

"My brother's name is Sam," I said, and instead of pulling back even more, I reached into my medic bag for the morphine Red had asked for. She immediately injected the German in the neck with the syrette, and soon enough he was out. Limp as a noodle. And the barn got very quiet.

I nodded.

"Yes?" he said.

"Yeah," I said.

Sergeant Meyer ran his hand over his face. "Good," he said, and the other soldier closed the barn doors. "Now hurry, ladies. We don't have a lot of time."

I worked side by side with Red as the sergeant watched us with his arms folded. We patched him up good with supplies from the medic bag, sticking him with plasma and sewing up his chest wound and his shoulder, which felt hot from an oncoming infection. After hours of working on him, we finally reached a point where we had done enough.

Then we waited.

Waited for him to open his eyes, and waited for him to talk.

"Red," I said, quietly, "what if he knows where Sam is?" I watched the German breathe and Red grabbed my arm. "I can ask him where. Find out about my—"

"No," she said. "It's too risky." She pulled me in close after Meyer looked at us. "And it's not up to you."

The German moaned, finally waking up. "Quick, give him something..." Red said, tapping me. I searched my pack for something to give him other than morphine, thumbing through the different medicines. I paused, fingers on the sodium pentothal.

"What is it?" Red asked, and I looked at her, suddenly aware I was more prepared for this situation than I thought.

"I have this." When I showed her the glass ampule of injectable medicine, she smiled.

"If only Roxy was here," she said.

We administered sodium pentothal for pain, but we called it the Roxy drug because patients babbled on for many minutes about anything and everything. It was worth a try.

Red swabbed the German's skin while I prepared the medicine and drew it into a hypodermic syringe. "Here goes nothing," I said, and I punched the needle into his fatty upper arm. His pasty face turned peach in a matter of seconds. He'd stopped moaning, and Sergeant Meyer pulled me off to the side.

"Tell him you're a special agent with the SS. You're embedded with the army. That will explain our uniforms. Make sure he thinks you're one of them..." The sergeant went on and told me things only a German agent would know, battle positions and plans lifted through telephone conversations. "Then, when he fully trusts you, ask him about the *giant*. What does it mean? Let him do the talking."

I nodded, trying to remember all he said, and thinking of the right words to use. I was the only girl in my town forced to go to German school, and I hated every minute of it. Never had I been more regretful about cheating on my final exam than at that very moment, standing next to a Nazi. Frau Hess, my long-suffering teacher, would flip over in her grave if she knew what I was about to use my German for.

"Anything else?" I said.

"Yeah," Meyer said. "Stick to the script. These Nazis are clever bastards." He pushed me toward the German.

"Stick to the script," Red warned, and I nodded, making the short walk over.

The German's eyes lifted and then fell, lifted and then fell. I waved smelling salts under his nose, and he roused enough to look at us coherently. My cold palm frightened him. I cleared my throat. "Officer…"

He took a sudden breath and I think he was glad to hear my accent, which my mother made me master. "*She must have a proper northern accent and know perfect German*," she had told my teacher, "*as if she is one.*" I swallowed, thinking of all the times I cursed my mother's persistence.

"Fräulein," he said all weepy.

"I'm an agent with the SS." I waved my finger at the sergeant and Red. "These are my informants." I went on to repeat the information the sergeant told me, and the officer nodded intermittently as if he already knew the things I told him.

"Officer," I said, messing with his blanket, buying time to remember the right words, and how to say "giant" in German. I tried looking into his eyes, but they were still a little shaky. "I need to know about the giant." He'd just realized we'd sewn up his shoulder and felt around for the sutures, asking about what else we'd done to him. "Officer," I said again, using his chin to move his head, and his eyes wheeled to mine. "*The giant.*"

And he spoke very fast from the medicine I'd injected him with. Too fast for me to translate in my head, and I interrupted to tell him to slow down. "The giant," he said, "was quartered and moved. Resistance. Alps. The tunnel, long days and nights." He pointed a finger in the air. "Deposit is secure in the Black Forest. Führer is prepared. Be restful with this, fräulein. The butcher knows where," he kept saying. "The butcher, the butcher…"

"What's secure, Officer? Ammunition?"

"No, fräulein." The man swallowed, taking a labored breath. "The Reich's war chest," he said, and I jumped up from the ground.

2

KIT

The sergeant caught me as I stumbled backward, feeling white as a sheet and wobbly in his arms. The German had closed his eyes, wincing from moving his arm—he hadn't seen my reaction when he mentioned the Nazi war chest. I felt an urgency to tell Meyer immediately what I'd heard, but I couldn't. Not yet. I stood straight, composing myself and resisting the desire to feel my thrashing heart.

The German rambled on again about his sutures, searching for them with his eyes and then feeling them with his fingers. I knelt back down, trying my best to look calm and in control, tucking my hair behind my ears, and turning my blubbering lower lip into a stiff one.

"Who did you say, Officer? A butcher?" His head rolled from side to side, still asking me what I'd done to his shoulder when I placed a hand on his arm. "Look at me." But he wouldn't, and I felt a panic bubbling up from my chest to my throat, knowing the medicine would be wearing off shortly. He had to know where the airmen from the Eighth were taken; he had to know about my brother. Somewhere in that German-Hun mind of his, he had answers. I slowly glanced up at Red and her brow furrowed, and in those fire-green eyes of hers I knew what she was thinking—*don't do anything stupid.*

I squeezed the German's arm, and his head stopped rolling. "Tell me about the American airmen captured two weeks ago. Where are you keeping them?"

"Karlsruhe," he mumbled, eyes closing, and I assumed it was a village—one of the many places the Germans had POW camps, secret camps.

"Are they alive? Tell me what you know," I said, and his eyes popped open. He focused on me much more lucidly than he'd been, and shifted in his bed after a long pause. That's when I knew I'd messed up. My stomach sank.

I let go of his arm, and he tried sitting up, now looking at us three with eyes wide, almost as if seeing us for the first time. "What's your name, fräulein?"

"I told you my name."

His face turned stern and browbeat, not affected by the pain anymore, or the delirium that infected him earlier. "No," he said. "You did not."

My mind went blank. I couldn't think of one German name, and I knew Kit didn't translate well. I repeated some of what I'd already told him, making a point about being an agent with the SS. "We saved you from amputation. We saved your life!"

I pointed to every part of his body that Red and I sewed up.

"You think the Allies would treat you so kindly? We saved you from a prisoner of war camp." I laughed cynically, glancing up at Red, but she looked lost since she didn't understand German. "Surely you realize we're on the same side…"

I gulped.

He looked at the plasma we'd strung up on a nail near his bedside and then fiddled with the needle. "Whose fluid is this? What did you give me?" His eyes slid to his jacket, which had been slung over the back of a chair after Red had ripped it off him. I stood up, not knowing what to say or in what language. He eyed his jacket again after glancing at me, and in one swift move, he reached for it with a sudden burst of energy.

Me and Red grabbed a hold of the same sleeve, yelling at him to drop it, but he'd dug his fingers into a hidden pocket and before we could stop him, he'd pulled out a cyanide capsule. The sergeant slugged him in the face before he could swallow, followed by a swift throw of his jacket across the barn. The soldier from outside rushed in to help, and they argued who was at fault for not finding the capsule during the search.

Red put her hands to her cheeks, looking astonished. "Kit, what did you say?"

"I didn't say anything!" I said, and I lied right to my best friend's face. "Honest!" I cringed, another lie.

"You stuck to the script?" Meyer asked.

"Yeah." I chewed my nails.

Meyer took me by the shoulders while the German lost consciousness behind his back, the only other person who knew what questions I'd asked. "What did he tell you?"

And I told the sergeant everything about the giant. Red's hands moved to cover her mouth, while the sergeant looked more stunned than one of our boys who'd come in completely shell-shocked. He felt behind him for the wall and leaned up against it.

"The Nazi chest? It's been split up and moved?"

I nodded. "Yes, Sergeant. I believe so."

"And who's this butcher?" he asked. "Did he say anything else? The slightest detail could be useful."

I paused, glancing up at Red, and she folded her arms. "That's all."

"Well, it's quite some news, I must say." He looked at the ground, thinking, eyes pointed, before looking back up at us. "Now, ladies," he said. "This is confidential information, as I'm sure you are aware. You do know what that means? Don't you?"

Red and I nodded incessantly.

"Unfortunately, there are spies among us. He's not the only hostile to infiltrate. You're at risk if anyone finds out what you know. Trust no one." We turned to leave after he'd asked the soldier to take us back to our hospital. "Oh, and Kit," he said. "You made the right decision."

I glanced over my shoulder and the last thing I saw was the sergeant standing with his hands on his hips, watching the German come to.

The soldier let us ride in the front of the lorry instead of the back, where both Red and I squished in next to each other with me in the middle. The sun rose in the distance, looking blood red through a veil of bomb haze. B-17s droned overhead from a lift in the rain—two, three, four I counted without looking up. I closed my eyes, thinking of

Sam. "Come back to us," I said, breaking the silence, and when I opened my eyes back up, Red was looking at me, watching, studying, but I looked out the windshield.

The soldier shifted gears and the lorry grumbled as we turned off a dirt road for a paved one. "If you're having regrets, don't," he said, taking his eyes off the road long enough to glance at both of us. "Sergeant Meyer was right. You did the right thing." He looked again. "Sorry about your brother. The men from the Eighth—"

"Yeah," I said. "Are you going back there, to the barn?" I said, but he kept his eyes on the road this time and I took that to mean he wasn't going to answer the question. Then I thought it was probably best I didn't know and was glad he didn't answer. "Well, can you tell me your name at least? I think I deserve to know it now—"

"Jack," he said, brushing the hair from his eyes, and I caught a good look of his face with the rising sun. He was a real person now, and not the stiff shadow from the back.

"Well, Jack, I guess we're connected now. All four of us. But if it's all the same, I hope we never see each other again," I said, and he chuckled, though I wasn't trying to be funny.

He drove us to our field hospital instead of our clearing station near the battlefield. Red hopped out of the lorry before Jack turned off the engine, walking toward the tent we shared with Roxy. "Red—" I scooted from the seat and ran after her. "Wait up!" I said, walking the last few steps with her up to our tent as she shook her head over and over. "I hope Roxy's asleep—"

"I hope Roxy's asleep," she said at the same time, and we looked at each other. "Listen, Kit. She can't know where we went or what we've done. Got it?"

I hesitated answering, exhausted by it all.

"Got it?" Red said again, and I mustered up the energy to nod. She looked back at Jack and the lorry, but he'd driven away. "Come on."

I followed her into our tent. Roxy sat on her cot, taking her boots off. "Boy, are you a sight for sore eyes," she said to us, but Red and I had already collapsed on our cots. She tossed my K-ration on my blanket, and Red's too. "Same breakfast as yesterday, dolls."

I sat up to grab my box, only to collapse back on my cot.

Red ripped hers open, shoving a piece of the chocolate in her mouth as Roxy studied us.

"Well, you only missed twelve patients," Roxy said. "Cute boys too, poor fellas. Had to amputate a foot before we could send him to evac." She whistled. "And the doctor was mad, cursing and swearing like a sailor if I'd ever heard one. Had to steal a nurse from another tent to administer ether." She paused for a split second, which I'm sure felt like a minute to Roxy. "Sure glad the rain stopped though. It rains like that in Jersey, but worse. Nonna always said a good dose of rain is God's way of—"

"Roxy," I finally said, as my boots plunked to the floor. "Quiet."

I was hoping Roxy could see that Red and I had been through the wringer and that we didn't want to talk, but I knew it was only a matter of time before she asked where we'd been. I was thinking it would take her about five seconds to pipe back up, when in fact it only took her three.

She sneezed after taking a whiff of her ration crackers. "So where were ya?" Cracker bits sprinkled her front pockets as she chewed, eyes shifting back and forth between me and Red.

"On vacation," I said in the air. "Soaking in a hot bath, salts for our feet." Roxy crinkled up her cellophane into a ball. "Yeah, and later we got glammed up in silky dresses, went dancing at the Paramount followed by a dinner at the Ritz!"

"No, really, where were you gals?"

"Drop it, Rox," Red said from her cot, which surprised Roxy. "Not another question."

I shook my head when Red wasn't looking, mouthing, "Not now," and our tent fell eerily quiet with only the crackle of cellophane balling in Roxy's fist.

She reached for her boots, looking up at Red as she shoved each foot inside, but Red only stared at the tent ceiling. "I'm filling my canteen," Roxy said, storming out the tent flaps. I expected Red to sit up with Roxy gone, but she remained still on her cot, eating crackers.

"Psst," I said to her. "What are we going to do?"

"What do you mean?" she said.

"What do you mean, what do I mean?" I said. "How can you sleep after all that?"

"Drop it, Kit. I mean it. You heard the sergeant. You want to get mixed up in something?"

"Red, we put him back together, stitched him up like Raggedy Ann. We're as mixed up as anything."

Red had pressed her pillow to her ears to drown me out. Moments later she pulled it away. "And how does someone from a dairy farm in Washington know fluent German?"

"Please don't tell anyone, Red. I didn't join the Nurse Corps to fix up German POWs. If anyone got wind of it—"

"I won't, Kit. I promise. But tell me, how did you learn it?"

I had sat up completely by this time, crisscrossing my legs and digging into my ration box. "I know it seems odd. My great-grandparents were German Russians from Odessa. They came to live with us when I was small. My mother enrolled me and my brother in German classes so we'd be able to talk to them properly. Frau Hess, my teacher—jeez, what a grumpy old woman she was—she wouldn't die until I'd perfected an authentic Berliner accent. Swear to God, she died the day she told me I was fluent." I lit up one of four cigarettes from my ration pack. "Damn German classes. Ruined my summers." I glanced up through the puff of smoke.

Red looked at me for a long moment. "If you're so good at speaking German, then how'd he figure out you were lying? You had a complete conversation with him, then on a dime, he changed." She paused. "You did stick to the script, didn't you, Kit?"

I tidied up my ration pack to avoid eye contact. Red had a way of reading people, and I thought if I looked up, she'd know I wasn't telling the whole story. "Of course, I did. He figured it out is all. One moment he was fine, then he switched, just like you said."

"That's it?" she said.

"Well yeah, Red." I slowly looked up, but she had rolled back over.

Roxy came back in and lit a cigarette. She waited for Red to fall asleep before snapping her fingers at me, her body half-hanging off her cot. "Hey… what's with that cock-and-bull story you fed me?" She took a drag off her cigarette, batting her giant brown eyes. "Spill it, will ya? I'm growing old already."

I exhaled from my mouth, eyes flicking over to Red as she slept, knowing I couldn't tell her anything that resembled the truth. Roxy had a mouth that ran like water. I had violated the rules of the Geneva Conventions—not something I wanted her to talk about the next time she went on one of her talking tangents.

"Well, it's this…" I smoked my cigarette, taking many drags while sitting on my cot, looking at her. "Damn that sergeant if I can say it. Let me tell you, Nurse Blanchfield will be getting a nice writ when I get home. What I saw was definitely not in the War Department film, let me tell you, Roxy. Oh! Let me tell you!" By now my cigarette was a tiny nub, burning my fingers.

"You're not going to tell me, are you?" She snuffed out her cigarette on the floorboard, and I hung my head down. "I tended to all those boys myself, me and the doctor. One had a wedding ring, lost the poor boy right in front of me."

Roxy had a soft spot for the married ones, because she felt sorry for their wives. I reached for her hand; out of everything she'd seen in France, the married patients she couldn't save were her worst thing in the world.

"I'm sorry, Rox. But yeah. I can't."

She rolled over and talked from under her blanket. "Well, wherever you gals went, I know it must have been a real picnic, I tell ya." The blanket over her head rose and fell with her huffing breath. "A real picnic!"

I lay back and tried to get some sleep, but I tossed and turned like laundry for an hour or more. I finally decided I should go for a walk to clear my head; only when I sat up,

Red was staring at me from her bed. Her eyes looked right through me, tired and worn, and her hair looked like she'd had her hand in it over and over again, slicking her ginger locks back.

"Red," I whispered, but she didn't move. "Red," I whispered again, and her eyes slid to mine. "You all right?" She shook her head slightly before getting up and putting her boots on. "Where are you going?"

She walked out of our tent without a sound, slipping into the daylight. I threw my boots on and ran outside to catch her, my laces dangling in the mud from not tying them. "Wait!" I said, shielding my eyes. Red had taken off between a row of nurses' tents. The swing shift was up and washing their hair out of their helmets in the grass, taking advantage of the break in the rain to clean up.

"What are you doing up, Red?" one said, followed by another and another. "You got your shift mixed up?" The nurse had her fingers in another gal's hair, working up a lather. Red swatted her hand as she rushed past, ignoring them all. They looked to me for an answer as I chased after her, but I could only shrug.

"Red!" I finally caught her arm, stopping her behind the field hospital and a parked ambulance with nobody inside. "Will you wait already?" I was out of breath and bracing my knees. "What's gotten into you?"

She pushed up her sleeves. "Do you realize what we participated in?" she said. "The laws we broke. He tricked us, Kit. We can't be ordered to break the law. I'm a nurse first; I felt I had to help that man. But damn... I think we really messed up."

30

"It's done now," I said.

"I can't lose this gig, Kit. Nursing's all I've got. We shouldn't have done it." She leaned into my ear. "What if he killed that German? No sense in letting him live after he figured us out, tell others about what we'd done. What if we get pinned for murder? I save lives!"

"Listen, it was the right decision, Red." I straightened up, as tall as I could get being as short as I was, and folded my arms, but she had turned her head. "It was!"

I thought of my brother, dirty and lonely. He'd be lucky if he was a slave, making German bullets in one of their munitions factories—I prayed this was the case. Deep down I knew he was most likely being starved and tortured. Without a shadow of doubt, if I were given the chance again to operate outside the rules of war to get information about my brother and the men captured from the Eighth, I would.

"Damn Germans. He's lucky we fixed him. You think they're doing the same for our boys?" I said, and my eyes uncontrollably welled with tears. "My brother." My throat balled up. "Sam…" And when I said his name aloud, I erupted in a gasping, heaving cry. Red took me into her arms and I wept into her shoulder, and for the first time since his capture, I let myself feel the loss of my brother as if he had died, and it poured from my skin and soul with prickling pain, leaving an empty space inside where I'd once felt alive.

"I'm sorry," she said, petting my head. "That's why I walked out of our tent. I didn't want you to know how I felt." She pulled away to look at me, and I dried my tears well enough with the back of my hand. "We wouldn't be in this mess if he hadn't figured us out."

"I know…" I sniffled.

"I hope we never see Meyer again," she said, "or that Jack."

We hugged again. "Me too—" Over her shoulder, Jack had walked out the mess tent with some others. They talked briefly, pointing to papers he had in his hands before splitting up in different directions. He spotted me watching him, eyes shocked wide over Red's shoulder, and I thought I was going to have a heart attack—of all people to see after what we'd said—and then he smiled, which caught me even more off guard.

Red pulled away, but he was still there, smoothing his dark hair back before putting his helmet on. He fastened his chinstrap. "Right, Kit?" Red said, and he flicked his helmet brim as if it was a wave.

"Yeah, Red…" I said, near stuttering, and I shut my eyes briefly, hoping he'd go away, but when I opened them back up, and he had left, I wondered where he went. "Yeah."

"Come on, let's go—" Red said, and we took a couple of steps only to gasp. A photographer was making his way toward us, nurse by nurse, taking snaps of the girls washing their hair. "A photographer. Damn! It's Benny—little creep." We turned around and stood still, shoulder to shoulder.

"What's he doing here?" I said, wiping my eyes completely dry.

She scoffed. "He can smell a story a mile away."

Benny from the *New York Times*. He loved to take photos of the nurses. He had a slick of dark hair that ran over the top of his bald head, and he was petite like me, which I thought was unusual for a man.

We started to walk away, trying to scoot into someone's tent unnoticed, but Benny had already snuck up behind with his camera. "Red, Kit," he said, and we sighed. "Turn around."

Red flicked my arm, and we put on huge smiles.

"Yes…" we both said, turning around.

He lowered the camera from his eye. "You can't pose," he said, which is why we did it. "Pretend I'm not here." He put the camera back up to his eye. "But still smile. People back home want to see winning smiles."

I reached for his camera. "Benny, why don't you—"
Flash.

"Try again, Kit," he said, pulling his camera back.

B-17s droned in the sky, flying in from the east. I closed my eyes briefly, tapping my heart, counting the planes by their sound. One, two, three… My eyes popped open after I'd only counted three. The fourth one came up from behind real slow, its tail dragging and its engine smoking up the sky with a thick, gray haze. "Four," I said, and I looked at Red, and she'd put her hands on both my shoulders.

Bennie took one snap of the three planes that flew over us, then dropped his camera, watching me as I felt for my heart, and Red as she looked into my eyes. "Maybe later," he said, and he walked back over to the nurses washing their hair.

"Kit, I'll say this one last time. Then I don't want to hear anything else about it. We can't tell anyone. You hear me? Nobody." I heard Benny taking snapshots of giggling nurses over her voice. "Promise?" Red said. "You won't say anything?"

"I already did promise you," I said. "But, Red, what are we gonna do about Roxy? She won't let up—you know that."

Red hooked her arm around my neck and we started back to our tent. "I'm sure you'll think of a story," she said. "You always do."

3

KIT

Our shift that night was changed to the following day while the troops refueled. We had a break. Proper recreational time wasn't something we normally experienced so close to the battlefield; it was something we talked about while huddled between sandbags at our makeshift canteen supplied with gifts brought over from the villagers. Gunfire popped randomly in the far distance—the usual song of the night. *Bap, bap...*

I set a crate of wine down between us. "Are you sure we're good to drink these?" Roxy said. "We're not gonna get in trouble, are we?" She rummaged through the bottles, pulling them out to read the labels, but they'd been ripped off. "Not like the last time you found us some wine. Right, Kit?"

"Yeah, sure," I said. "This is different." Before we mobilized near Arracourt, I'd *found* some wine in an unmarked crate. Turned out it belonged to the battalion surgeon. A search was made, and out of fear of getting in trouble, I fessed up to the mistake.

"Who gave them to ya?" Roxy said.

"I won them playing Bridge," I said.

"Yeah?" she said, and I thought I saw a questioning shift of her eyes.

The truth was, I got the bottles from an old villager and his wife, a thank you for tending to their daughter's burns. We weren't allowed to accept edibles from villagers since Mont-Saint-Michel, where our boys got poisoned by collaborationist chefs in a brasserie. These bottles were plumb. I inspected the corks myself. Plus, I didn't think that little old man and his wife wanted to kill the person who'd saved their daughter.

Red found a bottle of champagne hidden among the bottles of wine. "The champagne too?" she said, and I nodded, but that one I sort of ended up with. She held the champagne up to the lantern light, eyes bright. "If we get in trouble, I'm blaming you, Kit."

Roxy looked in the box for a corkscrew, but I handed her one from my pocket. She began to uncork it, twisting and twisting with a grit in her teeth. "Stubborn little fella, isn't it?" Roxy said, finally popping the cork. She licked her lips, looking at the bottle once more in the light, before giving it a sniff. She whistled. "Nobody makes wine like the French."

Roxy guzzled that wine, and God's truth, it sounded like she was pumping gas.

"Hey now, Rox," I said, reaching for the bottle. "Easy does it." I tugged and tugged until finally she let go, a little spurt of wine dribbling down the bottleneck from the back-and-forth. "Don't want anyone to think you're a lush, do you now?"

"I deserve an extra slug or two after the shift I pulled last night." She reached for the bottle I had taken from her, and I let go, no resistance after she mentioned last night. "You two weren't there so you wouldn't know."

I felt the sting in her voice, and I looked at Red, but she was looking at Roxy. I tried to think of something else to talk about, swirling the wine around in my bottle, but the quietness made Roxy's remark hang more awkwardly in the air.

"Oh, go ahead and tell her, Kit." Red popped open the bottle of champagne for herself. "I'm sure she'll keep it secret." My face must have been one of shock because Red glared at me to play along. "Kit, you know… the *story*."

"Oh, yeah, sure," I said, realizing she wanted me to make something up. "The *story*." I was good at making up stories. Some people would call them lies. I took a drink while I thought one up, something Roxy would believe, which wasn't hard because she believed everything I said.

Roxy sat up tall.

"Well you see here, Red and I, well we… ahh…" I looked at Red—she wanted a story. It was all I could do but keep a straight face. "Are you sure you want me to tell? I mean, aren't you embarrassed?" Red's eyebrows rose into her forehead, and I coughed out a laugh. "All right." I shrugged. "I thought you'd be embarrassed, but since you insist…"

Roxy moved to the edge of her sandbag, mouth gaping open.

"Why would I be embarrassed?" Red said.

I leaned forward, getting really close to Roxy, cupping my hand near my mouth but it was all for play. "So, it turns out I wasn't in trouble, just like the doctor said."

"You weren't?" Roxy said, near breathless.

"Nah, but Red here sure was." I slapped my palm to my forehead. "God, I can't believe you want me to tell her the truth, Red." I sighed. "Well… you see here, Rox." I inched even closer. "The sergeant blamed Red for infecting his platoon with a venereal disease they couldn't diagnose."

Roxy burst out laughing, falling feet over head off her sandbag.

"Serious!" I crossed my heart. "God's truth." I slugged down some wine.

"Oh, yeah, Kit?" Red said, giving me a little push.

"Yeah, Red." Now I was the one laughing. "You said to tell her."

Red dumped champagne on my lap, tipping the bottle up as I tried swiping it away in the air. "Knock it off, jeez…" I said, but I knew I deserved it.

"Don't listen to her Roxy," Red said.

Roxy straightened her headscarf and fixed her hair. "No really, where were ya? I can't say I was lonely, but I sure was really tired of doing it all. Nurse this, nurse that. There was only so much I could handle, and with the doctor swearing like he was and me trying to keep the soldiers from fading off—"

Red glared at me, saying words with her eyes and I turned to Roxy. "Friendly fire struck some villagers," I blurted. "Building caved in right on top of them. The sergeant wanted the wounded taken care of without alerting too many people. A messed-up shoulder, a perforated thigh, and a torn gut." I pointed in the air, making up a location. "A blacksmith and his wife. Nice lady, given the fact she'd almost died. We were working all night like you." My eyes were set on Roxy in the dark; she had no idea that while the details of the made-up scene tumbled out of my mouth, I thought about the German, and every stitch me and Red sewed into him under a flickering lantern. I took a drink.

Roxy set her wine down. "Why didn't ya say somethin' before?"

"We had orders to keep it secret," Red said. "You understand, right, Roxy?"

"Sure," Roxy said, taking sips of her wine. "Will you get a load of that? Friendly fire."

I didn't like telling Roxy a story this time, mostly because I wanted to talk about what we'd done—but Red would kill me. I felt a push to at least tell her a little bit of the truth and release some of the tension in my chest. My foot tapped, thinking... thinking about what I could and shouldn't say.

"Did you hear about the German spies? Dressing up in our boys' uniforms, pretending to be soldiers—" I looked over both shoulders "—walking around camp and coming into our tents."

Red's eyes lit up in the dark. "Kit!" Her voice was curt, as I expected it to be.

"What? It's the truth," I said.

Roxy's mouth hung open a second or two, then she laughed. "Oh, nice one, you gals. You're not gonna get me twice."

Red tilted her head. "Hear that, Kit?"

I took a drink. "Yeah, I hear." I did feel better, even if it was only for a second. I moved some sandbags out of the way so we could stretch out. With the lull in the bombings, the stars had come out, winning their own war with the haze.

"Man, oh man, look at those sparklers," Roxy said. "Makes you wish you were with your fella, gazing at you like you're gazing at the stars." I tossed my helmet at her, and she acted as if I'd socked her in the stomach. "Ugh... What'd you do that for?"

"You're dreaming," I said. "Fellas and stars..."

"Don't you get looked at, Kit?" Roxy said. "I get looked at." She dusted off her shirt where it was still unbuttoned from earlier.

I laughed. "We know you do, Rox," I said. "And no, I don't get looked at." I took a slug of my wine, then thought about Jack, and his eyes, wondering if he was taking a look at me near the mess tent, or just looking at me.

"What do you mean you know?" Roxy said, tossing my helmet back, and I shook my head.

"Forget it," I said, and I tipped my bottle up for a drink, washing thoughts of Jack away.

Two nurses from the swing shift sauntered by. "Well, what do you have here, Kit?" one said, and when she bent over and picked through the bottles, I reached into her pocket and lifted her lighter. She looked at me, still bent over, and I stuffed it in my pocket.

"You have a good look?" I smiled. "Because you're not getting any," I said. "I won this fair and square." I glanced at Red, who took another look at her champagne bottle.

"Actually, I'm in the market for smokes," she said. "You got any you can spare?"

THE GIRLS FROM THE BEACH

I pulled two from my pack. "It'll cost you some chocolate."

She traded me the chocolate for the smokes, and after her and her friend walked away, I had a little laugh.

"What?" Roxy said, and I tossed up the lighter in my hand.

"Looks like one dropped their lighter, that's all," I said, and I lay back again, hands under my head.

"Achoo!" Roxy sneezed, startling both Red and me.

"Easy, Rox." I pulled a tissue from my pocket. "You're gonna lose the war for us with your sneezing," I said, and she swatted me.

"Stop it," she said. "I am not."

It was how me and Red met her—the sneezing.

Our first night on the beach. The air was thick with smoke and heavy with the smell of spent ammunition. And dark. Pitch black—and when someone says 'pitch black' they have no idea what pitch black really means unless they'd dug in the sand and in the grass with me and Red that night on Utah Beach.

I sipped from my canteen, wetting my drying lips, trying like hell not to guzzle what clean water I had left. My limbs felt like gelatin, and my skin was raw with sand rash. We helped set up the hospital and tended to over a hundred patients. Still hadn't eaten. Still hadn't gone to the bathroom in the grass, but mostly out of fear of stepping on a mine.

Red lifted her canteen to her lips, but dropped her arms they were so tired, so I helped her lift it, and by the slosh and swish of the water, I knew she only had a few drinks left too. We'd never spoken of it, how tired we were the first day, not with so many of our boys dead on the beach, some still floating in the surf.

"Thanks for saving me," I whispered. I pulled back my uniform collar, where it had stretched from the ocean water, to brush sand from my neck. "I would have drowned had you not pulled me up." I clinked my canteen against hers. "I'll save you next time, all right?"

"Sure, Kit," she said.

Gunfire tapped in the distance—a monotonous, deadly beat all through the night. Bap, bap. Followed by a long pause. Bap, bap. I chewed my nails in the dark, hoping to catch winks in between the shots. Footsteps came up from behind in the sand and my whole body froze. We'd been warned about Germans sneaking up on us in the night and slitting our throats.

I pulled my last fingernail from my teeth. My hands shook. "Red," I whispered, and she searched for my head in the dark, pushing her lips into my ear.

"It could be a nurse," she said.

"Achoo!" we heard, followed by complete silence. Not one bless you from the ground where other nurses had dug in, which made me think they thought it was a German too. More footsteps followed, closer, louder, the crunch of boots on the beach followed by the spray of sand from moving feet. "Achoo!" we heard again, only this time we definitely heard a voice. A woman, and she had cursed, then moments later she fell into our hole. "Achoo—whoa!"

"You all right?" I said, untangling her feet and arms from my body. "Cover your mouth."

"Sorry," she whispered. "I've been wandering around for an hour trying to find a place to bunk. They said we'd have *tents tomorrow or somethin'." She paused, and I thought she'd clammed up, but she didn't. "Oh, and boy is it dark or what? I've never seen it so dark. Back in Jersey…"*

"What is it, the Roxy Hour or something?" Red said, and she sat up in the dark, dropping her canteen in the sand.

"The Roxy Hour?" she said. "Oh, yeah… Nonna used to listen to the show on the radio…"

"Shh!" me and Red both said, and she did, but only for a second.

"Does whispering count?" she said.

"Hey, did you hear about the Germans? You know… the war and all that? We're trying to get some sleep here," I said.

"Oh yeah," she said, and she buried herself into our foxhole. "Me too."

I covered my face with my helmet and closed my eyes.

"Achoo!" My eyes sprung open with her sneeze. "Sorry," she whispered, before rolling over. "Roxy… I like it!"

Roxy took the tissue I'd offered her and blew her nose good. "Dang, Kit, you're a walking PX. You know that?" She tossed the used tissue into a barrel for burning. "What else you got in there? Churchill? Is he in there too?"

I laughed, pressing my back against a sandbag, and the assortment of tools in my pocket jingled and twanged. "Only the essentials. I like to be prepared."

"She was like that when I met her, in the days before the landing," Red said. "If you needed something, Kit was the one to see."

43

"Yeah, yeah…" I said, looking up at the stars. "Girls, where do you think we'll go from here?"

"We follow the boys," Roxy piped. "Straight on to Berlin."

"That's not what I mean," I said. "When we go home. Will it be different? Will *we* be different?"

Even Roxy sat quietly.

"Not between us." Red clinked her bottle against ours. "We'll meet up, you know? Someplace nice, and not at a hospital or in a tent," she said.

"As soon as I get home, I'm moving someplace nice, sophisticated. Somewhere far away from eastern Washington where everything is brown. I want to live somewhere green."

Roxy looked shocked, her black eyelashes fanning into her eyebrows. "You mean it's not green like what Woody Guthrie sang about?"

I laughed. "Douglas firs and lush mountains? No, where I live it's more like sagebrush and rattlesnakes. And dry. Only a little bit of rain."

"Why would he do that?" Roxy stood up, and she looked as if she wanted to stomp right off to America and give Woody Guthrie a piece of her mind. "No, really. Why would he do that?"

Me and Red laughed at her reaction—her indignation—the gall of Woody Guthrie. "I don't know, Rox," I said, taking another swig of wine. "Because he's a liar? There's a lot of liars around here."

"Oh, here we go," Red said, leaning back. "More about Nurse Blanchfield?"

"Listen," I said. "I'm not bellyaching or nothing—"

"Sounds like you are." Roxy giggled, tipping back her wine.

I promised Red I wouldn't talk about Nurse Blanchfield and the War Department film almost every nurse in America had watched before signing up. White dresses and lipstick were what she promised.

"Yeah, yeah," I said. "Listen, you should have seen my face when I got issued my fatigues and boots instead of a white dress. My mouth hung open and the lady told me I'd catch flies if I didn't close it." Red giggled from under her mouthful of champagne. "That's when I realized Nurse Blanchfield was a better storyteller than me." I toasted my bottle in the air. "So, here's to you ole crocodile. You got me. You got me good."

"That's the one then," Red said, nodding. "You found your match."

"I suppose."

Roxy sat back down with a humph, her wine bottle cradled between her legs. "What about you, Red? Where are you going after the war?"

Red took a long quiet sip of her champagne. "Home to Oklahoma where I support my mama. She can't take care of herself since my dad died and without me and the dough I'm bringing in, she'd be destitute. Life can be tough there."

"Oh sorry, Red," Roxy said. "I didn't know."

Red nodded with her head down, and I reached for her hand. "In a strange way, the war saved us a little bit with the steady pay."

"You mean somethin' good came out of this here war?" Roxy said with a laugh.

"I guess so," Red said.

"Well, ladies," I said, clinking our bottles together, "here's to the war!"

And we drank every last drop we had, not knowing what kind of boys we'd get coming to us in the morning, or who would be alive come the afternoon. Only the wounded and the dead knew what we'd been through, what we'd seen. And I thought, *When I leave this godforsaken war, I'll leave my memories in the ground with the last-word whispers from the dying.*

And I'd never step foot in Europe again.

4

EVELYN

June 1989

Evelyn Jones walked around her house in a hurry, closing all the window blinds with her purse hooked on her arm, before double-checking the stove and filling up her cat's water dish. She took a parting look at herself in the hall mirror and studied her pink blouse, the one her daughter Michelle had given her for Mother's Day, ruffling the poufy cap sleeves before sniffing her wrists where she'd sprayed a little Windsong perfume. She unbuttoned her collar to show off the strand of pearls she'd clasped around her neck, another gift, this one from her husband, touching them lightly with two fingers, but then thought they were a little too fancy for coffee at the Pancake House with her church group and slipped them into her purse. She'd run out of rouge, and pinched her sagging cheeks to redden them up, before sweeping a lock of hair from her forehead and looking into her eyes, examining the shafts of color that used to be so bright.

A puff of air blew from her mouth; there was little she could do about that at her age.

She pulled her purse strap up over her shoulder and walked briskly down the hall for the front door, but before she could set her hand on the knob, a knock came from the other side and shocked her still.

She stood on her tiptoes to look through the peephole.

A man. A nicely dressed man. Young. She guessed he was about thirty, with shiny brown hair and fitted clothing—and a tie? He didn't strike her as the type of man she should be afraid of, but still, she wasn't used to getting visitors. She opened the door cautiously, keeping the screen door locked between them.

"Hello, ma'am," he said, and he adjusted the leather bag he had slung over his shoulder. The American flag her husband had strung on the flagpole waved and rippled behind him. "That's a nice flag you have," he said, smiling, but when Evelyn didn't smile back, he cleared his throat. "I was wondering if you could help me. I'm looking for someone."

"Out here?" Evelyn lived in the country, a few miles from the nearest town. She glanced over his shoulder and to his car; he had to drive down the long gravel driveway, past the barn, and through the cattle pastures to make it to her house.

He smiled. "Yes, ma'am…" He searched his pockets, padding them first before digging his fingers into one and pulling out a business card. "I'm a reporter from New York."

Evelyn held in a laugh. "New York! What on earth…"

"I'm doing a story." He held his card out for her to take, but Evelyn still didn't feel comfortable enough to unlatch the lock, and he stood with his arm extended.

She wondered what kind of story would bring him to eastern Washington, where the local news only talked about the weather. Clearly, he had the wrong house, the wrong county—God, even the wrong state. The only reporter she'd ever known was back in the war, and he was a sneaky little man, someone she never trusted. She hoped this man wasn't like him.

He finally lowered his arm after waiting for Evelyn to take his card and reached into his leather shoulder bag. "I'm looking for..." He glanced at some notes he'd pulled from a folder, balancing his bag and the papers in his full hands. "Do you know..." He looked at Evelyn through the screen, back at his notes, then back to Evelyn. "Are you Kit?"

Evelyn felt herself go pale, paler than she already looked without any rouge on. She hadn't used that name in over forty years—that name belonged to a girl. Someone else. Another life.

She slowly moved her head from side to side, too stunned to squeak out any kind of words.

The man stared at her, a little gleam in his eye, and Evelyn sensed that he didn't believe her. A few excruciating quiet seconds followed. She rested a hand on the screen door lever, making sure the lock was still firmly engaged, which he noticed.

"This is the fifth dairy farm I've visited in Grant County. The farm over there—" he pointed off in the distance "—said he thought you might be the woman I'm looking for." He smiled, but Evelyn only continued to stare, unblinking, until her eyes flicked to his papers and she caught a glimpse of what he had compiled.

Letters, they looked like, old yellowy envelopes addressed in pencil. Cursive handwriting. He swiftly pulled the letters back so she couldn't see, clearing his throat.

"That's Mark Jenson's place. He doesn't know my family. None of the farms around here do anymore. I've lived here my whole life."

"Oh," he said. "I see." He tried giving his card to her again, pressing the paper corner into the mesh screen until it folded, but Evelyn never did unlatch the lock. "Well, if you do happen to remember the person I'm looking for…" He managed to slide his card through the thin space separating the door and the latch. "Here's my card." He winked, and she snatched it from the door. "Just in case."

"I won't," Evelyn blurted. "I don't see how I could suddenly remember someone who doesn't exist. As I said, I've lived here my whole life."

"Have a good day, ma'am." He dipped his eyes before turning away.

Evelyn shut the door, hoping he wouldn't look back, throwing her body flat up against it and closing her eyes. One hand reached up to feel her neck where she thought her pearls were strangling her but they were still in her purse. Her eyes popped open when she heard his car start up, and she peeked through the window blinds to watch him, only he wasn't inside his car and driving away as she hoped, but turning around and looking at the farm from all angles with his hand to his forehead, shielding his eyes from the sun.

"Drive away," she whispered to herself.

He focused on the roof of her house only to slowly draw his eyes downward and look right at her through the window blinds. She backed up in a fright, the blinds shuddering from having her hand on them, which she knew he could see from the other side.

Evelyn wasn't sure what to do other than pace around her living room, nibbling her fingernails. She wondered how he'd found her, but that wasn't the troubling part.

It was the fact that he *knew* to find her.

She stopped pacing, hands to her face, feeling the pressure of her palms against her eyes, but then with relief heard his car drive off.

Her husband walked through the back door unexpectedly, throwing the door wide open. "Hi, honey," he said, and when the door slammed shut, the clack of wood on wood startled her so severely, she jumped as high as a cat before slumping forward and bracing herself against the wall. "Sorry," he said, "I thought you'd left already. Don't you have plans today?"

Evelyn put her hand against her chest where her skin felt warm. "I do have plans…" She swallowed, and he looked up from the table where he'd placed a wrench and another greasy farm tool. "I mean I did."

He wiped his hands down the front of his dirty overalls. "Which is it?"

"Which what?" Evelyn wasn't listening. Her mind was still very much on the reporter who had been at her door. She peeked through the blinds again, uncaring that her husband had soiled her table linens with his dirty tools, watching the reporter's car vanish behind a pillow of dust.

"Either you have plans or you don't," he said, but Evelyn continued looking through the blinds until the car had completely disappeared. "Evelyn?"

She turned around, waving herself cool, and he glanced at the card in her hand.

"What's that?" he asked.

She put her hand down, hiding the card behind her back as nonchalantly as she thought was possible. "Nothing..." she said, and a field hand yelled for her husband from outside.

He gathered up his tools, turning to leave, but took another look at his wife. "Is everything okay?" he said. "Are *you* okay?"

She smiled. "Yes, yes... I'm fine," she said, though he didn't look convinced. "Go. Someone needs you. Really, I'm fine..."

He left out the back door and she fell onto the couch and sat facing the front door with her purse in her lap. She wasn't going to the Pancake House today. Not now. How could she? Sweat poured from her armpits, ruining her pink blouse, and she couldn't remember the last time she'd sweated.

Evelyn dug into her purse and pulled out her address book, frantically flipping through the pages, one after the other until she found the number she'd been looking for. She reached for her phone and stretched the receiver's cord all the way across the couch to reach her ear. While dialing she thought about what she'd say, but when the receiver was picked up on the other end her voice got caught in her throat.

"Hello?" the voice said.

"It's me," she blurted, followed by a long, quiet pause. "We need to talk."

5

KIT

The mess cook seemed only mildly interested when I asked him if he had a map of Germany to go along with my eggs the next morning. He'd paused for a moment, cigarette dangling off his lips, holding a slotted spoon full of eggs over my tray. "I might have one." He slapped the eggs onto my tray—*clack*—pulling his nub of a cigarette from his mouth and exhaling the smoke. "How fast you need it?" Nurses had lined up behind me, eager for real eggs that morning instead of our usual K-rations, pushing me with their trays.

"Hurry up, Kit!" one nurse said.

"Yeah, stop holding up the line," another one said. "Move it already…"

"Today?" I said to the cook between pushes, holding my spot in line.

He winked. "I'll see what I can do."

"Thanks!" I said, skirting off. "It's worth a bottle to you."

I scarfed down my eggs from a table not far away.

Moments later the cook poked me in the side. I looked up with eggs bulging in my cheeks. "Make it two bottles, Kit." He handed me a folded map.

I swallowed, eyes widening. "Yeah, yeah," I said, taking the map. "You got it. Whatever you want."

I hurried off to my tent with the map stuffed in my pocket. The last thing I wanted was for some nosy nurses to see me with it. They'd think we were moving again and wonder who I'd slept with to be the first to know.

Roxy and Red sat on their cots, playing cards. I flopped onto my mattress, turning my back to them and pulled the map out, taking a guarded look.

"What are you doing?" Red asked, trying to take a peek.

"Nothing, all right?" I said, turning my back even more. "Play your cards, Red."

I had a good idea how far we were from the German border, which was behind enemy lines, but lines change daily, sometimes minute to minute. I didn't think we were more than a long day's drive from Karlsruhe according to the measurements I was taking with the tip of my pencil. It felt good to know the name of the place—to know he didn't vanish into the fog.

B-17s droned past, one after the other. I closed my eyes, wishing them safety as the tent fluttered from the planes flying so low. We plugged our ears until they had passed. Then what followed was a period of quietness, the bated minutes in between our boys' departure and their return. Roxy and Red slid cards into their hands, while I looked at the map.

The tent flaps flew open, and I scrambled to hide the map under my pillow before whipping around.

A nurse wearing a little white dress and even whiter shoes stood in the entry. She flipped her woolen blue nurse cape over one shoulder. "Gail Barry," she announced at half past seven in the morning.

After pausing dramatically with her chin tilted up and her cape hanging off her neck behind her, she sauntered over to Roxy's cot. She tossed her tote on the mattress with a flump, taking a discerning look around, tugging slightly on her white nurse's dress. Roxy and Red watched her from their cards, Roxy, with a cigarette hanging from her lips and Red with her eyes cast upward, studying her every move.

Gail flung her hair to one side with a dramatic head flip. Tawny or was her hair hazel? Brassy, I'd decided. Shiny and brassy and clean. The tent flaps fluttered open from a burst of wind and the shock of light turned her hair gold. And those lips. Damn, how'd they get so plump when mine felt like dried cherries? A pin-up girl if you ask me, and I thought she was lost—she had to be lost. I hadn't seen anyone in the field in a white dress before. Not a spec of dirt on her; I'd bet money she'd had a real bath not long ago, and not one out of a helmet. The stark contrast made us look even more ragged than we were.

She unzipped her bag and dug through the contents, picking up some of Roxy's things and tossing them to the end of the bed.

Roxy had never taken her eyes off her, but when Gail seemed to be claiming her cot for her own, Roxy put her cards down. "That's my bed, toots."

Roxy shared almost everything she had, from her pre-threaded suture needles to her hairbrush, but never—under any circumstances—would she share her bed. It was her one true space in this war without any blood on it.

Gail adjusted the belt around her tiny little waist. "I'm your new bunkie."

I leaned off my cot to look at her sparkling shoes. She smelled like clean cotton, and I closed my eyes, imagining her hair smelled like her dress, and it'd been so long since I smelled freshly laundered things. I opened my eyes when I realized she was watching me, and caught myself from falling. "What'd you say your name was?" She took her cape off, and now I smelled honeycomb, which could have only come from her.

"My name's—"

"I said, that's my bed!" Roxy untied her headscarf to ruffle her dark hair, which was sorely in need of a wash, and stood up, stepping closer to Gail, who'd taken a step back and closed up her collar with a searching hand. "And why are you in a dress?"

Gail's eyes fixated on Roxy's unbuttoned nurse fatigues, exposing the lacy red brassiere she wore so often. She cleared her throat, fighting hard to look away from Roxy's undergarments, her eyes darting off only to zero back in on Roxy's cleavage. "I'm here from General," Gail said.

Red set her cards down. "General?" Gail's shoes stuck to our floor from tracked-in mud. She lifted her feet one by one, examining the soles and looking completely mortified, though they still looked sparkling to me. "Darlin', this is the front line," Red said. "You took a wrong turn somewhere."

Roxy laughed, one step away from bumping Gail with her sidearm. "You sure did."

Gail pulled a piece of paper from her dress pocket and

read her orders aloud, which Roxy snatched from her hands to read herself. "See," Gail said. "I'm in the right spot."

Roxy looked up after reading Gail's orders, solemnly giving her back the note. "Well, this is my bed, ya hear?" She pushed Gail's tote but it barely budged. She pushed it again, and again, but still no luck even after using both hands. With a final grunt, Roxy leveraged her knee on the mattress and lugged the bag over to a cot with only a thin blanket, still pinching her cigarette between her lips. "There!" Roxy said, swiping her hands together, but the bag slipped heavily off the edge and onto a muddy floorboard.

Gail's hands flew to her cheeks. "Well!" she said, eyes stretched. "I never!"

Gail reached for her tote, heaving it onto the cot with such force I would have thought she was a man. She fixed her hair, running her hands over her bouncing curls, before looking at her palms. "Oh, ick! Dang the dirt…" She turned in circles, a mousy squeal coming from her mouth, looking for a place to clean it off as we watched, but everything from our blankets to the dusty tent ceiling had some kind of filmy dirt on it.

Red finally handed her a towel from her waistband, which she used right away to clean those fingers of hers. "I'm Red," she said, holding her hand out for a shake, but Gail had already turned back around and dug through her tote, moving her bottom from side to side. Red cleared her throat. "Gail?"

She turned around. "Oh! Sorry…" Gail shook Red's hand and then looked at Roxy with such disapproval you'd think she had ants crawling on her. Roxy offered her a hand to shake anyway.

"Are you washed?" Gail said, and Roxy's jaw dropped. "You guys know about germs?"

Roxy's mouth went from wide open to drawn up like a purse, and all three of us looked at the new girl with such astonishment I wasn't sure who was going to break first. Then Red spoke up, which I was glad about because Roxy looked like she was about to blow. "I'm the chief nurse in this unit, and I guarantee you us *guys* know about germs."

Gail's face changed. It was neither a frown nor a smile, but more of a straight line. "My apologies." Her chin tilted up.

"This is Kit," Red said, pointing to me. "And Roxy." Red waited for her to shake Roxy's hand, which was still extended, fingers wiggling, but Gail only looked at it.

I chugged my canteen, unable to watch with how uncomfortable the situation had turned. "Kit," I heard Gail say as I glugged, "and Red, Roxy, is it? Are these your real names?"

Water sprayed from my mouth and nose. "Ah hell," I said.

"What's wrong with our names?" Roxy said. She'd put her hands on her hips, which I thought was a bad sign.

"Gail," I said, wiping water from my mouth, "I think the real question is… what should we call *you*?" Listening and watching her spar with Roxy was one thing, but insulting all of our names was a different matter entirely.

"Yeah," Roxy said, "don't ya know? You don't get to pick your nickname. We get to choose it for ya." Roxy jumped onto her cot and lay back, hands behind her head, chuckling sheepishly.

"Oh?" Gail's face took a turn for the worse with her lower lip hanging slightly.

"Do you have a nickname from General?" Red asked.

Gail clasped her hands together, thinking. "Well, my middle name is Francine and back home I've been known to go by Fanny."

Roxy burst out laughing. "Yes!" she said, sitting up board straight on her cot. "That's it."

"What's so funny?" Gail glared at Roxy, who was no doubt enjoying this bit of news Gail had so freely given up. Red turned away, smiling, leaving me and Roxy to tell Gail why her name was so funny.

"Where'd you come from?" I said. "Did you go through England?"

"I was there for a day," Gail said. "Then I came here." She looked confused by our question. "Landed on the continent last night."

Roxy had lit up another cigarette and took a few long pulls, puffing smoke up at Gail who waved it away. "Well, doll face," Roxy said. "Fanny is exactly what we will call you. Guaranteed."

"Roxy," I said, giving her the eye. "We can't."

"You heard *Gail*," Roxy said, who was now holding her cheeks from smiling so much it hurt. "Fanny. That's her name."

Gail sat on her cot, hand on her tote, tapping her clean little fingers on the canvas. "Tell me now. What does it mean?" Her face was straight, and I swear her wavy hair had straightened too.

I cleared my throat, trying to shake the smirk from my face. I'd never had to explain this before, and I felt a heat of embarrassment. "If you'd stayed in England long enough, then you would've known. The Brits call—" I pointed between my legs "—this a fanny."

Roxy howled, moving her hands from her cheeks to hold her stomach. Two nurses stopped near our tent flaps outside, trying to hear what had gotten into us and asking if they could come in.

"Shush, Rox," I said, and she quieted, barely.

"I see." Gail's face turned placid. "You find this amusing, do you, Roxy?"

Gail stood suddenly and Roxy jumped up too. "Yeah," Roxy said, lifting her chin to make herself look taller, but Roxy was a bitty thing, barely able to reach Gail's eyes at the level. "I do."

Red immediately stepped in between them. "That's enough, you two." She pushed them both to sit on their cots, where they immediately drew opposing, nasty little faces. "Gail, you'll have to earn your name. Got it? And it's not Fanny." Roxy looked deflated, letting out a puff of air. "And you, Roxy. Leave it alone. She'll earn her name and that's that."

"Say you," Roxy grumbled, but Red still had a stern eye set on her. "Yeah, sure, fine." She put her hands up, surrendering to Red's insistent look.

"Gail," I said, and she looked at me. "Weren't you issued fatigues?" She smoothed her skirt against her legs, shaking her head "no" very delicately. "Because you can't wear that dress around here."

I pulled a spare uniform from my things. "Here," I said, tossing it at her, which she caught against her chest, eyes closing. "You can wear that until you get issued one. One size fits all, so it should be fine." I looked at the clock. "But hurry up. Our shift's about to start, and we need to get a ride out there."

Gail held the pants up by the crotch. "Button-fly pants?"

I held in a laugh, watching her whole face turn up. "The army wasn't prepared for women," I said. "We wear men's uniforms just like everyone else."

Red and Roxy laced up their boots while Gail got dressed in the corner of the tent, pulling one arm from her dress and then slipping that arm into the fatigues, looking over her shoulder, making sure we weren't watching her. "Don't wait for me," Gail said. "You guys go on. I need time to change."

Red took a long look at Gail. "Don't miss the last transport lorry to the line. You won't want to walk to the clearing station. It's too far."

"I understand," Gail said, but I didn't think she did.

I pulled the map out from under my pillow and folded it few more times to make it smaller. I looked for a place to stash it, but no matter where I thought of putting it, I realized Red could easily find it, and once she found it, she'd ask questions, and questions led to only one thing— the truth, and how the German found us out, that it was my fault.

"What about you, Kit? You coming?" Red said, holding open the tent flaps with Roxy. I looked up from my cot, palming the map, which she immediately noticed, squinting. "What's that?"

My stomach sank a little. "Oh, ahh… nothing." I slipped the map into my pocket and then busily gathered my things as she waited.

"Let's go!" she said. The clouds had rolled in, hiding the sun behind her and swelling with rain.

"Coming!" I said, and I flashed her a smile before following her outside.

*

We arrived at our clearing station near the battlefield already soggy from another transport in the rain. Red prepared for surgery with the doctor, repositioning the operating lights and laying out their medical instruments nicely onto a tray lined with white canvas. Roxy and I rushed to administer plasma to a soldier with a bullet hole to the abdomen, who talked about monsters in the night and mosquitoes with teeth. After we'd got him stable, and a little relief from the pain, his ramblings changed and he talked about the real monsters and mosquitoes, the German patrols and their 88s.

He pulled me closer to him, grabbing on to my arm. "Am I gonna live?" he said.

"Yeah," I said, "you're going to live." He was one of the lucky ones. The bullet didn't go very deep.

Roxy brushed his hair back, smoothing it against his head. "You're gonna be fine, soldier. A right fine young man you are, and an even finer gentleman you'll be when the war ends." She caught my eye, and we continued to patch him up.

Me and Roxy had cleared two patients before Gail decided to join us. I was proud of Roxy—she'd kept her mouth shut about it, never mentioning the fact that our new "bunkie" was late. But when Gail finally did make it to work, boy did Roxy let her have it.

Gail folded up her umbrella, giving it a good shake, standing next to the big, bright operating lights. "Clearing station, right?" She shook her feet too, but those sparkling white shoes now had mud caked all over them like chocolate frosting.

Roxy stood up from where she'd been kneeling, the vee of her unbuttoned uniform puffing with her chest, showing a good patch of skin. "Where have you been?" she said.

The doctor looked up. Red too. I stayed kneeling, realizing I was the only one who believed Gail when she said she needed time to change. Girls like that took time.

Gail's smiling face turned upside down, seeing Roxy. "I got lost."

"Lost?" Roxy laughed. "You hear that, Red? Fanny here got lost."

"Don't call me that," Gail said. "It's..." She played with the buttons closest to her neck. "It's Nurse Barry. Thank you very much."

"Red, scissors," the doctor said over their patient, in between a thread and a tug on some sutures.

Gail looked aghast. "The doctor doesn't address you formally?" she said to us.

I dabbed antiseptic on my patient's arm, getting ready to stick him with plasma. "Sometimes he does," I said before telling my soldier to hold tight. "Does it bother you?" I'd plunged the needle into his arm while still talking, which to my surprise made Gail squirm like a stepped-on worm.

"Well, will you get a load of that? Hey, Red!" Roxy yelped over her shoulder. "They sent a nurse who can't nurse." She folded her arms and turned to me. "You ever hear of that, Kit? A nurse who can't nurse."

"Never heard of it," I said.

"Yeah, never heard of it either," Roxy said.

Gail held her dripping umbrella, and Roxy leaned into my ear but talked loud enough for the whole tent to hear. "Maybe she's one of them?" She nodded, answering her own question. "You know, one of those spies you were talking about. She could be a Hun sent to kill us in the middle of the night with a long knife, the kind that will slice right through a person. Front to back." She looked at Gail, who had slits for eyes. "Like butta."

The doctor snapped at Red, who was so distracted by Roxy's declaration she'd forgot to hand him the scissors.

Gail held her head up, her entire body stiff. "I am certainly *not* a spy."

Two medics rushed into our tent, wet as blankets, and lay a wounded soldier on the ground with his stretcher. His skin bubbled with red and black blisters, and the smell, a sweet and sickly char of a body clinging to life in pulses. One eye was wrapped up as if he'd lost the thing, but it was hard to tell under the loose bandage the medic had tied around his head. The soldier reached for it himself not knowing where his own head was, his fingers grasping at air. Roxy injected his neck with a morphine syrette, and that's when Gail came to life, dropping to her knees to hold the soldier's hand.

The medics barked out where'd they found him. "In a burning Sherman. Only survivor." But beneath their voices was Gail's, whose quiet soft tone steadily rose above the light tap of rain on the tent canvas.

"Where are you from, soldier?" Gail said, very near his face.

His blast-shocked eye suddenly moved. He blinked once. "Toledo," he said, spitting blood from his mouth, "Ohio." His head bobbed and nodded like an earthquake. "Are you an angel?"

"I am," she said. "And you're a hero, my sweet soldier. You beat the enemy."

"I did?" he said, and his mouth opened as if he was trying to smile, but in fact it was a wide hole.

Gail ran her hand over his head and through his hair, smoothing it away from his face like a mother comforting her child. Her eyes had an enduring longing to them and looked glossy from welling tears. Then she sang, and her voice traveled like a warming breeze, filling every square inch of the tent with the most glorious sound that harped from her lungs.

"*When the night falls around you, hold my hand and I'll be there for you...*" Red froze, hand reaching for a scalpel, eyes moving from her patient to Gail while Roxy fell plumb backward on her bum. A bandage popped from my hand, unraveling as it wheeled across the floor, my thoughts and ears only on the sound of Gail's sweet, driven melody. And for a moment, there was no war. There was no blood. "*You're always safe with me...*"

The soldier's eye fell heavy with morphine, and Gail let out a little breathy "job done" kind of sigh. She stood up and patted her hair, tucking in loose strands behind her ears and making a few noises. "Oh! Looky here," she said, picking up the roll of bandages near her toe. She tried handing it to me, then noticing our shocked faces, pulled back and looked at us as if we needed medical treatment.

"She's a nurse," Red barked, and there was no more talk about whether Gail was a real nurse or not.

The patient load dwindled by nightfall and we were let go for dinner. We figured it had something to do with the refueling we'd heard about yesterday. Red and the doctor finished cleaning up after their surgery, and we waited for her outside after the rain had turned into a sprinkle. Gail pretended to smoke, taking waspy puffs off her cigarette and not bothering to inhale.

"Why'd you call me a spy?" Gail's voice cut through the smoke.

Roxy seemed caught off guard, coughing at first and searching for words with a bumbling mouth. Gail never took her eyes off of Roxy, which meant she had to answer, but I felt uncomfortable with the whole situation because I was the one who put spies into Roxy's head.

"It's my fault," I said, finally, after watching Roxy struggle.

"Why is it yours?" Gail tossed her head back as if she didn't believe me.

"I make up stories, all right?" I blew smoke from my mouth. "And I told Roxy something about spies at the field hospital last night and, well you see, Roxy… She'll believe anything!"

"Hey!" Roxy stomped out her cigarette.

"Well, sorry, Rox. But you do. And you eat up spy stories." Roxy tilted her head, knowing I was right. "Admit it, Rox. You really do."

"Yeah, sure," she finally said. "I suppose I do."

Gail appeared to accept this explanation, nodding, looking at the ground while still taking wispy little puffs off her cigarette.

"You honestly can't blame me," Roxy said. "I mean, look at you."

"What about the way I look?" Gail said, reaching for her collar and fingering the top button.

"You're all wound up!" Roxy had lit another cigarette and waved it at Gail's collar. "Tight as anything I've ever seen."

Gail made a line in the moist dirt with her toe, and I could tell from her flushing cheeks that she was trying hard to keep her temper in check. The beautiful ones you had to look out for, I always thought—the underestimated ones. "I'm different than you." She straightened her neck. "I'm a proper girl. I don't wear red brassieres and let people know it."

Roxy's mouth fell open. "Listen, sweetheart," Roxy said. "You spend a few more weeks out here, caring for boys who may not live the next day, hell the next minute, then we'll talk."

Gail didn't say anything, and rightfully so. Roxy had a point. Gail was new to the battlefront. Her nursing experiences came from General, where her little white skirt stayed white, and her patented shoes clicked down hallways of tile and stone. It was a place for recovery and rest, not a place for dying with burns glowing red on your skin. Gail, everything from her shiny hair, to that tiny waist and even tinier ankles, embodied General—the place Nurse Blanchfield talked about in the War Department film—where nurses played golf in their spare time, slept in actual dorms and wrote letters to family on real desks with sharpened pencils on crisp, white paper. Gail was exactly what the soldiers needed to see while rehabilitating, and plenty.

But not in clearing. Definitely not in clearing.

Roxy stared at Gail, waiting for a response, but I thought her silence was enough. "So, don't lecture me on—"

"I think she got it, Rox," I said.

"Do you?" Roxy asked.

Gail nodded with as little neck movement as possible, which Roxy seemed to accept. She looked for a place to snuff out her cigarette, one hand cupping it underneath to catch the ash, while me and Roxy watched her. Finally, she gave up and stuck it in some mud near a tent spike, taking a little breath and wiping her hands over her uniform.

"And don't call me Fanny." Gail looked at her nails before looking up at Roxy who hadn't said anything. "Please."

"Yeah, yeah," Roxy said. "Your little secret's safe with me."

Gail slapped her thighs. "It's not a secret."

"Look," Roxy said. "Can we start over or what?"

Gail nodded, and they finally shook hands.

We stood for a second or two, but it seemed like we'd been standing outside for a long time. "What's taking Red so long?" I peeked into the tent after smashing my cigarette with my heel. All seemed normal enough, Red and the doctor talking after another surgery. Voices were raised and then quieted, which wasn't alarming at first until Red backed up into the operating table from something he'd said, dropping a metal tray loaded with instruments.

I threw open the tent flaps and Red's face had turned snow-white, twisting and pulling her operating cap in her hands.

"Everything all right in here?" I said.

Red broke away after a pause. "Everything's fine." She walked toward me, clipping her medical bag around her waist. "Ready?" She motioned for me to walk through the tent flaps first.

"Kit," Doctor Burk said. "Can you come here for a second?"

"No, she cannot," Red said to him, taking me by the shirt-sleeve. "Our shift is over. Come on, Kit. The mess tent is waiting."

Roxy and Gail climbed into the back of the jeep, ready to take us back to camp. I turned to Red as we were walking. "What's going on?" I asked, but her lips only thinned. "Does this have something to do with the German?"

"Don't!" She stopped abruptly, eyes closing. "We said we wouldn't talk about it, remember?"

"Jeez, all right, Red," I said.

She pushed me toward the jeep, but I was only a step away.

6

KIT

The ride back to camp was a quiet one, only a few pops of gunfire in the east and the glow of bombs very far away. Red had her eyes closed for nearly the entire trip, arms wrapped around her waist. When we pulled up to the mess tent she sprung to life and hopped out.

Roxy pulled me aside. "What's with her?"

I shook my head, watching as Red walked into the mess tent ahead of us, pretending I didn't know, though I was sure it had something to do with what the doctor said to her.

"What's for dinner?" Gail said, holding her helmet to her head with both hands.

Roxy laughed.

"Why is that funny?" Gail said.

"We could get K-rations. We could get stew," Roxy said. "There's no way of knowing."

Gail looked horrified. "Stew?"

We walked through the tent flaps and I was relieved to see the cook dishing up real food for dinner. Something salty, something hearty. I tried to place it, taking a deep breath through my nose. "Smells like—"

"Ick!" Gail covered her nose. "What is that?"

Roxy smiled, breathing it in while stretching out her waistband with her thumbs. "That's dinner, doll," she said. "Be glad it's stew and not hamburger gravy."

Gail gagged in her hand, and I tugged on her sleeve. "Come on," I said, and we filed in line behind Red to dish up before it was all gone.

"Why do we have trays?" Gail said. "Shouldn't we have bowls?"

I shoved a tray at her. "If they hear you complain you won't get any of it," I said.

The cook spooned up a heap of stew and slapped it on my tray, holding his ladle steady until I looked up. A savory steam hovered between us. "You got that donation for me, Kit?" he said, and I immediately felt the map he'd given me in my pocket.

Red's eyes swung in my direction as she shuffled ahead of us in line. "Yeah, yeah…" I said, and he lifted the ladle. "Later, all right?"

We sat at a long mess table not far away. What a luxury to have real eggs for breakfast and now dinner on a tray. I spooned a hunk of potato into my mouth.

"What was that about?" Red said, and I shrugged, potato bulging in my mouth, which I thought was enough to deter her, but she wouldn't take her eyes off me.

"I don't know." I swallowed. "He's a cook."

Red went back to her stew and ate quietly, taking small bites. Gail shoved bits of beef and potato around on her tray with her spoon, which Roxy noticed right away.

"Are you gonna eat that?" Roxy said to Gail. "Because I'd be glad to take it off your hands." She eyed Gail with arched eyebrows, pressuring her to give up her food.

"Leave her food alone, Rox," I said, and she went back to her own meal after sticking her tongue out at me.

Noreen, a nosy nurse, second tent down from us, walked up to our table holding a bundle of letters. None of us looked up, except for Gail, but that was because she had no idea that Noreen was a real pill to deal with.

"Hello," Gail said, but I kept my head down.

The usual pause followed—the cold-shoulder kind we always gave her, a pause she never understood, or if she did, refused to acknowledge.

Noreen cleared her throat. "Hello, ladies."

"Noreen." I set down my spoon. The last time I saw her she was rummaging around in our tent looking for wine. She said she was looking for Red, but her big head was under my cot and her knees were on the ground.

She plopped the bundle of letters on the table, which Red took. "These were delivered to my tent by mistake." She smiled, and I saw the bits of beef that had collected between her yellow teeth.

"Oh, I'm sure, Noreen," I said.

"Get lost," Roxy said. She started to sneeze, mouth open, eyes squinting. "Ahh, ahh…" But she'd lost the urge, and Noreen giggled. "It's you I'm allergic to, Nosy. Get lost already."

"Who's the new girl?" Noreen pointed with her head to Gail, who was about to say her name, but Roxy cut her off.

"I mean it!" Roxy stood up, throwing a finger at the open tent flaps. "If you know what's good for ya." Several other nurses stopped and stared while holding their trays in their hands, but not just because of the rise in Roxy's voice, more so because they knew Roxy and Noreen's history. Roxy caught Noreen lifting a wedding ring from an unconscious patient. Noreen said she'd removed it because his fingers were swelling, but she couldn't explain why it had ended up in her pocket.

I stood up next, and Noreen looked very offended.

"Well, if that's how you treat other nurses!" She stormed off and Roxy sat back down, mumbling about what a no-good nurse she was. "If anyone's a spy it's her—lousy pretender."

Red glanced up when she said "spy," giving me a little look before untying the string from the letters. I waited for Red to say there was a letter for me, hoping there was something from my mother, as she thumbed through them. I wanted to read her words, see her handwriting from home, and I was due for a letter, but the mail was unpredictable and always delayed. "Anything for me?" I finally asked, and Red shook her head before handing one to Roxy. "Oh."

Roxy patted my hand. "It's all right, Kit. Your turn next time." She sat up, smiling, before ripping into it. "It's from Nonna!" She separated the pages, examining the length of it, before reading the letter aloud. "Dearest Dorothea Teresa," Roxy said, and Gail giggled.

"Dorothea?" Gail giggled again, patting her lips with a napkin. "That's your real name? But it's so refined... so... so..." Gail looked up and saw Roxy tracking her like two missiles in the night.

"You got somethin' to say, toots?" Roxy said, and Gail messed with her napkin, shaking her head. "Now, can I read or what?"

"Go ahead, Roxy," I said, nudging her to continue with a flick of my chin.

Roxy cleared her throat. "Says here she got a new pair of ice-tea glasses that prism in the sun when she's outside on the patio eating lunch. And... and..." Roxy's eyebrows furrowed and she got an inch away from the letter, reading to herself.

"Ice-tea glasses, huh? God, that's when I know I've made it," I said. "Ice tea on the patio without a care in the world." I scraped my tray of all its brown sauce and took a warm drink of water from my canteen. Roxy folded up her letter and stuffed it away. I swallowed. "What else?"

There was a pause, an abnormally long pause for Roxy. Her head hung over her tray. "Roxy?" I said, and she dug into her stew and chewed up sloppy mouthfuls.

"Is everything all right?" Gail asked, and Roxy wiped her mouth with the back of her hand, gulping.

"She said my brothers took bets on when I'd call it quits and come back home. The whole neighborhood has taken up a collection, and the purse is up twelve dollars." She pushed her tray away and folded her arms. "Chumps!"

Gail sighed. "Sorry, Roxy. That's a mean thing."

"What about you, Red?" I said, and that's when I noticed her eyes had welled with tears.

"News from my mama," Red said, and she wiped her tears away in such a hurry most people wouldn't have noticed. "She misses me. That's all. And the landlord raised her rent, she says she'd be on the street without my nursing money." Red stuffed the letter away, muttering her last words to herself. "But I already know that…"

"Aw," Gail said.

Roxy looked up at me, and I shook my head—not now. We'd have to explain Red's situation to Gail later.

"What's that?" Roxy said, startling Gail with a sudden reach across the table, grabbing her wedding finger and examining an enameled gold ring. "You got a fella?" Roxy said, swallowing a mouthful of stew.

Gail snatched her hand back, rubbing and twisting her ring. "No," she said. "It's a class ring. Mount Holyoke."

Roxy whistled, fanning herself as if she was warm. "Fancy girl college. So, you're *beautiful* and smart! And you sing like a songbird, better than Dinah Shore, let me tell ya. I bet you modeled for one of those women's magazines too." Gail didn't answer, and after a few moments of silence, Roxy's eyes grew wide with her unrequited admission. "You did, didn't you? A model! Fancy college, fancy dresses, and that hair and those perfect lips…"

"Stop it right now." Gail didn't like it when Roxy called her beautiful, and she let her know it by giving her a pointed glare. "I mean it!" she snapped, and Roxy nodded. After a pause, Gail's eyes skirted over the other nurses to see if anyone overheard, but there were a hundred nurses scraping their trays and many conversations going on at once. "I only modeled to pay for school." Gail lowered her head, hiding her face with her brassy locks. "I'm more than a pretty face."

"Don't, Gail," I said, and she looked up. "You're beautiful and smart. It's all right to be both."

"Kit's right," Red said. "You can be both. I'm sure Roxy here would be a model too, if she could."

Roxy squinted at Red before going back to her stew.

Benny wandered into the mess tent with his camera, snapping photos of the nurses still standing in the food line. "Oh no," I said, and the girls looked up. He didn't seem to mind that the nurses were posing this time, even if they were smiling because they were being served real food. "Hurry," I said, "before he sees us." And we shoveled our last heaping spoonfuls of stew into our mouths, except Gail, who didn't understand why we were inhaling our food at an alarming rate. "Gail, eat up!" I said, mouth full, and she reluctantly slipped her spoon into her mouth.

"Why?" she said over her food, trying to choke it down when Benny slid into the seat across from Roxy.

We all groaned, except Gail.

"Hey, ladies." The sour tang of old grease lifted from his hair. The top button of his shirt had been undone, exposing a carpet of chest hairs. "Real food tonight." He examined his camera settings, squinting, and adjusting. "You've got to be happy."

"Benny," I said, swiping my mouth with a napkin. "Don't take photos of us, all right? Not now."

He watched us as we ate, looking very disgusted. "No, God! I won't." He raised his camera and focused on Gail, who'd just swallowed the bite of stew she'd been rolling around in her mouth.

"Gail Barry," she said, and they shook hands across the table.

"Pleasure's all mine," he said.

"I said get lost, Benny. Jeez," I said.

"No. Actually, you didn't, Kit," he said. "You said not to take any photos while you're eating." I glared, and he put his hands up, letting his camera hang loose on his neck. "And I won't."

"What are you doing here, anyway, lurking about at this hour?" I said. "You shoot in the day." He smiled slyly, and my mouth pinched. "You have something to say?"

He leaned onto the table using his elbows. "There's a story circulating. Thought I'd come in here, see if I heard anything." He nudged Roxy. "Everyone knows how this one likes to talk," he snickered.

"You're always on the prowl for something, Benny. There's a war going on. Isn't that story enough?" I said.

"Yeah, but this is something else." His voice turned into a whisper. "Did you hear about the SS officer captured not far from here?"

I gulped, feeling every hot potato swimming in my belly. "What officer?" My fingers curled around my spoon.

"Word is he was found lying on the side of the road. They thought he was dead, but sure as the sun, he was breathing! But get this…" He paused, leaning over the table a little more. "They think he was tortured." His eyebrows moved into his forehead. "By one of *you* nurses."

"You're lying, Benny!" Roxy said. "Get outta here, will ya? What a disgusting thing to say! None of us would do anything like that. Not even Nosy Noreen."

"Nah, serious," he said, "and you know what else?"

Gail's eyes grew wide like a doe caught in headlamps. "What?" she breathed.

"The Hun's talking," he said, and my spoon slipped from my hand and fell to the floor. I looked at Red, but she was already looking at me, stone-faced and serious.

"That's enough, Benny," Red said, still looking at me. "Leave us."

"Yeah, you little creep," Roxy said.

He whistled. "Touchy this evening, aren't we, ladies? Makes me think you're hiding something." He got up, chuckling to himself. "I'm going to sniff this story out like a rabbit from a hole."

Red looked like she was about to vomit.

Benny lifted his camera and focused on Gail. "Boy are you a sight for sore eyes, my dear," he said, and Gail's pleasant face flattened.

"I'm smart," she said, and he lowered his camera a hair to see her with his naked eye.

"Yeah, yeah…" A slippery smile spread on his lips, half-hidden behind his camera. "Of course, sweetheart…"

Flash!

Gail's hands flew up to cover her face while Red stood up.

"Get out of here, Benny!" Red said, and he scrammed. "Damn him." She sat down with a thump, pushing her empty tray away, spilling what was left of her stew onto the table. "Can't we eat in peace, just once?"

"Hope you trip on a tent spike, Benny!" I shouted.

We sat for a moment too stunned to move and all for different reasons. Roxy got up first to walk out. Gail followed.

"You ready, Red?" I said, standing up next.

Her head had been in her hands. "Yeah," she said, looking up, tired and drained. "Let's leave."

We walked back to our tent, Roxy and Gail a few feet ahead of us. I didn't want to bring up the German, but the farther we walked not talking about what Benny had said, the tension became too much to bear. I finally reached out for her shoulder, and she shrugged me away.

"Red," I whispered. "The German…"

She shook her head. "Not going to talk about it, Kit."

I watched her walk away again. "Is that what you and the doctor were talking about?" I said, and she turned around, finger to her lips for me to be quiet.

"Shh!" she hissed. "Dammit, you promised not to talk about it. Don't you understand? If Benny or someone else hears us…" Red burst into a fit of tears and I didn't know what else to do but to hug her, and tell her nothing was going to happen, nobody would find out it was us, but how could I promise those things when I was as unsure as she was?

Rain spit from thin clouds into a hard rain, and Nosy Noreen appeared, wearing rain gear and running for her tent, but instead ran into us. "Oops!" she yelped. "What are you doing standing in the rain?" She blinked, holding her hood over her head while we shivered in our nurse fatigues. "You two are acting strange."

"Listen, Nosy—"

Red pulled me away from her. "Bye, Noreen," Red said, and Noreen reluctantly walked off in the dark, her feet slushing through small puddles as she took occasional looks over her shoulder.

"Great," Red said. "Nosy Noreen... Last person we need suspecting something."

"Come on," I said, and we walked on to our tent, hands over our heads to protect from the rain, but it did little use.

"Damn, Kit," she said, moments before we stepped into our tent. "This was what I was afraid of. If only the Hun hadn't figured you out."

"Yeah," I said, followed by a pause. "If only."

We walked into our tent and found Doctor Burk standing by Red's bunk, dressed in his civvies, and wearing an old man's hat. Gail looked frightened to see a man in our sleeping quarters, even if it was the doctor, while Roxy looked more confused.

"It's not our shift, Doctor," Red said.

"I know." He squeezed a messenger bag strung over his shoulder, watching us stare at him. "There's been an accident." He darted across the tent to stand in front of Red.

Roxy and Gail immediately sat down. Red remained standing. She didn't mind working fourteen-hour days or being called out for emergency surgeries, but a man coming into our tent uninvited was like walking into her bedroom while she was changing.

"Surely there are nurses on duty?" Red said. "Doctor, this is our tent, our space..."

"I know, Red," he said. "I wouldn't have come if it wasn't important."

"What accident?" I said.

I had a terrible feeling he was going to say something about the German, that he'd died and the army found out what we'd done, and we'd be court-martialed, sent home, and put in jail—all of it flashed through my mind. My throat balled up as if I'd swallowed a rock.

"Several men are stranded, in need of medical," he said. "I was specifically asked to gather my nurses for a rescue."

"What?" I sat down, feeling very much relieved, but still a little scared. "Us?"

Red scoffed. "We can't leave—"

"You can," he said. "I've been informed the battle is in reprieve. We can slip out and be back before anyone notices." The doctor rushed to close the open tent flaps so nobody could hear.

"Slip out where?" I asked.

He clenched the tent flaps behind his back with his eyes frantic and wide.

"Behind enemy lines."

7

EVELYN

Hours went by and Evelyn sat on the couch, clutching her saddlebag purse and staring at the front door, thinking of that reporter and what he wanted with her. She thought that telephoning Roxy was going to help, that she'd know what to do, but instead she went on about a reunion that fall for the nurses, which was too much for Evelyn to think about on top of everything. Her husband came in through the back door, looking surprised to see her still in the house, and watched her for a moment from the doorway.

"Have you been here all day?" he finally asked.

She looked up, her last long fingernail in her teeth. "What time is it?"

"Almost three," he said. "You know we have that barbecue at Michelle's house to go to."

Evelyn sighed—her daughter's barbecue. The last thing she wanted to do was go to a barbecue—and in June? The weather was so unpredictable. "I didn't forget," she said, but she had forgotten, even though it was on her calendar.

"Maybe it will be good for you," her husband said.

He took his ball cap off to rub his face, and Evelyn realized she still had the reporter's business card in her hand. Her husband looked up, and she shoved the card deep into the pocket of her polyester pants.

"Did you hear me, honey?" he said. "Maybe it—"

"Is someone here?" Evelyn thought she heard a car drive up outside and bolted to her feet to peep over her husband's shoulder, but it was only her daughter coming to pick them up for the barbecue. She clutched her chest in relief without realizing how that would appear, and her husband gave her a look.

"Did the doctor call?" he said.

Evelyn turned away from the window. "You always think that." She kissed his cheek. "I'm fine."

He kept studying her.

"Honest," she said, "now go get ready." Evelyn pushed him toward the stairs, and he went to the bathroom to wash up.

She watched Michelle get out of her car and walk up to the house. By the time she'd made it to the door, Evelyn thought she'd convinced herself that a barbecue *was* what she needed—a rest from her thoughts, and a rest from watching the front door.

Michelle turned the car radio on while they drove, an instrumental thing on the AM channel—a soothing melody that should have relaxed her, but soon enough Evelyn swore she could feel her husband's eyes on her from the back seat. After forty-four years of marriage, she knew he was on to her. But in the same breath, she knew he had enough sense not to bring it up in the car with their daughter right next to her.

Evelyn played with the reporter's card in her pocket, feeling the sharp paper edges, before looking over her shoulder. Sure enough, her husband was staring at her. They both smiled at each other, and she turned back around.

"Is something going on?" Michelle said.

"No." Evelyn pulled her hand from her pocket to fold her arms. "Why?"

"Because you're both really quiet," Michelle said. "I don't think I've ever heard you two so quiet." She moved her rearview mirror to look at her dad in the back seat.

"It's a quiet day." He smiled at her through the mirror. "Looking forward to the barbecue," he said.

"Hey, Mom," Michelle said. "I invited my neighbor. She's about your age. She's nice. I think you'll like her."

"Mmm." Evelyn put on a smile for her daughter's sake, but she normally tried to avoid women her own age.

They pulled up to Michelle's house and Evelyn walked straight to the backyard through the grass where the barbecue was in full swing. Children splashed in small pools, and dogs raced around fetching toys. Smoke billowed from a barbecue cooking dry-rubbed ribs and seasoned hamburgers.

She took a seat at the patio set where she could fan herself and have a glass of ice tea. Evelyn held the glass up to the sunlight after swirling the ice around, trying to get the right tilt to see the refracted light, tilting, tilting, the tea moving closer and closer to the lip, almost able to see a rainbow—

"Mom?"

Evelyn jolted, spilling a drop of cold tea on her polyester pants and losing her tilt. "Yes?" She'd closed her eyes briefly before looking up at Michelle.

Her daughter pointed to the woman sitting at the same table wearing powder pink pants and a white knit shirt with little butterflies. "This is my neighbor I was telling you about. Hazel."

"Oh?" Evelyn smiled politely at Hazel, saying hello, though she wasn't in the mood for a conversation, especially after the reporter's visit that morning. She thought she'd made that clear by crossing her legs and looking away, but Hazel slid her plate and chair closer after Michelle walked away.

"Great daughter you have there. Michelle and her husband—they're the best neighbors." She'd pointed to Michelle with her spoon, who was now opening the barbecue and flipping burgers with her husband. "I moved into the area not that long ago after retiring." She scooped up some macaroni salad and chewed her food, but her eyes were set on Evelyn as if she expected her to ask where she'd lived before.

Evelyn decided to indulge Hazel, thinking a little banter might satisfy her enough to leave her alone for the rest of the barbecue. "Where from?" The ice melted in Evelyn's tea, beads of water sliding down her glass and over her fingers.

"San Diego area," Hazel said. "I was stationed there during the war."

"Mmm." And there it was. Evelyn should have figured as much—all women her age had a story to tell about the war days, and it was her luck she'd have to sit next to one of the talkative ones. This was one of the reasons she liked her church group, where most of the women were a full generation younger than her.

"Liked the weather so much I stayed!" Hazel looked at Evelyn a little more closely, swallowing the mouthful of macaroni salad in her cheeks, and Evelyn felt the question coming—it was inevitable, and her heart ticked up just thinking about—the question everyone her age asked each other. "Did you serve in the war?"

Evelyn immediately took a long sip of her watery tea as if she didn't hear her—chit-chat time was over—but even after she'd set her glass down and patted the tea from her lips, Hazel was still looking at her.

"Well, did ya?" Hazel said, and Evelyn went on to jiggle her head into something that resembled a shaky nod, something she'd never done before, never admitted. Even her own daughter didn't know she'd been in the war— they'd only told her about her dad's service. Evelyn quickly looked around for something else to talk about. The burgers on the grill, the slobbering dogs, the children splashing in pools, when she noticed the sky, and the gray clouds that had rolled in.

Goose bumps erupted down her arms, causing all the little hairs to stand up. "Does anyone know the weather forecast?" she said, but Hazel shook her head and dug into her plate.

Everything's fine. Evelyn took a deep breath through her nose, and tried to focus on the sounds of the barbecue, but instead heard something heavy and clunky being brought outside. She twisted around and was surprised to find her daughter wheeling the television out the slider to the patio. "What are you doing?" Evelyn said.

Michelle bent down to plug in the extension cord.

"There's a D-Day special on," she said, and Evelyn's limbs shuddered. "Hazel asked me to put it on. It's on all the major channels."

"It's today? The anniversary?" Evelyn closed her eyes tightly. My God, how could she let this happen? *The D-Day anniversary.* Evelyn always stayed home on that day to protect herself from parades, memorials and the memories that haunted her—and she most certainly didn't think about Michelle's TV since the barbecue was supposed to be an outside affair.

"But the rain, Michelle," Evelyn said, pointing to the clouds. "I don't think this is a smart idea at all. You could ruin your set!"

"Mom," Michelle said. "I already told her. Besides, I thought Dad might like it too, and the other veterans here." She looked to the sky as she set the rabbit ears on top of her television set. "The weather will be fine."

Hazel scooted to the edge of her seat, happy as a clam, and Evelyn closed her eyes. *Of all the luck*, she thought. The very last thing she should be watching today was suddenly in her face.

Evelyn's husband had just walked over and placed his hand on her shoulder. "Honey?" he said, and Evelyn looked up.

"Can you help me inside?" Evelyn felt sick. She held her shaking hands out in front of her. She thought she could hide it like she'd done for so many years, that nobody would know something was wrong with her, but she wasn't sure if she could hold it together after the day she'd had, and especially now with the D-Day anniversary program about to play out before her.

"Yeah, yeah…" Her husband set down his paper plate, which was top-heavy with ribs and pasta salad, and tried helping Evelyn out of the corner she'd wedged herself in. He leaned down and whispered, "What happened today?"

Evelyn looked helplessly into her husband's eyes without a word to say, just as Michelle turned on the television. The guests quickly crowded around the table with the thought of watching TV outside, and Evelyn was absolutely, and unfortunately, stuck.

Michelle spun the dial. "Found it! Tom Brokaw—D-Day anniversary special."

Evelyn's husband shook his head, oh so sorry, mouthing that it would be all right and to look away. So, Evelyn closed her eyes again. She even covered her face. But little could be done about the volume, and while everyone heard Tom Brokaw talk about the beaches, Evelyn heard wounded soldiers crying out for her in her mind, begging for morphine.

"Lord, there were girls on the beach?" a man said, and when people chuckled, Evelyn felt as if she was floating in a thin fog, waiting for it to be all over, counting the seconds, wishing time would move faster. Then, just when she thought she might catch some relief, thinking a commercial was about to cut in, her husband gave her hand an urgent squeeze, forcing her to look.

Evelyn nearly fell out of her chair. A black and white group photo of the 45th Field Hospital shown on the screen—Evelyn recognized herself right away even from so far away, sitting crisscross on the ground with her medical kit in her lap. She couldn't believe it. After controlling her surroundings for so many years and protecting herself from this very thing, she'd stepped right into the past.

She grappled for a lie to tell in case anyone recognized her, so she wouldn't have to talk about her time in the war, but when the camera zoomed in and focused on Kit's face, showing all her features, Evelyn hadn't a story to explain it away. Even at twenty-two the resemblance was still striking. Michelle spun around, looking just as shocked as her mother.

"Mom, is that you?"

Evelyn sat with her husband in the back seat of Michelle's car on the way home. No words were exchanged, and Evelyn thought Michelle might not bring it up, but about halfway home, she adjusted her rearview mirror to look at Evelyn in the back seat.

"How come you didn't tell me?" Michelle said. "You lied to me all these years—a nurse in France? You said you were a nurse after the war."

Evelyn and her husband looked at each other.

"Mom?" Michelle said as she drove, but Evelyn didn't know what to say.

"I'm surprised you're upset," Evelyn's husband said. "You knew she was a nurse. You're making it a bigger deal than it is. So what? Your mom was a nurse in France."

"I'm not upset, Dad. I'm confused! Mom's always told me she worked in a hospital after the war. Maybe she didn't tell me specifically it was in the United States, but she's always made it clear that she'd never been to Europe, never left the country. Kind of a big deal. Why hide it?"

"Does it matter?" Evelyn's husband said. "I was in the war, you know that, but I don't talk about it much, and you've never asked me for details."

"Yeah, but at least I know," Michelle said. "Mom, why keep it a secret? And how come you're not saying anything?"

Evelyn didn't know how to answer her without sounding brash, but quite frankly she just wanted the conversation to be over, so she said what she thought was necessary in order to get her daughter to drop it. "Oh, Michelle, I'm sure there're things about you we don't know. Give it a rest, all right?" she said, but that only ignited Michelle's curiosity.

She pulled over unexpectedly into the gravelly road shoulder, whacking her hazard lights with a flat palm before coming to a complete stop. She twisted completely around in her seat and faced the both of them. "Sorry, I love you guys, but I can't let this go. None of this makes sense," Michelle said. "It's weird."

"I'm the same person," Evelyn said.

Evelyn's husband reached for their daughter's shoulder from the back seat. "We love you too, honey." He looked at Evelyn. "The reason we kept it—"

Evelyn shook her head sternly. Michelle knew she was in Europe; that was enough. She didn't need to know everything.

Michelle's face fell. "Shit, what?" Her fingers dug into her leather headrest as she twisted even more in her seat. "You're not going to tell me I have a French sibling out there, are you? I know soldiers do things in war—"

"No!" he said. "It's not like that."

Evelyn's eyelids fluttered. "If only it was that simple," she mumbled, and Michelle's mouth fell open. Thunder boomed overhead unexpectedly and a light trickle of rain tapped on the roof of the car. All three of them looked up, but it was Evelyn who saw the dark storm clouds brewing directly above them.

Her heart instantly ticked up. She put a hand to her pounding forehead, feeling the worrying chill of the impending downpour and the whip of wind that was sure to follow. First the television special, and now the rain? "Take me home," Evelyn said just as the surge of fear she'd been hiding all day had caught up to her, rolling visibly over her body like a crashing wave.

Michelle yelped, her eyes both shocked and horrified from seeing her mom this way.

"Hurry!" Evelyn's husband said, and Michelle slammed the car in gear and sped back into traffic, wipers swishing back and forth.

Evelyn closed her eyes. There was only one other time she'd seen that heartbreaking look on her daughter's face, and she had vowed never to see it again. She remembered the year and the day as if it was last week—October 20, 1966.

At first, Evelyn didn't hear the weekly television report over the whir of her Electrolux and vacuumed her carpets in relative ignorance. But something had caught her eye, a flash, someone running, and when she looked up at the television, her heart sank.

War had come, yet again.

Evelyn turned off the vacuum, sitting down on the edge of her recliner near the television, fingers pressed to her lips in utter disbelief, watching soldiers dressed in those damn olive drab fatigues she knew all too well disappear into the jungles of Vietnam with a reporter by their sides, running into the war.

She'd heard about what was going on in Vietnam, but this was the first time she saw war on television, and it threw her mind and body into a place netted in dark and danger.

A shuddering wave of nausea rose from her toes up to her head with the bap, bap, bap of gunfire echoing in her living room. She could almost smell the bomb smoke and taste the acrid grittiness of it in the back of her throat. Evelyn reached for the screen, dropping to her knees and crawling to the television. Silent tears dripped off her cheeks.

Evelyn felt incredibly small, no voice of her own, when she heard a muffled whimper behind her where Michelle had walked up unexpectedly, clutching her dolly under one arm with her little eyes fixed on what was playing before her on the television.

"Michelle!" Evelyn scooped her daughter up in her arms, ashamed she'd allowed her to see war on television. "I thought you were in your bedroom." She held her daughter close, trying to hide her eyes as she rushed into the other room.

"Mommy," she said, pointing at the television as Evelyn rounded the corner into the kitchen. "Were you there?"

Evelyn wiped her tear-driven face, scrambling for words. "No," she said. "I wasn't there."

"But on the phone... I heard you say you were in the war."

Evelyn closed her eyes tightly. Michelle had overheard her calling numbers out of the phone book she'd loaned from the library. "I was trying to find a friend, sweetheart."

She set Michelle down and held her hands, looking into her daughter's eyes, which had welled with tears. "I wasn't in a war. I was a nurse."

"Oh?" Michelle sniffed, holding her dolly close to her chest while Evelyn played with her daughter's pigtails, twisting them around her fingers, but Evelyn saw the uncertainty in her eyes, an expression that said she was still scared and worried her mom had been in a war. "A nurse?"

"That's right, sweetheart. I wore a little white dress and clicky little heels." Evelyn felt a bubbling of emotion near her eyes, thinking of Gail and the first time she met her—and that cape, that damn blue cape. A lump formed in her throat. "Don't worry, all right? Men fight in the war. I served coffee to the wounded after the war in a big hospital." Evelyn said the words for her daughter, thinking it would set her mind at ease, though inside Evelyn felt her heart twist with such a blatant lie.

"Did you find your friend?" Michelle said.

Evelyn's gaze trailed to the window and her mind thrust into the dirt patch outside, spinning out of control through the field and up into clouds of angel hair.

"Mommy?"

Evelyn's attention snapped back, and she hugged Michelle, burying her face into her daughter's shoulder where she smelled of baby powder and soap, still hearing the bap, bap, bap of gunfire in her living room even though the program had changed.

Michelle turned onto the long farm road, tires drifting over wet gravel to get to the house as quick as she could before lurching to a stop near the front porch. Lightning cracked overhead followed by a booming roll of thunder, which felt like a zap to Evelyn's heart.

Michelle threw the car in park.

"Stay here," Evelyn's husband said frantically to her, hand on the door. "I'll get an umbrella!" But when he jumped out of the car so did Michelle, and they argued in the pouring rain. Evelyn watched and heard them through the tracks of rain on glass.

"What's wrong with her?" Michelle said, near crying. "Dad, tell me. No more secrets!" She threw a pointed finger at the car. "Something serious is happening!"

"You don't understand," he said to Michelle. "She gets like this when it rains. She's always hid it. From you, from everybody!"

Evelyn's throat closed up and she found it hard to breathe. She looked to her husband for help, trying to get his attention through the rain-splattered window, her arm lifting and falling on the seat as he talked to Michelle.

"I have to get the umbrella—your mother!" he said, but before taking a step toward the house, he looked through the window and saw Evelyn crumpled on the seat. "Oh my God—" He threw open the door, and rain spat into the car. "Honey!" he shouted, arm outstretched. "Take my hand…"

Evelyn's arms tingled just before every muscle in her body locked up. To Evelyn, the rain drilling on the car roof was bad enough, but to step out in it? Feel it hit her skin? Her mind told her it would be all right—it was only water—but it wasn't just water. It was a memory—and even though her rational mind said it couldn't happen, she had the overwhelming fear that the rain would split her open like a cherry, spill into her insides and drown her.

"Mom! Take my hand," Michelle cried, and it was her daughter's touch that allowed Evelyn to answer.

"I can't."

8

KIT

Our tent turned deafening quiet, so quiet you could have heard a pin drop. I don't think any of us were ready for what the doctor had proposed. Gail especially, who looked as if her head had been played for a gong.

"Pardon?" Gail said, shaking her head a bit. "What was that?" She looked at us, cupping her hand behind her ear. "Where'd he say?"

Nobody answered her; we were still trying to process the news ourselves.

"This is dangerous," Doctor Burk said. "I'm not going to lie. A secret detachment—a surveillance convoy crossed enemy lines, only they were found out. One made it back alive. The rest are waiting to be saved, all badly injured."

Roxy bolted to a stand, holding her head at the temples. "Whoa! Wait a minute, will ya?" She walked to one end of the tent. "You want us?" She spun around. "A secret mission to save some of our boys?" she said, and the doctor nodded.

"Kit, will you get a load of this?" She could barely contain the smile on her face. "Boy, is this a change or what?"

"It's across enemy lines, Roxy," Red said.

Roxy looked us over, Gail still with her hand cupped behind her ear, and me with my jaw slung open. "What's the matter with ya? It's our boys we're talking about," Roxy said. "Wounded boys. Saving them is what we do."

"Don't be such a fool," Red snapped. "Think about what he's asking!"

Roxy folded her arms. "Red, I don't see—"

"Why us and not the medics?" I said, finally able to speak. Seemed like the logical question to ask.

"Yeah," Roxy said, followed by Gail, who nodded. "Why us?"

"This isn't something that can be covered up easily, four nurses and a doctor missing from our hospital," I said. "I mean, someone will ask about us. Won't they?"

"You won't be missed," he said.

"Hey!" Roxy moved her hands to her hips. "Who says we won't be missed around here?"

"That's not what I mean." He closed his eyes briefly. "The medics could get caught too easily. Nobody would suspect women, and that's why we've been asked. We have a unique opportunity—a window of time while the Third is refueling. As I said, the battle is in reprieve—five days at best. Rumor is Patton is taking Nancy next. Our men will be stranded indefinitely, if they survive that long."

"Stranded," I repeated. The doctor seemed sure of this, his voice very clear and direct as if he'd spoken to Patton himself, and I had to admit I was surprised by this turn of events, which I was sure he could see on my wondering face. "But… but… the quickest way to Berlin is to continue east."

"This is what I heard," Doctor Burk said.

Red had shut down completely, hunched over, elbows on her knees.

"What condition are the wounded in?" Roxy said.

"We have to field-operate," the doctor said.

I gulped. One of the worst things was to operate in the field. "Amputation?"

He nodded. "We've been asked to prepare for it, and I know the others need fluids. My hope is that we get there in time to save them, and their mission."

I walked around the tent, hand to my forehead, thinking about those men—our boys—stranded without any medical. "How would we get in? There must be German patrols all over. And pillboxes!"

Doctor Burk drew a map in the dirt between the floorboards, and for the next several minutes we listened to him explain some of the details. "We'll drive a few miles east where transport is waiting, which will take us to a secret single-track path leading us to a village."

"But what if we get lost, Doctor?" I said. "Shouldn't someone from the OSS be leading us?"

His eyes trailed upward. "I am OSS."

Red threw her hands up with this secret information and slapped her thighs—now the entire thing with Sergeant Meyer made more sense.

Roxy stood up after studying the plans in the dirt, swiping her hands together. "So! We waltz across enemy lines, fix up some of our boys and then walk back over?" she said, and he nodded. "I'm in." Roxy plopped down on her cot and crossed her legs at the knees, swinging one foot back and forth while talking to herself. "Me," she said, "on a secret mission? Well, I declare. Nonna's not going to believe this story when I get home, let me tell you... and then there's my good-for-nothing brothers, Rico and Charley, both those chumps can take their bets and shove them up their—" She popped the collar up on her uniform. "Well, someplace unpleasant, that's for certain."

Gail stood up next, looking at Roxy and smiling nervously. "I'll go too." She rolled her hands into each other.

"Kit?" Doctor Burk said. "What about you?" He stood up slowly after having knelt on the ground.

There was only one answer. "I'll go," I said, and Red walked to the far side of the tent where she folded her arms. "Red?" I said, and she half-glanced over her shoulder, shaking her head slightly, and for the first time since knowing her, after sharing more blood between us than either one of us cared to admit, I didn't know what she was thinking. I took her into the corner so we could talk privately.

"Think about what we've already done," Red whispered. "The German and now this. It's too risky. Listen to what the doctor's suggesting."

"Dolls?" Roxy called out, and Red gathered us into a small circle, taking Roxy's hands.

"Listen to me for a moment." Red swallowed. "Us, behind enemy lines? Nobody will know where we went. Nobody will know how to save us if *we* get in trouble."

Roxy slowly pulled her hands away. "Yeah, Red, but our boys..."

Red had a strange pleading look in her eyes, and it was then I understood the real reason she didn't want to go. It wasn't about saving our boys, or not saving them. What kind of trouble we were in, or could get into. There was danger, yes, but Red had landed on Utah Beach in a hail of bullets; danger wasn't something that held her back. "Kit," she said, reaching for my hand. "You understand, right?"

I nodded.

"I could be listed as a deserter," Red said. "The government doesn't pay a missing nurse." She looked very conflicted, her eyes moving between mine and Roxy's. "I can't do that to my mother."

"You don't have to explain," I said, taking a deep breath, and with that, I felt my lips wiggling from an oncoming cry. This would be the first time we'd been separated since landing on the beach, and I tried not to wonder how I was going to do this without her. On D+15, she threw me into a ditch, saving me from an unspent grenade. On D+24, she found me smoking in the dark and in the rain and saved me from a Screaming Mimi that blew our hospital to smithereens. And on D+32, when I heard the bone-chilling whirr of a German Stuka diving out of the sky, she'd dragged my paralyzed body to safety after she'd already found cover.

The doctor retrieved a bag from his vehicle and began passing around civilian dresses and shoes for us to wear while Red sat on my cot, watching. "These are for after we cross into enemy territory," he said.

Roxy's head bobbed continuously into one long nod, taking the dress and holding it to her body. "Hear that?" Roxy said, elbowing Gail, who nodded.

I packed up my dress and shoes, and padded my pockets,

checking for my pocket knife, but found the map of Germany instead. I paused, thinking of a place to hide it while I was gone, but no spot seemed safe enough, not in my things, especially with Nosy Noreen around. A nurse with a map—she'd think I was a spy. I stuffed it into my pack when Red wasn't looking. I took off my dog tags next. Roxy and Gail did too, then Roxy asked for Gail's ring, which she didn't want to take off.

"Why my ring?" Gail said.

"It's American, toots," Roxy said. "Someone will know."

Gail reluctantly took off her ring and handed it to Roxy. She rubbed her finger where her skin was shiny and smooth.

Roxy tucked our tags inside an empty K-ration box and put it with Red's things—nobody would touch a chief nurse's K-ration. She hugged Red quickly, pulling away before the tears came. "So, that's that." Roxy marched toward the tent flaps and stood in the open wet air, one foot in and one foot out. "So dark," she breathed. "Strange, isn't it?" She turned, looking at us over her shoulder. "No eggs dropping from the sky. No glowing bursts of orange. I'd almost feel better if there were, ya know?" Her voice turned into a whisper, which I could barely hear over the rain. "In the dark, the Huns can hide anywhere."

Roxy walked out of the tent toward the doctor's vehicle, which I could see a few feet away outside, sputtering with its red taillights glimmering off the puddles.

Thunder rolled and Gail's whole body shuddered as if it were the Germans dropping bombs on our heads. She took a breath, the kind you take before diving into deep water, and followed Roxy out of the tent.

"Love ya, Red," I said.

I turned around to see her once more. Leaving her felt as natural as ripping off a sticky bandage from dry skin. And I stared at her, wanting to go, but couldn't move for the life of me.

She stood up to pace, blowing air forcefully from her mouth, her eyes red from crying. "Dammit," she said to herself, before walking over to her medic bag and opening it up.

"What are you doing?" I said, gulping, hoping to God she had decided to come with us.

She shook her head, mumbling to herself about how she couldn't believe what she was about to do, pulling a hypodermic needle and ampules of medicine from the bag.

"Red—"

"Let me tell you one thing," she said, pointing a finger at me. "If we stumble upon any of that Nazi loot we heard about—*the giant*—I'm keeping some of it. Got it?"

"Red… I… I…" I wanted to tell her not to come, though I needed her to come, and I'd be lying if I said a pang of guilt didn't hit me square in the chest for not telling her directly that we'd be all right without her. "But your mother," was all I could say.

"Yeah, I know!" She slipped her dog tags into the box with ours. "But there's something you don't." She looked into my eyes, and I'd never seen them so glossy. "I can't let you go alone."

She threw open the cabinet we used to store extra medical supplies and grabbed enough morphine syrettes to kill us all.

"That's too much," I said, reaching out.

Red turned around, counting the last few syrettes she had in her hand and shoving them into her bag. "Kit, we're women. If we get caught by the Germans, the last thing you'll want to be is alive."

She grabbed my hand and we walked out together.

9

KIT

Nowhere had it rained more in one night, than that night in France. We piled into the back of a lorry pockmarked with shrapnel, packed up with our equipment tied to our bodies, and drove down a rustic road into the country. I fastened my helmet strap and closed my eyes.

"We'll be fine," I said, tipping my head back, my face wet and salty from the rain. "We'll be fine." The road was rugged and full of twists and turns, which made us bump up and down like jalopies.

"Is this what it was like the other night?" Roxy said, and I looked at her.

"Other night?" I said.

"Yeah," Roxy said, holding on to her helmet. "The friendly fire." After I didn't say anything, she leaned forward to catch Red's eye. "You know, those civilians you fixed up."

"No." Red looked at me when answering, her face hard as stone.

"What happened the other night?" Gail said.

I shook my head, giving the kill motion to my neck, and Gail sunk down next to Roxy. I wasn't about to have that conversation. My mind was on the enemy line we were about to cross, not the laws I broke days before.

"Well, do we know where we're going?" Gail said. "Does the doctor have permission to drive this lorry?"

"It doesn't matter now, permission or not," Red said.

"I'm sure Doctor Burk will brief us when we get there," I said. "You know, in case…"

"Yeah," Red said. "In case."

We stopped abruptly surrounded by dark hills, and the doctor came around in a hurry. "Let's go… go, go, go!" And we filed out of the back of the lorry and into a tiny European car that had been waiting for us with its engine running. Doctor Burk claimed the front seat with a driver, a girl who looked about fifteen, scrawny as a chicken, wearing a thin lavender peasant dress; not what you'd expect in this rain. Red slid into the back seat, and I realized there was only enough room for one more. I turned to Roxy, hand on the door, and she looked up at me in the rain.

"What?" Roxy said, and I pointed. "Oh no! Where are we gonna sit?"

Doctor Burk rolled down his window and slapped the side of his door. "In the trunk. Hurry! We don't have time."

Roxy grunted a little bit, having to climb into the trunk with Gail, who got in carefully as if she was stepping into a hot bath.

The driver pushed a gun at the doctor. "You'll need this," she said in broken English, and he took it, reluctantly, stuffing it into his pack.

"We save lives, not take them," Red said, and the girl slammed the car into gear.

She drove into a decrepit vineyard with quiet urgency, straight through rows of knotted, tangled vine with fruit that had been left to spoil. The rain fell so hard the driver rolled down her window to see the road, splashing through mud puddles that spurted brown droplets into the car.

I squeezed my medic pack, trying not to think of what waited for us, and how we were going to walk through a village unnoticed. *What am I doing here?* I thought to myself, and I was thrown back to the day my brother and I enlisted, when we confessed our secrets to each other. Seemed like a million days ago. Another me. Both of us naïve, young, unsuspecting.

I'd noticed his bedroom door was shut for quite a while, and the field hands were still milking the cows, and he was supposed to be in the barn, supervising. I rapped on the door once, waited for a second, and then rapped two more times after I didn't hear anything.

The lock clicked over and I cracked open his door. He'd walked to his window and gazed outside. "Why aren't you in the barn? It's milking day."

He'd turned around after a pause. "Sit down," he said, pointing at the corner of his bed, and I knew it had to be bad. "We need to talk." I sat down gingerly, tucking my skirt under my thighs, nervous he was going to tell me he was sick, or that Mom or Dad were sick—some terrible secret only he knew. Then he blurted, "I've decided to enlist."

"In the war?" I wasn't sure what was better, to be sick or join the war.

"Well ya, sis," he said. "What else is there to enlist for?"

I suppose I wasn't totally surprised. Sam had dreamt of being a pilot since he was a boy, making planes out of paper and sticks and modeling kits. "He's an engineer," Mom would say, ignoring his blatant fascination with aircraft, "building skills he'll need to run this farm someday." She was proud he'd gotten his degree in Pullman, and even prouder when he moved back home, immediately settling into the role of foreman. What she didn't know was that Sam flew Jenny crop dusters in the Palouse during college. He was already a pilot.

"Have you told Mom?"

He hung his head slightly, gaze trailing to look out the window. "I'm gonna tell her after it's done. Dad, he'll understand, but Mom..."

And we were quiet for some time, both of us staring out the window, watching the cows eating grass in the pasture. Grant County was small, everybody knew everybody, and most importantly, they knew my uncle died in WWI and how his death had devastated my mother. Parents told their children about the war growing up, ending with "and then there's what happened to poor June Perkins from over there on Jacobs Road."

"Why, Sam?" I asked. "Why now? You registered, isn't that enough?"

He looked at me, a little wink in his eye. "For the same reasons you're joining."

"What?" I'd only told one person I was thinking of

joining the Nurse Corps. My mouth pinched. "Damn that Barbara—she told you? I knew I shouldn't have trusted that little—ugh! She still owes me a dollar she lost on a bet." I stood up. "Wait till I collect. I'll give her a piece of my mind—"

"I saw you in town coming out of the cinema. There was only one film showing, and I knew what you were planning," he said, and I sat back down.

"Oh." It was true. I'd watched that damn War Department film a hundred times in the last week. Nurse Blanchfield was very thorough, sitting at her desk in her official uniform—she'd been a nurse for over twenty-five years. Everyone loves a nurse, I think is what she had said, and I wanted to be part of it—and get out of Grant County.

"You'll be a great nurse, sis. You don't have to sneak around." He slowly looked up, meeting my eyes. "It's my secret that will break her, and I'll have to live with that." He scooped me up in his arms and we hugged. "I love you, sis. Don't ever forget."

I went to bed that night praying for the mothers of the war, and that if their sons didn't come back, they'd rest a little easier knowing they'd raised heroes.

The car slid with a sharp turn, and that's when I saw Red looking at me. She patted my knee. "Did you steal that champagne?"

I smiled, and she knew. "I won it," I said.

"Yeah, sure."

The driver looked over her shoulder, giving me a strange look from having broken the silence. She had tan eyes. I didn't think it was possible to have tan eyes, but she did, and when she looked at me, I felt a pang of fear.

She shouted something in French before slamming on the brakes, and I grabbed Red's hand, but we'd flown into the front seats. "It's time," she said, flicking her hand at the doors. "You leave." She threw open her door and ran around the back in the rain. The doctor got out, followed by Red and me, and we watched her unlock the trunk. She looked out into the horizon where the sun had started to rise, over her shoulders and to both sides, which made me look over my shoulders.

"Be careful," she said, and the trunk popped up.

The air smelled as heavy as the rain with the exhaust pumping from the tailpipe. "Are we across enemy lines?" I said, but she'd walked back to the front of her car.

Roxy and Gail climbed out from the trunk looking like they'd been through a washing machine. Wet and tossed and sick. Gail ran her fingers under her eyes where her mascara had run, and her bottom lip trembled when she saw the black streaks on her fingertips. Roxy snorted her running nose, wiping her face with her wet sleeve.

The driver pointed east, shouting a few things in French nobody understood. "What?" Red said, but she'd backed up her car and sped off under the grind of rusty gears, and she was gone.

"Let's go." The doctor motioned for us to follow him, but we'd only walked a few feet on the trail before we were brought to a halting stop by the sudden appearance of a rushing river.

We stood like gray figures cast against first light, up to our knees in the tall wet grass at the river's edge, feeling very exposed with nowhere to hide. Then the lightning came, streaking across the morning sky in jagged strips of orange. "Where's the bridge?" Rain pelted my face, and we looked at each other, mouths drawn in disbelief.

"But... but... nobody said anything about a river!" Roxy said.

Red grabbed my arm, her fingers slipping from the rain. "This way," she said, but I could only read her lips. She pointed to where it was more of the same, soggy wet grass with a vanishing bank, but a leafy bush and some brambles that provided a little cover. We knelt down in the reeds, with our medic bags and slippery helmets that wouldn't stay on.

Doctor Burk pulled a folded piece of paper from his front pocket. "The village is a few miles walk. I have the map." He held the paper up before tucking it back into his pocket to keep it dry. "We should be home by nightfall if we follow the plan. Get in quick, stitch them up and get back."

"Tonight," I said, looking at Red as if to reassure her, but then turned to the doctor. "What's the name of the village? Where are the men?"

"Lichtenau. Third building on the right after entering the square. A sympathetic has taken them in." He walked several paces away, sizing up the narrowest part of the river and the bank on the other side.

Lichtenau. That didn't sound French, but every village sounded strange and foreign and more of the same. I chased after him, holding my helmet to my head.

"Lichtenau, Doctor? This is in France?" I said, but he swatted his hand in the air.

"Not now, Kit," he said, and he walked back to the group, leaving me by the swirling river and making me feel silly for even questioning—he would have told us if he was leading us into Nazi Germany.

"Now, everyone ready?" he said as Red futilely wiped the rain from her face. "Let's get going!" He adjusted his pack as if he was going to cross the river.

Red gasped. "We can't cross here—we'll get swept away!"

"The bridges are blown," the doctor said. "Our only way across is to cross it together. Arm in arm." He demonstrated how we were to cross, hooking Red's arm. "Like this."

Another crack of lightning burst over our heads. "You knew there was a river?" Roxy shouted so she'd be heard, and the doctor half nodded.

He tightened the straps on his medical pack. "I'll go first, followed by Red, Kit—" he pointed with his head "—Roxy and Gail."

Roxy folded her arms for warmth, shivering and chattering. Gail stood up like a pole, lanky with her arms by her sides and her hair stuck to her neck under her helmet. I had to wonder how'd she make it across. The rain alone on her skin looked like it had been a shock to her system, with her body shaking as much as it was, more so than that ride in the trunk of the car.

"All we need is a couple hundred feet of bridge," I said. "We should at least try to see what's around the bend."

Doctor Burk gazed at the raging river while Gail stood right next to him trembling from her head to her toes.

"Doctor, look at Gail," I said. "I'm not sure she can make it."

After a second of examining her, he'd finally given in, and tightened up his medical pack with one last swift pull. "Okay, Kit. Fifteen minutes in that direction." He pointed.

"If we can't find anything, we walk back here and pick up the trail. Across the river."

And we labored on, our boots sinking into the mud and the ground, slipping and sloshing. It had been well past fifteen minutes, but nobody wanted to stop. We all wanted to find a bridge around the next bend, but when there wasn't one someone would say, "How about the next bend?" and that turned into yet another bend and another. Roxy had slowed down, and her pack drooped low on her back, hanging near her rear end. She was getting tired, and as far as I was concerned none of us could afford to be tired. And when she stepped, she stepped with force, with anger.

"Hey, psst!" I said. "Did you think this was gonna be a picnic?"

Roxy turned around as she walked, hand on her helmet, and looked me in the eye. "Where's the bridge, Kit?" she said as if it was my fault we'd been walking in the rain, tired, and across enemy lines. "Huh, doll face?"

"Quit jabbering your gums, will ya?" I said.

"Yeah, yeah," Roxy said turning back around.

"Get down!" the doctor commanded, and we dropped to our bellies in the grass.

"Is that a bridge?" I said, pulling a pair of binoculars from my front pocket. "Holy smokes, it is a bridge!"

Red pulled them from my hands. "Give me those." She took a quick look. "It's a bridge."

Gail put her hand on Roxy's back and they both sighed with relief. Red elbowed the doctor. "Kit was right."

I took back the binoculars to get a better look, adjusting the lenses. It was a nice long bridge, looked like an original one too, not something that had been blown up and then rebuilt in a hurry. I handed the binoculars to the doctor so he could take a close-up look for himself, and he did, barely, shaking his head disbelievingly.

"What's wrong? It's a bridge." I pointed. "You can see it yourself."

He put his hand up, watching the rain hit his palm, which had turned into a sprinkle in the short time we'd been crouched down. "But for how long?" he said, and we looked up.

"What's that mean?" Gail said. "You're scaring me."

"The rain keeps the German bombers away," Roxy told her, and Gail looked into the sky with the rest of us, ducking fearfully as if the sky was going to fall on her at any moment.

I tucked my binoculars back into my pocket and got up. "What are you waiting for? If there's an egg in the sky with that bridge's name on it, we'd better be across it."

Red grabbed Roxy by the elbow and we rushed down the riverbank. The rain disappeared to all but a drop here and there, but the jingle from our medical equipment clanking against each other sounded like rattling pans. The bridge was definitely getting closer, and the air drier, more stagnant from shifting weather.

A drumming buzz came from the sky. The doctor stopped suddenly and we froze as a plane dropped from a splinter of blue sky, plunking two bombs.

Boom! Boom! We hit the ground with our hands over our heads, feeling the earth move underneath, rumbling and shaking from the blasts. The bridge split into two halves, cracking and buckling, before collapsing into the river. "Damn as anyone," I said, as the plane flew over us. "It's one of ours!" And we watched it fly away into a puff of clouds.

Roxy knocked on Gail's helmet, and she looked up from the ground, bits of grass sticking to her cheeks from being face down with eyes still black from running makeup. Her whole face shook, and mumbling came from her lips in high-pitched squeaks.

"Flip her over!" I shouted, and we flipped Gail over on her back. Red reached for her medic bag, but Roxy had taken Gail's hand, talking to her the way she always talks to patients and getting her attention.

"Gail," Roxy said, "Listen to me…"

"I don't belong… here… in the war," Gail said, slobbering and sniveling. "I'm not like you…" She looked at Roxy in a way I never knew she could look at Roxy, from the bottom up at her weakest moment.

"Well, you're not *in* the war. Just part of it, all right?" Roxy said. "Some of the bravest parts. Coming out here with us broads, on a mission to save some of our boys."

Gail shook her head, face scrunched up, and lips pressed tight. "I'm not supposed to be—" she gulped air "—here. I'm not…" Her skin looked pale and pasty and her limbs grew weak with her fingers barely able to curl around Roxy's hand.

The doctor moved in close, hunkering on the ground. "Gail Barry, I've worked with a lot of nurses, in hospitals and in the field. You're one of the greats. Don't think anything less. And I'd be honored if you assisted me one day."

I looked at Red who only slightly rolled her eyes. Gail had her own way of nursing, as we'd found out, and we all knew Red was the best nurse in France. But with Gail lying on the ground, there wasn't much else that could be said. Red wiped Gail's hair from her eyes. "Hear that, Gail? Believe the doctor."

"Only broads tough as nails could've ridden in that trunk," Roxy said. She pointed at Gail and then herself. "Me and you. Got that?"

We talked her through some breathing patterns, and after a few minutes of lying in the grass Gail looked a little pinker, and we helped her up. She put her helmet back on, and stood weakly while trying to find her balance.

"You all right?" Roxy said, making Gail look at her, and she nodded, which I thought was a good sign given the fact that she'd been paralyzed in the grass a few moments ago.

"Sorry," Gail said, clearly embarrassed. "I don't know what got into me."

"I do," Red said, pointing at the bridge, and we all paused for a moment and looked at the roughened water where the bridge once passed over.

"How are we gonna get across now?" Roxy said.

The doctor took a deep breath. "We'll have to go back to the original plan and swim across." He grabbed his own hands, clasping them together with a fine tight grip. "Arm in arm, hand in hand."

Roxy immediately put her head in her hands.

"We're already wet, what're you worried about?" I said.

Roxy looked up from her hands. "What am I worried about? Dying, Kit. I'm worried about dying."

Red scoffed. "A little late for that kind of thinking, Roxy."

"No," she said, and I noticed her eyes, which had never looked so sad and drawn before. "You don't understand." She gulped. "I can't swim."

We were the ones in shock now. Doctor Burk walked a few feet away, hand over his face, but us girls kept our eyes on Roxy, who looked like she was going to get sick all over the grass.

"You can't swim… at all?" I finally asked, and she shook her head.

"Dammit, Rox," Red said. "Why didn't you say anything?"

"I didn't know there was a river! The plan never included drowning." She pointed at the river, which was rushing fast and gray.

"You'll have to walk back," Red said, "and wait for us then."

"She's not walking back!" I said. "That's the stupidest thing I've ever heard you say."

Red folded her arms. "Is it, Kit? Is it?"

The doctor turned around after hearing Red's tone. "We'll think of something," he said. "You can't walk back."

"I'll hold you," Gail said, and Roxy looked up. "Like the doctor said. Arm in arm, hand in hand." She gave herself a reassuring nod. "We can do it, Roxy. I won't let go."

It had been a few days since Roxy was speechless, and if I could have held the moment forever, I would have. They took each other's hands.

"Well, what are we standing around for," Red said. "Let's get going."

We walked back the way we had come so we could pick up the trail on the other side. Without the rain, our walk felt faster, but now the flies were out, and the bees, and the air was humid from the rising sun. I knew I shouldn't have thought it, but by the time we made it back to where we'd started, I wanted to get in that river, despite the rapid, growing swell of it.

The doctor slid down off the vanishing bank into the river, holding my hand and then taking my arm once I had fully got in. God, it was cold, too cold to breathe, and I instantly wanted to be back onshore. Red, Roxy, and Gail followed, hooking on to us as we waded in a swirling eddy, our packs strapped around our necks to keep them dry.

"Gail," Roxy said, inching across the river. "Don't let go!"

I felt Red squeeze my arm, and I looked at Doctor Burk who gave me a nod. And we waded across, one careful step after another in chest-deep water. "Almost there," I said down the line, looking at Roxy. "Almost there."

Twigs and sticks floated by us in patches. Nothing alarming at first. It just looked like river debris, but it turned thicker and more unnatural-looking. "Ouch, ouch," I said when a piece of wood hit my neck. "What is that—" A sound came from upriver. Not a plane, or the hum of a panzer tank. A mighty roar that eclipsed the rushing river, wood on wood, and metal on metal. "Red?" I said, and we froze, trying to make sense of the change in the water upriver, from gray to black like a dark cloud rolling over the swells.

"Oh no," the doctor said. "It's another blown bridge!" Beams and the side of a bridge washed down the river in forceful clumps, headed straight for us. He let go of my arm and made a swim for it, but the swirling current grabbed hold of him and pulled him away. Red shrieked, doing her best to reach for him, but it was my hand he tried to grab.

"Doctor!" I lunged for him, but our fingers slipped from

each other's in the water and he vanished under a swirl of white water. And he was gone. Long gone.

We screamed and yelped under the roar of waves as Red yanked us to shore, and one after the other, we washed up on the bank. Red immediately burst into tears in the grass. Roxy was the first one to throw up, lying half out of the water with Gail. I was the second, bawling on my knees in the river and in the muck, looking at my shaking hands.

And there we were, just the four of us, behind enemy lines.

10

KIT

The last of the blown bridge washed down the river in jagged chunks. The sun was higher, and the air much warmer. I wrung out my socks near the river's edge. We were all very quiet. Roxy and Gail sat together in the grass, looking at the ground and recovering from exhaustion. Red covered her face with one hand, refusing to move for many minutes after the doctor got swept away.

I looked at my hands, my waterlogged palms. He'd been so close. I squeezed my socks out one last time and laid them flat in the sun. *So close.*

"We should do a prayer," Gail said, and me and Roxy joined with her in a circle. Red watched from a distance.

"Hello, God," I said, eyes closing. "Please watch over Doctor Burk." The words crumbled in my mouth as I remembered the look on his face before he got swept under, eyes stretched, a sense of disbelief.

"Bless him," Roxy said. "He was one of our boys, like all the others."

Gail prayed in whispers, kissing her hands and blowing her words to the sky. "In God's hands," she said.

"Red," I said. "Do you want to add something?"

She got up slowly. Roxy and I took her hands, closing our eyes. "Watch over him, God," Red said. "He was an excellent doctor. A good man." She paused. "But dammit, he left us here without a map!"

Our eyes popped open, and Red ripped her hands from ours.

"Oh no!" Gail said.

"He had the gun too," I said. "What are we going to do?"

Red paced around in a circle, hands on her hips. "I don't know." Her arms flew up. "Does anyone remember what he said? Something about a building after the square?"

"Third building," I said. "On the left."

"I thought it was on the right," Roxy said.

I tried to remember the doctor's face in the grass when he spoke to us, what he'd said. The river was rushing, coldly swirling with rain, and gray. I remembered him talking about the village, and a building. I briefly squeezed my eyes shut. "I misspoke. It's the third building on the right."

"Are you sure?" Red said, and she waited for me to answer, but now I second-guessed everything. "Kit!" she snapped, and I looked at her, fingernails between my teeth, chewing rabidly.

"Yes," I said, and I dropped my hand. "Third building on the right."

"You know what's gonna happen if we show up at the wrong place?" She pointed behind her off in the distance. "We might as well save the Germans some trouble and load the train to one of their POW camps right now."

"I'm sure," I said. "Third building. On the right. I know it, Red. I promise."

Red cooled down, breathing normally again, only to cry a little more. And we stood in the grass, waiting for Red to stop sobbing. I put a hand on her shoulder for comfort when a sudden pop of gunfire shook us all. *Bap! Bap!*

Birds flew from the trees and over the river. We grabbed on to each other, half searching the air for a direction, the other half looking for a place to hide. "Over here…" I said, and we scooted into the weeds where it seemed abnormally still. No birds overhead, and no more shots.

Red crept up ahead to look through some bushes but came charging back moments later. "In the river," she said, shooing her hands at us to get back in the water.

Roxy hyperventilated the moment Red said river and wouldn't move even while me and Gail jumped in.

"Hurry!" Red said, and she grabbed Roxy by the scruff of her neck and threw her in the cold water with us. We locked our arms together, hiding in an eddy protected by a tangle of tree roots and brambles. A heavy car, a military type of wagon, sputtered on the bank somewhere behind us. "Maybe they'll drive away," Red said, but then the engine turned off.

Car doors shut, and I swear I could hear German words. It was then I remembered my socks were still in the grass, flattened from trying to dry them out. "My socks," I whispered, and Roxy's eyes bulged.

Two men in gray-green uniforms walked over to the riverbank, but what kind of uniforms I couldn't tell. One had a gruesome scar cut into his cheek. "Get down," I hissed as they moved closer, and we slid even more into the water, eyes and ears barely above the waterline. The men laughed and pointed into the river, before pulling out their guns and getting very excited about something floating in the current.

Bap! Bap! Bap! Pistol haze drifted like cigarette smoke after they popped off several more shots. "Thousand-year Reich!" one said in German, and Gail clamped a hand over her mouth under the water.

Two bodies drifted by face up. A man, dark-haired, and a young woman with brown hair, eyelids sprung open, transfixed. The current took the man away, but the woman's lifeless body floated near us in the eddy. Her tangling hair snagged in the roots, then her blue dress, her body listing like a sinking ship. Roxy closed her eyes, but Gail's got big as anything as the water rushed over the woman's arm, drawing her toward us even closer. Red quietly released the caught clothing from a branch and her body bobbed along, hugging the shore, before the water finally took her under.

My socks shined up in the grass, warming in the sun. The Germans gazed at the river. All they had to do was look down, then to my horror, they walked over to the muddy bank with one of them catching my sock on the heel of his boot. They lit cigarettes and talked about the rain, not one mention about the people they'd killed seconds ago.

Roxy puffed above the waterline, eyes bouncing from holding in a sneeze. "Ahh... Ahh..." we heard muffling from her throat, and I prayed she could hold it in. Just once. Please, hold it in! Red reached over to cover Roxy's mouth. "Achoo!" A horn had honked and the men ran off just as Roxy let it blow, sneezing into the water and all over Red's hand, but thank God the Germans were already getting in their car.

Roxy looked at me, lips pinched, after they'd sped off.

"What?" I said, and she rose up out of the water and slapped me coldly across the face.

I gasped. "Roxy!"

"Don't ever take off your socks again." She shivered and shook in the water, and I held my cheek where it felt cold and numb from having been slapped on wet skin. As shocked as I was from Roxy's slap, it was nothing compared to the look she had on her face.

"Leave it," Red said to me, then we all climbed out of the river.

"Who were they?" Gail said, dripping on the bank, taking her pack off and tossing it on the ground.

Red shook her head. "Wehrmacht? I don't know. Germans. Isn't that enough? In case you didn't figure it out. That river—" she pointed "—is the damn Rhine." She looked at us standing in shock on the muddy beach. "That's right, ladies. We're in Nazi Germany, not France."

I covered my mouth. Behind enemy lines in France was dangerous enough as it was, but inside Germany? I should have known with name like Lichtenau, and then especially after the doctor brushed me off when I questioned it.

"God," I said.

"What do we do now?" Roxy cried.

Red rubbed her eyes, shaking her head, and I thought of the map I had in my pack. I went to dig it out, searching my deep pockets when it flopped heavily onto the ground between my legs.

"What's that?" Red said, and my stomach sank.

It was soggy and had started to tear. "I... ahh... I just remembered I have a map," I said. Red walked up behind me as I unfolded it carefully. Sure enough, on the other side of the Rhine was a tiny dot of a village called Lichtenau, Germany.

Red held my gaze as if trying to read my thoughts, then she squinted. "Why do you have a map—how'd you get a map?"

I pointed to the dot on the map, tapping my finger, and she finally looked at it.

"We're not far, maybe only a few miles away," she said, and I turned away hoping she'd forget about her questions, but Red rarely forgot anything. "You going to answer up about this?"

I shrugged. "Doctor Burk gave it to me earlier."

Red looked at me for a long while, straight into my eyes, and I gulped. Out of all the stories I'd told her, all the little white lies about wine and extra cigarettes, this was a big one and I felt she saw through it. I waited for her to chew me out for lying, demand I tell her the truth, but instead she pushed the map at me.

"Here," Red said, and I turned away, blowing a relieved breath of air from my mouth.

"Well, what are we going to do?" Roxy said.

Red huddled us into a circle. "We have a choice. We can go back. Or, we can continue what we started," she said. "Like it or not, this is our hand."

"Continue," I said, followed by Roxy.

"Continue," Gail said.

"Okay," Red said, rubbing her forehead. "Let's dry out our gear and change into those dresses." She started unpacking her gear.

We lined up our bottles of antiseptic. Only one had

broken, but we lost the plasma with the doctor. Red asked Gail to sanitize our instruments, setting aside the broken bottle for her to use so as not to waste it, but Gail had gathered up the instruments and headed for the river.

Red stopped her. "What are you doing?"

Gail looked confused and embarrassed at the same time.

"The river isn't sanitary," Red said. "Use the antiseptic."

Gail smiled a little "I'm sorry" kind of smile before walking back. She opened up her hands. "I suppose I'm still not thinking straight."

Red took the instruments from Gail to clean herself, dousing antiseptic over them from the broken bottle. One ampule of penicillin survived the river. She held the injectable in her palm. "This won't be good forever," Red said.

"It's better than nothing, I suppose," I said.

"How are we going to carry our supplies?" Gail asked, and Red turned her around and wrapped her legs up like a mummy with bandages.

"We'll have to tuck everything under the bandages," Red said. "Our skirts will hide it."

Gail stood with her arms up as if Red was her seamstress and fitting her for a new dress. "But it's so bulky," Gail said. "People will notice."

"Do you have another idea?" Red said, and she paused to look up at Gail with her arms spread out until she shook her head.

Once we'd taken as much equipment with us as we could, Red stashed what was left under a rock, and buried our fatigues in a hole. The dress I wore was still damp and smelled fishy like the river with little purple flowers and a lacy hem. I'd been wearing fatigues for so long, the air between my legs felt odd and wrong. My hair crunched in my hands.

Roxy looked me over with those big brown eyes of hers, pulling a sprig of river weed from my hair. "You look like a drowned rat," Roxy said. Red also looked horrible in her ruffly pinstripe dress and Gail in her peachy thing. "We all do. We'll never blend in." Roxy pointed to her feet, wet toes in wet shoes that squished with water. "And our shoes!"

Red pulled a kerchief from her pack to cover her red hair, and immediately she aged ten years. "We'll blend in," Red said. "Hand me your packs." Gail gave hers up instantly, while Roxy shook hers out in the dirt before handing it over. I folded the map up before holding out my pack. "Anything you want to say?" She glanced once at the map in my hand.

I slipped the map down the front of my dress. "About what?"

She snatched the pack from my hands, and the way she did it let me know she wasn't finished with me about where I got the map.

A huge tree feathered with golden orange leaves grew out from the riverbank. "Remember this tree," Red said, pointing. "It's our way out."

God help us.

And together all four of us walked away from the river and into Germany.

We stood on a hill looking down at the village. Binoculars in my hand. No cars drove in and out, the farms looked derelict and the vineyards were all dried up. "What do you see?" Red said, and I looked into my binoculars from behind a leafy tree branch.

My gaze rolled over the village, over the rooftops and down the cobbled roads. *Third building on the right after the square. Third building on the right after the square. Third building on the right after the—* "Ah hell," I said, gasping. "There're two squares."

Red reached for the binoculars, yanking them from my eyes. "Give me those." She took a long look at the squares. "Wonderful," she said, handing the binoculars to Roxy.

"Nobody said anything about two squares," Roxy said, after looking. She handed the binoculars to Gail, who after studying the village for a moment, noticed something we had not.

"One's bigger than the other," Gail said.

"Let me see," I said, and I looked again, adjusting the lenses, and sure enough the second square was different than the first. "It is smaller!" I said. "You can clearly see a fountain in the first and a bell tower, but nothing in the second."

"Man," Roxy said. "You trying to give me a heart attack or somethin'?"

"Red," I said, but she'd started to pace. "Red!"

"What?" Red said, stopping, and looking no better than she had moments ago, agitated and worried.

"It's smaller," I said.

She came walking back. "What does that mean? Smaller. So what if it's smaller? Doesn't change the fact that there are two squares," Red said.

"Let me see again," Gail said, and I handed her the binoculars. "The biggest square is always the true square of any village. Anything else is considered an open alleyway or a close. The second one doesn't have anything extraordinary about it, no fountain, no central meeting point. I've seen these kinds of openings all over—not a square."

"I thought you just got here?" I asked.

"Ya," Roxy said. "How are you so sure?"

"I did just get here…" Gail pulled the binoculars from her eyes, and she paused, looking at us. "What I meant was, that's what I read in the *Baedekers*. Read the Paris guide cover to cover on my trip over—"

"You read a travel guide coming over?" I said, laughing, thinking of Gail sunning herself on her ship's deck in her little white nurse dress, thumbing through a travel guide on her way to war. *Of course, she sunned herself.* Red rolled her eyes. "We came over on the *Pendleton*, arriving four days after D-Day." I paused to see if she'd catch on to what I meant by that, but it appeared she was lost. "We were under constant threat of a U-boat attack—torpedoes, Gail. And during the night, when we were fast asleep in the bowels of the ship on our swinging cots, our captain sailed us into an underwater German minefield—yeah, and in case you're wondering, German bombs sound just as menacing exploding all around you in the ocean as they do on land."

"Yeah," Roxy said.

Gail flashed us a quick smile before looking back into the binoculars—what I'd said made no impact on her whatsoever. My mouth fell open.

"Open alleyways are very popular," Gail said. "The first one is the location we're looking for. Third building on the right. See there?" She pointed toward the village. "White brick with an awning. Looks like a business, a pharmacy maybe. It's hard to tell what every building is, but this is my best guess…"

It was the most I'd heard Gail talk in one conversation, and by the look of Roxy's wide eyes, it was clear I wasn't the only one stunned by her sudden chattiness and her total disregard for what I'd said about our crossing to the beaches.

Red snatched the binoculars from Gail. "Let me see those." She looked again, though very quickly. "Better hope you're right," Red said.

"So… What are we gonna do?" Roxy said. "We can't waltz down there and ask the Huns about our boys. That'll be suicide!'"

Red folded her arms. "Oh, you don't say?"

"Stop it, Red," Roxy said. "I knew it wasn't going to be easy. Give me a break."

"I say we walk into the village as anyone else would." I ripped a handful of colorful weeds from the ground that looked more like wildflowers. "And carry some flowers. I'll lock arms with Red and we'll go straight on through. Nobody will think we're suspicious if we move causally yet swiftly. German girls carry flowers, right?" I dusted away the dirt and snapped off the roots, holding the weeds like a little bouquet.

Gail pulled up some weeds too and so did Roxy.

"But what if…" Roxy said. "What if we see some Germans? Not the locals. The ones like we saw at the river."

We looked at each other. Nobody wanted to say they were scared.

"If you see a German, keep walking," Red said. "And whatever you do, don't talk—no matter what. The second you say something in English we'll all be dead." She looked at me. "You either. Don't say anything."

The rain had evaporated from the grass and the sun was out. Puffy white clouds floated way up high, so beautiful, no planes, no sign of war—exactly the kind of weather four young German women would be out strolling around in. Yet, not one of us moved from the top of the hill, and my heart raced from being scared.

"Let's get on with it," Roxy said, wiggling from being wrapped up like a mummy with supplies under her dress.

"I need a second, all right?" I took a deep breath before looking at Red. "If anything happens…" I said, swallowing. "Red, I want you to know…"

"I know, Kit," Red said. "I know."

Red took the first step and together we walked down the hill through a field of blue cornflowers to get to the street. The air smelled sweet, not cloudy with diesel or smoke from charred villages, but of the last days of summer.

The buildings were taller up close, with many windows for people to peek out. Red and I watched carefully, looking for people looking at us between fluttering curtains, when a group of German girls ran past us on the sidewalk— one, two, three—little blonde heads bobbing down the road.

I watched them with a hand to my chest, before looking at Red; we weren't prepared to see smiling children, especially ones who looked rested and wearing clean dresses. Not like the shoeless French children who were starving, dirty, and crying.

We turned the corner, only I'd gasped from walking under a Nazi banner hung proudly over a restaurant. I'd seen them in the newspapers and on the newsreels, but in the French cities we'd passed through they'd been torn down and burned up. "My God," I whispered, and Red tugged on my arm.

We stopped to read the road sign, but there were three and they pointed in different directions even though there were only two streets to choose from. A woman asked if we needed help, and when we looked at her stunned and still, she pulled stiffly on her jacket lapels. "Where are you going?" she reiterated, nose pointed.

Roxy sneezed into her flowers, and we all shook from the unexpected shock of noise.

"Well!" the woman said, and she stormed off.

Red grabbed me by the sleeve when she heard the fountain, and we scampered off toward the sound of the gushing water. I counted our steps, counted the buildings. *Third building on the right after the square.* I saw the white one with the brick and striped awning. It *was* a pharmacy, just like Gail thought. Of all the places—a pharmacy, most likely with medicines and supplies? I wrapped my fingers around the cool glass knob, pausing slightly, waiting for Roxy and Gail to catch up the two steps they'd lagged behind, but I had a terrible, sinking feeling I'd got the directions all wrong. *A pharmacy? What were the odds?*

"Jesus, the police," Red said, voice deep, and we whipped our heads around. They patrolled the square, pointing to German women gathered in a group. Their fingers shifted toward us and my stomach felt like it had fallen out of my body and landed on the sidewalk.

Roxy's scalpel slipped out from under her skirt and the metal clanked on the ground. "Go in!" She snatched it up in a hurry, but I looked at Red, desperately trying to gauge if she was thinking the same thing—had we gotten it wrong?—when she reached around and opened the door herself.

We shuffled in like penguins under the ding of a ringing bell that echoed into the street, then immediately turned to look out the window after closing the door. The policemen had walked to their car instead of toward us, none the wiser.

"I think we did it," I said, but we still searched the streets, looking for any signs that someone else had noticed us, but it seemed as if nobody had. "Ah, we did do it," I breathed, only to turn around and scream.

One stunned pharmacist and his equally shocked wife stared at us from the middle of the store. The woman clutched a broom in her hand while he slowly grabbed a metal rod from a shelf.

"Red," I said, and the wife backed up, whispering a few words in German to her husband I couldn't make out, and he tightened his grip around the metal rod. The wife froze, one foot behind the other, eyes shifting.

They both made a break for it out the back and Roxy jumped over the counter and wedged her body between them and the door.

"We're Americans," Red exclaimed, and when the man looked at me, I lifted my dress up to show them the medical supplies I had under my skirt. His mouth turned into an "O."

"Quick! This way," he said in broken English.

We followed him down a short hallway and into a cellar with a man lying on a mattress, who immediately reached for a club resting against the wall. His mattress springs squeaked and shifted from the weight of his body trying to sit up enough to use it, only he collapsed from exhaustion and I saw his face.

"Jack?" I said, shocked, flabbergasted, and searching for words.

"It's you!" he said. "Thank God. I hoped it would be you…"

He looked rougher than he looked the last time I saw him, stubbly beard and dirty fingernails. "What are you—" I bent to my knees, reaching for supplies. "I didn't expect this…"

Roxy unraveled a bandage from her leg. "You know this guy?" she said, and when I nodded, Red looked at me. A slight shake of her head followed, which I took as a warning not to say how.

His arm had been bandaged up a while ago and was now soiled with brown blood—old blood. "Were you shot?" I said, and he nodded. Roxy and Red started unwrapping his arm while I pulled a hypodermic needle and an ampule of penicillin out from under my dress.

He tried to smile when I moved in close, but his arm got the better of him and he grimaced. I smoothed his hair back to get a look at his eyes, see if he was in shock. "Look here," I said, and his eyes shifted to mine and they were sky blue with dark lashes, and suddenly I was staring.

I turned away, faking a cough. "Where are the others?" I said. "We were told there were a few of you boys. Maybe even an amputation." I prepared the needle for injection, pulling the medicine into the syringe after giving the ampule a shake.

He swallowed dryly. "They didn't make it."

Roxy immediately covered her gaping mouth with this news, leaving Red to pull his sticky bandage off.

"Ugh!" Red said into her sleeve. The markings of an infection had set in and the bullet hadn't been removed.

"It's warm too, Jack," I said, feeling his skin, and I had to wonder what would have happened to him if we hadn't come.

I waited for Red and Roxy to finish looking Jack over for other wounds as the couple tried talking to Gail in their broken English, but she unexpectedly replied in perfect German.

I looked up, nearly dropping my hypodermic syringe.

Red and Roxy were still too busy to notice, but it was very clear to me. She wasn't speaking a few broken words; she sounded fluent with an accent. Gail stopped talking mid-word when she noticed me staring, turning slowly, and the air between us felt uncomfortable and charged.

"Kit, you gonna stick him?" I heard Roxy say, but I couldn't say a thing and swallowed a million times, standing like a goose among the reeds, frozen with a syringe in one hand and an ampule of penicillin in the other.

A bell chimed from the front of the store, and the pharmacist and his wife looked terrified. "Go, go," Gail said to them in German. "We'll be quiet as mice."

The wife patted her hair in place and fixed her apron before walking back to the front of the store with her husband. Gail closed the door gingerly behind them and without a sound. She fit her ear into the crack to hear. "Quiet as mice," she said again in German, and with that Red and Roxy had turned around.

The nervous tick in my chest spread throughout my body. Gail's shiny hair, and that noticeably nourished figure of hers took an unexpected, suspicious turn. She showed up to France wearing the wrong uniform, and the day after we'd questioned the SS officer and learned about the Nazi war chest. I wasn't sure why I didn't see it before. She knew about the squares, she spoke German, and even though we'd accepted her as a nurse, I couldn't forget how she'd squirmed at the sight of needles.

Red snapped once to get my attention, mouthing silent words to me I didn't understand, but the sentiment was there; Gail was German, a spy, the kind the sergeant had warned us about.

I motioned for Jack's club on the ground, and Red quietly reached over and handed it to me, while Roxy took the syringe and ampule from my hands. My brother had taught me how to hit a baseball. "*Keep your hands together and load up,*" he'd once said to me. "*Swing all the way through.*"

Red nodded once, and I tightened my grip around the club, looking at the back of Gail's neck and her brassy head of curls.

11

KIT

Gail pressed her ear to the door, listening carefully to the commotion on the other side, while I took a step toward her. A seesaw squeak from Jack inching up in his bed, the sound of Roxy's lips mouthing words to Red, and I pulled back the club. Gail turned around, immediately jumping back with fists defensively in front of her body. Every tendon in my arms locked up.

"What are you doing?" she demanded.

The door burst open, and the pharmacist and his wife rushed into the room. "Customer is gone," they both said, only to freeze when they saw me with the club and Gail with her fists up.

"Who are you?" I said, rotating my wrists and swinging the club around.

The couple looked at Gail, mouthing off some frantic German words asking what was going on with Gail replying in an equally frantic tone that she didn't know.

Red lunged at Gail, taking her by the arms and getting

her on the ground. "You're hurting me," Gail said, tearfully. "Cut it out, Red… please…"

I lowered the club after hearing her pleading voice only to raise it once more. "Tell us who you are," I said, chin up. "Where'd you learn to speak German like that?"

"In college," she said, "I swear it." She burst into tears and Red let go of her. "What's wrong with you guys?" Gail coughed and spit through her tears, which made it hard not to believe to her.

I dropped my arms, and the club slipped from my fingers and fell onto the floor. "Why didn't you tell us you knew German?" I said.

"I don't know." Gail's knees curled up into her chest. The couple tried to help her and she talked to them in German through her tears, telling them that we were indeed the nurses they'd been expecting. I tried to help Gail up, but she scooted away to stand flush against the wall with her hands feeling the bricks behind her.

"Listen, Gail," I said. "We're not going to kill you. We're on edge, all right? And when you started speaking like a local out of the blue it sounded fishy." She wiped her eyes with the back of her hand. "Can't you understand? From the start, you've been off. You're the most squeamish nurse in France, and you knew things about the squares and then to find out you're fluent in German?" She nodded, which surprised me. "So, you do understand?"

She lowered her body onto a stool, nodding, taking an enormously deep breath to calm her crying, but it seemed to take forever. "There's something I need to tell you." She rubbed her hands nervously together. The little room got very quiet as we watched her, waiting to hear what she'd say, even Jack had sat up in his bed the best he could. "Don't look at me like that. All of you," she said.

Roxy stood up, folding her arms tightly. "Spill it, doll face," she said, and it was the angriest I thought she'd ever been. Italian mad, with pointed eyes and a bit lip.

"I'm not the Gail Barry who was meant for your hospital." She flinched, cowering slightly as if she thought one of us was going to hit her. "She was a replacement sent to you from North Africa. I switched orders with her." Gail looked up from her hands, trying to gauge our reaction, but we only had looks of disbelief.

Roxy threw her hands up in the air. "Why would you do that? You crazy or somethin'?"

"For the same reasons I came on this mission," she said, "why you all did."

Gail's words hung in the air between us all, touching us personally. Even Roxy had sat down on the foot of Jack's bed, looking at the ground.

"The other Gail," she said, "the one I switched with, she was gritty and strong. She had confidence. You knew she was smart by looking at her. People treated her with respect." Gail sat up a little straighter. "I'm smarter than I look, you know? The Nurse Corps took one look at my face and shuffled me right into General after a few weeks of training. I was even told I might have to nurse captured Germans. I was so mad!" She swallowed. "I wanted a chance to prove myself, so I took matters into my own hands."

Air blew from my mouth. She knew German, all right. And she probably had more book knowledge than any one of us locked up in that college brain of hers. But there was one important thing missing. "You might be smart, Gail,

I'll give you that," I said. "But you're also the dumbest box of rocks out here, pretending to be a battle nurse when you've been trained for pouring tea and wound dressing. We trained for weeks like the men, preparing especially for the beach invasion and life as a battle nurse. You can't fake that kind thing out here in the field. It's dangerous. And Red here already served in North Africa. You put our boys in danger. And us."

Gail shook her head, eyes cast down, a little cry coming from her mouth. "I know..." she said, wiping her nose with her hand. "I know that now..." The couple asked her if she was all right, and she started talking to them in German, nodding her head and taking his hanky for her nose, when I spoke up in German and butted right into their conversation.

"She'll be all right," I said in an accent just as perfect, and Gail snotted into the hanky with eyes wider than any owl. "We had a misunderstanding. We've sorted it."

There was a quiet pause. Gail gave her nose a rough swipe, trying to make sense of my German. The pharmacist offered me a hanky from his other pocket, and I waved it back with more German words. Roxy stood bolt upright from the bed.

"You know German too, Kit?" Roxy said, and after I didn't answer she looked at Red who knowingly shrugged. "And you knew, Red?"

"She hasn't known that long," I said. "Please, don't get mad. No use hiding it now. Besides, I'd feel bad keeping it to myself after I almost clubbed Gail for it." Roxy shook her head, and I reached out for her. "Please... Rox, don't get mad. If the Nurse Corps found out, I'd be fixing up

Germans in the POW camps instead of our own boys. It's why I kept it a secret."

But Roxy did get mad, her face pink and pulpy as a chewed-up strawberry. She dropped to her knees, and went back to her patient, reaching for the syringe I'd already loaded with penicillin.

"Roxy?" Red said, but Roxy threw her hand in the air to shush her.

I looked at poor Jack, grimacing, knowing he was about to feel the brunt of Roxy's anger with that needle. And when she asked him to roll over and show her his butt cheek, he hesitated. "Now," she gritted, and he rolled over all right. She hastily dribbled antiseptic on him, mumbling about how we always kept things from her, but when she stuck him, she was nice and gentle and thorough, as any trained good nurse would be.

"What happened to the others?" I asked Jack.

"There were three," he said. "The pharmacist and his wife buried them in secret, to keep the German patrols from finding the bodies."

Roxy gasped. "Poor fellas," she said. "I bet they didn't have time for remarks or nothing." She looked to me for comfort but turned back around when she decided she was still angry. "Horrible," she said to herself. "Horrible!" She helped Jack sit up.

"We were safe-housing nearby and an informant turned us in. We killed those Krauts, but unfortunately, they got almost every one of us too. I took a chance the pharmacist would be sympathetic based on our surveillance, and I was right. Nice folks. But they're worried I'm here. I know they are."

Jack looked at the pharmacist and his wife, who were looking at us. I asked them in German if they had any food to spare, and they disappeared back into the front of their store.

Gail and Red unwrapped the rest of our supplies from their bodies, pulling out syringes, bandages, and ration packs. They offered me one of the ration packs, but it looked waterlogged from the river, even with its cellophane. Thank God the pharmacist brought in a loaf of stale bread for us to eat because the thought of eating a ration cracker soaked with Rhine water turned my stomach. We passed the loaf around, tearing off big hunks from each end and savoring the flavor in our mouths, not knowing when we'd eat again.

The pharmacist asked me in German when we were leaving, and I told him I didn't know. The uncertainty made him look nervous, pulling out a pack of cigarettes from his white pharmacist's jacket and tapping it in his hands but never taking out a smoke.

I thought about asking for one, pointing briefly at the cigarettes, but he shoved the pack back into his pocket. "Be quiet," the pharmacist said, and he swiftly shut the door.

Roxy had been pacing since learning of the men's crude burial. "Look, Jack," she said, stopping abruptly. "When we get back to camp, I want to see their tags, do a prayer for your men that didn't make it. You understand, right? They deserve some remarks." She rubbed her palms together. "I'll need to hold them."

"Yes, a prayer!" Gail said.

Jack hesitated. "Their tags aren't back at camp. They were with them."

"What?" she said. "Why would they do that? Go

undercover with their tags on... Even we were smart enough to leave them behind."

"I don't know," Jack said. "The pharmacist told me. They must have searched their pockets before they buried them."

Roxy turned visibly upset again with a puffing chest. "They need a prayer," she said, "and their families need the tags." She looked at Red. "The tags, Red."

"There's nothing we can do about it now," Jack said. "They're buried. I don't even know where."

Roxy folded her arms and looked down at Jack over her cheeks. "Well," she said, sternly, "you're very casual about it, aren't you?"

Even I was surprised to hear Roxy's tone. "Roxy, he was shot, remember?" I said.

"Oh, I remember," Roxy said, and she pointed to Gail who was still sitting on her stool. "You!"

Gail stood up. "Me?" She pointed to her chest first, then looked over both shoulders as if someone stood behind her. "What about me?"

"You," Roxy said again, flicking her chin. "Ask the pharmacist where our boys are buried."

Gail looked to Red first, who nodded once, and Gail called in the pharmacist. "Where did you bury the Americans?" she said, and he looked at Jack and then back to Gail.

"Not far," was all he said.

"Not far," Gail and me repeated.

Roxy took a step toward the pharmacist. "Where'd you bury our boys? No good Huns. Are you even Christian—"

Red gasped. "Roxy!" she said, but Roxy continued to spout.

"Did it bother ya digging those holes..." Roxy went on.

The pharmacist shook his head, looking at me and then to Gail from not understanding Roxy's rambling English words. Gail butted in, translating word for word what Roxy had asked, which he immediately frowned at, especially the part when she asked if they were Christians.

His voice was a little harsher this time. "Of course, we are Christians!" he said. "If this is how you treat us then leave." He waved his finger at all of us.

"No!" both me and Gail yelped.

Gail smoothed it over by saying she translated wrongly. "I meant to say," she said in German, "that we know you're good German Christians and we assume you said a prayer."

"We did not," he said. "There was no time."

Gail looked to me, and I shook my head for her not to tell Roxy that part, but Roxy was on to us and folded up her arms.

"Where are they?" Roxy demanded, and Gail repeated in German.

"We buried them behind our cottage. In the garden. A kilometer away," the pharmacist said. "But their tags are under a tree. To keep them separate in case the Reich found the bodies." He reached into his pocket and pulled out their gold wedding bands.

I snatched the rings from him before Roxy could see, and turned to Gail. "Nothing more from you, all right?" I said, knowing she'd blurt out what he'd said and send Roxy into a tailspin. "I'll tell her."

"Tell me what?" Roxy said.

I swallowed, buying some time. "You see it's this..." I said, and Roxy glared. "They buried the tags separate from the bodies. Under a tree." I opened my hand and showed her the rings.

"Oh no!" She gasped, and she had that look on her face I'd seen so many times, one of fright and of complete disgust. "Did they eulogize?"

"He said there was no time," I said. Roxy breathed heavily, her chest puffing again, and I talked quickly to try and settle her down. "Remember, they were burying them in haste, Rox. They could have been arrested for what they've done, helping Jack here, and burying those men."

Roxy took the rings and stood quietly in the corner, holding them tight in her hands. Gail finished up talking to the pharmacist, telling him thank you, when Roxy abruptly turned around. "I'm getting the tags."

"You're not!" Red said, moving away from the wall.

"I am too," Roxy said, folding her arms. "The wives need the tags. Otherwise, they'll hold out hope till their dying days and each day will be deader than the last, waiting for their husbands to walk through the door. The dog tags—it's final. They need to see them. I'm not leaving Germany without their tags."

"You're out of your mind," Red said. "Did you already forget what it took to get here? The river—you almost died."

"I'm going," Roxy said, then she pointed to Gail. "And you're going with me."

Gail's eyes bugged from her face. "Why me?"

Roxy bit her lip before blurting, "Because I said so."

Gail's jaw dropped, processing Roxy's command.

"Don't do this, Rox," Red said, shaking her head, but no matter how much Red pleaded for her to stay, Roxy wouldn't budge. I reached for Red and we hugged, not knowing what else to do.

"You know why I have to go," Roxy said to us. "D+50."

"What happened on D+50?" Gail said.

Red and I slowly let go of each other. *Saint-Lô.*

The name sounded romantic. Exotic. Cobbled roads and simple farms. An idyllic village that bloomed with apple blossoms in the spring, and rested with peaty, ripened soil in the fall. By the time we'd arrived, the carefully planted apple orchards had been churned up, burned up and spat out. Trees toppled over into cavernous shell holes. Livestock left behind by the Germans had been blown to pieces, bits of cow and pig belly dotted the ground in patches and baked in the sun. The corpses that survived whole rotted among the soldiers.

Trucks brought our poor boys in from the battlefield. Body after body stacked on top of each other like bricks. Red handed me and Roxy some gauze to cover our noses since our medical masks were in short supply. "Breathe through your mouth," she said to us, and as soon as I heard the words, I tasted the smell in the back of my throat where my tongue was thick and dry.

Doctor Burk delivered us the sorrowful orders of body identification. Dead soldiers were unloaded from the trucks behind him and laid out in rows as he talked. "Notify graves registration if you find someone you know," he said, covering his own nose with a hanky. "I'm sorry, ladies." He looked over his shoulder where the bodies seemed to go on for miles. "The Germans are taking the tags off our soldiers."

Roxy whimpered immediately when she saw wedding rings on bloated fingers. "Who would do that?" She struggled whether to keep her hand over her nose or to move it to wipe her eyes.

"The Huns," Red said. "Ruthless, spineless Germans."

And we walked, looking at our poor boys' faces, stepping over shredded body parts buzzing with flies, trying to be respectful, but at the same time wanting to get a look and move on—give the body a name to go with the registry.

Roxy walked ahead of me by four steps, wobbling, looking weaker and weaker with each boy she looked at, pulling back his head only to shake hers tearfully when she couldn't give him a name, as if she blamed herself for not knowing his identity.

I looked up, face to the sun, and when I closed my eyes, no matter what I tried, no matter what I thought of, I was still in Saint-Lô.

That disgusting heap of earth.

Roxy screamed, turning around. "Kit!" She grabbed on to me, her legs to the point of buckling. "It's Private Bentley." She buried her head into my shoulder and wept. He was only eighteen—a kid with dreams.

"Roxy," I said. "At least we know. His family will know." I petted her head and she looked up, eyes spilling with tears as she surveyed the mass of bodies we'd yet to walk through.

Too many bodies to count. All without a name.

"Are you scared?" Roxy asked Gail.

Gail crossed her arms only to uncross them seconds later. "Yes."

Roxy nodded. "So am I."

I knew there was no talking Roxy out of getting those tags, and asked the pharmacist for directions.

"Why?" He looked very concerned, shaking his head. "You can't leave. It's too dangerous—suspicious. Someone could see you!" His voice rose and his wife tapped his shoulder for him to quiet down. "No." He shook his head, crossing his arms. "I won't tell you. You leave and you leave for good." He dropped his shoulders after looking at Jack, and finished in English. "Us... Caught..."

I looked to the ceiling, about to tell Roxy the bad news when Gail beat me to it.

"You tell me where those tags are," Roxy gritted, grabbing Red's surgical scissors and slapping them against her thigh. "Or I'll... I'll..." She inched closer and closer to him, and he backed up into the wall along with his wife who had her hands out, begging for Roxy to put the scissors down and be quiet, while I tried talking Roxy out of slitting his throat.

"Tell her!" the wife said to her husband. "The noise, the noise!"

"Fine! I'll tell you," he snapped, and Roxy put the scissors down after I told her what he'd said. "But you must leave out the back. And you can't leave like that." He asked his wife to fetch some ribbons for their hair, and the wife made them look more German, more German than they looked when we arrived, combing out their hair and styling it like peasant girls with braids.

There were no words exchanged between us girls. Only quiet embraces. Jack told them to knock in sequence when they came back, otherwise we wouldn't answer the door, and they understood. Then they were gone.

We weren't supposed to talk about dying, but when Roxy left out that door, I felt as if she took a part of me with her—a part of me that would die in Germany if she didn't come back.

Red slid to the floor, head in her hands. "She'll come back, Kit," she said. "Both of them will. We have to believe."

I fingered the collar on my little dress before tapping my heart twice. Once for Gail, and the other for Roxy. Red reached for my hand.

We have to believe.

12

EVELYN

Twenty minutes went by. Twenty minutes of Evelyn sitting stiff as the dead in the back seat of Michelle's car before she'd allow her husband to carry her inside. She sat on her couch wrapped up like a hotdog in a pink quilt with her daughter and husband staring at her from the love seat.

Evelyn thought about the stories she'd told Michelle throughout the years to reinvent her past. But now, after more than forty years since she'd come home from the war, she wondered if the stories had become just as vicious as the reality.

Evelyn swallowed. "I'm sorry you saw me that way," she said to her daughter.

Michelle got up from her seat the moment her mother had spoken, and took her hands, holding them tenderly. "Don't be sorry." She hesitated, looking deep into Evelyn's eyes. "I knew you didn't like the rain, but I thought it was because you didn't want to get your hair wet. There was always an excuse, now that I think of it..."

Evelyn closed her eyes, remembering the games she'd made up when Michelle was young to keep them inside. At some point, Michelle outgrew the games, and she'd resorted to lies, curating a pocket full of excuses that up until today had served her well. The late pickups when the rain lingered a little too long, saying she'd lost her keys. An important phone call she'd have to wait all day for, but never came. Although she'd gotten good with her excuses, she was thankful she lived on the east side of the state where it was drier and the rain was seasonal.

"I never would have dreamt the rain could—" she looked over Evelyn's body wrapped up in the blanket "—debilitate you. Cause you to—"

"Michelle, honey," Evelyn's husband said. "I'm sure you have questions, but as you can see, your mother's been through a lot tonight."

"Oh yeah, Dad. Of course." Michelle got up, and when her hands slipped away, Evelyn's curled up into themselves. She kissed her mother's cheek before meeting her dad at the door where they talked in hushed tones, but Evelyn heard them just fine.

"What happened, exactly, Dad? I'm worried," Michelle said.

"Doctor says it's stress," he said.

"Stress?" Michelle said. "Out here? On the farm?"

"No," he said, "you don't understand. Stress from before—from the war. It's why she never wanted anyone to know she was in France." He put his hand on her shoulder, turning his back to Evelyn. "I recently convinced her to see a doctor about it." He rubbed his eyes. "I was at my wits' end not knowing how to help her." His voiced wavered, on the verge of a cry, and Michelle threw her arms around his neck. "We're still trying to learn about it."

She pulled back. "Jesus, Dad, do you have it too? You were in the war," she said, but he shook his head.

"I have memories of war," he said, "but nothing like hers."

"I don't understand," she said. "If you were both in the war…"

He closed his eyes briefly, taking a breath. "I didn't land on the beach. Your mom did, and she was on the front line all the way to Berlin. Do you understand? The casualties she saw, the wounded she attended to firsthand, many just young boys. It was an endless circuit. The rain is a reminder—it sets it off, brings all the memories back, only they're not just memories. She relives them." Michelle covered her mouth with this information while he glanced back at Evelyn still on the couch. "We can talk about it later. Go home to your family," he said, and they hugged their goodbyes before he walked her outside.

Evelyn went to bed that night embarrassed that her daughter had seen her in a fit and unable to move in the back seat of her car.

"I'm glad she knows," her husband said, lying next to Evelyn in bed. "I went along with keeping your past a secret because it's what you wanted, and I thought it would help, but it hasn't. I think it was a mistake hiding the truth."

Evelyn absorbed what he'd said. Whether it was the right thing to do or not, the fact was Michelle knew now. That part of her secret was out. There was no way to erase it.

"Go to sleep," she whispered.

"I think you should tell her all of it," he said. "The whole story—what happened those five days in September."

A thick, unmistakable silence wedged between them. Even her husband didn't know all of it. She stared into the open space above her bed, wishing she had her husband's memories instead, ones he would be willing to talk about if she let him. But they had never talked about anything too specific over the years for fear it would ignite her own.

"Evelyn?"

"I called Roxy today," she blurted.

"You did?" he asked. "When?"

"This morning," Evelyn said, though she wasn't about to mention the part about the reporter. "She said there's something in Atlanta this fall—a salute and a reunion."

"I think you should go!" He rolled over and faced her in the dark, searching for her hand under the sheets. "You need someone to talk to, Evelyn. A support group. This could be the answer. Think about how many others will be there. Who you'll see."

"Not everyone will be there," she said.

Evelyn felt the weight of her declaration, and she knew her husband did too. It was, after all, at the core of what haunted her the most, especially about those five days in September.

"You can't turn back time," he said. "And it wasn't your fault what happened."

Evelyn didn't answer. She couldn't answer. But she did squeeze his hand, and after a long pause, with both of them facing each other in bed, they said goodnight. But what he didn't know, and what Evelyn could never bring herself to tell him, was that when she went to sleep her memories turned terrifyingly vivid and alive, even as she held his hand under the sheets and without any provocation at all.

She tried to remember what her doctor had told her to do, and took a few deep breaths through her nose, thinking about the things that brought her joy, but as she thought about Michelle, her grandchildren, and her husband, a current of old memories flooded over her just the same. She never knew where she'd end up. Would she be bobbing in the sea, trying to get her nose above water, or would she be in the surf, feeling the grittiness of beach sand between her teeth?

One thought led into the next, then somewhere in her kaleidoscope of swirling darkness, Evelyn's thoughts landed on the pharmacy in Lichtenau. The coolness of the glass doorknob in her palm, the breeze fingering her bangs as she looked up at the striped awning. The sterile odor of the bare shelves inside.

Her heart ticked up, but instead of counting away the memory like her doctor suggested, she held on to it, and felt her consciousness slip inside the cellar—a ghostly apparition—watching Red and Roxy tend to Jack. Then she saw Kit.

The girl she used to be.

Evelyn watched Kit pace the center of the room, hands on her hips, feeling the strange gap of air between her legs from wearing a dress. The crustiness of the river water hardening the tips of her brown bob, and the wave of her dark eyelashes, which would eventually turn sparse and gray in the many years to come. *In this scene,* Evelyn thought, *Kit doesn't know what lies in wait for her.*

If only she could go back in time, whisper in her ear. Warn her.

Evelyn took a deep breath through her nose and when she exhaled, the cellar's cement walls caved in over top of her, sucking all of them into an endless black hole where Evelyn dreamt her dreams.

The next morning, Evelyn sat drinking coffee at her kitchen table, listening to the light buzz of farm equipment tattering in the field where her husband was working. Her chest still ached from yesterday, like she'd been out in the cold and a sickness was trying to take root. She fought back by taking a sip of her incredibly black coffee and trying to relax. A bird sang not that far away, a robin, she decided, and a woodpecker hammering on a tree.

She opened her window to let the morning breeze in, thinking the fresh air on her face would carry her away, and indeed it did, but not in the way Evelyn hoped. The sudden sharp clang of rattling chains from the barn reminded her of the SS *Pendleton*, the rope ladder to her landing craft, and how her boot clumsily fit in each rung. She felt the burn in her palms as she hung on, and the impact on her bones when she fell three feet into the craft. She set her coffee cup down and clenched her fists, chanting to herself the way her doctor had told her to do when these sensations washed over her, but the woodpecker's hammering sounded like the pop of gunfire in her field. "I'm safe," she said, eyes closing. "I'm in Washington…"

She thought about last night in bed with her husband, when he said keeping her past a secret had been a mistake, and in a desperate move to try something different, she spoke her truth out loud and into the quiet air of her kitchen.

"I was a battle nurse." A deep breath followed.

Evelyn said the words again, though this time she opened her eyes. "And my name was Kit." Each syllable rang in her ears.

Evelyn boxed up her life as a nurse after the war in 1945, and although she rarely looked at it, she knew exactly where the box was in her cellar. Behind the *Kerr* jars, second shelf up.

Evelyn bolted from her chair and walked down the hall. She paused a second before wrapping her hand around the doorknob, giving herself a moment to reconsider, and in spite of the little voice in her head telling her not to go into the cellar, she threw open the door and padded down the wooden stairs in her bare feet and stood where it was cool and dark and moldy. She pulled on the light string.

Evelyn walked right to the box, moving the glass jars out of her way: big, made of cardboard, and webbed in the cobwebs of her thoughts. She gave it a shake, the clattering of her old life.

There were times throughout the years she had thought about opening the box. She'd set dates that would come and go, picking the perfect time and the perfect place— but as the years passed, she began to think the box would remain closed until her very last days, just before she died— just before her daughter took her to hospice. This is what she imagined. Yet there she was with no planning at all and standing in her bare feet and house pants, very much alive, with the one thing that could rip her open or save her from drowning.

Evelyn blew dust from the box and had a little cough. She pulled on the flaps.

Snap. Snap.

She gasped suddenly, robbing the room of all its oxygen, when she saw her old fatigues lying right on top where she'd folded them over forty years ago. She ran her fingers over the olive drab twill, over the buttons. Her dog tags slid out from a pocket, which caught her off guard. Evelyn ran her thumb over the embossed letters of her name before rubbing both tags together.

Then she saw it.

A locket she'd been given on that fateful day. It almost took her breath away, seeing it again in the dim cellar light. Tarnished silver, cool and matte. She set down her tags and pulled the locket up gently, its delicate chain rubbing against the cardboard box as she pulled it out and held the locket in her hand, closing her eyes. She slumped forward a little, remembering.

"Goddamn you," she said, and the guilt and pain from something that happened many years ago pulsed in her throat. *How is this a good idea?* She looked up, her eyes skirting over the beams that held her house up, wishing she had as much strength.

Evelyn stifled a cry and forced herself to dig deeper into the box, finding her old canteen and putting her helmet on, when a knock on the front door startled her.

She spun around, looking up the stairs, feeling very much like she'd been caught doing something she wasn't supposed to be doing. "Coming!" she yelled, stuffing her fatigues back inside and throwing her helmet in before closing up the flaps.

She slid the box back on the shelf, anxious to see about the door, but in her haste she'd forgot to put the locket inside. As if an afterthought, she slipped the locket over her head as she dashed up the stairs, even though it had been decades since she'd worn it. Another knock. "Coming!" she said again, and as if opening the box and wearing the locket again wasn't bad enough, she went on to make the most fatal error of her day.

She opened her front door without looking through the peephole.

"Hello—"

The reporter.

She gulped, though she wasn't surprised to see him; she knew he'd be back. She felt it in her bones. If only he knew where she'd been moments ago, feeling out her old nurse fatigues.

"Well, hello there to you!" he said.

This time she opened her screen door and joined him outside, looking around the farm as if he wasn't the most important thing to step up on her porch that day.

She folded her arms and the door clacked closed behind her. "Yes?"

He pulled a folder from his leather bag, opening it up for her to have a look at what was inside. A large black and white photo of her and Red outside the nurses' tents.

She instinctively gasped, reaching out to touch her and Red's faces, but he pulled the photo back. "We need to talk." He paused. "Kit."

She folded her arms back up, and he smiled, and it was slippery and cunning, a smile that belonged to only one other. Evelyn already had too many memories to count, now here was a lost one, and it was staring at her, standing right on her porch. Evelyn's spine straightened; she should have known—she should have recognized his offspring.

"I believe you knew my dad," he said.

Evelyn gazed into his hazelly eyes—like seeing a ghost. *Of all the people,* she thought. *Of all the people to turn up on my doorstep.* A puff of air escaped between her lips, saying that old coyote's name in her mind. *Benny.*

"How'd you know it was me?" she said.

"The library in town has records. I saw your photo in a yearbook." He laughed. "Good old yearbooks!" He tucked the folder back into his leather bag. "You ready to chat?"

Evelyn thought she'd be coy, feel him out. "About what?"

"Oh, I think you know," he said, and when he smiled a ray of sunlight glinted off a white tooth. "Tell me, how's your German these days?"

Evelyn dropped her arms to hold on to her thighs. She was about to tell him to leave when her husband walked around the house, and upon seeing a stranger at their doorstep, he walked up to them both, wiping grease from his hands on a rag. "Good morning," he said, and the reporter shook his hand. He looked at his wife, and then back to the reporter, studying. "Can I help you?"

The reporter stood nice and tall, meeting Evelyn's husband with a commanding, yet agreeable stature. Evelyn knew better; he was a snake. All reporters are snakes. Especially one related to Benny.

"I'm a reporter from New York," he said, handing her husband a business card. "I'm doing a story about World War Two nurses. To be precise, there's a mystery I'm trying to solve about four nurses from the 45th, and my search brought me here," he said. "To find Kit."

Evelyn's husband's eyes grew round as saucers when the reporter said "Kit," and she knew he was looking to her for how to react, but then he saw the locket around her neck, and his whole face changed.

"Maybe you should come inside," Evelyn's husband said, and she glared. She certainly wasn't giving him permission to invite the little snake in.

"This is what I was talking about last night," he whispered into Evelyn's ear. "You need to talk to someone. Maybe this is the first step. You must be thinking this too if you were in the cellar." His eyes moved to the locket around her neck.

"But…" she said, only he led the reporter into their house and into their kitchen, despite her protesting, where he poured them both a cup of decaf at the table. She knew her husband was only trying to help, and it took a moment for her not be mad at him, and a few deep breaths.

Unlike her husband, Evelyn had no expectations other than to see the photo again. She scooted up in her seat. "Can I…" she said, motioning to his leather bag. "Can I see the photo again?"

The reporter placed the photo in front of Evelyn on the table. She gazed at the glossy image, taking in every detail. She remembered when it was taken, she remembered the planes flying overhead, how Benny had snuck up on them near the field tent, and how nervous Red was about the German. She touched Red's face. It had been so long since she'd seen her.

"Do you feel okay?" Evelyn's husband said to her, and

she nodded, though she couldn't quite pinpoint what she was feeling. Her stomach had knotted up and her head felt heavy. And her throat. God, the pain in her throat!

The reporter placed another photo in front of Evelyn and she immediately covered her mouth. It was the photo Benny took of them in the mess tent the night they left with the doctor. A window into the past. The tears that had pooled painfully in her eyes spilled over her cheeks. She pulled three tissues from a box she had on the table, one after another, and dabbed her cheeks.

"These are the other nurses from tent seven?" The reporter pointed to each of them, saying their names. "Red, Roxy, and Gail?"

"Are you asking me their names?" she said. "Because I'm sure you already know."

His smile rose and then fell. "I do."

Evelyn continued to pat away the tears from her cheeks. "What is it you really want to ask?"

The reporter stared at Evelyn as her husband rubbed her back, almost as if reconsidering his questioning given her state, but he couldn't resist, and Evelyn expected nothing less of him. "What happened those five days you disappeared?"

Evelyn snagged another tissue from the box and pressed it to her eyes while her husband reassured her everything would be okay.

"It's all right if you need a minute," the reporter said, and Evelyn looked up.

"You're damn right I need a minute."

13

KIT

The room turned quiet with Gail and Roxy gone. Red didn't move for ten minutes, and when she did, it was only to pace. "I should have gone with them," she said. "Roxy isn't used to being in charge of herself. She'll need me."

"At least Gail knows German. She can do the talking if she has to."

Red glanced over her shoulder. "You think Roxy isn't going to talk?" she said, and I immediately heard Roxy's voice in my head. *"What do you mean by that, doll?"*

I sighed.

"Come on," I said, motioning for her to help me with Jack, "we need to get this bullet out." I pulled his shirt up over his head, and he winced and moaned from having to move his infected arm. Then he shivered from having to sit on his mattress bare-chested. I'd seen a thousand men with their shirts off, and I surprised myself by glancing at him longer than I should have, my eyes skirting over his shoulders, down his sculpted chest, and ending where his belt looped around his waist.

"You ready?" I said to him.

"As ready as I'll ever be, I suppose." He smiled nervously before his lips fell into a thin line, preparing for the inevitable. I held his arm still, reached down for my medical kit out of habit, patting my skirt, only to remember we buried our kits by the river. Red laid out what equipment had survived the Rhine on the bed.

"Can we get anything from the pharmacy?" I said, and Jack shook his head.

"They have to account for everything they sell and they said it would look suspicious if some of their supplies went missing," Jack said.

"Just as well," I said, looking over what we did have. "I think we have all we need."

Red tried to stick him with some morphine, but he refused. "I want my wits for this," he said, and I looked at him a little surprised, thinking he might be crazy. "I mean it."

I wasn't going to argue with him even though I thought it was a dumb idea. "Red, get the whiskey," I said, but she had walked away and started to pace again. "The whiskey, Red."

Red resolved to help me, and it wasn't like her to leave me with a patient all alone, but the girls out there on their own had gotten to her. "Lie down on your side," I said to Jack, and he did.

Red handed me the flask of whiskey, and I held it to Jack's lips for a swig.

"Thanks," he said, and I let him take a few drinks, but

pulled it away mid-glug to pour some on the wound. He hissed, sucking air through his pinched lips. "Dammit to hell!"

"Sorry," I said, wincing, as bubbling white foam dripped down his arm. "I couldn't tell you it was coming. You would have tensed up and it wouldn't have worked." I took hold of my forceps. "All right, now *this* will hurt…"

"And the whiskey doesn't?" he said.

"I'm not the one who refused morphine," I said.

"Wait." He motioned for more whiskey, which Red gave him, and he slugged nearly all of it before closing his eyes. "Okay, go."

I pressed both thumbs to each side of the wound, and the bullet poked out from the bloody hole like a prairie dog, and while I had one thumb still pressed firmly on his bicep, holding the bullet in its place, I dug my forceps into the hole, clamping down on that little monster. "Like pulling a splinter," I said, extracting the bullet slowly. "Your very own souvenir."

"Let me see it." Jack opened his eyes, and I dropped the bullet into his hand, still streaked with blood.

"You'd think the pharmacist would have at least got you some sulfa powder," I said. "It would have kept the infection down."

"They gave me something, a thick, revolting white drink. I think it was to knock me out because I don't remember much after coming here."

I reached for one of Roxy's pre-threaded suture needles to stitch up the hole, and he made a hurtful face. I laughed. "You've been shot. I poured whiskey inside the wound, and this is what makes you squeamish?"

He shook his head. "No," he said, and he looked straight at the wall.

I held in another laugh. "This is the first time you've had sutures I take it?" I said, and he nodded. "Don't worry. I'm pretty good at it. Though there'll be a scar."

"Another souvenir?" he said.

"Yeah," I said, and when I was done, I think he was surprised I'd stitched him up so quickly. I bandaged his arm. "Keep this dry," I said, and while he examined the bandage, I found myself looking at his chest again.

He looked up. "Oh, ahh…" I said, turning away, and faking an itch behind my ear.

"Yes?" he said.

I cleared my throat. "Where're you from?" I thought he'd say Ohio or Indiana since there were a lot of boys from those states.

"Colfax, Washington," he said.

"I'm from Washington!" My mouth hung open for a bit before smiling. "My brother flew a Jenny in the Palouse while in college. He must have flown over Colfax a hundred times. I know exactly where it is, and it's not far from my home."

"Good! After the war I'll come to visit you," Jack said. "It's good to make plans for after the war."

I felt a blush at first, thinking he was serious, but knew it was just one of those things people said to give themselves hope, something to look forward to. "Yeah," I said, and I helped him slip his shirt back over his head. Something metallic caught my eye, glinting from under the bed where it was dusty and cluttered with storage boxes. A radio.

I dragged it out into the open—this was the kind of distraction we needed. "Will you look at this?" I said. "Red, a radio! Can you believe it?"

"Does it work?" Jack said.

The possibility of hearing music brought a little light into the cellar, when all I'd heard for so long was the explosion of bombs, the pop of bullets, and the moans of dying soldiers. I closed my eyes, praying it worked before plugging it into the wall.

"Keep the sound down," Red said.

I reached for the switch, and the pharmacist's wife barged into the room, which shook us all.

"*Nein!*" she said, reaching for the radio. "*Nein! Nein! Nein...*" She yanked the cord from the wall and her face turned from angry, to concerned, to apologetic. "Sorry, fräulein." She wound the cord around the set. "Sorry," she said one last time before leaving the room.

Red put her arms around me as I hung my head. "Another time," Red said.

"Yeah."

Jack's bandage had come loose and I moved to tighten it up. A nurse knows how to tighten a bandage, and I had to admit this was the first time one of my bandages had come loose, but as I rewrapped it, I thought maybe I'd wrapped it hastily on purpose. I felt his eyes on me.

"We should talk about the plan," he said. "Our next move."

I tugged and pulled on the bandage. "We'll go back the way we came, be on free land by dinner time. We'll be eating K-rations before you know it."

Jack didn't say anything, and I felt a strange tension coming from him. "No…" he said. "That's not the plan I'm talking about." After a short pause, I let go of his arm.

"What do you mean?" I said, cautiously.

"We have to finish the job." His eyebrows furrowed. "That is why you're here."

"We came to fix you up," Red said, but he only stared at us more intently.

"Oh no," he said, rubbing the back of his neck. "You don't know, do you?"

"Know what?" I said at the same time Red put her hands on her hips, and I'd never seen her lip tip out before, but there it was, like a shelf from her face.

"You're the replacements," he said. "You're here to complete the mission."

We stood frozen in disbelief, staring at him.

"What *were* you told?" he said.

I thought back to what the doctor said in our tent. He talked about transport, the possibility of an amputation, and… and… "Women," I breathed, and I turned to Red. "What Doctor Burk said, why we were asked and not the medics—because nobody would suspect women."

Jack nodded. "My team was killed because they were men. We stood out like sore thumbs." He pulled a piece of paper from his pocket, flattening it the best he could with one good arm and one injured one. It was a map of the village, marking the farms around it. One was circled. He tapped the circle with his finger. "This is where we're going. Where I'll lead you," he said. "A man is expecting women to meet him—a package to pick up."

"What package?" I said, and I grabbed his map to look at

it a little closer. I saw the square, the little shops all named, and... a notation. About a butcher. And a giant.

I looked up at Red, gulping.

"What is it?" Red said.

"Umm..." I gulped again, not sure how to answer her. "Red, it's the... the..." She ripped the paper from my hands. "The giant."

Red's face instantly fell flat. "What?" She looked at the paper herself. "They tricked us? Again?" She shook her head vigorously. "This isn't what I signed up for! A mission to steal Nazi loot?"

I sat down next to Jack as Red sounded off about being tricked. "That bastard Sergeant Meyer!" Her voice echoed in the little room from yelling, and the German couple rushed in immediately telling her in German to shut the hell up, which of course Red couldn't understand, but I was sure she understood their frantic waving and their scrunched-up faces, scolding us like disobedient children.

"*Ruhe!*" the wife said, pointing. "Quiet! Quiet!

"Red, stop," I said. "You're angering them." But Red continued to spout, hands in the air, turning in circles. "Shh! Red, would you clam it?"

The couple started arguing about letting us stay, and the tiny cellar got so loud anyone who was anyone could have heard us. The pharmacist pulled his pack of cigarettes from his pocket but this time he lit one, smoking with frantic, urgent pulls and I felt like he was a pot about to boil over.

I grabbed Red. "Look at me!" I said, and she finally shut her trap, but only after I clamped my hand over her mouth. "He's going to kick us out!" She closed her eyes tight, and the tiny vessels near her eyes turned red, purple, and then blue, before she suddenly moved out from under my grasp to fold her arms in the corner.

"I'm sorry," I said in German to the couple. "It won't happen again. We're scared. Like you. This will be over soon, and you'll never see us again."

The pharmacist exhaled suddenly with what I said, stepping on his spent cigarette and storming out, leaving the wife to answer. "If we have to come in here again because of noise, my husband says we have to throw you out."

"Understood," I said, and when she shut the door, I heard her lock it.

Jack watched Red with a furrowed brow, and I felt I had to explain. "She didn't want to come," I said. "She's fine with the rescuing part. It's…" I looked at Red slumped against the wall. "She has other responsibilities. Other people on her mind who need her too. This is the last thing she needed to get wrapped up in."

Jack took his map back. "I thought you knew. I requested women and you showed up."

"Oh, we showed up," Red said. "Did you know we lost our doctor in the river? And for what? So you and your buddies can make a money grab?"

"You don't understand," Jack said. "Thousands of men will die if you don't come with me."

Red whipped around, and a lock of her fire-red hair flopped out from her kerchief. "I'm not going to be tricked again. I'm sure there are a hundred laws we'd be breaking if we followed you. Thousand men. What men?" She turned to me. "I'm not risking my life for a pot of gold. I was being sarcastic back at camp when I mentioned the giant. I never dreamed we'd actually have to go and get it."

When Red said "pot of gold" I had to agree with her. Nazi chest or not. "I think it's best if we get back to France, before we get caught up on the wrong side of a battle." I shivered thinking about it. "It's strange being here. Behind enemy lines."

"It's not just a pot of gold," he said. "I'd understand if it were, but the hard truth of it is the Reich's preparing for a postwar resistance. They call themselves Hitler's werewolves. The chest was sent here to fund them. We know through intelligence that there's at least two hundred in training in a castle outside of Aachen. If you don't help me, if we can't get to the package first, our enemy will rise up from the ashes and slit the throats of our soldiers in the night."

"Mother of God," I said, fingers to my lips. "A postwar resistance."

"I'll be with you," Jack said, and he reached for my arm. "I'll go as far as I can, lead you all there. I'd do the job alone if the butcher wasn't expecting women—"

Red threw a pointed finger in the air. "The Allies can get the chest when they invade Germany. They're practically at the front door!"

"Red's right," I said. "It's too dangerous, especially with our boys so close to crossing the Rhine."

"And the day they cross, the werewolves will attack the POW camps with artillery and soldiers they funded with the giant," he said.

I clutched my chest. "What?"

"Starting with the one in Karlsruhe," he said.

Sam! My knees buckled as if a bat had smacked them and I collapsed to the ground. Red tried to catch me, and I looked into her eyes, barely able to speak.

Red reminded Jack about my brother's capture, which he remembered from when we questioned the German. "But we don't know where he is," she added. "A POW camp somewhere."

"Red," I said, and she sat me on the bed. "Karlsruhe *is* where he's at. I didn't want to tell you, but I found out." I gulped hard, pulling my map out from the top of my dress, which was now too damaged to use.

Her eyes constricted. "How do you know this?" she said, but I couldn't answer. "How, Kit?"

"You know how," I finally said, and she looked away, shaking her head. "I asked the German. All of our boys captured that day are there—the camp in Karlsruhe. I paid the mess cook to get me a map because I needed to know where that was. All right? The doctor didn't give it to me."

"And that's how the German found you out? You asked too many questions, didn't stick to the script like you were told. That's it. Isn't it?" she said, and I nodded continuously. She took me by the shoulders when I wouldn't look at her.

"Yeah, Red," I said, meeting her eyes. "That's how, all right? It was killing me not knowing where Sam was, and once I had the name of the place, it felt like he was still alive. I just needed to know."

She let go of me to hold her head. "I knew something wasn't right with that map," she groaned. "I knew it."

"I wanted to tell you, but you were so worried, and… and… I had to ask, Red. I couldn't let the opportunity pass me by." I wiped my eyes, which had teared up, glancing back and forth between her and Jack. "Like this Red, you know we have to do this. We can't let the werewolves attack the POW camps. We save people. Isn't that what you always say? You'll never forgive yourself if they raze the camps."

The room turned piercingly quiet as she moved her palms to cover her eyes. And the question of the job, and what to do next hung in the air. Jack was clear he didn't intend to go back to France right away. Red, I was sure, would be out the back door as soon as Roxy and Gail stepped through it.

"I'm doing it," I said, but Red remained still. "Did you hear me? I'm—"

"I heard you." She inhaled deeply, sucking air back into her chest. A subtle nod followed. "I'll go too," she said.

"Are you sure, Red?" I said. "What about your family? Your mom—"

"I don't want them to attack the POW camps either." She turned around when I touched her shoulder, and she laced her fingers with mine. "Plus, I'd never let you go alone." She looked at Jack very seriously. "But I'm telling you one thing right now, if I'm going to steal that giant thing—part of the Nazi war chest—I'm keeping some of it."

Jack didn't say anything about Red's declaration, which I thought he might.

"What do we have to do?" I said to Jack.

"Two women—werewolves—parachuted into the forest not far from here. They're on the move, and they have plans to retrieve the funds from a man they call the butcher, at a farm on the outskirts of Lichtenau, tomorrow. We have to get there first." He pointed to his map. "Right there. It's not far, but we have to go through the village and into the country." He looked at his watch. "But time is running out."

"How big is it?" I asked. "I mean, are we able to carry it? It's not like we have a truck to drive over the river with it."

"From what I understand it's in a bag. Jewels, probably. We've been told to ask for a package."

Yesterday I was in my dirty little nurse tent, fixing up boys from the Third, and taking slugs of wine in the off hours that rolled into fourteen-hour shifts. Today I was in a German's cellar, hiding out with an OSS officer, planning a covert operation to steal some of the Reich's war chest. Roxy wouldn't believe it. She'd get mad at us first for not telling her about the giant. After she came back with the dead men's tags, there was no telling what kind of shape she'd be in; I'd seen her at her worst in Saint-Lô, and I'd seen her at her best moments ago when she walked out that door.

I turned to Red. "What do we tell Roxy?"

Red's eyes shifted to mine. "The truth."

14

KIT

And we waited. Time ticked on and I thought Red was going to lose her mind if the girls didn't show up soon. I begged the pharmacist's wife for something else to eat, saying it would help keep us quiet, and she came back with a big bowl of soup from the deli across the square. Red waved for her to give it to me, too sick over Roxy and Gail to eat. The wife waited for me to have a taste before leaving.

"How is it?" Jack asked me, but I could barely swallow it.

"It's good," I said, and he laughed.

"It's not good," he said. "Boiled cabbage tastes like a slug of salt, doesn't it?"

I nodded, trying hard not to spit it out in front of the wife. "Thank you," I said to her, and she nodded, but she also gave me a strange smile as if she might have understood some of what I'd said to Jack in English. I wasn't about to complain out loud to her in German. They were taking a big risk helping us, and I knew their hospitality would only last so long, especially after Roxy waved scissors in her husband's face. Those Nazi flags outside weren't there for show. She went back into the pharmacy, locking the door up, and I pushed the soup away.

Urgent knocking on the back door sent Red flying into the air. "It's them!"

I held Red back with my arm to keep her from opening it. "Wait for the signal," I said, but the knocking persisted. Red closed her eyes, murmuring to herself for the sequence to change, like they'd agreed to before they left.

Then three knocks in succession followed by one, and I let my arm down. Red opened the door, and Roxy and Gail fell into the room, landing on the floor.

Roxy held her hand up from the ground, huffing and puffing from the last-minute sprint down the stairs. "I got them." Her fingernails were covered in dirt, and her hair had unraveled partially from her German braids. Gail sat up on her knees and hugged Roxy, which surprised Red and me. I never thought I'd see the day.

Each of them smiled. "Nobody saw us," Roxy said, swiping hair from her eyes.

"How do you know?" Red said.

Roxy stood up. "You don't see anyone chasing us, do you, toots?" She and Gail hugged again. They told us about the tree, how they'd found the spot fairly easy, and said a nice prayer. Roxy kissed the tags before blowing that kiss into the air. "I think they'd appreciate what we did."

"I know they would," Jack said. "They were good men. Fine men." Jack motioned for her to give him the tags.

"Oh no," she said. "I'm in charge of these." She slipped

the tags down the front of her dress into her brassiere where she'd put the wedding bands.

Gail brushed her hands together. "Now that that's done. Shall we be off?"

She said the words as if we were going to lunch—an afternoon tea. Red and I stepped back, eyes shifting.

"Let's go," Roxy said, and she'd glanced at Jack's bandaged arm. "You got the bullet out, right?"

I stepped back further, and there was a pause.

"What's the hold-up?" Roxy was still smiling from retrieving the tags, but the more seconds that passed with me and Red acting strangely, her face slowly began to fall. "What?" Roxy said.

I folded my arms only to drop them. "There's something we need to tell you," I said.

Red pulled up a stool and motioned for Roxy to sit in it, which she did. And she stared up at us. "Spill it," Roxy said. "And I swear to Christ it better be the truth."

She last said those words to me outside of Caen, when I lied to her about the orphan boys we'd found on the side of the street.

They'd been through hell, little towheaded angels that they were. Freckles speckled across their noses. Dirt on their cheeks, and wearing trousers that had been cut off and frayed. We'd been on marching orders to set up a hospital two miles down the road when we found them, jittering and shaking. Their mother lay in the weeds next to them, with only one nicked heel on her foot, the only parts of her poking out onto the road. I checked her pulse immediately, and it was very faint.

"Your mother?" I kept asking the boys, but when they spoke, only gibberish came out.

We loaded her onto our truck. She had a bullet hole in her arm, and it didn't look right from the start. It was a blast, torn-up flesh that exposed her bone as if something was eating her from the inside. By the time we made it to our next bivouac, she'd died. The boys didn't seem to understand.

"Ah, little sweeties," Roxy said. She cleaned the oldest one's feet and picked the stickers out since he'd been walking barefoot for God knows how long. "Breaks my heart, these ones. He looks about six." She looked at his brother. "And he looks about four."

I brushed the littlest one's hair and gave him something cool to drink. "You sound like you want to take them home," I said.

"Well, who wouldn't?" She held his shaking hand. "Damn Germans. Damn this war."

"Shh!" I said. "What if they know what you're saying? You can't be cursing around little kids."

Roxy handed her patient a blanket and he clutched it like nothing I'd seen before. Like a life raft, as if he'd float away if he let go, or sink into the earth. Even Roxy was taken back and had to turn away so he wouldn't see her cry.

Poor little kids. They stayed with us for two days before we had to move our hospital again. But we couldn't take them with us. I was ordered to drop them off at the orphanage in the village, but I told Roxy their father had picked them up. Lied straight to her face.

★

"You see, Rox, it's like this…" I folded my hands together and told her everything. From the sergeant to the German I interrogated and everything I'd learned about the Nazi war chest and the butcher. Her mouth opened and closed to match her widening eyes that often constricted into little black dots. I paced around in front of her, throwing my arms up and stressing to her how I didn't want to lie, how we didn't mean to keep things from her, but there were a set of circumstances that had unfolded right in front of us, and that I'd burned Red too, having kept a secret from her about Karlsruhe.

"And you see, Rox," I said, "we weren't sent over here just to fix up stranded boys. We were sent here to finish the job—the butcher is expecting women to retrieve the package. We need to get in there and steal the goods. We're the only ones who can finish Jack's operation."

Gail sat on the bed with a flump, and I was immediately reminded of the moment she first entered our tent and threw her bag on Roxy's cot. Only this time she put a hand to her head and slumped forward, a smear of dirt on her dress and on her knees. Her hair in fuzzy braids. She pulled the ribbons out and tossed them over her shoulder. She looked exhausted all of a sudden, the excitement from retrieving the tags, lost.

Roxy had a strange look in her eye too, though I couldn't read her at all—was she mad at us, or was she ready to go?

She stood up. "I'm so mad I could spit."

"Well then do it," I said, but Roxy smacked me upside the head. Then she smacked Red too!

"Oww," Red said, holding the top of her head. "Why'd you have to go and do that?"

"That's for lying to me." Roxy sat back down and crossed her legs, only this time she swung her leg up and down, and Red and I knew to let her be. She twirled a piece of her hair rapidly around her finger to the point that it looked painful.

"What if we don't go?" Gail said.

"They're planning to attack the POW camps," I said. "Starting with the one in Karlsruhe—where my brother is."

Roxy stopped swinging her leg, pulling her finger from her hair. "Whoa! This changes everything—the POW camps?"

"If we cut off their funding then we can stop them before their plans even get off the ground. If we don't, hundreds of our boys will die the moment the Allies cross the Rhine."

"That could be soon!" Gail said.

I stood next to Red. "We're going. But listen, you don't have to—"

Roxy stood up. "Yeah."

"Yeah what?" I said.

"Yeah, I'll go," she said, and I threw my arms around her. "Doesn't mean I'm not still mad at you for lying."

"Sure, Rox," I said, pulling away. "I understand. And from now on I'll never tell you another lie. I promise." We hugged again.

Gail stood up next. "I'll go too."

"Thank you," I said to all of them. "Thank—" But I choked on my words, unable to speak with the lump that had formed in my throat.

"I know, doll," Roxy said, and she wiggled my hand. "All right?"

I nodded.

★

I spread Jack's map out on the floor to study it. There was a good distance according to my measurement—a half a day's walk—between the city square and the butcher's, which looked like it could be a farm. A thin forest separated the two after more village streets. Jack also mentioned a cornfield, which I thought would be good for cover.

"What's it like out there?" I said to Roxy.

"Did you see any more police or what about soldiers?" Red asked.

"Nah, none of that," Roxy said. "But the pharmacist's house." She whistled, flicking her fingers in the air. "Man, oh man, is it a sight. Lined with brick, real pretty, and big…"

Red wrapped her arms around Roxy's neck, giving her a great big hug, and she looked completely stunned, eventually patting Red's back and looking to me for an explanation. I shrugged even though I knew exactly why Red had grabbed onto her. "You all right, Red?" she finally said, but Red squeezed a little tighter. "Red?"

"We were worried about you two," I said, and Red finally released Roxy.

"I'm all right," Roxy said. "Let me know if you wanna hear more because—"

"Can any of you shoot a gun?" Jack asked, and all four of us spun around.

"Why?" Red looked offended. "We save people. Not kill them."

Jack chuckled as if he thought she was joking. "Wait, you're serious?" He straightened up, clearing his throat.

"You're behind enemy lines." He paused. "You need a gun. You're sitting ducks without one."

Red looked surprised when he pulled a gun from a leg holster and handed it to her, pinching it between her fingers as if it were a rotten, stinking fish. "The doctor had our gun. And why do we need a gun if you're coming?" Red snarled. "I'm not shooting this."

"We should prepare for the worst," Jack said. "If we get separated, or for when you ask for the package... I won't be with you inside the butcher's house. Who's used a gun before?"

I carefully raised my hand. "My brother took me hunting once. It was a rifle, but aiming's the same, right?" Red swung her arm over to me and now I was the one with the gun.

"Aiming is the same," he said, "and don't hold it like that." Jack showed me quickly how to handle the gun, which ended with him saying not to aim it at anything I didn't intend to kill.

I fit the holster strap around my leg and was able to cover it with my dress.

"That's for an emergency, you understand? All we need to do is make it here," he said, pointing to the spot on his map. "Pick up the package and leave."

Gail had closed her eyes. "You make it sound so simple. Is it *really* that simple? Tell me it is. Even if it isn't, I want to hear you say it." Her eyes remained closed, waiting for Jack to repeat what he'd said, but Roxy elbowed her way to the front.

"Didn't you say they're women?" Roxy asked. "These werewolves."

"They are women," he said.

"See, Gail," Roxy said. "We got these dresses on." She fluffed her skirt before feeling her unkempt braids. "German braids in our hair... And we have Jack. You know in Jersey..."

Roxy could make anything sound like a trip to the market. We were in fact behind enemy lines, and about to steal a portion of the Nazi war chest. I hugged her unexpectedly, so glad she was back, but she immediately stiffened.

"Oh, from you too, Kit?" She patted my back like she had patted Red's. "What's gotten into—"

I pulled away. "I'm just glad you're back."

Me and Gail convinced the pharmacist into letting us stay the night by talking to the wife. Me, with my flattery and thanks, and Gail with the cold hard facts that five shadows creeping out the back in the moonlight was more suspicious than five people dressed like Germans walking out into the daylight, especially after Gail and Roxy had already done it successfully.

We all took spots on the floor, but I couldn't sleep and lay with my eyes open, thinking about the journey tomorrow— all that could go wrong and all that could go right. I stared at the door to the pharmacy, and then the locked doorknob. What I needed was a smoke to relax me, and the longer I lay looking at the locked door, the more I thought about that pack of cigarettes the pharmacist had in his jacket. I should have just asked him for one when I had the chance.

Jack woke up to me examining the lock by flickering candlelight. "What are you doing?" he whispered.

"Shh," I whispered back, and he lay back down while I

slipped into the dark hallway where it was eerily quiet. I had a few thoughts as I stood against the wall. One was that Red was going to kill me if she woke up and found me missing. The other was that I needed to hurry.

I scooted along the wall toward the register where the pharmacist had hung his white jacket. Dim moonlight cast through the large windowpanes near the street, lighting up the floor and the mostly bare shelves. I peeled myself away from the wall, breathing a little rapidly now, being alone in the pharmacy with all those windows. Four big steps was about all it should take to reach the jacket. One step became two, then three, and the next thing I knew I was reaching into the pharmacist's pocket, but it was empty, save for his lighter. *Damn.* I wondered where he might keep his extras, if he didn't keep them at home.

I searched the counter, then the shelves under the register, thinking about the seconds that had become minutes with me gone from the cellar, and how I was taking too much time, fingers reaching, when I felt his stash of smokes tucked behind a wood box filled with bric-a-brac. I was surprised to find it was a whole pack.

I scurried back down the hallway, taking giant tiptoe steps, only to throw my back up against the cellar door once I was inside. Red was up. She lifted her head from the noise and searched the air. My neck instantly turned warm and sweaty.

"What are you doing?" she whispered.

I smiled. "I... I thought I heard a noise," I said, and she studied me in the flickering candlelight, failing to notice my hand behind my back. I moved to sit next to Jack's bed, stepping over Roxy and Gail's legs on the floor.

I smiled nervously at him, and Red rolled over, away from us.

"Did you find anything?" he whispered after Red had gone back to sleep, and I nodded, showing him the cigarettes. "Rather dangerous to go out there for a pack of cigs."

"Does that mean you don't want one?" I said, fanning my neck cool.

"I didn't say that..." he said, but then I realized I'd forgotten the pharmacist's lighter.

"Ah hell, I forgot to take the lighter." I hung my head.

"I have one," he said, and he pulled a lighter from his pocket.

"It's fate then," I said, and we shared a smoke together, and it did relax me. "Jack," I said, and he looked at me. "The other day I saw you outside the mess tent. Seemed like you wanted to say something to me."

He rolled over slightly and now our arms were touching. "Yeah," he said. "You caught me seconds before I left to come here."

"Well, what was it?" I said, and I wasn't about to move my arm if he wasn't. "What did you want to say?"

"Already said it," he said.

"What do you mean you already said it?" I'd turned all the way around and looked him in the eyes.

"I hoped it was you," he said, and I smiled, and we both finished our cigarettes, talking about Washington and the places we called home.

After a short sleep, the pharmacist's wife unlocked the door. She looked at me suspiciously, as if she knew I'd snuck out, but instead of scolding me like I thought she was about to do, she handed us each a hunk of bread. "It's morning," she said. "You leave before my husband comes in." After staring at us for a moment, and after I promised her we'd be gone, she left.

There was some discussion about what to pack since we weren't on a medical mission anymore, and decided to only carry enough for one wound because of the bulk. But one thing Red wouldn't part with was the morphine. She'd taken the syrettes out of her dress to rearrange them, and noticed me watching her. "Let's move out," she said, and we headed to the back door, but Jack fell backward on the bed, dizzy, and holding his head.

"Wait," he said. "Whoa, I think I stood up too quickly." He repositioned his bandaged arm, wincing before trying to get up again, but he only flopped back down.

Me and Red looked at each other. "He can't go," I said, and there was a collective gasp. Roxy put her hand to her mouth. The entire job seemed much more doable with him. But he was weak. His face was pale and his arm was still gimpy.

"I'm sorry, Kit," he said. "All of you."

"No, no, no, no…" Gail said. "We can't go without him."

"This is bad," Roxy said. "This is really bad."

I examined his arm and retightened the bandage before helping him lie back down on the bed. He stared up at us from his back. The silence was deafening when he handed Red his map.

"You made it this far," he said. "I know you can do it. Besides, you know what they say about the girls from the beach, don't you?" He paused. "You're the heroines."

"Oh yeah?" I said, and I thought of Doctor Burk. I certainly wasn't his heroine. "But the pharmacist and his wife," I said. "They want us gone. What if they don't let you stay?" I grabbed his good arm. "Jack, I don't want to leave you behind."

He itched his beard stubble. "I'll have to talk to them, and hopefully with my broken German and their broken English we can reach an understanding. Fact is, I can't walk out of here in this state. It will look suspicious. Someone will notice if I can't stand." He looked up after pausing. "Listen." He swallowed dryly. "Meet me on the other side of the Rhine. There's a vineyard, in the middle of it is a house, yellow with green dormers. No pillboxes, no dragon's teeth—it's a clean walk and only a few miles west. I'll wait there for you," he said to us all, but he looked at me, and our eyes connected in a way I didn't expect.

I felt the others staring.

"I guess we don't have a choice," I said. It was a short reply, but there was nothing else to say, really. He reached for my hand as the others left out the door.

"Be safe," he said, and our fingers slid off one another's, and with his touch in that cold cement cellar, I imagined him dying alone. I moved to leave, but one of the more painful memories of the war had suddenly blanketed me in a fog. I braced the doorframe, eyes closed tightly.

We set up our hospital in a damaged building, pockmarked with blasts from German 88s. The windows were shattered and the walls looked like they'd cave in with one gust of wind. Surgery was set up in the back, away from the opening, where the medics brought in patients. Soldiers lay on the ground, moaning, festering, and holding their body parts together. We covered the windows with empty potato sacks we'd found in crates.

Doctor Burk pushed his sleeves up, calling for Red, who'd been washing her hands in a dribble of water leaking out of a lone spigot in the wall. Me and Roxy ripped the soldier's uniform from his body. Our only light was a single bulb strung up over our makeshift operating table. Sniper fire popped throughout the village in menacing, spaced-out attacks.

Red ordered me to help administer the ether. "But I haven't been trained for anesthesia."

"Trained or not, this is war," the doctor butted in, and that was the first rule of many I would later break.

Roxy poured the ether, while I held the soldier's jaw and gauze over his mouth, making sure he didn't swallow it, gag, or drown.

"Kit," she said. "Don't let go."

And I held that boy's jaw till my elbows ached. Then my arms. And my fingers felt stiff as nails, unbendable. My legs started to collapse from the pain in my arms, only when we were done, there wasn't a moment to rest. Another boy to fix, followed by another—tally after tally after tally I made on the wall. Intestines spilled into Red's hands, and she stuffed them back in. Ears had been blasted off, and soft tissue opened up to yellowy fat that bubbled like chicken skin in Crisco from a tank battle.

"Sweet boy," Roxy said to the ones who could still hear. "I've got you…"

The potato sack covering the window slipped from the nail. I couldn't move my arms. The doctor froze, Red and

Roxy too, and in horror we stared at a sliver of glass left unprotected.

"Hurry," I said in a shouted whisper to anyone who could help. "The window!"

And another nurse climbed up on a chair and fastened the sack back to the nail. She fell to the floor in disbelief that she was still alive, knowing she could have been shot by the nearest sniper.

Some twelve hours later, with my back slumped over, I was given a break.

I walked away in the gray morning hours of the shut-up building, stepping over reaching hands, and bodies with bayonet slashes exposing their insides in the most ungodly, unsurvivable way. "Nurse," I heard someone say from the floor, larynx gargling with blood, "Help…" Fingers grasped at my ankles and slid off my shoes. A mix of antiseptic, urine, iron, and rotting corpses hung heavy in my clothes, on my skin, and in every particle of air I breathed like dust. I collapsed against a wall, wanting a space to escape, if only for a second—a breath of fresh air—when I slipped out a side door that opened up into another room, this one much darker, and still.

I took one step in and my ankle twisted on a floor made of soft bodies, and I fell face-first onto men who had died waiting for surgery. Ones we forgot about. Ones we'd left behind.

Red barked at me two steps up the stairwell. "You coming?" she said, and my eyes popped open. The door shut behind me, and the last sight I had of Jack was of him lying on his bed. I exhaled, feeling jittery and unsure. It was more than leaving a soldier behind. I liked him—which made leaving him feel even worse.

Red looked at me. "You all right?"

"Yeah," I said, and I reached behind me and felt the closed door between us.

"We'll have to hurry," Red said, and Gail and Roxy nodded.

Every time someone said we had to hurry, the situation always turned into a chaotic circus full of blood and screams. Roxy and Gail followed Red up, and an eerie shiver prickled up my spine as if the daylight we were marching into was just trading one escapist's hell for another.

And we were following each other into it, blindly.

15

KIT

W e walked onto the sidewalk, each of us with our backs together forming a circle in the most obvious way that shouted *outsiders*. Red batted our hands to fall in line, and we did. Thank God, nobody was on the street behind the pharmacy to see us.

"It's brighter than yesterday," Roxy whispered, squinting into the sun.

"Shh," Red hissed, and Roxy clamped a hand over her mouth, nodding.

We followed the road through the square only to see it was market day. Umbrellas popped open and Germans set out their wares. Red looked at each of us, motioning with her hands for us to stay calm as we walked cautiously between women who were picking out vegetables and children who looked like clones from yesterday, chasing each other through the stalls, laughing, when the drone of bombers whirled through the clouds.

Every eye went to the sky.

"*Amerikaner!*" someone yelled, and three B-17s dropped out of a cloud in formation.

Women scattered like roaches, reaching for their children and yanking them inside where boards went into windows and doors bolted shut. We stood still among the empty market stalls holding each other, a swift breeze unfurling Nazi flags from street poles, knowing if those bombs hit the village there was no amount of running that would save us.

"We're gonna die by one of our own," Red said.

My heart pounded and blood glugged in my throat, waiting to hear the dreaded whistling from dropped bombs. Red hugged me, and Gail reached for Roxy, and we cried. "No other nurse I'd rather die beside," I said.

They flew right over us, a second chance at life, and I fell to my knees not able to breathe, clawing at my chest and neck. Red lifted me by the scruff of my neck, and we bolted down the street into the trees where I took a moment to try and catch my breath.

Nobody had followed us. And if they'd seen us from their loft windows, we couldn't tell. We watched the bombers fly off over the treetops, heading east.

"Let's go," Red said, and she tried to make us leave right away.

"Wait a minute, will ya?" Roxy said, bracing her knees, breathing heavily from the run.

"We don't have a minute," Red said, and we walked while still trying to catch our breath—a mile at least—until the forest gave way to a field of brown grass infested with giant grasshoppers.

Gail's hands flew to her face. "They're everywhere!"

They clung to our arms and legs, hopped under our skirts, and tangled with our hair. The steps we took to outrun them only seemed to aggravate the situation, making every step worse.

"Relax," Red said, but she was addressing Gail mostly, who yelped and hopped with each grasshopper that landed on her. "There's nothing we can do but walk our way out. And stay close. If you pay more attention to the grasshoppers you'll stray off." Red's gaze rolled over the field. "There could be mines out here."

I reached for Gail's hand. "Come on," I said, leading her, and we walked together through the field. The grasses turned marshy in places from the recent rain, looking a little moldy, and smelling foul. One step was firm and solid, then the other squishy and slippery with just enough grass to keep the mud from caking to our shoes. Out of the blue, Roxy turned to me, flicking a grasshopper from her nose.

"What's with that Jack?" Roxy said.

"What do you mean?" I said.

She flashed me a snide little smile. "Oh, Jack, I'm from Washington like you, oh, we live so close, oh this, and that…" She laughed. "I heard you talking in the middle of the night."

"We all did," Red mumbled.

"That's enough, girls," I said.

"Nah, really, Kit," Roxy said. "I think he likes you."

I scoffed. "I saved his arm from an infection that might have taken it off. Of course he likes me."

"Yeah, sure," Roxy said, and the conversation about Jack was dropped in favor of food. She sniffed the air. "Smells like fries out here. Don't you think?"

I made a face. "God, no," I said. "Smells like mold."

"Steak, on the grill?" Roxy said, and I swatted her arm.

"Stop it," I said. "The heat must be getting to you."

And the heat was indeed getting to us. Gail's face had turned red and splotchy against her brassy hair, and my armpits were sweating.

"I'm tired," Gail said, and we all moaned, even Red, who was at the front three paces ahead. Rule one of nursing: you never said out loud how tired you were. Everyone was tired. Everyone. "And this heat… It rains for days and then the sun comes out to scorch us to death?"

Roxy laughed. "Welcome to Europe, Gail," she said, hands out. "Today's weather is warm and balmy, followed by a brisk wind and buckets of rain that'll drown ya like a rat. Slight chance of bugs."

I smiled. "That's about right. I wonder if it's always like this?"

"I don't think so," Roxy said. "But what do I know? It's not like they gave us travel guides with our orders." She looked at Gail. "But you got one. Don't tell me the Nurse Corps handed them out to all the General nurses, did they?"

"Another nurse gave it to me after she got orders for Hawaii," Gail said.

"Hawaii, huh?" Roxy had laughed at first, but it quickly trailed into a sigh. "I would have liked Hawaii."

"Yeah," I said. "But then you would have missed all this." I whirled my finger around as we walked.

"Mmm…" Roxy said.

Gail stopped abruptly. "Did you hear that?" She swatted a grasshopper from her arm while searching the air.

"Hear what?" I said.

She darted several paces away and cupped her ear before motioning for us to follow her, but we stood still trying to hear what she'd heard, Roxy searching the sky for planes and Red scanning the field.

"I hear a child crying." She pointed indiscriminately, walking even further away, taking giant leaping steps through the grass, not caring a bit about the grasshoppers. "Don't you hear it? I think it's a little boy…"

"I don't hear anything," I said.

"Me either," Roxy said, while Red demanded she come back, warning of mines.

"But… but…" Gail said, frantically turning around trying to find the crying child when she shouted. "There he is!" She pointed with certainty this time, and we all gasped.

Sure as day there was a little boy—a blond German boy watching us from a fence post, pouting and whining about a scraped knee.

"And he *is* crying…" she said, and while Gail rushed toward him for comfort, we stood frozen, trying to make sense of the strange scene.

He pouted some more, pointing to his knee, but then giggled, and not in a cute way. A sinister way. He spat on the ground, and a chill pricked the hairs on the back of my neck. His icy blue eyes, cold, unfeeling, no soul to be seen, and his short, short hair. He smiled, showing teeth, and his lips spread from ear to ear, thinly, mischievously.

"Are you hurt?" Gail asked him in German, arms out, and he goaded her to follow him into an overgrown cornfield, stopping long enough for her to get close before running off again as if it was a game.

"Call her back," Red said frantically to me. "Call her back!"

"Come back!" I yelled in German. "Gail!" But her brassy head of curls disappeared over a berm and we'd lost them both.

Pop!

A single gunshot echoed over the quiet field, and we instinctively cowered in place. Birds flew out of the brush to perch on barbed wire. None of us moved, looking at each other in stunned silence, when Gail cried out for us. "Guys…"

We ran up and over the berm only to find her rolling around on the ground with a bullet in her arm and grasshoppers hopping up from the grass and landing in her hair. The boy had vanished.

"Quick… over here!" Red said, and we carried Gail a short distance away into the very cornfield the boy had tried to lure her and found cover.

Red took a look at the bullet hole, examining it real close as if she were a jeweler looking through an eyeglass, while Gail cried, head thrashing from one side to the other, giving us her arm to look at as if it didn't belong to her anymore. "How bad is it?" Gail said. "Please tell me. I can take it. You must tell me…" She tried her best to give a stiff upper lip, but her lips were too loose, and wet and she was slobbering.

"It's strange." Red's eyes shifted to mine, and I took a look. Muscle poured out of the wound like hamburger.

Gail's heels scraped the ground. "It stings! It stings…"

"Give me morphine," I said to Red, and I stuck Gail before she had a chance to know I was going to stick her in the neck.

"Ouch!" She slapped at it. "Ouch, ouch!" She knocked

the syrette from my hand with a final swipe, but I thought I managed to give her enough to dull the pain.

Red had reached under her skirt for her scalpel because we didn't pack the forceps. She held Gail's arm still, looking into her eyes with a pause, before gently prying the bullet out. Me and Roxy watched, and Red was a master surgeon, but this bullet was stubborn, hiding from the sharp end of her scalpel.

"It's lodged pretty good..." Red said, picking at it carefully as Gail whimpered into her shoulder asking her to hurry. "Almost got it... got it..." She picked it out of Gail's arm.

Plunk. And when it hit the dirt, we stared at it in shock and wonder, watching it roll.

"Oh shit," Roxy said, and that got Gail to pull her head up.

"What," she said, and there was a quiet pause before she scooted her bottom up to take a look, but we wouldn't let her, and blocked her with our arms. "Is it big?"

A bullet's a bullet. Except this bullet had been soaked in poison, which stained the tip pink. A wooden bullet that failed to split as it had been designed, but had wormed its way into her arm nonetheless, infecting her.

"Yeah," Roxy said. "That's it... just big is all."

"Don't lose it," Gail said. "I want to keep it. A souvenir." She exhaled, and I could tell the morphine had kicked in, and while she rested, none of us had let go of her arm. I looked at Red, and she looked at Roxy.

"We have to tell her," I finally said.

Red shook her head, but then smiled big when Gail looked at her.

"What's going on?" Gail said, but we didn't answer. "Guys?" Her voice had changed, she was worried and confused, and only God knew what kind of explanations were running through her head. "Roxy?" Gail reached for her. "Tell me."

Roxy gulped, and I could tell Gail knew it was something serious when she saw Roxy's face, which had turned flat as a pan and white as cake. Gail looked at her forearm for the first time where the bullet had chewed up her skin and immediately looked terrified and disgusted.

"Well, you see here..." Roxy said.

I'd turned away at first, not wanting to see Gail's reaction when she realized she'd been poisoned, but had a change of heart, feeling a great sense of shame for not holding her other hand. And when I squeezed her palm in mine, she'd started to cry.

"You're scaring me," Gail said.

"Listen, Gail," Roxy said. "There's no easy way to tell ya, but this bullet looks poisoned." Roxy hung her head down momentarily before looking back up. "What I mean is, it *is* poisoned. That bastard kid poisoned you."

Gail scooted up. "But... but... how do you know?" she said.

Tears spilled from Roxy's eyes into the dirt; she couldn't answer. Gail looked to me. "You've seen these bullets before?" Gail said, and I nodded. "Did the person die?" I'd never stopped nodding, and Gail's face had gone blank. "But I don't want to die." She looked at Red. "I don't want to. Red..." She sat up completely straight.

"We're going to stitch you up and you'll get a nice dose

of penicillin when we get back," Red said as she ripped open a sulfa packet with her teeth. "Nobody's dying on my watch. Got it? Nobody." She looked up at me. "Nobody left behind."

Tears pooled in Gail's eyes when Red said 'nobody left behind' as if we'd have to leave her in the corn.

"They said I shouldn't come," Gail said. "My brothers. My father. They said I was too delicate, called me a frightened kitten." She patted her cheeks when the tears fell, sniffling, trying to talk through her sobs. "They said I wasn't smart either, and I'd proved them wrong when I got my degree." She shook her head. "But I guess they were right about this one…"

Roxy took Gail by the shoulders. "Listen here, toots. You're tough. One of the toughest gals out here. I didn't believe it before, I have to tell ya, but you're the real deal, Gail Barry. Not even battle trained and look at ya. You're in the thick of it." Roxy's eyes rolled over the cornstalks. "Really, you are."

Gail laughed through her tears with that joke, and Roxy wrapped her arms around Gail's neck.

"Don't let anyone tell you differently, you got me?" Roxy said. "You got shot!"

Roxy held Gail's hand while Red stitched her up with the only needle and thread we had. "Don't worry, Gail," she said. "This is temporary. A doctor will fix you up better when we get back." Red wrapped it up with the bandage she had around her thigh. "Can you move your fingers?" she asked, and Gail moved them, barely.

"They're a little stiff," Gail said.

"Keep wiggling them, okay?" Red said. "Keep the blood flowing. The bullet didn't split like it was supposed to, but we need to keep an eye on it. Understand?"

Gail looked like she knew what Red was trying to say. We didn't know what the poison would do, but one thing was sure: Gail was on borrowed time. Every moment we spent in Germany and away from our medical team was a moment too long for Gail. We were lucky we brought some supplies with us, but now we were nearly out.

"Dolls?" Roxy said, kneeling and leaning into us. Cornstalks swished and swayed, but there wasn't a breeze. "Someone's coming."

None of us talked. None of us breathed. There was a moment where I thought she'd been mistaken. Then we heard it. Footsteps in the grass and the crackle of hands pulling back the stalks. I searched the air for a direction, but it was near impossible to know where the sound was coming from, when Red patted my shoulder. "The gun, Kit," she whispered. "The gun!"

"But he's a boy…" I said.

She tapped me urgently, eyes set into the unknown of the thick cornfield. "The gun…" Red said.

I reached for the gun around my thigh, fumbling with the strap with sweaty fingers. "Hurry, Kit," Gail said, "shoot him…" But Roxy begged me not to shoot, tapping my other shoulder and whispering in my ear about how he was a little boy.

I pointed the gun into the corn, trigger pulled back, jerking left and right with each crack of cornstalk and each bristle in the grass. I felt him watching us, and my breath grew rapid, heart pounding, searching and searching, thinking of the only other time I'd ever used a gun.

"Don't let the deer hear you," my brother said. "You have to be patient. Wait for your target to come to you."

The rifle he'd given me was the size of a dog, and heavy as one too. He said it would give me muscles, but I didn't want muscles. I wanted to shoot and get it done with.

The farms of the Palouse were vast and hilly. Deer liked to bed down in the young green wheat fields at night and feed on them in the day. We'd walked a mile before Sam found a spot for us to sit. "It's hard to sneak up on a deer in the Palouse because we're so exposed." He crouched down on his knees, motioning for me to sit next to him. "Now we wait," he said. "Stay still. They won't know we're here."

"Yeah," I said. "But how will I know when to shoot?"

He smiled over his shoulder. "You'll know when." We'd spent the entire day in the grass in the Palouse without a single shot. My knees ached, and my legs tingled with pins and needles from sitting in one spot for too long. Then out of the blue, a buck with great big antlers walked quietly by a few yards from where me and my brother were.

Sam smiled, mouthing at me to take him, flicking his finger at the buck.

I lifted the rifle, pressed it against my cheek, and aimed at my target through the grass. The buck looked at me, as if he'd sensed me. Sweat instantly poured from my forehead.

"Take the shot," my brother whispered. "Take the shot…"

I dropped the rifle momentarily from the sting of sweat in my eyes, not sure if I could do it, only to lift the rifle up once more. My finger squeezed the trigger, pulling it closer, tighter, watching the buck chew up the wheat in his mouth, eyes scouting, looking for predators. I saw him breathing, his sides billowing and shrinking.

I released my finger, and looked up at my brother who rubbed the top of my head.

"It's okay," he said. "Not everyone can do it."

Red pointed to something blue playing peekaboo between the stalks, weaving in and out, catching fleeting glimpses only to lose sight in the cover. "I see him," I said, breathy as if I'd been running, aiming, holding the gun between my sweaty palms.

"He's a boy, he's a boy..." Roxy said in one ear, while Gail cried for me to take the shot.

A rifle cocked through the stalks about to shoot, and I dropped the gun, but Red snatched it from a tangle of weeds without hesitation. *Bang!*

A thump and a tumble followed our screams, a lumpy sack of potatoes falling to the ground.

Red breathed heavily, abandoning the gun and throwing her hands to her head for what she'd done—she'd shot a boy. We looked at each other after covering our faces, eyes like eggs, runny and wide. Roxy flicked her chin at me to go see, but I shook my head.

"Fine," Roxy said, and she crept over to where the body lay.

"He was going to kill us!" Red shrieked, and I patted her back. "What was I to do?"

"It's a man!" Roxy shouted back to us, and with that we sprung up to see, holding on to each other, taking guarded steps toward the body that lay motionless on the ground.

A farmer, perhaps, dressed plainly with buzzed, graying hair. I picked up his rifle and opened the chamber like Sam had taught me. Gail peeked over my shoulder, her mouth pinching sourly when she saw more wooden bullets loaded in his gun.

"Bastard Hun!" She kicked him in the leg. Again, and again, his body sluggishly moving in the grass with each blow, until Roxy finally pulled her away. "Gail!" she yelped, and they hugged, with Gail crying into Roxy's shoulder.

I leaned over his body. There was no bullet hole, not a spot of blood, an exposed wound—nothing. I'd seen a lot of bullet wounds, but never had I seen one without an entry point. "Where'd it hit?"

"Who cares!" Red took me by the arm to leave, then he moaned suddenly, deeply, like a growly bear. He kicked out his leg and Roxy fell to the ground in one swift move, words spitting from his mouth in German, "Dirty American bitches!" He pulled a dagger from a knife belt, holding her neck with one hand and reaching up to slice it with the other.

I raised the rifle. *Pop!* The blast blew me backward on the ground in a daze with a piercing, deafening silence. "*You'll know when,*" my brother had said to me.

I saw the sky.

Red reached for me, and I said Roxy's name, but I couldn't hear my own voice. I stood up in a stupor, one hand cupping my ear and the other wrapped around Red for support. Roxy knelt on the ground, holding her neck, hacking her breaths. It had happened so fast; one moment Roxy was on her two feet, breathing, talking, and the next she was limp as a noodle with a purple face, scratching at the German's hands with her nails.

Red shook my shoulder, her voice like a whisper though it looked like she was yelling. "He's dead... you got him..."

And when she said the words, I looked into his dead eyes and saw my dark silhouette in his widened pupils.

Roxy stumbled to her feet and threw her arms around me, followed by Red while Gail held her shot arm close to her chest. And as we hugged over the dead man's body in the corn, a hardened wave fell over me. A shift. A change. I had killed a man. I slid down below them, dropping to my knees, and bawled with my hands to my eyes, convulsing. Yet, I knew I'd done the right thing, and I'd be reminded of it every time I looked at Roxy.

Roxy knelt down next to me, squeezing my hand, her big brown eyes sagging a bit. "Thanks, Kit." She turned away before her own tears fell.

Gail handed me Jack's gun, and Red motioned for us to get going. "Wait," I said. "Shouldn't we say a prayer?"

Red paused between the stalks, but Roxy and Gail kept walking, Roxy still holding her neck, and Gail clutching her poisoned arm.

16

EVELYN

Evelyn sat up in her chair across from the reporter, and for the first time in over twenty years, she asked her husband for a cigarette. She picked up the photo the reporter had brought, all four of them sitting in the mess tent eating the dinner Gail all but threw up the moment she'd swallowed. Evelyn smiled with *that* memory, the only time she remembered smiling about those days.

Evelyn closed her eyes to find strength, reaching up to feel the locket around her neck, when her husband flipped open his old metal lighter and lit her cigarette. She was surprised to find she missed it—a familiar taste that hit the back of her throat.

"First..." She picked up the business card the reporter had given her husband, since she didn't actually read the one he'd given her yesterday. "What's your name?" she said, cigarette bobbing between her lips, seemingly picking up her little habit right where she'd left off. "Says here it's..." She put her readers on after squinting. "Robert?"

He nodded, rummaging around in his leather bag before pulling out a small recorder and placing it on the table between them. He paused, looking at her before hitting the record button. "That's right. Robert."

"Well, Robert." She reached over the table and stopped his recorder. "This is my kitchen, and before I agree to tell you anything about me, I need to know about you."

"Oh?" he said, smiling curiously.

"Yeah," she said. "For starters, you're obviously here because your dad told you something. What do you know?"

He smiled as if wondering how much he should say. "My dad took photos of the nurses from Utah Beach until Berlin," he said. "He collected them along with letters my mom had lifted from nurses she thought had been compromised—she believed everyone was a spy."

Evelyn was surprised, which she was sure showed on her face. "Your mom?" She lowered her cigarette, brow furrowed. "Who's your mom?"

"Noreen Battistelli."

Evelyn blinked once. "Noreen?"

He smiled. "Yeah, did you know her? She was at your field hospital."

God, she thought. *Nosy Noreen. Yeah, I know her! Match made in heaven those two, and now their son is in my kitchen. Roxy would be mortified.*

Evelyn smiled the best she could. "Yes, I remember Noreen. How is she?"

"Passed away. Dad too."

"I'm sorry," she said, though she wasn't surprised. So many of those who had served and survived were passing away.

"Thank you," he said. "My dad had a great career at *The New York Times*, and after he died my mom passed his proofs to me. He came back from France with a lot of stories—too many to count. But there was this one story that intrigued him the most."

"Oh?" Evelyn said, lifting her coffee cup to her lips.

"It was about nurses who tortured an SS officer to get information about the Nazi war chest," he said, and Evelyn choked on her coffee.

"Sorry," she said, wiping her mouth. "Go on..." She picked up her cigarette.

"Mom said you and your tent mates disappeared for several days on a secret mission she'd heard rumors about, and that you left without your dog tags. She was convinced the two stories were related. And because you left your tags behind, she and my dad thought you crossed enemy lines. Did you?"

Evelyn smoked her cigarette, staring at the reporter through the smoke. After a moment without an answer, he cleared his throat and took yellowed envelopes out from his leather bag, placing them in front of her.

"These letters!" Evelyn's cigarette nearly fell out of her open mouth. "They're mine!" She shuffled through them, all addressed to Nurse Blanchfield. "Nosy Noreen stole these?"

He laughed when Evelyn called his mom "nosy," but chuckled it away when he saw Evelyn wasn't kidding around. "I suppose she was a little nosy."

Evelyn scoffed, tossing the letters on the table in front of him. "These are complaint letters. Is that how you learned so much about me? You read all these and figured out where I came from?"

He reached for the recorder again, pressing his thumb on the power switch. "Is it okay if we start?"

Evelyn didn't like his tone; it chafed her nerves, especially since she hadn't decided one way or the other to give an interview. She coughed into her closed fist. "Listen, sonny," she said, and she swore she'd never, under any circumstances, sound like an old lady, but it had slipped out, and it slipped out from thinned lips that made her sound even older. "I've got a story to tell; you're right about that. But I haven't agreed to talk to you about it yet." Evelyn swallowed, not sure if he'd understand, but then she didn't really know if Benny's son was capable of understanding. "I'll be changing history, you see?" Her eyes fell to the photo again, and she took a long, lingering look at her friends' faces. She'd always been fascinated with photos, capturing a moment in time. Frozen. Untouched. Lives still living.

She took his recorder and pressed record, talking right into the speaker. "But let's clear something up," she said. "I didn't torture anyone. None of us did. I'll tell you that now, just to get it off my chest." She turned the recorder off, taking a deep breath, and reached for her husband. "Honey…"

Her husband held her hands. "You're doing great," he said, but Evelyn shook her head.

"So, to confirm. The stories are connected and you were involved in both?" Robert said.

Evelyn immediately held her pounding head. "I don't like this," she said to her husband. "Right now, in my kitchen? I've kept this story locked away in my mind for so many years. I… I need time."

There was a moment of quietness as Robert watched

Evelyn struggle on the opposite side of the table, smoking her cigarette to a nub and gulping her coffee.

"We don't have to do this today," Robert finally said.

"Well, we don't have to do it at all, either," she said. "This is my choice, my kitchen, my house that you're in."

Robert smiled half-heartedly. "You're right. You don't," he said, "but this story isn't going away." He pulled a piece of paper from his bag and pushed it across the table. An official announcement of the first-ever Women's National Salute in Atlanta and reunion. "Would you consider telling your story here?"

"We talked about this reunion," her husband said.

"So, you know about it? Good," Robert said. "I was actually hoping you'd agree to a formal interview here. My paper has partnered with cable to do a special called *Women of War*. We'll be taking oral histories live at the event. Would you consider telling your story at the reunion this October? I think it would look really striking on television—"

Evelyn looked at her husband, eyes bulging from her head before standing sharply from her chair. Evelyn couldn't believe the reporter's gall, though she wasn't sure why—this was Benny and Noreen's son, after all. "This isn't a circus bit, Bob," she said, without asking him if she could call him Bob. "This is a story about real people—a story that will knock you blind. A moment of true courage, friendship. Heartache. Do you understand?" She scoffed. "Of course, you don't understand."

Evelyn paced her kitchen with her heart ticking rapidly, thinking about telling her story in such a sensational way. She turned to her husband, looking for guidance.

"I think you should do it," he said, and she shut her eyes.

"With all due respect, Kit," Robert said, and she threw him a hot look. "I mean, Mrs. Jones—ma'am. You'll have a lot of support at the reunion. And if it's at all like you say, the heartache, courage, and friendship... It will only draw more attention to the women who served. The interview will be done in a very respectful way. I promise you."

"Think about what he's saying," her husband said. "And this gives you some time to prepare."

"If it makes a difference," Robert said. "My mom had headaches for decades after the war. The blood. The loss of life. It infected her, stayed with her. This is the first reunion of its kind for the nurses who served. You won't be alone."

This hit Evelyn in the soft part of her chest. Nosy Noreen was a real pill, but she was in France with the rest of them, and to hear that even Noreen Battistelli wasn't immune to the last words of the dying, got her to think of his request differently.

Evelyn sat back down. "You need to understand something," she said, as her husband handed her another cigarette. "I haven't told anyone about this. Ever. My own daughter didn't even know I was a battle nurse in Europe until last night." She stuck the cigarette in her mouth only to pull it back out. "Last night," she reiterated.

"So, you will do it?" Robert said. "I want to make sure I understand. You'll tell your story at the salute?"

Evelyn took a long, jittery breath as her husband placed his hand on her back.

"I'll go to the salute, but as for the story... I'll try. I can't promise you," Evelyn said as she wondered what trying would look like, feel like. "I'm glad the reunion is months away because I need some time to prepare mentally for it."

She felt her chest, feeling the thumps between her breaths while her husband kissed her cheek. He looked very relieved, and she gave him a conciliatory smile.

"Can I..." Evelyn motioned with her fingers. "Borrow the photo? The one of all of us."

Robert looked at the photo again as if he was thinking about it, before shifting his gaze to Evelyn and her tired eyes. "Sure," he said, and he gave it to her as he gathered up his things, but just before he walked out of her kitchen, he piped back up.

"Oh... One more thing," he said, slinging his bag over his shoulder. "I was looking through the Nurse Corps archives, and Red... There's nothing about her after 1944. It's as if she's vanished from all official records. Do you know anything about that?"

Evelyn slowly looked up from the photo, a ribbon of smoke escaping between her lips. She knew Benny's son couldn't resist one last question. She would have asked it too, and honestly, this was the question she expected when he sat down. But Evelyn had been very clear, she wasn't prepared to answer his questions today, especially this one.

She smiled, and a long, awkward pause followed as they looked at each other.

"Mrs. Jones?"

Evelyn turned away from him in her chair. "Goodbye, Robert," she said, and her husband showed the reporter out.

17

KIT

The butcher's house looked more like a farm, with a big pasture dotted with black cows, and fencing. Lots of fencing. Barbed wire, wood, and stone. We knelt down at a distance in the damp grass. Birds tweeted in the trees and clouds puffed by. Far away, and for the first time since crossing the Rhine, we heard bombing. Explosions that sounded like thunderclaps.

"That's close," I said. "Maybe the Third changed their plans, decided to take the Rhine and not wait for the refueling?" I turned around to find Roxy sitting in the grass, her back up against a tree trunk.

She looked up at Red. "Can't we rest for a second?" She rubbed her feet and felt her aching back. "Please."

Gail stared off in the distance toward the butcher's house, holding her arm, which Red had tied in a sling. When she did talk, her voice was quiet and soft, but still, she didn't take her eyes off the farm. "What if the butcher tries shooting us?"

I didn't think we'd get shot at again. In fact, I thought Gail's wound would be the sort of thing the butcher would expect to see on a werewolf. We spoke perfect German, Gail even better than me, if I was honest with myself. Besides, I'd fooled that SS officer already, and had I kept my questions to myself about my brother, he would have never figured me out. I could fool this butcher. We'd ask for the package. Collect it, and leave. Jack made it perfectly clear that the butcher was the holder. He was waiting for the werewolves. There'd be no reason for him not to give us the package.

"What if it's the wrong place?" Roxy said.

Red unfolded the map. "This must be the place." She paused, looking up at the farm after studying the map once more. "The next farm is a mile away. Unless I got the directions completely wrong…"

The sun rose higher in the sky. More bombs exploded in the west, faint thunderclaps, but still closer than they should be, and I closed my eyes. War *was* coming. It had to be, and I felt the precious hours we had to save the POW camps slipping through my fingers.

"The war," I said. "Don't you hear all that? We don't have time to rest."

"Please," Roxy said. "A rest. I beg you. We've been walking all morning. Sorry for speaking it out loud, but this is different."

"No, let's go!" I said, making a move toward the butcher's, but Red grabbed me forcibly by the elbow.

"Sit down!" she said, pulling me to sit on the ground. "I'm in charge. We're not going yet."

My mouth hung open in shock. Even Gail broke away from her deep thoughts to look at Red. "But the POW camps. If we don't get down there and get the package before the werewolves… You heard Jack. They'll attack the camps." I threw a finger in the air towards Karlsruhe. "My brother's POW camp!"

"You're going off half-cocked," Red said, sitting down next to Roxy. "Just like in the tent when a critical comes in. You always rush. Think. Will you?" She rubbed her face, covering her eyes.

"Well, what a thing to say!" I said, but Red kept her face in her hands, and the longer she ignored me with Roxy staring at the ground, the warmer my neck grew. I pulled my collar forward. "Say it to my face why don't ya?" I said, and when Red looked up, I stood.

Red studied me for a second and then stood up too.

"Sit down." Red put her hands on her hips.

"No." I looked up at her, shaking my head.

Roxy jumped up, despite her aching feet. "Whoa! You gals wanna start somethin'? You're best friends!" She held her arms out to keep us apart. "We're in this together. Goddamn it! If we can't work as a team then I don't know what the *hell* I'm doing here."

It was the first time I'd ever heard Roxy talk like the men. Red backed away in a huff, and so did I, each moving to opposite sides of the tree.

The longer I stood with my thoughts and my back to the girls, the heavier my eyes felt, and soon enough they'd welled with tears. We'd never talked to each other that way before. The stress of the real werewolves beating us to the package weighed on me more than anything I'd ever endured before. *How dare she.*

I turned around, about to confront Red again, tell her I

was going by myself if I had to, but was surprised to find her standing right behind me.

"Sorry," she said. And that was all she had to say, and the tears I'd been wiping away turned into a flood. She put her arms around me. "I'm scared, Kit."

It was the first time I heard Red say she was scared. The first time. After everything we've been through since the beach, and I think those words alone hit me the hardest.

"I'm scared too," I said. "Trust me, Red. Time isn't on our side. I know what to do, and you know we can't sit here."

She only looked at me. No words, before finally nodding ever so slightly.

I walked over to Gail and touched her shoulder, which startled her. "It's us, you know? We're going to have to do all the talking."

"I know," she said, eyes flicking to mine. She tried moving her fingers, and it looked like they were getting a little stiff, especially her pinkie. "I think the poison is starting to take hold."

I took a look myself, holding her wrist and moving her fingers, but it was hard to tell if it was the poison or because she'd been shot. "Don't worry, Gail," I said. "We'll get the package and get back to France in no time. Before that poison does any harm. Besides, the bullet hadn't broken up like it was supposed to."

She looked up, and I thought she was sniffling, but realized she was more upset than scared and hurt. "I hope you're right."

"Are you in pain?" I said.

Gail shook her head. "I got enough morphine to dull it." She looked off toward the farm again. "Can we go now?"

I motioned for Roxy, and together with Red and Gail we huddled together. "This is what we're going to do," I said, and I told them my plan, which was absurdly simple. "Me and Gail will speak. That's it. That's all."

They followed in line behind me without question. I took a deep breath when I felt a twinge of nervousness, which they couldn't see from behind. *Get in, get out. Ask for the package and leave*, I thought, and we walked down the hill.

The grass turned longer and harder to walk through the closer we got to the farm. Red swatted a fly near her face. "Ugh!" Red said. "What's that awful smell?" And when Red said it, the most disgusting odor wafted up from the grass and rained down from the trees.

"Ugh is right!" Roxy said, covering her nose. "That *is* awful!"

Red looked for a place to get sick from the stench. One fly turned into two, and then three, and then a hundred, all buzzing up from the grass, landing on our arms and hair. Big giant flies, the ones I normally saw when we drove through smoldering battlefields, swarming around mounds of earth mixed with flesh and fluids.

Sometimes cow pastures smelled that way, although faintly, especially near a slaughterhouse, but there were only three cows in the pasture, and they looked like dairy cows. It was then I noticed the cows weren't mooing. In fact, it looked like they weren't even moving. I waved the flies away, trying to get a better look, and I was sure they were still. More still than I'd ever seen a cow before.

"Is this what farms smell like?" Roxy asked. "It smells like… like…"

Saint-Lô.

None of us wanted to say it.

In the hospitals, on the battlefields, we knew what to expect. But out in the country where the colors were so vibrant, the green grass, the blue sky, it was jarring to the senses and the mind.

"Not our farm," I said, and we continued our walk. As we got closer, the house appeared more and more German. Wood and cream-colored stucco, with a dilapidated porch and painted decorative beams. The smell wasn't as strong toward the front of the house, less pungent, but it was still there, only intermittingly broken with a little breeze that seemed to brush it away in sweeps.

A woman popped out from behind the fence and scared us all. "*Willkommen!*"

Roxy and Red screamed, immediately covering their mouths to keep their English words from tumbling out.

"*Guten Tag,*" I said.

Her eyes were wide and unmoving as if resisting the urge to blink.

"Sorry, for the fright," I said in German. "We didn't see you."

She moved closer to us through the grass, using a pitchfork for a walking stick. Her dress looked oily and stained, dark circles covering lighter ones, and it was about three sizes too small. When she took a breath, the bodice tightened and the hem lifted above her knees, showing her dirty legs.

She talked through her teeth. "I scared you?" She covered her mouth with one hand, only to uncover it long enough to speak. "Good day indeed!" She motioned for us to follow her. "I've been waiting for you. Come... come. This way." She walked toward the house.

"Wait!" I said.

She stopped, her back to us, pitchfork gripped tight in her hand.

"Are you the butcher?" I said, clearly, directly, and her shoulders dropped.

Gail lifted her chin. "We're on orders from the Führer."

She turned around slowly, moving one hand to her hip. "Maybe I am and maybe I'm not. Come in for some tea," she said, "then I'll let you decide."

She walked on to the front of the house but turned sharply and we headed toward the back. "Decide what?" I said, and she glanced at us over her shoulder.

"If I'm the butcher or not of course!" She cackled like a witch about to throw us in a pot.

Roxy took my hand and squeezed while Red looked utterly confused. When we stepped up on the back porch, the smell had turned into something more ghastly than uncomfortable. Death. Roxy was right, the smell was exactly like the exposed, decomposing corpses of Saint-Lô, though there were no bodies. Only a few motionless cows in the pasture.

"Is there something wrong with the cows?" I asked, and she giggled again as I tried to make sense of what I saw. The blue and white fabric woven through the pergola beams fluttered whimsically with the wind, yet the flowers cascading out of window boxes had turned black with flies. Cats fought viciously over something wet and red in the corner underneath a broken rocking chair, and she scatted them away.

I gagged into my hand.

"Will you be all right?" she said, blinking for the first time since we'd met.

"It's the smell," I said, and she looked at me as if I'd had two heads.

"Whatever do you mean?" She opened up the door and we walked inside where the smell wasn't as bad, but where its imprint had marked the space clearly. She closed the door. "Oh, do have a sit, will you?" She bobbed around her kitchen taking five teacups from her cabinet. "I've been waiting for you…"

Two chairs had been set out as if she had definitely been waiting for us, or at least the werewolves. She smoothed a lacy tablecloth over a round table and pushed it toward the chairs with a manly grunt. "You are early, no?" she said, "and I expected two of you." She brought out more chairs before reaching for a steaming yellow teapot.

"Is that a problem?" I said.

"No!" she half yelled, followed by a smile. "Early is good, and four is fine. Absolutely fine." She set the teacups on the table, placing one in front of each of us, but held on to mine and took a moment to marvel at the cup's hand-painted alpine scene before pouring me some tea. The tea bubbled up near the rim, and Red looked at me, shaking her head slightly, warning me not to take a drink, and Roxy followed, but I thought they were being overly cautious after what happened to Gail. This woman thought we were werewolves.

The woman's tongue probed her wet lips, waiting anxiously for me to drink, nudging with her chin. I moved the cup closer to me on the table, sliding it slowly so as not to spill.

Roxy looked around the house, examining every corner of the room. A painting of a boy in traditional clothing hung on the widest wall, near the stove where soot had streaked the bricks. Cobwebbed candle sconces hung in the strangest of places, under shelves, and much too close to the curtains. And the windows, dirty as if a thousand dust storms had blown through. She reached for my hand when she saw Hitler's portrait hanging on the wall behind us.

"We're here for the package," Gail said, shifting her hurt arm, and I could tell she was growing tired of the delay. "We're not here for tea."

The woman plopped down in her own chair opposite of us, and her belly mushroomed from the middle of her body with her feet flying out from under. She smiled. But this time her smile was different. Oddly different. Condescending in a way that made me think she felt smarter than us. She reached into her pocket and played with something I couldn't see, something bulky, and when she caught me staring, she pulled her hand out, glaring.

"I want us to drink some tea!" she shouted, and we jerked in our seats. "Only then will you know where your precious package is. Führer or not, this is my rule. My name's Gilda, what's yours?"

She reached for the teapot again, and this time topped off each of our cups, making it almost impossible for us not to spill the tea in order to drink it. She pulled a bread bun out from under the table, but from where I didn't know. She leaned back.

I gulped, staring at the cup of tea before me, and I swear I smelled something tart and tangy, something that didn't belong.

"I don't get many visitors. And the ones I do get aren't—" she coughed "—very talkative. I want a little company. I'm owed this much. You have some tea with me, we finish off this pot together, and I'll tell you where your package is." She put a finger in the air. "Oh! And after each sip, I'll give you a hint. That will put some excitement into my day." She giggled into her cup of tea, chewing her bun and swallowing loudly.

Red shot up from her chair, dragging me to the corner to talk, leaving Roxy sitting on her hands at the table and Gail staring at a fidgeting Gilda.

"I have a bad feeling about this," Red whispered.

"What kind of feeling?"

"What if the tea is poisoned?" Red said. "Maybe she wants to kill the werewolves, not help them."

Gilda craned her neck around. "No whispering! Get back here!" She pointed at our seats.

I shared glances with the others as I considered what to do, but we had little choice. "Put your lips to it, but don't drink it," I whispered back to Red, and before she could protest, I'd walked away.

We took our seats again, and while Roxy examined the walls and Gail continued to stare, I lifted my cup with a little clear of my throat. I sensed the warmth of the liquid nearing my mouth as it rippled from my breath, and I smelled that tang again. I closed my eyes briefly, wondering if Red was right, but I felt I had to at least put my lips to the rim. A low-flying bomber rumbled overhead, rattling the glasses in her cupboards and spooking the cats. We looked to the ceiling, following the sound of the engines, which gave Gilda a laugh.

"We'll all be dead soon," she said.

"What?" I said, my lips inches from the rim.

"War…" Gilda said, smiling. "So many dead." She motioned with her chin for me to take a drink of the tea. "Go on." She slurped a long drink from her cup, which made me feel better since the tea was poured from the same pot—the odds of two Germans poisoning us did seem like a long shot. Red was being paranoid, I decided, and she'd made me paranoid.

I moved in for a drink and Red stepped on my foot under the table, pressing, pressing, trying to get my attention, but I took a sip anyway, knowing it *was* the only way to get what we wanted out of Gilda. Surprisingly, the tea didn't taste as horrible as it smelled.

"It's hibiscus," Gilda said, smiling.

"I took a drink." I set down the cup. "You saw."

Gilda set her cup down too only to pick it right back up. "Oh, yes… yes. I did see you. Of course." She stared at us with her silly smile. "Oh! You want a clue." She put a finger to her chin. "What's black and white and dripping red?"

I repeated Gilda's words while Gail squinted, tapping her good fingers on the table.

"You lose!" Gilda shouted. Her feet kicked out from under her chair with excitement, and she spilled tea onto the front of her dress. "Oh no…" She dabbed the wet spot with a tea towel from her lap. "Look what you girls made me do!" Her voice had turned angry, and Gail stood with command, having had enough of Gilda.

"We came for the package!" Gail bellowed, and Gilda covered her ears, shrieking.

"Sorry, sorry, sorry," Gilda cried, "don't hurt me." She

slipped off her chair and crawled away on the floor like a cowering dog from Gail's booming voice, and I don't think any of us could believe it; all we could do was stare.

The door opened with a bang, and a man walked into the room. We stood up behind Gail, huddling together and reaching for each other's hands. He wore black overalls with a blood-stained white apron and had a machete gripped in his hand.

The butcher.

"Black and white and dripping in red…" Gail said, and Gilda sprung up from the floor and clapped wildly.

"Yes, yes!" she yelped. "You understand!"

"What do you want?" The butcher looked at us with a keen eye, studying the details as if to make a mention of us later.

"We came for the package," Gail said.

He took one step closer and the floorboards creaked under his weight. He looked at Gilda, he looked the table, the teapot, and my cup. He took a sniff, holding my cup close to this nose, before dipping his finger in and dabbing his tongue with the tea.

"Husband," she cried, and he threw the cup across the room in a fit of rage. He grabbed her shoulders, bringing her upright, spouting in her face. "What did you do, Gilda?"

"I did nothing," she said. "Ask them… ask them…" But he kept looking at her. "I only wanted them to stay. Only wanted the company. I swear it, husband."

The butcher turned to me. "Did you drink the tea?" he said, and my stomach sank as I nodded.

He stood over Gilda as she crumpled on the floor. "What have you done to us now, woman? They're the werewolves.

We'll end up in our own pasture, collecting flies in our insides!"

I sat back down in my chair, holding my throat. My God, Red was right. "Did you poison me?"

"No!" the woman cried. "Nothing was in the tea but the tea!" She reached for my arm only to pull her hand back. She looked at her husband. "If there was something else, she'd feel it already." She nodded at me. "You feel fine, don't you, fräulein?"

"Do you feel fine?" he asked while Gilda pointed to the blue teapot she had on her cooktop.

"It's the blue one I use for the *other* company, the special company," she said. "Not the yellow."

Other company? I felt my own forehead, but didn't feel any different than before I took the drink. I thought maybe she was telling the truth—the tea was just tea. I nodded.

"See! She's fine… she's fine!" Gilda said.

The butcher paused, looking at my face, studying my features, before saying, "Follow me." He motioned for us to follow him, but when we did, he yelled. "*Nein!*" Roxy and Red jerked, grabbing on to each other. "Only her," he said, pointing to me. "Nobody else." He left out the back door and stood on the porch waiting for me.

I put my hands up, mouthing that it was only me who was supposed to go. Red whispered for me to use the gun if I had to when Gilda wasn't looking.

I closed my eyes for a brief second. *The gun.*

"In case," she mouthed, and I nodded.

"Sorry about my wife," the butcher said to me on the porch. "She…" He waved a finger in the air while I swatted at flies. "Gets lonely. Doesn't think straight." We walked toward a barn, a large Bavarian barn that looked like it was built for horses. He paused with his hand on the door. "Stall fifteen. Prepare yourself." He rolled the door open and the scent of death hit me like a blast of car exhaust. Rotted garbage, diarrhea, and burnt sugar. I immediately gagged amid a swarm of flies. He stood next to me, looking stoically into the barn.

"Come," he said, and I followed him inside.

Instead of horses, the stalls held bodies, all in different stages of decomposition, some had turned green, others black as tar, all stacked right on top of each other. We stopped at stall number fifteen. Flies landed on my eyelids and on my lips; no amount of swatting kept them away.

"Traitors are sent here for my wife's special tea, at the Reich's request," he said. "I'm showing you so that you know our commitment. I've made many scientific discoveries in this barn in the name of country."

I looked around, hiding my horrified face with my dress collar. Each stall had a chart, documenting the different stages of rot, and how long they'd been dead. "You will report favorably about us, won't you, fräulein?" He reached into a horse trough without any water and pulled out a lumpy bag with a long shoulder strap. "We do what the Reich says…"

I nodded, and he stepped toward me, getting nearer, tightening his grip around his machete. I patted my leg for the gun, trying to grab it through the fabric of my dress, but he was only handing me the bag.

I fell against a wood post.

He opened a trapdoor under some hay with a staircase that disappeared into a dark underground lair. "Good day."

He walked down the stairs, and the trapdoor slammed shut over top of him, but I was already running out of the barn.

I coughed and gagged around the corner, trying to catch my breath, but I only wanted to run, not stop and inspect the bag. I slung it over my shoulder and ran toward the house to collect the others. I fell through the door, stumbling over my own feet, gasping, one hand over my nose, the other holding the bag tightly, only to find Gilda bent over and staring at Red and Roxy real close as they sat shaking like two scared cats.

Gail told the woman to back up, get out of their faces. "They're mute I told you!" she said, which only seemed to intrigue Gilda more.

Gilda pulled Red's kerchief from her hair. "Ooh, a ginger!" she said, touching Red's hair, and feeling it in her fingertips.

I patted the bag near my waist, motioning with my other hand for them to follow me, and Roxy and Red shot up from their seats.

"Don't leave! Not yet!" Gilda crumpled to the floor, pouting with clenched fists as we shuffled out of the room. "He always ruins everything," she cried.

"Go," Red whispered, while Roxy pushed me from behind. "Go... go..."

I threw the front door open, stopping cold. Two blonde girls walked up the gravel road toward the butcher's house with their arms unmoving by their sides, dressed in blue with long, long braids. "Mother of God." I turned around sharply.

"The werewolves." I gulped. "They're here!"

18

KIT

I'd never been speechless before. Truly speechless, where my tongue and brain felt dumb and numb. I closed the door immediately. Gilda was in the other room, out of earshot and out of sight, but we heard her singing her own name and clinking teacups together. "Gilda this and Gilda that, la la la la…"

We looked through the one window that wasn't covered in dirt and watched the pair walk slowly, methodically, like toy soldiers in the day, right up onto the butcher's property. Their blonde braids made them look even more menacing and evil, lying flat against their breasts. "What do we do now?" I said, just as Gilda burst into a crying fit in the other room. My heart hummed.

"I know what to do!" Gail exclaimed, her voice commanding, resolute, and she had all three of us listening. "Take Gilda into the pasture. A tea party." The werewolves walked closer, marching, marching, close enough to hear us if the door had been open. Gail turned to me. "Don't come back in here until I say so."

"What are you going to do?" Roxy said. "I'm worried."

"Don't be." Gail's eyes were set on the two girls walking up the walk. She held her wounded arm, wrapping her fingers around it delicately, gently. "Go."

With the girls about to step up on the front porch, we had no choice but to do what she said. We rushed back into the other room to get Gilda, and her eyes lit up. Roxy and Red grabbed the teapot and cups. I took the tablecloth. "You're back!" she said all breathy, and truth be truth she looked sincerely overjoyed.

"Yes!" I said. "We can't leave without a proper tea party."

Gilda stood bolt upright. "You can't? Oh, this is wonderful." She saw Roxy and Gail scoot out the back door. "But why are we going outside?"

I pushed Gilda outside with me. "Because we're having a *garden* tea party," I said, and she all but clapped. "Doesn't that sound lovely?" The door clicked shut behind me and I caught a full breath of the putrid outside air, holding back vomit.

Roxy and Red turned around, not knowing where we should go, and I pointed toward one of the cows, which I thought would be far enough away to catch a decent breath. "Oh, I'm so glad you girls stayed," she said. "Such beautiful girls too." Gilda clasped her hands in front of her body as she walked, and sometimes skipped. "Tea party, tea party…"

"Oh yes, we'll have so much fun!" I grimaced when she wasn't looking, and walked on toward the cow lying in the pasture, following Roxy and Red. Damn thing still hadn't moved, and I wondered how it could stay so still. Back in Grant County, our cows never stayed still; they were always grazing. Sometimes we had to send our dog out to round them up.

Roxy stopped suddenly in the grass and Red turned around, frantically pointing with her head to the cow. Then I noticed what they'd already figured out.

The butcher's cows weren't cows, but heaps of black canvas made to look like cows at a distance. Camouflage. Roxy lifted one end of the canvas up, only to drop it immediately after exposing the long-barrel gun underneath—the exact kind we saw abandoned on the battlefields in France, but this one looked shiny and brand new, ready to be fired. "Gilda. The cows... they are... they are..." The tablecloth slipped from my fingers into the grass.

"Guns. Big guns!" She laughed that strange laugh, in between a cry and a squeal, only to press her fingers to her lips. "Do what the Reich says... do what the Reich says..." She took the tablecloth from the ground and spread it out onto the grass before motioning for the teapot and cups.

I took Red by the arm and all three of us walked far enough away to talk plainly without Gilda hearing us. "Jesus, Kit," Red whispered. "The guns." She looked urgently over the pasture as if the Wehrmacht was about to march in any minute and use them, then to the sky looking for planes.

"There's something else." I exhaled, thinking of a delicate way to tell them about what the butcher had been doing, but there wasn't a way. "A hundred bodies are decomposing in the barn." Their faces instantly contorted, both disbelieving and horrified. "All in different stages."

If someone wanted to know what sudden shock looked like I would say it looked exactly like Roxy's face at that moment. White, drawn cheeks, and a wave of weakness that buckled her knees. "But... but... but..." she babbled. "Why? How?"

I turned my back to Gilda, if only because I couldn't watch her setting out the tea any longer, smiling, pretending the day was wonderful. "He said he does it for the Reich. Crazy Gilda serves them poisoned tea and then they become, well... his experiments."

"They poison everything here!" Roxy said. "I'm scared." She moved to catch a glance of Gilda over my shoulder, her eyes growing.

"What are you girls doing?" Gilda snapped. "Teatime. Right now. Understand?"

I closed my eyes, hearing Gilda's voice.

The barn door was closed, but who knew how long the butcher would be out of the way, busy in his secret lair where he did God knows what on those bodies. And Gilda, she was the weathervane that got zapped over and over and over again; I didn't know what she was going to do or say next. The werewolf girls were still in the house with Gail.

"We need to run, Kit," Roxy said. "This gal's crackers. You hear me? And this place is creepy." She rubbed her arms from an unexpected shiver while trying to swat at the flies landing on her nose. "We need to start running and fast."

"Without Gail?" I said, but I knew she didn't want to leave without her either.

Red pointed to my waist. "We have the package, right? I say you and Roxy head to the hill, we meet under the tree, and I'll go get Gail. Werewolves or not." Red folded her arms, and I could tell it was hard for her not to know what was going on in the house.

"No, Red. This isn't your plan. It's Gail's and we have to trust her," I said. "We have to wait."

"I'm worried about her," Roxy said, and she chewed on her nails, which I hadn't seen her do since we bivouacked out of Utah Beach. "She's still green, even if she did get shot."

Roxy had me doubting myself for a second. From the moment I'd met Gail she'd been delicate, squeamish with the little things. The bullet in her arm toughened her up a bit; I saw it in her eyes when Red stitched her up in the cornfield. But I'd be lying if I said I wasn't worried about her in that house with those werewolves.

"No... we can't, all right?" I had to listen to my own words, and trust she knew what she was doing. "Neither of you know German. You have to trust her and me."

Roxy closed her eyes, resigning herself to what she knew we had to do.

"Now, let's get on with this tea, all right?" I said. "Remember, not a word from you two. Who knows what this nut will do if she hears you speaking English."

We walked back over to Gilda. "Where's the other one?" she said.

"What other one?" I said, knowing full well she meant Gail. Roxy and Red sat down gingerly on the tablecloth in the grass, picking up the teacups while Gilda lowered hers.

"The other girl," Gilda said.

I threw my palm to my forehead. "Oh! The girl..." I laughed with a little smile, still not answering her and hoping she'd forget, but the look in her pointed eyes said otherwise. "She's cleaning up the spilled tea," I said, finally thinking up a lie. "That's all." I swallowed when she looked at me blankly, as if she didn't understand. "As a favor for the hospitality. She knows how much it stressed you, so she's cleaning up the front room." I picked up my teacup and clinked the edges with Red and Roxy for a toast. I pretended to drink. "Mmm…" I said, eyes twinkling, "delicious."

Gilda seemed satisfied with the story, and smoothed her dress over her dirty legs, giggling and giggling. She noticed the bag near my waist as I swatted flies from it, while slipping her hand into her pocket, again playing with something I couldn't see, something bulky, humming a little tune before going back to her tea.

I looked over to the house, fully expecting to see no movement, but in fact saw silhouettes pass by the window, behind the dirt and grime. I couldn't tell who was who, or if Gail needed help. My stomach did a little whirl, and I hid my fading smile by keeping the cup pressed against my lips.

"Gilda," I said. "How long have you lived on the farm?"

It was an honest question. Something I would have asked if we were having a proper tea, a girls' talk, but when her eyes slowly shifted upward and locked with mine, I realized it was the wrong question to ask.

"Why?" Her voice wisped through the tiny slit between her lips.

Red and Roxy's eyes swung like pendulums between me and Gilda. Even if you didn't know German, you could tell I had struck a nerve with her.

I scooted up and swatted at some flies near my face. "It is so peaceful out here!" I tried to sound cheery. "You must have many restful nights." I closed my eyes immediately, realizing I said the absolutely wrong thing. Peaceful nights? How could someone have a peaceful night out here with all those corpses?

Gilda hung her head down, her lips bathing in the tea, lapping it up like a dog, and I looked at Red, who'd stiffened straight up.

"And what about these?" I pointed to the heaps of camouflage, but that was another mistake, I thought. "You must feel secure."

She laughed that crazy laugh again, half shriek half giggles, only to compose herself like a lady, sitting up real tall and looking a little prissy. A fat-lipped smile spread on her face. "Boom." Her eyebrows rose.

Red and Roxy lowered their cups, looking into the sky. You didn't have to know German to know what she meant by "boom."

Gilda slipped her hand into her pocket again, only this time I heard the tink of metal. When she saw me watching her, she pulled her hand out to twist grass with her finger. I thought about her life on the farm, how she must have been normal at one time, hadn't she? At one point she was someone's baby, someone's daughter, and a bride. She wiped her lips with her arm before bursting into a cry, tears streaming from the corners of her eyes, and she looked genuinely sad and discouraged. She looked human.

"Gilda…" I said, my voice dropping, "what made you like this?"

She dug her palms into her eyes, wiping every last tear away and all the moisture from her cheeks. "The Reich did this to me," she said, clearly, sanely. She reached back into her pocket only this time she pulled out what she'd been playing with, and I was surprised to see it was a toy train car. The red paint had been chipped from many years of play, and the wheels were rusted from being left outside one too many times. "My boy," she said. "His legs didn't work right, bent the wrong way. But he was mine. The Reich took him away."

I gasped, realizing what she meant, and it somehow rationalized what she did to the Nazis who were sent to her for tea, traitors or not, they were her enemy. Red and Roxy stared at me, and I felt my face drain of all its color. I tried swallowing the lump in my throat, thinking of the Reich taking a crippled child away from his mother. "I'm... I'm sorry," I said.

I reached out to touch her hand, but she sprung up and ran into the pasture and into some trees where she disappeared.

"What now?" Red asked.

"The Reich killed her son. Took him away because he was crippled. That's what made her go crazy."

"Oh, she's crazy, let me tell ya," Roxy said. "Can we go see about Gail now?"

I twisted all the way around in the grass and stared at the house, waiting, holding the bag close to my body near my waist, looking for a sign. *Come on, Gail...*

"I'm worried," Red said, rubbing her hands together. "I'm going in." She stood up.

"No, Red," I said, jumping up to stop her. "You can't take control of everything all the time. We have to trust her—"

A crash came from inside the kitchen. Red grabbed both my arms. "I told you, I told you..."

We ran through the grass into the house, pushing open the door and throwing ourselves inside. "Gail—"

Gail slowly turned toward us just as the two werewolf girls tumbled onto the floor and lay motionless at her feet.

19

KIT

Gail held Gilda's special blue teapot in her good hand. Roxy clamped her hand over her mouth. Not one of us said anything, and I don't think any of us were breathing, especially the two werewolf girls. Their bodies lay in a twisted mangle, braids flopped over their heads, faces to the floor, and their legs unnaturally crisscrossed.

"That's for the poisoned bullet." Gail set the teapot down and turned toward us, first looking at me and then to Red. "Now we can leave," she said, and in a strange twist of fate, the poisoned had become the poisoner.

I couldn't move. Red pushed Roxy toward the door, reaching for me next, but I stood still and stunned, with my eyes on the dead girls lying on Gilda's floor. "Go," Red whispered, pushing me. "Kit…"

I finally looked up, and she hugged me quickly.

"Come on," Red said, "before someone sees us."

Gilda would come back from her hiding spot looking for us and would find the dead girls in our place. She'd be sad we'd left, but perhaps happy at what she found on her floor—two dead girls from the secret resistance the Reich had planned. Nobody would know what happened to them. Not even their parents. Their skin looked bright as white paper, but soft as dough—perfectly German—and young. Teenagers I suspected, trained to kill our boys.

Red took me by the hand and I followed her out of the house. I glanced over my shoulder as I crested the door, seeing their blonde heads lying on the floor, and now Gilda out the screen door in the pasture making her way to the back porch.

We ran through the grass and up the small hill to the tree where we had started. The farm looked quiet from the top of the hill. The butcher still hadn't come out of the barn, and it was now strange to view his farm this way, at a lovely distance, knowing the gruesome crimes that had been committed under that roof, and in that barn.

"I never want to see this place again," I said.

"You won't have to," Red said. "None of us will. And we never have to talk about it either. Got it?" She folded up the map after a quick look and tucked it back into her leg bandage.

I adjusted the bag over my shoulder. "Got it," I said, but I was sure she meant that more for Gail, who'd turned away from us in thought.

Roxy flicked her chin at the bag. "Do we get to peek inside?"

I reached for the buckle when Red told me to stop.

"Not here," she said, but then clarified. "Not yet. Let's get some more cover. Never know who might be watching."

We found a ravine with some rocks that provided a little

cover. We tucked ourselves inside, and in the closed space I could really smell the odor coming from the bag, which had transferred to my palm from patting the fabric. A lone fly buzzed near my hand.

I unlatched the buckle. The thought crossed my mind that the butcher had fooled us and gave me reichsmarks instead, which was as useless as Confederate cash. The girls watched me reach for the zipper next, holding my breath, flicking my eyes up at Red one last time before closing them completely. My brother—the entire fate of the POWs depended on if we were successful.

"What if it's not—" Roxy said, but I unzipped the bag.

All was quiet. Nobody breathed, nobody said a word. Then Red gasped, and when I opened my eyes my legs folded underneath me like a collapsible table. Diamonds, a million of them, glittering in the dusty, darkened ravine along with the greenest of emeralds and the reddest rubies.

"God," I breathed, and Red put her arm around me, giving me a squeeze.

Me and Roxy reached into the bag, letting the diamonds slip through our fingers, sparkling like the sun shining on a snowcapped mountain. I thought about all the people I would give a diamond to—each boy under my watch. A souvenir, something to show for their wounds.

"We did it, dolls," Roxy said. "Right here, right now. We saved hundreds of our men in one swift move." She smiled. "And nobody knows in the world, but us." She pulled a handful of jewels from the bag, four good-sized rubies sat on top of a scoop of diamonds like cherries on a sundae. She studied them in her palm, picking at them for a moment, before stuffing them into her brassiere. Red stopped her.

"What are you doing?" Red said.

Roxy paused, her arm halfway down the front of her dress. "We can't have a little for the trouble?" She looked confused, but Red shook her head.

"Why not?" I said. "You said it, Red, before we left the field hospital. Then again when Jack told us the plan, you were going to keep some of it."

Red shook Roxy's hand of all the diamonds, before reaching for mine. "We can't. I was spouting off. Mad, you know? And I didn't know the giant was part of the plan back at the hospital. Me and Kit already violated the Geneva Conventions with that German. What will happen if they find out we stole some of the jewels too? Besides, they aren't ours."

"Well, whose are they?" Roxy asked.

"Yeah, Red," I said. "Who do they belong to? Our government? And what are they gonna do? Spend it somewhere? But what about us? We almost died getting here. And what about our boys? They deserve some too. In their own hands. Something to leave with."

"I understand what you're saying, but it's not right," Red said. "We came to do a job. We'll finish it honestly."

"Oh, I'll freely tell Jack I'm keeping some," Roxy said, reaching for the bag, but Red had zipped it up. "But the rubies, Red. One for each of us. Don't you think we're due that?"

"Yeah, Red," I said. "That sounds fair."

"The jewels belong to the victims of this war," Gail said,

and we all looked up. "The suffering villager who lost their son, daughter, or mother."

We were quiet again, but this time there were no sparkling jewels to gaze at.

Red handed the bag to me. "When we get back, we'll figure out who to give it to. I'm not so certain that person is Jack—not after all the lies and tricks from the OSS," she said, and we agreed.

Gail tried wiggling her fingers, and we watched her struggle, wincing and straining. "Can we leave now?" she said, breathless and irritated. "I want to get back."

"Yes, let's get the hell out of here," Red said.

"But I'm hungry," Roxy said. "We have to eat, find an apple tree or something. I won't make it across the river. I can't swim, and I'm tired as it is."

We all moaned.

"I'm not bellyaching," Roxy said. "This is different. We can't ignore the exhaustion. We can't pretend we don't feel it."

Gail turned to walk out. We all followed to stand on the rocks outside where a breeze rustled through the trees. I held my hair back from tickling my face.

"The rain," Red said, and that's when we noticed the clouds, which had turned gray and thunderous in the short few minutes we'd been in the cave. Bombs exploded in the distance from the advancing battle, and we all looked west. These explosions sounded even closer than they had earlier, with the faintest tailing of smoke visible in the clouds. We'd be dead the moment our boys crossed that river, caught in a firefight, and on the wrong side of the war. I looked up the hill where Gilda and the butcher would be if they had been following us. A blackbird flew by, and a caw came from somewhere else.

"Come on!" Red waved for us to follow her out of the ravine and along the tree line that crested the farmlands. We walked for miles without talking, too fatigued, nervous, and scared. Spending time with your own thoughts can be dangerous. Every noise in the quiet country, every twig snap, every bird chirp, caused me and Roxy to jolt, thinking the butcher and his wife were following us. The coolness of the approaching evening felt like another hurdle we'd soon have to face.

"Man, I'm so hungry," Roxy said, holding her stomach. "It hurts, Kit." She looked at me, her eyes drawn with pain as if her stomach was digesting itself. "I need some food."

"Me too, Rox," I said. "What do you want me to do? Walk up to the nearest German and ask him for a snack?" I paused. "I know! I'll ask him if he has any K-rations."

"Stop it, Kit," she said, pouting, but I didn't have a thing to give her.

Red waved for us to get down behind her. "Guys! Shh!"

We dropped to the ground in the grass, and she asked for the binoculars. "What is it?" I asked, and she shushed me only to pipe up a second later.

"A house," she said, but my heart had stopped, thinking she saw the butcher.

Roxy rolled over in the grass, holding her stomach. "Maybe there's food in there!"

"Looks like it's been bombed," Red said, and I reached for the binoculars in her hands.

"Let me see…" I fit them to my eyes, roving over the land, before settling on a little stucco farmhouse that looked like it had been bombed all right, a caved-in roof and charred black spots on the ground. "It has been bombed!" Farm equipment sat idle, and nobody was working the fields, which made me wonder if the house had been abandoned.

I handed the binoculars to Gail even though she didn't ask for them. "But I don't want to go to a house," she said. "I want to go back. To France, back to our hospital."

Red looked toward the sky. "I do too," she said. "But it's getting late. I don't think we have a choice." Roxy moaned again about her stomach. "Kit, go down there and see if anyone lives there."

I sat up. "Why me?"

"Because you speak German, remember?" Red said. "And I don't want Gail here having to do it with her shot-up arm."

Gail sat up next and held her head, hand stuck in her hair, and I knew Red was right. We couldn't send Gail, but I didn't want to go alone either. Roxy looked up at me from the ground where she clutched her stomach.

I sighed, rubbing my face, before taking another look at the house, trying to think up a story—how I was going to approach it. "What should I say?" I chewed on my fingernails. "If people are inside... What's my story?"

Red scoffed. "You're the storyteller, Kit." She pushed me to get going. "You'll think of something."

Roxy moaned again.

"Fine." I took off the bag of jewels and handed it to Red. "But just so you know, I think this deserves a ruby," I said, and Red shook her head.

"Get going, will ya?" she said, and she gave me another push.

"All right, all right." I stood up, straightening my dress and smoothing back my hair. "I'll tell you one thing," I said. "Nurse Blanchfield never said anything about *this* in the War Department film."

Red gave me a laugh for that one, but that was me being nervous about going off alone. I walked over, through the field to a dirt road marked by aerial gunfire. The cloudy sky felt heavy and staticky, like those seconds before lightning strikes even if there are only a few rain clouds. I looked back once to see the girls lying in the grass, and Red watching me with the binoculars. They were yards away, but it felt like miles.

I made my way up the small gravel walkway and past a pot of bluebells, which sat next to a scorched pot of tomatoes, destroyed from a fiery blast. The main window had been cracked, and a chunk of glass lay in the roses beside its broken green shutters. I peeked through the window that was still intact. I saw a hallway, wood floors, a kitchen table, and a sideboard with framed photos.

I took a deep breath, closing my eyes. *Mother of God.* I rapped two times on the door. Cawing birds flew out of the eaves. "Ugh!" I ducked, then threw my hands up at Red, but she waved for me to go inside.

I took a few more deep breaths, rubbing my trembling hands together. "You better believe I'm writing Blanchfield a letter when I get back..." I peeked through the window again, this time cupping my eyes with my hand, checking for movement. A breeze blew leaves in through the open ceiling and they trickled down the hallway.

I knocked again after clearing my throat. "Hallo?" I said, and the door opened a crack. I froze, listening, then pushed a little on the door. "I was down the road. Is everyone all right in here?" The door swung open with a squeal. I paused, looking, listening.

I stepped inside, arms folded, feeling chilled but not from the cold. I took another step, but this time the floor splintered and creaked, and it ran the length of the board to the wall. "Hallooooo?" I said, searching the air.

I stood close enough to look at the photos displayed on the sideboard, untouched from the blast that took the roof off. One was of a young man, smiling, posing next to his mother in what looked like a brand-new Wehrmacht *feldgrau* uniform. I only glanced at them, not wanting to see what they looked like.

I checked the rest of the house, which looked very lived in, homey. I waved for Red and the others from the front porch.

Red walked in with Gail, handing me the bag of diamonds while taking in every detail, from the wood floors to the photos to the opened bedroom doors down the hall.

Roxy walked straight to the kitchen. "Well, will you have a look…" She took a jar of pickled onions from the shelf where leaves speckled the countertops. Rain spit in through the open ceiling. She popped the lid off and fished out an onion as the rain tapped against her shoulders.

I talked to Red near the photos. "Typical German family." I pointed.

Red picked up one of the portraits, taking a look. "Smells like burnt bread in here." She sniffed the air as the rain continued to spit in. "Wet burnt bread."

"Yeah," I said, looking up at the blasted ceiling. "Like this place got hit hours ago. Maybe even this morning."

"Can you imagine?" Roxy said, eyes skirting over the ceiling while fingering an onion in the jar. "Getting an egg dropped right on top of ya like that?"

"There's bedrooms down here," I said, and the girls followed me down the hall. We found a closet full of women's dresses in one of the rooms. Linen, cotton and some silky ones. I pulled a cotton one out, shaking it from the hanger. "Guys," I said. "Look, dresses we can wear. Better ones than we have on."

"Is there one that'll fit me?" Roxy took a great big bite of her onion. "Well?" she said, chewing, and I tossed one at her that she caught with her face.

Red looked out the window into the field. "Seems strange, doesn't it?"

Me and Roxy changed into our new dresses. "What seems strange?" I said.

"This house," Red said. "Abandoned with their things still inside."

I froze with one arm through the armhole, looking at Red through the neck of the dress. "Well... yeah, Red," I said, pulling the dress down. "I suppose."

"Not I suppose," she said. "It *is* strange." We looked at each other, listening to the rain tap on the part of the roof that was still intact.

"Not as strange as Gilda," Roxy said, and she threw a dress at Gail who'd sat on the bed. "Get dressed, before something happens and we have to run. Maybe the Germans come back."

Glass bottles of perfume had been cracked and spilled on the dresser. I sprayed Roxy with the blue bottle, the only bottle that hadn't been busted, and she waved the scent away, chewing her onion. I picked through the ribbons, the trinkets, and the brushes that were displayed. I found a metal lighter with an engraving that said "Life be Lived" on the front in German. I flipped it open, striking it once to see if it worked. Red brushed out her knotted hair.

"I need help," Gail whimpered, sitting on the bed with the dress in her lap, covering her face with her good hand so we wouldn't see her cry.

Roxy rushed toward Gail while still clutching her jar of onions. "Here ya, Gail," she said. "I'll help."

Gail stayed on the bed as we dressed her, ignoring her painful grimaces and moans until we were finished with moving her arm. We stood back, not sure what to say, looking at her from her toes to her brassy head of hair for a sign that said she was better.

"How is your pain?" Red said. "Can you move your fingers?"

She tried moving her fingers with her hand in her lap. Four wiggled, but her pinkie had turned board straight and she cried out. "Red!"

"Let me see…" Red looked slowly up after taking a good look at Gail's fingers. "Looks like you might get a stiff finger out of it," she said, and Gail covered her face again, sniffling. "But you're alive. And if that bullet had broken, I know you'd be a lot worse off than you are now."

Gail pulled her hand away, her lashes wet with tears and her eyes glossy. "I want to leave, Red," she said. "What if my finger is just the start? What if I die out here?" We three sat next to her in the German girl's bedroom, dressed in our new dresses, thinking of what to do and how to make it better, but there wasn't anything we could do.

"Nobody is dying out here," Red said. "You hear me? Nobody left behind. I promise you that. We can eat and rest, but we don't have to stay. One hour only, then we'll be off again. I want to get back too." She glanced at Gail's fingers, and I knew that look. Red was concerned.

"Guys," Roxy said, swallowing a chunk of onion. "Look." She pointed to the wall, and to a photo of a young woman with her mom—the mother of the house. "She's a nurse. Look at the uniform."

I got up, then Red and Roxy too, and we examined the photo more closely. The woman looked like us, wavy hair, smiling, arm over her mother's shoulders. It was probably taken the day she left for the war, to take care of all those Germans our boys had wounded. My father took a similar photo of me and my mother when I left.

I hung my head. My mom had probably heard about Sam being captured by now, and my heart broke for my parents, but especially my mother. I swallowed bitterly, turning away. "I don't want to know what they look like. There's photos in the main room too."

I walked into the kitchen and rummaged through the vegetable jars. "Tomatoes, cucumbers, cabbage…" I opened the cupboard doors, and a mouse scurried out, scaring me half to death. "Ack!" I yelped, and the others ran into the room, even Gail, to see me clutching my chest. "Sorry," I said. "It was a mouse."

"For God's sake, Kit," Red said, and she took a few relieving breaths.

"I said I was sorry."

Gail winced. "The pain!" she cried. "I stood up too fast and there's a throbbing. Ow, and it hurts!" Her face contorted from the sensation, and it was clear that the little bit of morphine she'd had in the cornfield had run its course and all her nerves were exposed. "Red…" she said, and Red helped her to the couch. "Can I have a bit of the morphine?" She whimpered through pressed lips.

"Sure… Sure…" Red reached down the front of her dress, pulling out a syrette. "Check if there are some crackers in the cupboard, Kit," she said, turning away from Gail for a split second, and in that moment, Gail had stuck her own neck and drained the syrette of all the morphine.

"Gail! What are you doing?" Red cried.

Gail took a deep breath then sighed heavily, sitting back on the couch, looking very rested and relaxed. "That's better," she said, then she closed her eyes.

"Why'd you let her do that?" Roxy said, and she was angry, marching over to Gail and taking a peek at her closed eyes.

Red threw her palm to her forehead. "Damn you, Gail," Red said, but Gail was completely out, lying like a vegetable with her feet turned in and her arms hanging off to the sides. "You said you wanted to leave, then you do this?"

"At least she's not in pain," I said.

Rain continued tapping on what was left of the roof, and Red looked up after taking a deep breath. "Well, ladies," she said, "looks like we're staying."

20

KIT

Roxy ate every last onion in the house only to hold her stomach and moan about eating too many onions. I ate the green beans with Red, and with the blankets from a chest in the front room, we camped out on the floor next to Gail on the couch. The wind blew the rain through the open ceiling in sprays, but the couch and where we sat managed to stay mostly dry.

Roxy sneezed, catching it in the blanket. "That was close." She smiled with a sigh, thinking that was the end of it. "Achoo! Achoo! Achoo!"

"Clam it, all right?" I said. "What if someone hears?"

She wiped her mouth. "Who's gonna hear us through all this rain?" Roxy said, looking around in the dark. "It's beating on the roof like anything."

"Yeah, but I swear I heard a tap, something other than the rain," I said, and I shivered from my head to my toes. "Feels strange in here." I looked around in the dark, over the shadowy cabinets and down the hall and across the wood floors. "Did you hear it?"

"It's the rain," Red said. "We searched the house and nobody's here." Her gaze trailed out the window as she chewed on a green bean from the jar. Tree branches scraped the side of the house, and I closed my eyes, thinking it sounded like Gilda's screeching giggle.

"What if the butcher's trying to find us?" I said.

"Not in the rain," Red said.

"Man," Roxy said. "All this talk about people watching us and noises… Gives me the creeps, ya know? In the dark, out in the open like this surrounded by Huns, and our boys miles away." She ran her hand over the spray of bullet holes that peppered the floor, pausing to seek out the divots with feeling fingers. "Aerial fire too. You know a girl could use a smoke right about now."

I dug under my dress and reached for the pack of cigarettes I'd stolen from the pharmacist's. "Here—" I tossed them in her lap, followed by the lighter I'd found in the back bedroom.

"Where'd you get those?" Red said, and she put her hand on Roxy's to stop her even though she'd already torn open the package and was about to strike the metal lighter. "Where, Kit?"

Roxy looked at me with the cigarette dangling between her lips.

"Does it matter?" I said, reaching for the pack. "Smokes are smokes."

Roxy struck the lighter, eyes sliding to mine. "You didn't steal these from crazy Gilda's house, did you?"

"No!" I said, and Roxy lit her cigarette. "I stole them from the pharmacist."

"What?" Red said. "When did you do that?"

"While you were asleep."

I reached for three candles on the sideboard and set them between us. "I'm glad I stole these smokes, let me tell you." I lit the candles and read the engraving off the lighter. "*Life be lived* it says on this lighter. And God's truth, Red, we need to live what's left of it." I popped a cigarette in my mouth, lighting it up.

"That was a dangerous thing to do, sneaking out of the cellar," Red said. "What if something happened to you—"

"But nothing happened," I said.

I offered Red a cigarette, and she took one after a bit of coaxing, and all three of us smoked on the floor. For a while we smoked in silence, listening to the crack and snap of the burning embers under the rainfall. Melty candles waxed onto the floor. I never did ask them what they were thinking about, but for some reason, sitting on the floor in the cold brought forth thoughts of Jack. He said he'd visit me at home after the war, and even though I knew he said it to give himself hope—to have plans for after—it also gave me hope, and something to believe in.

I hoped he'd left the pharmacist's. I hoped he was still alive. *He has to be,* I thought. I took another drag, inhaling deeply, wishing I had shared more cigarettes with him, at least one more before we left the cellar. Just to say I did.

I moved the bag of diamonds into my lap, and Roxy unzipped it amid the flicker of candlelight.

"Will you get a look at that," Roxy said, "all those

sparkling diamonds. We did it, gals. I still can't believe it."
She pulled the blankets up over her shoulders after snuffing
out her cigarette on the floor to light another. "Hundreds
of men we saved. Germans gonna attack the POW camps?
Not with the nurses from the 45th on the task!" she said,
and me and Red laughed. "We pulled off what those men
couldn't. And they're the experts—the OSS, and we're the
girls from the beach."

"Yeah," I said, "we're the girls from the beach, dammit!"
I smiled.

"And your brother, Kit," Red said. "Someday Sam will
find out what you did. And your mother too. She'll know."

"Mmm," I said, and I thought again about my mother,
and her reaction to hearing about Sam's capture. I could only
imagine how the scene unfolded when the War Department
vehicle drove up to her front door, or worse, what if it was
a letter senselessly delivered in the mail? "I hope my mom's
recovered from the news."

Roxy nodded, but they both had no idea what I meant
aside from the obvious. I'd never told them the story. Though
this story wasn't one I'd made up. It was what neighbors
told neighbors before I was born. The story housewives
talked about over Bridge, coffee, and cigarettes.

I swallowed. "My uncle died in the war, my mother's
brother," I said, and they both looked at me. "She went
delirious when she found out he'd died. My grandmother
had to send her away to a sanitarium. After she had Sam,
she was convinced he'd be lost to her one day, and spent all
her time trying to keep his eyes off the planes in the sky and
focus on the farm—she knew there'd be another war. But he
couldn't stay away. Being a pilot was in his blood."

"God, Kit, your poor mother," Red said. "How'd Sam end up telling her he joined up?"

I took a deep breath; it was still so very clear. "He'd waited three days, trying to find the right time, but there was no right time. I heard her shriek and watched it unfold from the stairs. She'd begged him not to do it, shoving a list of sicknesses at him that would have kept him out of the service, but he wouldn't listen," I said. "My mother cried hysterically from her knees at the front door, asking him why over and over again, reaching up for Sam's hands, begging him to reconsider, but he'd already signed the papers. And when he pulled them from his pocket to show her, my mother's eyes ballooned into dark moons before her entire body dissolved into the floor and she lay there like a rag for days. Sam tried to comfort her. Over and over he tried."

Red touched my arm. "I'm sorry."

I nodded, hanging my head, and taking a puff of my cigarette. "The mothers of this war, I tell you... They are the innocent victims of this fight."

Roxy pointed her cigarette to the photo of the German woman and her children on the sideboard, the nurse, and the soldier. "Like her," she said, and I turned around, even though I said I didn't want to look at their photos again.

"Yeah, I suppose so," I said, and I took a moment hanging on to that thought, absorbing the scene in the photo.

"You all right, Kit?" Red said.

I nodded.

"A farm," Roxy said. "I think I'd like living on a farm."

I scoffed. "My parents talked about retiring to the mountains, leaving me and Sam the farm. But he already told me he wasn't interested, and I don't want it either."

"Why not?" Roxy said.

"I don't know..." The farm was peaceful in the daytime with the Canada geese flying through the clouds, and the cows mooing in the pasture. And in the evenings—stars for miles, like pinpricks through black paper. I looked up, through the open ceiling where the rain was sprinkling in, hearing the tap between my ears, which sounded like gunfire when I imagined it. "On second thought, maybe that's exactly what I need. A little peace and quiet. Nobody yelling, no screamers, no horns honking, no loud noises... only the cows and the geese."

I refolded my legs and adjusted the gun holster, when an owl flew in from the open ceiling, flapping his wings. "Ack!" I said, scooting away. "A damn owl." After collecting my breath, I waved my hands at it and he flew off. "I thought I heard something."

"I think I heard it too," Roxy said. "A scratching, tapping noise?"

I nodded. "Yeah!"

"Maybe it wasn't the owl," Red said, and we moved closer together on the floor. "Maybe it's something worse..." Her eyes flicked from side to side.

"Stop it, all right," I said. "You're scaring me."

Red laughed, and Roxy got mad, pushing her. "I was joking," Red said. "It was a bad joke. I shouldn't have said it."

"You..." I said, and I slapped her thigh with the tail of my blanket.

"I had you guys going, though," Red said, taking a bean from the jar and chewing on it. "It was the owl! We have hundreds of them in Oklahoma. My mama would be laughing herself into a fit if she knew how scared you two were. You can take bullets flying through our tent, bombs exploding, and Messerschmitts barreling toward our hospital, but set a mouse in front of you or an owl—"

"All right," I said. "We got it." I laughed after a second, thinking it was rather funny, and we had to find our laughs when we could. "So, I'm jumpy." I patted the bag of diamonds. "I know we're talking like the job is done—the mission's over—but we haven't made it across the river, and until then I'm gonna jump at mice and owls and anything else that comes our way. We're not safe yet, and neither are the POW camps."

I looked at Red, and then to Roxy. We all knew what I said was the truth. We hadn't saved anyone yet. We smoked the rest of the cigarettes while Gail was still out, and at some point, we each fell asleep, succumbing to our exhaustion.

I woke to the sun rising in my face and a strange tapping that sounded like a pencil on a tile. I sat up, thinking the noise had been part of a dream. "Guys…" I said, and I listened some more and the house seemed strange and static again, as if we weren't alone. "I think they're back. The people who live here."

Roxy stirred, groggy and trying to make sense of the world. Gail sat bolt upright holding her arm. She shoved a hand in her hair and looked around as if she had no idea what had happened with the morphine.

I shook Red awake. "Wake up." I searched the air, thinking I heard a groan—a noise somewhere in the house.

"Red—" Another moan, this time a little louder and I blamed Roxy for it.

"It wasn't me," Roxy said.

"Then who…" I listened carefully. "It's coming from under the house."

"It's the mouse," Red said, but I shook my head and got on my hands and knees to search closer.

"I'm scared!" Roxy said, and she stood up to fold her arms.

"Move out of the sunlight," I said, waving the girls out of the way, and the sun shined a little brighter and into the cracks on the floor. I moved slower, wood creaking under my knees as I crawled. "I don't see anything—"

Then I saw it. Between the cracks, something glossy, something alive. I screamed, jumping up from the floor. "It's an eye!" I pointed. "There's a person under there!" Then we all heard it, a finger tapping the floorboards. I crossed myself, then looked at Red.

A moan came from underneath and the clear and grappling voice of a woman begging for our help. We clawed at the floorboards and pulled up a section—a secret door—and found a woman hiding under the house in the dirt with wounds across her chest.

"Jesus," Red said, and we stood stunned, gazing at her in the dirt. Brown blood mixed with fresh red, soaking her yellowy dress and white apron. "It's the mother from the photograph!"

"Hilfe," she said in German. Help.

"Hurry!" Red dove into the small space and lifted her out, laying her out on the front room floor. "She must have been lying here for over a day."

We assessed her for more wounds. The burn marks on her chest appeared superficial compared to the bullet lodged in her neck. She reached up to clutch her throat, trying to talk, but only scratches came out followed by the familiar, "*Hilfe! Hilfe!*"

"How come we didn't know?" Roxy said. "We were here all night!"

"It was the rain," I said. "The damn rain must have muffled her voice."

I talked to her in German. "We're nurses," I said. "We can help." I asked Gail to help me, but she was still wobbly and making her way over to us. "We have to get the bullet out of your neck," I said, and the woman shook her head. "It's the only way to stop the bleeding."

"You're slowly bleeding to death," Roxy said to her in English.

Red held her head steady, stinging her with a syrette of morphine, and I reached for my scalpel. "Hold still, Mutti," I said, and her eyes swung to mine. "Mutti, hold still."

I dug into her neck with the only instrument I had, searching for the bullet, but couldn't find it as she rasped and gagged. "You're digging, Kit," Red said, and my lips pinched. "I'm trying not to." I went in for one last search, and the woman called out for her daughter with a waning cry, which sent a shiver up my back and neck.

The bullet popped out, and I was relieved and exhausted, thinking the worst was over, but a pool of blood flowed from the hole, faster and faster and faster like a hose. Red screamed for a rag, and Gail tossed one to me from the kitchen. I pressed it to her neck. "Mutti!" I said. "Mutti, stay with me! Mutti!" Her eyes sank, fading with eyelids half-closed, and Roxy shouted that we were losing her. "Come on," I said, and in that whirring moment, I glanced up at the photos on the sideboard and saw the woman smiling and alive next to her children while feeling her soul slip through my hands. "Come on..." I pressed the rag to her neck. "Damn you... Live, why don't ya! Live!"

"She's gone," Roxy said, and I reluctantly pulled back. "We lost her."

Red sat on her haunches, pressing the back of her hand to her forehead. "She was a bleeder, Kit. That's all. We did what we could."

I took a few deep breaths, looking at my bloody, shaking hands, then to the body of the mother I tried to save. The blood-soaked kitchen towel, and her fixed eyes.

I got up, feeling sick.

"You all right, Kit?" Roxy said from the floor.

I turned her photo over on the sideboard before stumbling to the window. "Yeah," I said. "I just need a minute."

I looked over the field that used to be her farm, feeling overwhelmed by a surge of emotion as I wiped my hands of the woman's blood. I'd lost so many patients, so many wounded dying in my arms or on my watch. But this one, this one got me to gush like a baby and I didn't know why. *She was a German*, I told myself. *She's the enemy.* I swallowed, closing my eyes to stop the waves of tears, yet they dripped off my cheeks onto my folded arms.

I heard Red and Roxy talking about what to do with the body. They decided to place her back where we found her, and while they lowered her back under the floor, I noticed a dust-up down the road.

I blinked, trying to see through the blur of tears, thinking it was a dust devil, like the ones we had on the farm in Washington, but it was thicker, and moving down the dirt road like a car was causing it.

"Guys..." I said, but it was more of a croak, and they were too busy laying the woman back under the house, when I gulped dryly, bracing the windowsill. "Red!" I said, and everyone looked up at me. "Someone's coming!"

A car skidded to a stop outside.

I rushed toward them. "Hide! Hide!" I said.

"Where?" Roxy cried, and it was Red's idea for us to hide in the floor with the dead woman. Gail hopped in, followed by Roxy then Red.

"Quick!" Red said, as they piled in, until I was next.

A car door opened and closed, followed by another, and a man shouting for his shotgun. "Hurry, Kit," Red said, grabbing for my arm, but there was no room. Not with the body.

"There's no room!" I said, and I saw my life pass before my eyes, listening to them walk up. *Crunch, crunch, crunch...* "What do I do?" I said, and Red grasped at my hands, eyes stretched and in tears, before getting an idea.

"The chest!" Red said, pointing, followed by Roxy and Gail, but their voices sounded like a hundred whispers in the cold house with footsteps coming up the walk. "Get in the chest!"

The chest we took the blankets from. I replaced the floor over them before diving into the chest where it was dark and smelled of pine. Footsteps pounded up the walk as I lowered the lid. I closed my eyes tightly, painfully, praying to God. *Please, don't let them find me... please...* The door swung open with a loud creak, and my eyes sprung open, heart thrashing and thumping in my ears.

"There's nobody here, husband," I heard, and my stomach sank. *Gilda.*

I covered my mouth to keep myself from crying and watched them breathlessly through the thin gap between the chest and the lid. The butcher stepped in first while Gilda scuttled up from behind. They paused. He seemed to be looking around, but only with his eyes as both of them stood in the front room.

"What's this?" he barked, and they walked over the blood spot on the floor. "Looks fresh."

"Someone died, husband," Gilda said, and her words trailed with giggles. They walked down the hall, and I heard noises that sounded like they were walking through each room, before walking into the kitchen where Gilda went through the cupboards.

The candles! God, the candles we lit were still on the floor. I squeezed the bag of diamonds near my waist, feeling light-headed and dizzy, thinking they'd see the candles any minute, pull me from the chest, and force me to drink Gilda's tea. I gulped. If he didn't shoot me first—an experiment in his underground lab either way.

The butcher picked up a blanket from the floor, talking about the damage the bomb had made and how they were lucky they hadn't been hit. Gilda agreed, then screamed from seeing that damn mouse. He tossed the blanket in the air and it landed on the chest, over the lid.

"Where is it? Where is it?" he kept yelling as Gilda screamed, but I couldn't see a thing.

Boom!

My whole body convulsed from a blast of his shotgun.

"Poor mouse," Gilda said. Her giggles were gone and it sounded like she might be sniffling.

"Let's go," he said. "They aren't here."

They left out the door, and I cried silently in the chest thinking that shot might have got one of the girls. I lifted the lid when I heard the car drive away, shouting for Red.

"We're all right," Red said from the floor, and I flopped out of the chest only to lie on the ground where I couldn't move. My heart beat like a rabbit's as I stared at the sky through the open ceiling, clutching my chest. A thin gray cloud breezed overhead. "Kit," Red said, and I was finally able to move. "Help us out."

I crawled over to where they were all crying. "He didn't get us," Red said, and my eyes trailed to the hole in the kitchen floor where the mouse had been. I pulled the trapdoor from the floor and after Red crawled out, we immediately embraced.

"Don't do that again, all right?" I said.

Red pulled away to look me in the eyes. "Do what?"

"Scare me like that," I said, and we hugged again.

We pulled Roxy and Gail out from the floor, and Roxy started to run out the front door.

"Wait!" I said, and I looked at my dress, my hands. "Our dresses. We can't leave like this. What if someone sees us covered in blood?"

Red took me by the elbow into the back bedroom where we found two more dresses and put them on in a rush.

Roxy snagged a jar of beans off the counter as we ran out

of that house, leaving the woman where we'd found her in the floor, and hoping her daughter or her son wouldn't find her, but that someone else would. In the pasture right before the trees, we learned of her husband. A tombstone with a bouquet of simple flowers marked his grave. I looked at my hands, stained pink and sticky, and giving them a swipe down my dress.

Roxy looked back at the house, almost looking sad, when Gail walked past us both, holding her arm. "They're German," Gail said, as if to remind us.

Roxy put her arm around me. "Come on," she said, and we walked the tree line away from the German mother's house until we couldn't see it.

We stopped at a rain puddle so I could wash the tinge of blood off my hands. I scooped up a handful of water, splashing it over my hands, down my fingers, coloring the water a muddy pink. I wondered if anyone at our hospital noticed we were missing. Nosy Noreen most certainly had been in our tent. I felt it, her hands on my bed and looking over my things. "What time is it?" I said, shaking my hands out. "And where are we going? Where's the river?"

Red looked into the sky, guessing what time it might be, before pulling out Jack's map. Lichtenau was to the west on the other side of the trees. There was another village in the east, and we'd be able to hug the tree line, but it would take longer and we'd be traveling deeper into Germany.

Gail took a step toward Lichtenau, but Red stopped her with her voice.

"We have to go through the next village, in the east," Red said. "It's the best way to make it to the river. What if someone recognizes us in Lichtenau—the women who ran?"

I shook my head. "No, Red... It's longer. And we have Gail's arm to think about."

Red pointed up. "See those ducks? They're eating corn. You want to go through that cornfield again?" she said, and Gail and Roxy immediately shook their heads. "We have to go east, the long way around. But look at us. We look a lot better than we did before in these new dresses. And we'll do what we did in Lichtenau." She pulled some flowering weeds. "Walk straight on through. The river bends that way, and we'll be within running distance after we clear this other village. I know it."

"But what if the butcher and crazy Gilda are there?" I said.

"They won't be, you hear me?" she said, but I knew she had no way of knowing if they were down there or not.

"All right. I'll go through the village," I finally said, but when I closed my eyes, I heard Gilda's girly giggle in my head and a shiver shot up my spine. We were going east.

"But nobody talk," Red said. "Not even you two." She pointed to me and Gail. "Unless you have to. Like I said, we walk straight on through." She nodded once, and we nodded back.

We gathered up our flowers and started walking toward the village but came to a grinding halt. A wide-open field, many yards long, separated us from the next tree line. Red kept walking as if it wasn't an issue, but it seemed like a very big issue to me. "We have to go through it," Red said.

"We can't!" I said, looking left then right, and up, standing still, holding the lumpy end of the bag close. "Red—" The strap slipped off my shoulder and slid down my arm.

Red turned around as she walked. "See those trees on the other side," she said, pointing. "Keep your eyes on those."

Gail followed Red, and after standing for a moment shaking in the weeds, me and Roxy stepped into the open field.

Nobody talked, but it was our silence, and the odd crack in the trees behind us, and the crunch of the weeds under our feet that made our thoughts feel like spoken words. If we ran, it would be suspicious. If we walked too slow it would be suspicious. If we didn't walk straight through it and tried hiding, it would look suspicious.

"I don't feel good about this," I said, halfway through.

Roxy looked left then right, and up, gulping. "Me either, toots. Almost there, almost there. Keep walking…"

Gail sang softly, trying to keep our minds off how exposed we were, holding the werewolves' diamonds—Americans in Germany for all to see, when Roxy joined in, humming shakily along. Then me too, step by step, with our eyes left then right, and up. Left then right, and up. Left then right, and—

We all stopped, hearing the sudden rev of a plane buzzing overhead. Roxy covered her mouth and Gail too.

"Where is it? Where…" I said, breathless and scared, twisting and turning in place trying to find it in the air.

Gail pointed. "There it is!" and she tried to run, but Red stopped her.

"Wait! We're in Germany," Red said. "The Luftwaffe isn't going to fire on us. They think we're Germans. Wave," she said, and we all looked at her as she waved to the pilot, who most likely only saw her a speck, a waving speck from a German woman. She elbowed me. "Wave, dammit!" And we waved, watching the plane fly over the trees, the roar of its engine revving and fluctuating as it dropped lower in the sky flying toward us.

"Bastards," I said. "I hope we blow you out of the sky."

"Yeah," Roxy said, "you dirty, no good pile of—"

"Just wave, will you?" Red said, and we continued waving, but it was flying much lower than I thought a plane should.

I put my hand back to my eyes, shielding a glare. "Why is it so low?" I said, and my arm dropped to my side. "Why—"

Bullets sprayed the field in front of us. *Zap, zap, zap, zap...*

"Run!" I yelled, and Gail and Red took off for the trees screaming, but Roxy stood shaking in her shoes, fixated on the firing plane coming straight for her.

21

KIT

I slugged Roxy's arm, and she snapped from her fog to run with me into the trees, leaping to the ground and covering our heads as the bullets punched the very spot where we'd been standing. I rolled over as they flew off, catching sight of the American star on the fuselage, and closed my eyes, blowing air from my mouth.

"I'm really sick and tired of getting shot at!" Roxy said, and she let go of the flowers that somehow managed to stay clutched in her fist. "Ahh, and I broke the jar of beans."

"They didn't know we're American," I said, and I flopped backward after trying to get up too soon, feeling my chest.

"No, but they saw that we were women," Gail said, and we were quiet, lying in the grass.

"It's war, ladies," Red said, after a pause. "We can't judge. Not us. Not after what we've been through. And what we've done."

I got up slowly, slinging the bag of diamonds over my shoulder.

Red asked Gail how her arm felt, and she shook her head vigorously that it wasn't good. "We'll be in France tonight," Red said. "We'll get you the best surgeon in reconstruction. There might be a remedy for the poison—"

"I'm worried," Gail said, and her eyes had teared up but she wouldn't let them fall.

"I know you are," Red said, and Roxy looked at me, and I knew she was worried too. We all were worried. It had been a day since she'd bought that bullet, and although one stiff finger sounded like she got away lucky, we were trained to know the worst wounds often revealed themselves days later.

We dusted the grass from our dresses and fixed our hair, using some of the ribbons we took from the German girl's bedroom. Red fixed her kerchief, tucking her hair underneath until only the wispy strawberry-blonde parts showed. "A quick and easy walk-through," Red reminded us, and we followed her into the trees and down to the village.

We should have known it wasn't going to be a quick and easy walk immediately after Red said those fateful words, because anytime someone was certain, there was always something unexpected waiting for us. We walked through a grassy area nearing the village.

"What's that noise?" I said, and it sounded like a crowd, laughing, and the din of many voices talking, but Red shook her head.

We made it to a cobblestone road, and although we'd heard the crowds first, we didn't know what we were in for until we got up close. Roxy elbowed me, but I was too stunned to elbow back. Red and Gail stood with their mouths hanging open.

Nazi flags unfolded from second-story windows over the heads of children standing at attention along the curb, waving miniature Nazi flags, while others talked proudly about the Wehrmacht.

A parade. *Ah, hell.* We'd walked into a damn military parade. I shook myself to, pushing Red backward where nobody could hear us, and Gail pushed Roxy. "A walk-through, huh?" I said. "The Wehrmacht's here!" I looked back, making sure nobody was walking up on us.

"How was I supposed to know?" Red said. She peeped over my shoulder. "Looks like they're passing through."

"Yeah," I said. "And where do you think they're going? We have to go around," I said, and I clutched the bag of diamonds close. "I have the Reich's jewels for crying out loud. This is the last place we should we walking through."

"Yeah, Red," Roxy said. "What if—"

"No," Gail said, and we all looked at her. "It's the quickest way now. We have to get across the river."

I closed my eyes, sucking air through my teeth. She was right, but it didn't mean I had to like it. I hiked the bag strap over my shoulder. Roxy hooked arms with Gail, hiding her wound from the locals, and I linked arms with Red. We walked off cautiously, but with forced smiles through the crowds, and I started to think maybe we *could* get through the village quick and easy with so many people to hide between, as long as we never stopped.

Squeals and cheers followed the scamper of women running arm in arm for the nearest curb, ribbon tails bouncing off their shoulders and bouquets of flowers shaking in their hands. We got caught up in the fervor, and before we knew it, we were boxed in and forced to stand on the curb with the others, waiting for the parade. I looked sorrowfully up at Red, and we scooted in close when we felt the crowd sway.

"Victory!" a woman shouted, and a hundred heads turned to look down the street. I held my breath, waiting, waiting for what was to come, then the first line of soldiers marched around the corner, and I covered my mouth. I was both scared and shocked, nothing could have prepared me, then something happened I didn't expect, and I burst into a shaking, uncontrollable cry on the street from having looked the enemy up close and in the eye.

Other women burst into tears, saluting as they passed, shouting for the deaths of Americans, and my stomach roiled. "Death to the pigs, death to the pigs!" I heard.

Gail tossed her flowers at the Wehrmacht's feet as they marched, following the others. "Victory," she said in German, followed by an elbow to Roxy, then Red, and to me to follow suit.

"Victory," I said, tossing my flowers.

A Tiger tank rolled in next, rumbling with the clunk of its track beating over the pavement. *Tack, tack, tack, tack...* I felt light-headed and faint. The tank stopped in front of us, and I couldn't tell if I was breathing. My chest hurt; my blood pounded. The hatch burst open, and a commander popped out, waving as a collective gasp and awe followed a roar of applause. Children held their Nazi flags high in the air and mothers blew kisses.

He caught a thrown rose, kissed it, then searched the crowd for a deserving German woman to receive it. Women competed with young girls, jumping up and down, begging for it to be them, when he pointed to me, hurling it through the air from his tank. I gulped, eyes fixated on the rose as it arced like a rainbow, tumbling bloom over stem, right to me.

The crowd went wild, women wanting to touch the rose he'd thrown but also cajoling me to blow him a kiss. Red jabbed me in the ribs, and I blew a great big kiss off my palm, only to hang my head after, and wipe my eyes.

We walked away soon after, stiff, numb, and not saying a word until we made it to the other side of the village. "Promise me you'll never tell anyone about that for as long you live," I said.

"Yeah," Red said. "I promise."

"Gail, Rox?" I said, and they both turned to me, nodding.

We'd walked for what seemed like hours, and there was no sign of the bend in the river Red had talked about. Our stomachs growled, and soon enough Roxy was complaining about her stomach again. "It hurts, Kit," she said, and I sighed.

"We're all hungry," I said. "Besides, we'll be in France soon. At that vineyard Jack talked about, and I'm sure they'll have something there for us."

"But where is it?" she said. "We've been walking all day. What if someone back at the hospital has noticed we're gone?" She dug her hands into her sides as she walked, grimacing from hunger pains. "And look." She pointed. "The sky is turning and it's getting late."

It was getting late, and the all too familiar evening breeze brought with it the usual graying skies. "I know, Rox," I said, and I shivered, looking up and holding my hand out, waiting for that raindrop to fall. An explosion in the west made us look.

"The river has to be close," Red said.

Roxy stopped abruptly. "What's that?" She pointed straight ahead beyond a dirt field to an orchard. "Could it… Yes, it is!" She glanced at me over her shoulder, smiling. "Apples!"

She trotted off ahead, running past Red and Gail straight toward the dirt field. Red tried to grab her. "Wait…" she said in a shouted whisper. "Roxy—wait a minute!"

"Oh, let her go," I said, as Roxy skipped off toward the trees.

"No!" Red said, and she grabbed my arm, and that's when I saw how manicured the field in front of it was, corded and groomed. "It's a mine!"

Roxy stopped on a dime, arms flung out, careful not take one more step. "Oh my God!" She looked over her shoulder to us, then back at her feet, inches from meeting the dirt.

We ran after her, but it was Red who walked her last steps with a determined gait that would have made any one of us shake in our boots. But instead of smacking Roxy upside the head like I thought she was going to do, she ended up hugging her. "Dammit, Roxy." She squeezed Roxy tightly before letting go. "Don't do that again. You almost gave me a heart attack."

"You?" Roxy looked completely mortified, clutching her chest. "I could've been blown to bits!"

"Come on," Red said, and we walked around the dirt field into the orchard, which was cool and damp with shade, and dirty. Weathered leaves collected around the base of each tree. Enough kindling to light up the entire orchard with the strike of one match, had it not been for the rain last night.

"Can't we please rest, Red," Roxy said. "Two minutes. I beg you."

"No," Gail barked, and she looked over both her shoulders while clutching her arm. "We have to keep going. I know the river is close…"

"Two minutes," Roxy said. "Please. Two. Minutes. I don't have any strength in my arms or legs and I'm worried about the swim."

"I'm too nervous to stop," I said. "Someone could be following us."

Red stopped walking and Roxy thanked her repeatedly, while Gail held her arm, wincing, taking occasional glances through the trees, looking for the butcher, the enemy, and anyone else. I held the bag of diamonds close.

"All right. Two minutes. But that's all," Red said, and then she turned to me and Gail. "She needs the food to make it across the river." She pointed to a tree. "Might as well have an apple."

We stood under one of the heartiest trees with low-hanging branches. Roxy moaned and groaned like an old woman flopping to the ground with one hand on her back. She pulled an apple off a branch above her head, taking a big bite. "Man, oh man. Will you get a load of this?" She shook the apple in her hand. "Something the Germans did right. Apples."

"Everything tastes good when you're hungry," Red said, and Roxy shrugged, taking another bite.

Me and Gail sat down hesitantly, still looking through the trees, but we had no choice. Red was right, Roxy needed to eat if she had a prayer of making it across that river. I picked an apple for myself.

"I can't wait for this war to be over," I said, and everyone looked at me. "What? Shouldn't we be thinking about it? Thoughts of hope, something to look forward to."

I took a bite of my apple. God, Roxy was right. It was delicious, juicy and sweet.

"I know what I'm looking forward to." Roxy chewed up the last bite of her apple, giving the core a toss. "Finding a fella."

"You don't have one already, Rox?" Red said. "I thought you would've had all the boys in Jersey by the sound of you—the way you talk to the soldiers."

We'd all thought it one time or another. Roxy had a way with the boys. The way she wore her uniform, unbuttoned one button too many, the way she talked, sexy at times, and the way she let the boys touch her.

"I know what you dolls all think," Roxy said, looking at us. "But ya know what?" She picked an apple directly over her head, studying it, feeling it in her palm before taking a bite. "I've never had a man."

"Knock it off, Rox," I said, and she looked directly at me, eyes pointed.

"Truth," Roxy said, and she tapped her heart then pointed to me. "On your life."

My mouth hung open before I smiled. "Mother of God."

Red and Gail looked surprised too.

"I'm not the only virgin in Jersey who carries herself like a real broad, let me tell ya… you'd be smart to try it," Roxy said.

I moved kindling around in front of me with my apple

core, thinking about all the boys back home. Most I'd known since kindergarten, most who'd gone off to war like Sam. The ones who stayed were all older. "Oh, I could never do that in Washington," I said. "Never."

"Well, we're not in Washington, now are we?" Roxy said. "There's always Jack."

"What?" I yelped. "Because we chatted about home?"

"It's more than that," Roxy said, winking. "Don't think we didn't see that lingering touch thing he did with your hand when we left." She laughed. "Red, tell her you saw it too." And Red nodded. "Gail too," she said, and Gail nodded.

"I don't know what you're talking about," I said, and we continued to eat our apples under the tree where some birds had perched. "Besides, I'm starting not to like him. Leaving us to get this—" I patted the bag of jewels "—all on our own. I know he was too weak to come, but still…"

"Yeah," Gail said, touching her wounded arm, "but still…"

"Yeah, but still," Roxy added. "He left us. Fed us to the werewolves and that crazy butcher. Even if he didn't know the extent of it, let me tell ya…" Roxy clenched her fist then punched the air. "Pop! Right in that plum mouth of his."

We all laughed. Even Gail, who winced afterward and held her arm close.

"I don't think he knew," I said, and then turned to Red. "Did he?"

"If he did know and didn't tell us, he's going to get more than Roxy's fist in his face," Red said. "You better believe it."

"He is cute though," Roxy said. "Gotta give him that."

"Yeah, I suppose he's cute," I said. "Those eyes, and that chest—"

"Man, what I wouldn't give to have a dreamboat like that someday," Roxy said, and she dug her heel into the dirt. "Damn this war. What if we never get across the line to France? What if we can never leave?" Her angry voice turned into a muffled cry, and when I swung my arm around her, she sobbed into her hands.

"Don't cry, Rox," I said. "We'll get out, and there's someone for you," I said, petting her head. "Promise. I'll introduce you to my brother, Sam. Oh, you'll love him. Tall, handsome, kind…" I hung my head, suddenly overwhelmed thinking about where he was, and where I was, with the werewolves' diamonds, and the possibility that we wouldn't get out at all.

Roxy wiped her nose, looking up. "Don't stop, keep going…"

"We'll get out of here, Rox," I said, trying to sound sure. "We have to believe."

We threw our arms around each other.

"I bet if I told him what I did to save the POW camps, he'd like me real good," Roxy said, and we both laughed, pulling away.

"Yeah," I said. "He would, Rox."

"Fräuleins!" a man yelled from a puttering truck, and my stomach dropped like a rock through a paper sack. His arm hung out the window. "You girls there!" he spouted in German. "What are you doing in this orchard?"

We stood up and gathered behind Red still holding our apples. "What did he say?" Red said from the corner of her mouth.

"What do we do?" Roxy whispered. "Do you think he heard us talking?"

My first instinct was to run, but he was in a truck and could easily catch us. He drove closer, his tires rolling slowly over fallen leaves.

"Say something, will ya?" Roxy said, but even Gail seemed to have lost her voice.

I cleared my throat. He was wrinkly, a seasoned old man, an apple farmer if I'd ever seen one, and I'd seen a lot. Only this one was German, and there was no way to know if he'd be sympathetic to a few American women or not, like the pharmacist and his wife had been. He could be friends with the butcher and had been out looking for us.

I smiled, quickly making up a story. "Good day, sir," I said in German. "We lost our dog. Have you seen a shepherd?"

His eyes skirted over Red, Roxy, and Gail, who'd hidden her bandaged arm behind Red. "*Nein*." And he paused, noticing our apple cores on the ground, which made the air between us feel very uncomfortable.

I cleared my throat again. "Sorry to bother you," I said, even though it was him who'd stopped us. I promptly turned around and mouthed, "Go, go... go..." And the girls followed me deeper into the orchard as if we knew where we were going and that it was all right to be there, through the kindling collected between the trees, the fallen leaves, and apples left to spoil. I felt him watching us from his puttering truck, one arm draped over his steering wheel with a keen German eye. I turned around once, catching a glimpse.

"Keep walking," Red said, reaching for my shoulder.

He had the same strange look on his face as he did when

we talked, one that said he didn't believe me. When we found cover behind a row of mature trees, his truck rolled slowly forward until he could see us again.

"Ah, hell," I said. "He's following us. Maybe he did hear us talking?"

"We need to do something else," Roxy said.

"Like what?" I said.

"What he'd expect young German women to do," Roxy said, and she picked up a wad of leaves in her hands and tossed them on Gail's head, who gasped momentarily before following suit.

"Laugh loud," Red said, and she squealed like a little girl, and we ran around the trees trying to catch each other, grasping at dress hems, and tugging on hair. Soon we were out of breath from playing tag and tossing leaves.

I looked back, and his truck was gone. "He drove off!" I said, and we ran as fast as we could through the orchard, but now it was near dusk and dark among the trees, which made our steps more deliberate, and careful, strenuous.

Roxy ran out of steam. "Wait," she said, falling against a tree. "I can't do it anymore."

We moved into a small circle around her. The boom of thunder and a cold sweep of air roared over the treetops. "It'll rain soon, that should keep him away," I said, and the stark cut of yellowy headlamps beamed through the trees, lighting up the kindling and our last steps.

"Quick! Follow me..." Red said, grabbing Roxy's hand while I took Gail's good one, and we dove into a narrow ditch and lay like cigars, packed real tight. Red put her arms over us, holding us in place and praying.

"*The Lord is my shepherd I shall not want...*"

A downpour of rain followed a crack of lightning, dirt turning into mud, and water channeling into the ditch. Headlamps skirted over the ground above us through the rain, followed by the roar of a truck engine. I squeezed my eyes closed, gripping the bag near my waist, thinking desperately of a place to hide the jewels if the Germans found us in the ditch, but I couldn't risk standing up or even moving out from under Red's protective arm.

"Please God," I said to myself, eyes closed even tighter, "please God…"

The truck rolled up next to us in the ditch, squealing with rusty, tired wheels. My eyes popped open. Headlamps flickered. And then a door opened and closed.

Wet footsteps slopped through the mud.

I felt frantically for the gun under my dress, wet fingers searching a wet leg. Roxy wept openly while Red searched her brassiere for the lethal doses of morphine. "Ladies," Red said as the rain fell on top of us. "It was a pleasure to serve with you…"

22

EVELYN

Sometime around midnight, Evelyn woke up with a jolt, shrieking and clutching her chest in bed. Her husband barely roused next to her. After several deep breaths, she opened her eyes to the darkness of the cold October night. The wind whistled against her windowpane, and she heard the light tatter of blowing leaves. But she was burning up, moistened with fear that had left her nightgown damp and limp.

It had been several weeks since the reporter had visited her home, and the salute was creeping up on her; in a matter of days she'd be in Atlanta in front of a news crew trying to tell her story. She still hadn't made peace with what happened behind enemy lines, and even though she tried with all her might to mentally prepare for the interview and tell her big secret, she wondered how she could talk openly about something that had scarred her so severely. She asked God for help, making deals she knew she couldn't keep, which she was used to doing—she'd been doing it since Lichtenau.

Evelyn crawled out of bed and tiptoed into the kitchen, where the linoleum was lit up with moonglow. She reached into the little basket above her refrigerator for the cigarette her husband had put there for an emergency, feeling blindly for it.

She felt some relief after she lit it and inhaled in her kitchen, flicking ash into her sink, but it didn't last nearly as long as she hoped.

She couldn't go back to bed yet, and walked to her slider. A single raindrop fell outside onto the patio—one black spot. Crinkled brown leaves pinwheeled across the patio from a gusty breeze, and Evelyn played with the door lock, feeling safe inside, flipping it up and down, up and down. She thought back to when Michelle was a little girl, when they'd run around the house and lock up all the doors when it rained—just one of those games Evelyn had made up so her daughter wouldn't ask questions.

Evelyn flipped the lock into the lock position—*clack*—and held it there as another drop became two and then three, splatting onto the concrete.

Michelle was eighteen months old when Evelyn realized she had a problem, when the rain had triggered a reaction in her that wasn't normal, wasn't sane. It was April 3rd—she remembered the day as if it was yesterday.

Michelle had a fever. Her face had turned beet-red, and her forehead and belly hot as a griddle while scream-crying herself into an oblivion. Evelyn rushed out of the house for the doctor's office, baby in one arm and purse hooked on the other, when she saw a single raindrop fall on the front step. Her muscles locked up, fibers stretching between unmoving bones, right there in the doorway with a screaming baby in her arms. Her body throbbed from an inner gush of imaginary fluid, rain that would fill her up as if she were a glass and flow over the sides, rain that would kill her if she stepped out in it.

Evelyn couldn't move. She couldn't leave.

She thought she would die.

Several hours later, after the rain had stopped, she escaped from her house with the baby and drove to the pediatrician's office in town, barely making it through the doors before they closed for the day. She waited impatiently in the waiting room, her stomach turning from the vile smell of antiseptic and the stink of latex before being led into an examination room.

The doctor wrote Evelyn a script to bring Michelle's fever down, who was now asleep in her buggy. But after examining the baby, the pediatrician seemed to be examining Evelyn, looking at her oddly. "I thought you were coming in this morning. It's almost five."

Evelyn sat in the examination room, hands folded nervously in her lap with trembling fingers. She wanted to cry out. Tell him what had happened, but the thought of him judging her felt like a rock forming in her chest.

"Evelyn?" He handed her the script, and she took it, eyes flittering over the room, pulse quickening. "I know your husband had been away on business. Is everything all right at the farm?"

It was then Evelyn realized the doctor thought there was

a problem in her marriage, which was far from the truth. "Oh, no... no... it's not that," she managed to say. "Nothing like that." She lifted her head after taking a heavy gulp of air and looked into the doctor's eyes. She'd known him for many years, before the war, when he was friends with her parents, both since passed. He put his hand on her shoulder. "Should I have the nurse come in?"

Evelyn thought she might be going insane. She felt it in the days after Lichtenau, and progressively in the years since, first starting in her chest, a heavy, rapid heartbeat followed by a bubbling of fear gripping her muscles, yet this was the first time she couldn't pull herself out of it—the first time she stood unmoving, watching the rain and feeling the ticks on the cement patio as if they were a sharpshooter's bullets in the night, unable to help her daughter.

Evelyn swallowed her pride and told the doctor what had happened and how she thought it was connected to her time in the war, her time as a nurse. "I'm deathly petrified of the rain. I know it's only water, I know it can't hurt me, but at the same time I feel I'd be walking to my death if I step out in it." She tapped her chest. "I feel it in here."

She had stood up and paced the little examination room, trying to make sense of it herself, clutching the locket she'd worn around her neck, a locket she'd been given during the war, a locket she swore she'd never take off. "So, you see doctor, that's why I'm late." She walked toward him, hands reaching, pleading for help, but stopped short from grabbing his lapels, remembering who she was, and who she was talking with. She dropped her hands, and at her wits' end she asked, "Can you help me?"

The doctor stared at her for a long while. So long that

Evelyn started to feel self-conscious and cold and she rubbed her hands for warmth. "Doctor? Please. I beg you..."

He backed away, his eyes narrowing. "How dare you."

"What?" Evelyn folded her arms, but not from anger, for protection. She'd made herself vulnerable telling him her secrets.

"My son was in the Pacific. Guadalcanal. There isn't a moment that goes by the suffering he endured doesn't affect him. But you..." He flicked his finger at her. "You were a nurse. You can't possibly suffer the way our soldiers suffer. You're making a mockery of—" He set his clipboard down. "Don't think I won't remember this, Evelyn Jones." He walked out of the examination room leaving Evelyn with Michelle who'd woken up from the doctor's voice and had started to fuss.

"Liar," she heard him say as he walked down the hall.

A nurse came into the room after watching the doctor storm off. "Everything all right in here, Mrs. Jones?"

Evelyn picked up her baby, trying to soothe her, wiping tears from her own eyes with the back of her hand. "Mmm-hmm," she said through quivering lips.

That night after dinner, while Evelyn cleared the plates, her husband asked her what was wrong. She swallowed the lump she'd been carrying with her since the doctor's office, and thought about telling him everything was all right, that she was just worried about Michelle, but her eyes sagged in an unfamiliar way, a way she couldn't hide from her husband.

Evelyn sat down at the table and sobbed uncontrollably with her head on the checkered tablecloth.

"What is it?" her husband said, rubbing her back. "Honey?"

She rolled her head over to look at him, tears sliding to one side and pooling on the tablecloth, hiccupping between her wails. "I don't know."

"Maybe it's the baby," he said. "Maybe it's too much. You try to do everything…"

"No," she moaned, "it's not that."

"Then what is it?"

She lifted her head only to rest her eyes in her palms. "I think it's the war. It's in my head."

Evelyn's husband got quiet, and she looked at him through the gaps of her fingers. "Don't you think of it?" she said, and he shook his head slightly, but then nodded.

"Sometimes," he said.

"How do you do it?" she said through her sobs. "How do you keep it from ruining your life?"

"I don't know…" he said, looking her over before motioning at the locket around her neck. "I don't keep mementos of the war with me—souvenirs to remind me."

Evelyn sniffled, wiping her runny nose with the flap of her apron. "But I said I wouldn't take it off."

"You're not in France anymore, Evelyn. You're home. The war is over."

Evelyn felt sick to her stomach. She'd sworn she'd never take it off; she'd never get rid of it, not until—

"You have to move on," her husband said, and he wiped his eyes swiftly with the back of his hand, which made her feel guilty for speaking about it. "The locket is a constant reminder."

Michelle fussed from her crib in the other room and Evelyn stood up. "Michelle needs me." But as she left the kitchen, her husband pulled her back.

"I love you, Evelyn," he whispered, hugging her warmly. "You're safe with me, okay?"

And she melted into his arms, knowing there was nothing he could do to save her.

Evelyn unlocked the sliding glass door—*clack*—and a flit of cold air whistled through a crack where the door had pushed open slightly. The patio had turned speckly with raindrops. If she walked outside, surely one would hit her. She felt a lump in her throat with that thought, but instead of closing the door up tight like she'd always done in the past, she decided to face her fears, something she'd discussed with her doctor but hadn't been brave enough to try.

She forced herself to stick her fingers through the gap and wiggled them in the jamb, feeling the cold damp air. Goose bumps rolled up her arm, over her shoulder, and down her back under her nightgown. With the door open she could hear the patter of rainfall, the light tick of it hitting the windowpane as the wind blew, and smell it, the bitterness of dust and dirt.

She slid the door open a little more and stood in the doorway, feeling naked and exposed to the elements and her thoughts. Normally she'd think about dying, but what happened caught her by surprise. She thought about living. Being haunted by her memories for more than forty years felt like a prison. She couldn't just try to tell her story at the salute, she had to do it; she had to confront her fear. Talking was, after all, the only thing she hadn't done, and when she thought of her next steps, she thought she'd try them in the rain.

Evelyn felt a pop, a sudden release in her chest with this resolution despite the bubble of panic trying to rise up inside her, and for the first time in so many years she had courage. She lifted her nightgown up above her ankles and stepped outside, first with her toe, feeling out the cold cement patio, and then her entire foot. One wobbly step turned into two and then three, her nightgown catching a breeze from the bottom up, billowing around her, revealing her twiggish legs as she walked across the slick patio and into wet grass, shivering and cold.

She reached into her nightgown pocket and pulled out her silver locket, looking at it briefly in her palm before hanging it around her neck and pressing it flat to her chest instead of clutching at her heart. Evelyn tipped her head back, looking into the night air, and waited for the first raindrop to hit her skin when she felt a sting on her cheek, a needle from the sky that slid cold and wet into her eye. She gasped, shuddering from her toes to her head before turning stiff, but after a second of being frozen in the grass, she fluttered her fingers and batted her eyes, realizing she hadn't drowned.

The wind roared over her pasture, over her lawn, and tossed up her hair. "Please, God, please…" Evelyn said, crying, flinging her arms out and begging God for help, a release from the debilitating memories she'd been carrying with her for over forty years.

The rain. There had been so much rain.

23

KIT

I pulled the gun from under my dress and pointed straight up into the rain, not knowing where to aim, blinking through the splatter in my eyes, listening to Roxy cry and Red say how much she loved us, when a woman and two kids peeped into the ditch.

"Up, up," she said in English. "Hurry, before someone sees!"

Red and I looked at each other, then back to her, too stunned to make sense of what was happening. She put her hand out. "Come now, in the truck," she said, motioning. "The patrols are out. Do you want to get caught?"

Gail sprung up to take her hand, and that same old farmer who'd been watching us appeared next to her, also with his hand out, helping Roxy and then Red and me out of the ditch.

"Where are we going?" I said, and she latched up the truck tailgate. "Get down, girls. It's a bumpy ride." And we slid down into the truck's bed and drove off down the uneven orchard road.

Red still had the morphine gripped in her hand, and I don't think any amount of talking would have got her to let go of it before she knew where they were taking us.

We drove into a clearing and onto a smooth road. Moments later we lurched to a stop outside a big farmhouse. We climbed out of the truck and shuffled into the house close together only to stand in the foyer. The kids stared at us, a boy and a girl, as we dripped all over the wood floor. The smell of something salty and warm wafted in from the kitchen, and my stomach growled with the thought of eating something other than apples. Warm firelight crackled from the main room.

"Where are you from?" the boy asked in German. The girl sucked at her thumb, blonde pigtails in ringlets.

"Far away," I said back.

"America?" he asked, eyes wide, but I couldn't tell if he was shocked, concerned, or scared.

The woman clapped at the children. "To your rooms, you two," she said in German, and the kids moaned before resigning to a slow climb upstairs. She wrapped blankets around us she had retrieved from a hall closet.

Red and Roxy stood stiff as boards near the door, barely taking a step inside, and rightfully so after the other German homes we'd been in. Gail held on to her bandaged arm, her hair in clumpy wet globs covering her eyes.

"Cut the lights," the woman said in German, and the farmer went around the house and flipped off all the lights. She turned to us and spoke in English. "This way, this way…"

Roxy gasped when she heard her plain accent, which was much more prevalent than it was in the rain looking down at us in the ditch—she sounded American. She waved for us to follow her into the kitchen, toward the smell of soup, and we shuffled along behind her through the front room and down the hall. A long wood table had been set with padded chairs, but we stood around it as if we didn't know what to do. She patted the blankets over our shoulders, drying up the rain. She reached for my bag.

"No!" I yelped, and she pulled her hand back. "I mean, my bag stays with me."

She paused before smiling. The farmer had already closed the window curtains in the kitchen, and lit candles, which made the room flicker dimly. "Sit," she said, pulling out the chairs. "Please…"

Gail and Roxy sat down at the table, and Red too, reluctantly, and eyeing the basket of bread on the table.

"I have some soup…" The woman slowly lifted the lid on a pot of soup that bubbled with brown broth and one meaty bone.

"Why are you helping us?" I said.

She turned away from the kitchen counter with a hot bowl of broth in her hands, which Red immediately shook her head at and mouthed for me not to eat, but I took the bowl because she'd pushed it at me. Though, I wasn't so trusting this time, and like Red had warned, I didn't have any intention of eating it until she answered my question. She went to ladle up another bowl.

"Ma'am," I said, and she looked at me this time. "Why are you helping us?" I repeated, but much more forcefully. Roxy, Red, and Gail looked up at her from their chairs.

The woman froze momentarily, studying us and our expressions before finally setting the bowl down. She clasped her hands together. "Because I'm American too," she said, plainly. "My uncle heard you talking in the orchard."

I sat heavily into my chair at the table, overcome with relief. Her dress was unapologetically traditional with little sunflowers and a lacy hem. And her hair, flaxen as a maid in a German fairy tale. "I know what you must think," she said, pulling her skirt up a hair to show the bulk of fabric disguising her tiny frame. "I was visiting my aunt and uncle when the war broke out, and I got stuck. I'm from South Dakota." She smiled. "The children are orphans we took in. My aunt died, sadly, of consumption two years ago. I took her name because the Reich was arresting foreigners."

"You mean, you're in hiding?" Red said.

"But what about the village?" I said. "The town... people talk."

She nodded. "They do. We buried her, a private affair in the orchard." She touched her skirt and fluffed some of the lace. "I wear her clothes and at a distance, people think I'm her. My uncle goes into the village when we need something. The children have never been there." She held out her hand for me to shake. "My name's Jean."

"I'm Kit," I said. "This is Roxy, Red—" they both gave a nod "—and Gail."

She noticed Gail's arm, and how she cradled it close to her body even in the sling. "Are you going to be all right?"

Gail shook her head stiffly.

"We ran into some trouble," I said, and Jean reached for Gail's arm.

"Let me see it," Jean said, and I think we were all surprised to see Gail give up her arm for a look. She unwrapped the bandage and examined the pink-stained sutures, and Gail's stiff pinkie.

"This is from a poison bullet?" Jean asked, as if she'd seen one before.

"She bought it two days ago," I said, and Jean looked up.

"Two days?" Jean held a candle to it for more light, inspecting the dye a little closer. "I know this poison. It's common around here. Did the bullet split or break?" Jean's eyes trailed up to Gail's.

"No," Gail said.

Red immediately stood up to comfort Gail when Jean held her breath. "Then this is the worst of it. Right there. That finger," Jean said, and Gail collapsed into a heap of tears right on the woman's table.

"Are you sure?" Red said, and Jean nodded.

"I've been so scared," Gail said, "thinking I could die at any moment."

"You're not the first." Jean got a dry bandage and redressed the wound, and she did it expertly, which impressed me as much as Red. "Herr Esser has been known to use these on trespassers. He owns the big cornfield on the other side of Lichtenau. Is that where it happened?" Jean said, but Gail kept sobbing with her head down.

Esser. The man I killed. It was a strange feeling, knowing his name. Gail sat straight up after she had a moment, and wiped her eyes, taking a few gulping breaths. She never answered Jean's question, or said a word about Herr Esser. It was our secret, to go with the others.

Jean motioned for us to have some bread and eat up her soup, which we were more than happy to do now that we knew she was American, and she watched us from her chair, arms folded, while we ate like ravenous pigs, slurping straight from the bowl and chewing up every last bit of bread she had in the basket. Roxy belched, and her hand flew to her mouth. "Sorry."

"Quite all right," Jean said. She sat back in her chair and crossed her legs at the knees. "Now, what the heck are you girls doing over here?"

I swallowed, holding on to the bag of diamonds near my waist as if it were a baby in my belly. "Probably best if you don't know," I said, and she nodded. "Thank you for the food, and for bringing us in out of the rain."

Red and I scooted from our seats to clear the table and talked about how we should get going. Jean spoke up and said we could rest in her loft for the night.

"No," I said, shaking my head. "It's too dangerous."

"I insist," Jean said. "But my uncle would be glad if you left by morning."

Her uncle had walked by, passing through the room, and paused when he heard her say his name. Roxy mouthed, "Please," while rubbing her neck. We needed to rest. We had to rest. Red and I discussed it further and decided to give in to her offer since we knew the damage from Gail's poison bullet had reached its peak.

"Understood," I said, and her uncle walked upstairs. "We will leave first thing."

Red pulled the map out but it was a useless, sodden glob of paper from the rain. "The river is only a three-mile walk from here," Jean said, pointing west. "Head that way and it's a straight shot."

"We're almost home," Red said, taking each of our hands. "Three more miles."

"I never thought I'd say it," Roxy said, "but boy I miss France. I miss the dirt. I miss our shabby tent."

Jean led us to a loft through a secret staircase that had been built for servants. Her uncle built shelves inside to make it look like a closet, complete with folded linens but left a space big enough for a few thin bodies to squeeze through off to the side.

We made our way up the dark and narrow passageway into the loft. The staircase was straight as a spine and cracked like old bones. We moved in shadows, feeling our way about the loft using the walls and each other. Jean lit one candle and then warned us not to light any more, and pointed to a small round window in the far reaches of the rafters. "A secret room must stay dark." She pulled a few blankets for us from a trunk to sleep with and gave us each a sweater.

Red shook Jean's hand before she left, the candlelight flickering between them. "Thank you for saving us." It was a simple thank you but weighted with the world.

Jean nodded once before shutting the door quietly behind her, and we listened to her retreating footsteps cracking down the stairs. It was then the room seemed to lighten a little more from our adjusting eyes. And the house was quiet. A few creaks here and a few creaks there before we heard a round of explosions thundering in the distance. I shook violently from the unexpected shake of it, coming up from the ground and rattling the house internally.

"I miss my mother," Gail said, and she curled up on the floor next to Red, who petted her head.

"Me too," Red said. "Tell us about her, Gail. Tell us the first thing you're going to do when you get home. Give us all some hope, something to believe in."

Rain tapped on the roof as Gail went on about her mother, how she was the smartest person she knew, even smarter than Gail, but she'd never stepped foot in a college classroom. "She wanted me to do what no other woman in our family had done—only the men—and go to college. Oh, and she's beautiful. I can see her now, sparkling eyes and Greta Garbo hair. The first thing I'm going to do when I get home is hug her into the next year…"

Red sniffled as Gail talked about her mother, reaching for her cheek in the dark to wipe tears away. "That's what I'm going to do too, hug my mom clear into next year," Red said. "That, and pay off my mother's landlord so she'll never have to worry again. In fact, I'll get us a new place. Yeah, that's what I'll do! I should have a few nice bucks coming after all this. And wouldn't it be great if we walked back into the field hospital and found out we were promoted?"

"Now you're really dreaming," I said.

"Oh, but I'm not done," Red said. "After I get cleaned up and look nice and neat, I'm going to walk over to Jim Marshall's house and kiss him right on the lips."

"Who's Jim Marshall?" I asked.

"An absolute nobody of an ex-boyfriend," Red said, and we all laughed. "That's one thing I miss. Looking nice. It's something I think about when the nights are long. There's a cosmetics case I have, a real expensive one. All my Max Factor cosmetics are in there." She sighed. "I can't wait to put on a full face of Max Factor."

"Yeah," Roxy said, followed by Gail.

"Yeah," I said. "That'll be the day. That's when I'll know the war is over."

We sat with our thoughts in the dark. It was the simple things we missed—all those things we took for granted before the war. And when that day came, when I could wear that full face of Max Factor like Red talked about, I knew I'd be thinking of my girls. Maybe I'd even buy a case like Red's. I just hoped I could keep the memories—all the thoughts of this damn war—from consuming me like my mother's thoughts consumed her.

"I love you guys," I said. "I don't know if it's okay to say that—the doom of saying it out loud. But God's truth, I love ya," I said, and they all answered up that they loved me too, and my voice quivered. "And Red, nobody's a better chief nurse..."

She reached for my hand in the dark. "We're in it together," Red said. "Remember what I said back at our field hospital? We'll meet up after the war, like we talked about when we drank wine at our sandbag canteen." She gave my hand a squeeze when I heard her tearing up. "We will. And tomorrow, we'll leave early, a short walk to the river and we'll be in France. Safe. And this part of the nightmare will be over."

So many days had passed since we landed on Utah Beach. Every day as clear as the next, marked by a smell, remembered by the odor of war. The loft had its own smell, one of still dust and mold. Only thin German walls separated us from the war outside and the short miles between our troops and the Rhine. My heart ticked up, thinking how close we were to the line, and how easy it would be for us to get caught in a battle if we stayed here one second longer—but leaving in the night and in the rain? We had to wait.

"Hey," Roxy said, and I looked up in the direction of her voice. "Will ya get a load of this?" She pulled something out from the darkest corner of the room, dragging it to us by a cord.

"Is that…" I covered my open mouth.

"A radio!" Roxy said.

I glanced at the door, remembering the last time I tried to listen to a radio and the pharmacist's wife had rudely taken it away. Gail sat up. "Do you think it works?"

"I don't know," Roxy said.

"Where's an outlet?" I said, and Red patted the walls, then we all did as quietly as we could in the dimly lit room. I started to think maybe there wasn't one, being an old house and in the loft, but then I found one. "Here! There's one here!"

"Keep it low," Red said, patting my arm, even though the rain had picked up and trickled off the roof. Nobody would hear us. I plugged the cord in, and we huddled around it on the floor, getting a finger's width away from the speaker. I rotated the dial slowly, through the buzz of static and undecipherable words until we heard snippets of music, then… song.

Clair de Lune.

Roxy gasped. "Oh my—"

"God," I breathed.

My eyes fell closed, my mind dissolving into the invisible space where the piano thrummed, overcome with emotion from what I'd been through since the landing, since Utah—the firefights, the night raids, wounded soldiers crying out for their mothers, the finality of dying, death and decay. The river, losing the doctor, and feeling his wet hand slip through mine. Gail's bullet, the dead bodies in Gilda's barn—every memory as if it were one. I wept silently, listening to the music with tears dripping off my cheeks and pooling on the floor.

The next time I pull back our tent's flap, sit on my cot and feel the warm blanket between my fingers, I'll remember this cold room, this hell, I thought, *and it will be over.*

Red put her arms around all of us, and we shared the song together, thankful to be alive.

And thankful it was our last night in Nazi Germany.

Red shook me awake, her fingers digging into my shoulders with such urgency I sprung forward into a sitting position from a dead sleep. "Get up!" she hissed. "Kit..." Red climbed on a chair to see out the tiny window way up high. Roxy and Gail sat up, scooting together in paralyzed fear from the cut of Red's voice in the shadowy morning air. I clutched the bag near my waist, watching Red in a silent fury as her hands gripped the window frame and the sun rose over the trees.

"What is it?" I said.

Red turned around, hands bracing the wall behind her, her feet sliding off the chair one by one onto the floor. Her face in disbelief.

"They're here."

"Who?" I said, and I pulled Jean's sweater tightly around me. "The butcher?"

She'd covered her mouth and squeezed her eyes closed, her voice whispering through her finger gaps. "The Reich."

I jumped up from the floor to peek out the window myself. Standing on my tiptoes on the chair. My eyes barely crested the glass, watching two men in military-style uniforms get out of a car and point to the orchard and then to the house. "They found us!" My whole body shook.

"In the corner!" Red said, flicking her fingers at us to move, and we crammed together, arms entangled, feet and legs. A rattling knock at the front door traveled up through the floorboards, followed by pounding footsteps into the house. Red put her finger to her lips.

We heard German being spoken, but the words were muffled. "What are they saying?" I whispered to Gail, but she only shook her head. Then her jaw dropped, and I heard it too.

"Women," one of them said, and I looked at Gail with a hand clamped over my mouth. A pause followed, which allowed me to wonder who he was talking to, the uncle or Jean, or maybe even the children—I wouldn't put anything past the Reich.

Several minutes passed, then the next thing we heard was the frantic race of footsteps cracking upstairs. The door was kicked open, and we jumped, only it was Jean, and there was no mistaking the look on her face, which was mixed with both surprise and fright.

"The SS were here. Looking for you!" Jean said. "In the village and in the fields…" She ran to the window and looked outside, where we heard a car start up and the pop and crack of tires on gravel.

"But how could they—"

"They called you American spies," Jean said. "Murderers."

My heart skipped before thumping viciously against my ribs. *Esser*. They knew we—that I—killed him.

Red grabbed my arm. "We're leaving!" Red said, and I nodded.

"Out the back," Jean said, and we followed her like a herd of elephants down the narrow staircase. "The river's that way..." She pointed out the back door. "Take the workman's lorry at the end of the orchard. Follow the dirt road. Straight on through a few miles." We ran out the door, each holding the other's hand. "You'll hear the Rhine rushing soon enough," she said, but we were already running through the trees breaking with morning sunlight.

The lorry was an apple truck with bald tires. We ran up to it out of breath and panting, looking at each other, wondering who was going to drive. "I don't know how to drive," Red said, which shocked me because I thought Red knew everything.

"But... but..." I said, looking at Roxy and then to Gail. I'd been taught in secret—women weren't allowed to drive on the farm—my father strictly forbid it. "Sam taught me." I looked at them. "But it's been years!"

Red threw open the door. "Get in!" We piled into the truck. The windows had been left down and the interior was wet and covered in soggy leaves. I could barely reach the gas pedal. We sat, looking out the windshield, waiting for the truck to start itself—me at the wheel next to Red with the gear stick between her legs, then Gail, and Roxy.

"Where's the key?" I said.

"We have to hotwire it." Roxy leaned over the others to

pull a few wires out from under the wheel. "I learned a few things from my brother too," she said.

"Guys," Gail said, but nobody listened to her because we were too busy watching Roxy twist the exposed wires together. "Guys," she said again, only this time louder. She'd turned her whole body around to look out the back window. "Someone's coming."

We flipped our heads around and saw a car speeding toward us on the dirt road. "Hurry, Rox," I said, as she twisted and twisted wires together that made no sense. "Hurry—"

The engine started with a pop and a jolt. "Go!" Roxy yelped, and I stepped on the gas, all of us jerking forward, the engine chugging and chugging. "Go, Kit! Go!" Roxy tapped the dash repeatedly.

"I'm trying!" I said, and I punched the clutch with a shift of the stick and we took off down the road with a burst of black exhaust popping from the muffler. We sped through potholes with the clank of clattering metal both from the truck and tools left in the back. The tailgate unlatched, and we screamed from the drumming thump of apples tumbling onto the road.

"It's slowing them down!" I said, peeking through the rearview mirror.

Red pointed to a line of trees toward the river. "Over there!" One golden tree stood out from the others. *The path.* I turned sharply to the right and found smoother ground. The steering wheel rolled loosely in my hands, and I felt the road, the dirt cords, the flatness. "I see the tree!" Red said, before whipping back around to see the car behind us, but there was no sight of it now. "You did it, Kit!" She smiled, but the road felt too smooth—off—and there was a pause, a split-second moment where Red caught my eye and we'd both realized I'd driven into a mine.

Boom!

The truck catapulted forward before skidding through dirt and rock and tipping over on its side. I only heard screaming, then absolutely nothing after we'd stopped.

I tried to move, but my head felt like my brain had been through a blender. Heavy, scattered. "Are you all right?" I said, sluggishly. "Girls…" Roxy and Gail answered right away and climbed out, seemingly untouched. "Red…" I coughed dirt from my mouth and dug it out from my eyes. "Red…"

She moaned, slumped on top of me like a wet rag. I pushed her dead weight toward the open window, and Roxy reached for her arm, trying to pull her out.

"Leave me," Red finally said, lifting her head, and I saw that she'd hit the windshield.

"No," I said, and I was able to crawl out and pull her by both arms. "I'm not leaving you." We heard the long honk of a pressed car horn, and my stomach sank.

"They're coming!" Roxy yelped, and I looked at Red's face in a panic, before turning to Roxy and hurling the bag of diamonds toward her.

"Go!" I said, but Roxy hesitated, agony in her voice and in her face, as if it was the last time we'd see each other.

"No, Kit…" Roxy said.

"Roxy," I said, and she tearfully answered back. "You have to go."

"But I can't, Kit…" She wiped tears from her eyes, glancing toward the direction of the horn. "I can't…"

"You must," I said. "I'm ordering you." And it was the first time I'd ordered Roxy to do anything. "Get the bag across the river!" She turned away, and she and Gail ran off toward the river.

I hung my head down momentarily, holding Red's hand.

"Leave me… leave me," Red said, but I managed to pull her out of the truck through the window, dragging her body to a lethargic stand. She swung her arm over my shoulder, blinking, weary.

Roxy and Gail disappeared behind the tree with the flaming orange leaves, and I felt some relief they'd made it. I turned to Red. "Like old times, Red. You and me." I wrapped my arm around her waist and hoisted her against my hip. "Just you and me." We staggered out of the mine and into the grass. The car stopped at the edge of the orchard, exhaust sputtering, and I thought we might make it—the mine had deterred them.

"Come on," I said, struggling, "come on…" I spun my head around, their engine revved, and they drove straight through the minefield at high speed as if they knew exactly where the mines were. "Hurry, Red! Hurry!" I squeezed her tighter, limping, alternating my looks between the speeding car, and the break in the trees where the leaves were still tittering from Roxy and Gail.

And I realized that if we followed the girls now, they'd catch them too.

I closed my eyes briefly, tapping my heart twice. One for Roxy and the other for Gail. "Be safe, girls," I said, and a little cry came from my mouth as we collapsed onto the grass.

24

KIT

I took a breath, feeling the air expand my lungs and thinking it was the last breath I'd take as a free woman. The car pulled up next to me and Red in the grass, the tire dangerously close to running over my ankle. "Don't say anything. Not a word, all right? Nothing." I wiped tears from my cheeks and kissed her forehead. "Promise me."

The engine cut off.

"I promise, Kit." She held my hand to her face. "Goddamn you."

Two men got out, both dressed in German uniforms, green, faded, and loose. I closed my eyes as they approached— *play it cool*—only to open them when I heard the cock of a pistol.

"Get up, fräuleins," he said in thick, unmistakable native German. Only when I saw the jagged scar on his cheek did I realize they were the same two we'd seen on our first day, laughing over their victims floating down the Rhine.

Every fiber in my body felt sick. I helped Red up, and we stood like fragile half-dead beings.

"Why were you speeding away?" he said.

"We were scared," I said in German, and he glanced at the river as if he thought there were more of us, but he didn't ask. "The battle's advancing. We thought you might be Americans—we thought you were the enemy."

"Where are your papers?" he said, and that's when I knew he'd got me. All I had was the U.S. manufactured gun hidden under my dress. I shook my head as he asked about Red's.

"She's mute. Lost her hearing from a bomb blast."

He and the driver talked quietly to themselves, and I thought he might let us go. I kissed Red's forehead again, hoping, praying Roxy was now wading across the Rhine with Gail, when a hand grabbed me by the neck and pulled me forward to walk. "Go!" he said, and he flicked his gun for us to get in the car. We got into the back seat, Red with my help, moaning and still in a daze, holding her ribcage with one hand, wincing every time she took a breath.

We drove out of the field and back through the apple orchard toward Lichtenau. They talked in hushed tones, laughing, occasionally glancing into the back seat at me and Red as we bumped along the road. I didn't think to ask questions from the grass, or when he pulled me by the scruff of my neck, but in the car, listening to them chat, noticing their unkempt necks in need of a shave and the casual way they smoked, it became very clear to me that these men were not official.

"Where are you taking us?" I finally asked in German.

The man in the passenger seat turned around sharply,

emotionless, overgrown eyebrows and a dirty face. He burst out laughing before turning back around and taking a drag off his cigarette, which made the driver laugh too.

They parked outside an abandoned building near the square. I could tell right away it wasn't a police station or a German command post. This is what scared me.

They brought us to a store that looked as if it had been ransacked at one time, with only a shattered glass counter and a few raggedy chairs left.

"Sit!" one of them barked, and we did, pushing the chairs close together and holding each other's hands. I fixed my dress to conceal the gun on my leg before inspecting Red's facial wound. I applied some pressure to her ribs to see how bad she bought it while they stood outside the door with their backs to us.

Red managed to sneak a few whispering words into my ear. "My ribs are cracked," she said, wheezing, and my eyes closed briefly. "Who are they?" She paused between her words. "Why are we here?"

"I don't…" A car pulled up, and the men seemed nervous, stomping out their full cigarettes and arguing about who was going to talk. A man in a uniform and glossy boots stepped out of it. The kind of uniforms I'd seen on the newsreels—the kind I'd seen on the dead inside ambushed buildings.

"SS," I whispered, and Red sat up the best she could.

He didn't seem real, dressed in that stiff uniform with double lightning bolts on his collar. He was blond, his hair shaved very close to his scalp and barely visible under his hat. He stepped into the building with one leaping step.

He skillfully studied us as we looked helplessly up at him.

A click of his boot heels and he called for someone outside. "This way, come, come…" he kept saying, snapping his fingers, and I gulped, thinking the butcher and his crazy wife would come walking in any second, only I didn't have the jewels and when they'd searched me, they'd find the gun and would probably kill me with it.

A car door opened and shut, but I saw nobody else outside the window. The padding of feet followed a light scuff. "Recognize either of them?" the officer said, and a little boy walked in through the door, his eyes puffy from crying, and tired. Blond.

"Look at them, boy," the officer said, and when he did my stomach knotted up and I wanted to vomit. The boy from the field—the one Gail had chased after.

I looked at my feet, trying not to fidget.

The officer took the boy by the shoulders and pushed him to stand in front of us. The boy twisted his hands around in his pockets. "Make them listen to you," the officer said to the boy, and he kicked me in the shin.

"Ack!" I cried out, and a puff of laughter spurt from the officer's lips.

"Stand!" the boy barked, his voice changing from a pouty little German child into a sinister monster.

I stood up slowly, but Red sat still, holding her side, not knowing what he'd said. He threw his leg back to kick her and I yelled that she had a cracked rib, and for some reason that got him to back away. He turned around and addressed the SS officer. "She had hair like straw and was tall." He pointed his finger at me before sniffing his nose and wiping a glob of snot away. "Not short and dark, or ginger."

Gail. Red slowly glanced up at me. I wanted to crumple in relief on the ground, thank God that this boy's memory hadn't been skewed, but I dare not even move.

The officer yelled for the men to come into the room, where he scolded them for catching the wrong woman. "You're a disgrace," he added.

"Neither of them has papers," the driver said. "And... and... we found them driving through a mine. That has to count for something, suspicious behavior indeed."

"Hmm." The officer glanced at his watch and then looked out the door where we heard the eruption of incoming artillery. "Put them on the seven. Someone will figure out who they are." He tucked his watch back under his sleeve.

"There's still a seven?" one of the men said, and the officer glared.

"Get back out there and find me the real murderer." The sun slipped behind a rain cloud, and the room shrouded in gray. "And if you fail, come sun-up you'll be the ones who're dead."

More explosions. *Boom, boom, boom.* The windows rattled faintly that time.

The officer left with the boy and the others went back outside to guard the doors. Hours passed, and we were sitting ducks listening to the sounds of war drawing nearer.

"Kit," Red rasped. "I'm not going to make it." Her eyes sagged as I'd never seen and her chest huffed even more than before. I started to think she'd crushed more than one rib and hadn't told me.

"Listen, all right?" I said. "Don't talk like that. You're with me. What could go wrong?" I tried smiling, but there was nothing to smile about. The men paced outside, looking up and down the street. I wiped my eyes. "Well, who's gonna get mad at me for stealing wine, or the ration cigarettes?"

"Kit..." Red said, and she held her side, shivering.

I shook my head, not wanting to hear what she had to say, not if it had anything to do with dying and leaving me.

"Back in our tent," she said. "My army blanket. The Nurse Corps will take it. Don't let them have it. You'll freeze at night in the winter." She took a deep breath in through her nose before continuing. "And don't tell anyone I'm gone right away. You can have my ration packs. Something extra for you and the girls..."

"Stop it, all right?" I said, and my eyes welled with tears no matter how many times I wiped them. "Who's gonna kiss Jim Marshall? You don't want me to do it. I swear it, Red."

"I love ya, Kit," she said. "I knew we'd be friends when I met you. But it wasn't until we washed up in the surf together all full of saltwater that I knew we'd be *best* friends, a bond that would last forever. You can't go through something like that and not be. You're a heckuva nurse. You're gonna be okay... You're gonna be okay..."

I wiped my cheeks. "You're beating your gums for nothing, Red," I said. "Because you're gonna make it. We're gonna make it. It's me and you, Red. It's always been. Nothing's gonna change."

Rain tapped on the roof, and we both looked up. One drop became two, then three and four.

"Get up!" the driver yelled from the door. "You're leaving!"

I helped Red out of her chair and we walked outside

where they shoved us in the car we'd arrived in. We sat in the back not saying a word, and I held her close. I was glad to leave the building, and I thought I'd be glad to leave the village, but they'd driven us to a train station.

"Seven o'clock train," the driver said. "That's you." He opened the door and pulled us out.

"Where's it going to?" I said, but he only smiled, and it was coy and chilling and made me want to buckle in two.

They brought us inside where it was crowded with women and children traveling without luggage—many with torn skirts and dirty faces, heavy eyes and frightened, cowering bodies. There was no heat, but with so many bodies the smell of clammy, yeasty skin was almost overwhelming. Shoeless children clutched headless dolls, sucking dirty thumbs. I picked up a little girl, thin, scraggly, and lost between shuffling feet. The poor thing swatted at me for being a stranger until another woman ripped her from my arms, her wail echoing. "Leave my child alone!"

Red grabbed on to me, and we were pushed into a collecting line. "Where are we going?" I asked in German to anyone who might answer.

"They said we're being evacuated," a young girl said, shuffling past.

Evacuated? A rail worker handed each of us a piece of paper with a number on it, both with a four.

A guard with a rifle took over where the rail worker left off. "On the platform! Get in the compartment and shut up." We boarded by number. "Number four! That's you two." He shoved us into the rear of the train car; that's when Red started to cry, but it wasn't from her crackling ribs.

"Why didn't you leave me?" Her eyelashes were wet and clumpy with tears.

"You know why," I said, and a few women standing in front of us turned around, looking both confused and admiring as we spoke in English.

"American…" I heard in a rolling whisper.

The train jerked forward, and we swayed into each other. A puff of steam floated by, looking thicker, denser, from a train about to leave, then a piercing whistle that sounded like a kettle about to explode erupted into the air. "Where are we being evacuated to?" I said in German, and a woman with sunken eyes looked solemnly up at me.

She tucked a matted swatch of hair behind her ear. "Don't you know?" she whispered, and I shook my head. "We're not being evacuated. We're going to prison."

My mouth hung open. "Prison?"

"We were in hiding, in the woods." She ran her hand over her bruised arm, and mumbled the rest of her words with a painful cry. "They took all the women and children. Every last one of us."

The train's whistle peeped once, then twice. Doors closed. The night air faded into a dark shade of midnight blue, and the train crept slowly down the track.

"Red…" I swallowed dryly, finding it hard to even say the words. "They're sending us to prison…" Women held on to each other, crying, saying tearful goodbyes to the empty platform. "What do we do…" The glow of exploding bombs lit up the hills. Our boys were so close. So close. And the train moved east. "We're moving into the heart of Germany…"

"Listen to me," Red said, but I was near delirious. The

train slowly gathered up speed, creeping, creeping, gaining momentum. There was no way out. Red shook me by the shoulder with one hand. "Listen to me!" And I looked into her eyes, which flicked once to the left, pointing to an emergency door that had a whistle of its own, one of air swishing through an open latch.

I gasped, stealing a look toward the front of the train car where the guard had started moving through the throng of standing passengers, using his rifle to push women out of the way. "Red…" She moved her body in such a way that it blocked the guard from seeing me so close to the door. "We just… jump?" I said, feeling the flit of air through the gap.

"Not we," she said, and I looked up at her.

"What do you mean?" The guard moved closer, some girls shrieking, others crying as he backhanded them to get out of his way.

Red smoothed a lock of hair out of my eyes. "We had a good run, didn't we?" Her lips quivered.

"Red, no. What are you saying?" She pushed me gently toward the door. "Stop." I grabbed her arm, trying not to hurt her but it was near impossible. "Jump with me, dammit."

"I'd never survive a jump." She wheezed, and flinched terribly from a spasm of pain in her side. "Make it to the river, all right? Find the girls, lead them back to our field hospital. Use the gun if you have to."

She pushed me again, and I dug in, my feet sliding toward the door, surprised she suddenly had so much strength. "No! I'm not leaving you."

"You're not, Kit." She smiled, and a gush of tears spilled over her cheeks. "I'm leaving you."

And with one final push, my backside hit the door and

I flew outside, tumbling and rolling, feeling the stinging wrath of fresh scrapes all over my body before coming to a stop. I lifted my head, seeing Red pull the lethal doses of morphine from her dress as the guard rushed up behind her. She tapped her heart, as if telling me her plan, before reaching out for me in the dark.

"No, Red, don't…" The train whistled, and I screamed. "Red!"

A minute or so passed, and the train was but a speck in the night, chugging softly away. Rain spat from dark clouds. "Damn you, Red," I cried. A spotlight from the station searched the tracks, moving close as I lay on the ground. Dogs barked.

I pulled myself up—aching, hissing, and scared—and hid in the bushes. A flashlight skirted over the tracks instead of the spotlight and I held my breath, listening to two guards chat about the night. I heard their dogs whining, sniffing. They hadn't seen me.

"Next load leaves tomorrow," one said.

I squeezed my eyes shut with my hand pressed to my mouth.

"If there is a tomorrow," the other said. "The battle's advancing." And with that, the other yelled at him for saying treasonous things and stormed off. A tossed lit cigarette flew through the air, and then they were both gone. I dragged myself to my feet and stumbled away down the track and into the night.

I made the slow walk toward the center of the village, arms folded, shivering even with the sweater Jean had given me. The sprinkle turned into rain, and I saw the signage on the pharmacy, the brick façade, and striped awning. I ran laboriously the last few steps down the street and threw open the door.

The bell clanged wildly and the pharmacist and his wife jumped in place from behind the counter, taking a shocked moment to look at me dripping water all over their floor.

"Close the door!" The wife motioned for her husband who hurriedly closed all the windows and locked the front door, but not before looking outside and making sure I was the only one.

I stumbled into the store, trying to hold myself together, but when I remembered Red's face looking back at me from the train, I threw my arms around the wife's neck, sniffling. "They took her…"

She reluctantly patted my back, and I felt her apprehension as she looked to her husband for what to do. I pulled away, looking at them both, wiping my face of rain, wondering what had turned her so stiff when, despite her calls for us to be quiet, she'd always seemed to be the nicest one.

"You're not welcome here, fräulein," the pharmacist finally said.

The wife held her chin up. "You must leave." She scrunched something in her hands, curling her fingers around it so I couldn't see.

"Your American friend is gone," he said. "And we are not in the business of helping. Not anymore."

"Jack?" I said. "When did he leave?"

"He left right after you left."

I felt a grit in my teeth with this news, and resented Jack in that instant, his smiling face, and those nice words of his.

The wife moved closer to her husband when she saw my lips curl, and he put his arm over her shoulder. "No more help, fräulein. We beg you. We can't." He swallowed and looked like he was gathering up the last bit of strength he had left. "If you don't leave, we will alert the authorities."

The wife nodded, nervously clenching her fist on the counter.

"What's in your hand?" I said, flicking my chin at her, and she threw her arm behind her back.

"Nothing."

I walked closer, and she looked a little worried, eyes glancing at her husband and then to me. "What's. In. Your. Hand?"

She shook her head, and I reached for her wrist and squeezed until her palm opened like a flower. A balled-up piece of paper tumbled out of it and onto the ground.

She cried to her husband about how I needed to leave. "Now… now!" she demanded, and he shushed her while I unraveled the paper.

It was a typewritten note—a threat. "Collaborators will face penalties. The first to surrender will be the first to hang."

"Someone knows about us," he said, "and we simply can't continue."

"But the war?" I pointed into the air, toward where I saw the glow of exploding bombs. "American soldiers are practically across the river…"

"But they have not yet crossed. Have they, fräulein?" he said. "Tides of war can change in an instant. My wife is frightened. I'm frightened. They'll make us bait, put my wife on the seven o'clock if we aren't careful," he said, and his wife cried out, reaching for him and burying her head into his chest.

"What did you say?" I said, and there was a pause. "Bait?"

"The train is made to look like ammunitions cargo, fräulein. For the enemy to blow up."

"Mother of God," I breathed. *Red*. "You Germans are damn sick. You know that?"

"Get her out of here!" the woman cried, and the pharmacist reached for my arm, but I pulled away.

"Don't touch me!" I wasn't about to leave. I wasn't about to let these Germans tell me what to do. Not after what I'd been through. Not after what we'd sacrificed. Especially Red.

I pulled the gun out from under my skirt. The wife shrieked, hand to her mouth, but the pharmacist reached for it and I pointed the barrel at his face. He put his hands up. He didn't know I only wanted to control him. He couldn't know. The moment he figured out I didn't want to kill him, the gun would be useless and possibly turned on me. I cocked it back.

"You know Esser? Hear what happened to him?" I said, and the wife's eyes grew quite large. "Yeah, that's right sweetheart. That was me." I waved the gun toward the back of the store. "In the cellar." I snagged a box of gauze from the rack and a bottle of antiseptic, before following them into the cellar and shutting the door behind us.

We sat in the dim, cold room with a few flickering candles, and they watched me from the corner as I tended to my wounds on Jack's old mattress. I set the gun down next to me, glancing up at them every few seconds as I dabbed my scrapes with antiseptic and gauze, hissing and grunting from the stinging pain.

The pharmacist moved, and I reached for the gun. "Not so fast…" I said, and he backed away. I stood up, painfully, feeling every inch of my body where I'd hit the train tracks. "Now, take me to your house."

"We will not!" he said, and I aimed at his head. "Fine! Fine!" And we left out the back door for their house, which was a short walk away in the rain, even for someone as wounded as I was. A big house too, nice, just like Roxy had said, and as I suspected, they had a car. I told the wife to get in and drive, and the pharmacist protested saying she didn't know how and that he'd drive, but I shook my head.

A light turned on inside their house, and all three of us looked. The silhouette of a young girl appeared in the window. "Who's that?" I said, and the wife suddenly remembered how to drive, racing around to the driver's side door with her feet sloshing through the mud, offering to take me anywhere I wanted to go.

She pulled out onto the main road as the rain pounded on the car roof and tracked down the windshield. "The Rhine," I said. I motioned with my hand, and she sped off.

We'd passed the orchard. Explosions in the west were now clearly visible, with flames of fire and clouds of smoke. "War is coming," I said to her, but she only kept her hands on the wheel, wrapped white tight. "You know you don't have to fear us. We're liberating you from the Reich."

She stepped on the brakes and cried into her palms, the car puttering on the lone country road and the wipers moving back and forth across the windshield, squeaking, and squeaking. I rolled down the window, and the rain spit into the car and onto my face. I heard the light rush of the river over the car engine, but the area didn't look familiar. "Go!" I half-shouted. We were so close. I was so close. I jostled forward in the seat. "Keep driving! Keep driving!"

Her cry changed into a wail seconds before a mortar exploded not that far away, close enough to light up the road, and I saw the apple truck we'd wrecked and the orange leafy tree Roxy and Gail had disappeared into. No sign of the patrol. I opened up the door, one foot out. "I was never going to shoot you," I said, and she looked up, eyes flooded, and I took off running as fast I could with how broken I was.

The patrol drove out of nowhere, a revving car engine barreling over heaps of earth in the night. *Bap! Bap! Bap!*

I jumped down the riverbank and into the mud, only to leap into the Rhine. I lost the gun as I bobbed and swam, pulling myself up onto the opposite bank using a gnarled tree branch, and crawling halfway out of the water.

I spat out the sour river water, looking over my shoulder one last time at Germany. The patrol car puttered in the distance, headlamps dimming. Relief waved over me like the waves, followed by the pang of guilt and the debilitating numbness of shame. "Damn you, Red." I hit the sodden ground with my fist, over and over again, bursting into a puddle of tears. "Damn you for leaving me."

25

KIT

I lay in the grass and in the rain with my face to the ground. Tired. Dog-tired. And when I said the words out loud, I thought I'd feel better, breaking the unspoken rule of our clearing station. "But I'm not in our clearing station," I said into the ground, with the rain tapping on the back of my head.

I gave myself a pass. One pass only.

I'm not sure why I thought of Jack at that moment, but with my face in the mud and my body shivering from both the cold river water and the rain, I thought of his smile, and his drawn eyes when he said he was too injured to go with us. *Liar.* "Left right after us," I said, repeating the pharmacist's words, and with that, I got up off the ground, slowly, begrudgingly, and started the solitary walk through the vineyard where our journey first started.

How would I explain to the girls what had happened to Red? Roxy, she'd be beside herself, and Gail, she wouldn't know what to do, probably ever. And what was I going to do? The question haunted me vine after vine as I trudged throughout the night, deeper into the vineyard.

When the sun rose, I found a bandage strung between two vines. Followed by another and another up ahead. *A trail*. The sun had dried up most of the rain, and the mud started to crack, and the slosh from my shoes turned into more of a clip and slip on the hardening field road.

The yellow farmhouse I'd been waiting to see for so many miles peeked out from the middle of the vineyard like a dollop of Mom's lemon frosting, and it was a strange thing seeing that yellow farmhouse. I felt overwhelmed with having made it, and I landed on my knees.

"Mother of God, I made it," I said, and a tearless cry creased over my face. I opened my hands, palms up high, and thanked God for my life and asked him to spare Red's. "I'll do anything," I said, and I knew I wasn't supposed to make a deal with God, but I did anyway. "I'll pray every day. Here on out. I'll be a better person. Swear. Please. Bring Red back to me."

Red had resisted going across enemy lines to begin with. And when I was honest with myself, and acknowledged that she'd only gone to watch over us girls, the burden soaked into my chest like a dark stain.

"Kit!" I heard, followed by the clack of the farmhouse's front door.

Roxy. I breathed a little easier hearing her voice, and collected myself as best I could, standing up and wiping a hand over my face. Gail ran out behind her seconds later.

They paused in the grass and looked at each other when they realized I was alone. "Where's Red?" Roxy said. She looked behind me, off into the horizon as if Red was just lagging behind. "Kit?"

My lips quivered, and a weeping cry spurt from my mouth with having to tell them what had happened. I wrapped my arms around Roxy, trying to gather my words.

"She's gone," I finally said. "The Nazis took her. A train…" I told them the whole story, and they latched on to me as if they never wanted to let go, and we cried together. "She saved me, pushing me out of the train car before it got going too fast." I shook my head. "But that's not the worst of it." Crying hiccups stifled my words, and I wondered if I could even tell them the truth, looking at Gail with her lost and worried eyes, and Roxy, who patted my back and told me to take a breath to calm down.

I swallowed the lump in my throat, the hard core of it pulsating with sorrow, and I thought about telling them a lie, but Red would want them to know the truth. "The train is disguised as a munitions car, bait for our boys to blow up."

Roxy's face was one of disbelief. Gail covered her eyes, shaking her head.

"How do you know this?" Roxy said.

"The pharmacist told me," I said. "I went back there after Red pushed me from the train."

Roxy dried her cheeks. "They're German. At the end of the day, they can't be trusted," she said.

"Even if they're lying, there's still the morphine," I said. "It was in her dress when she pushed me out of the train."

"She wouldn't," Roxy said. "Red liked to think she would use it, but deep down I know she couldn't go through with it. Not with her mama counting on her like she does. Red couldn't do that to her."

My cry settled into my chest as I thought about what she said. Roxy made sense, and that little bit of hope got me to stand upright enough to walk.

"I hope you're right, Rox," I said. "God, I hope you're right." Roxy petted my hair, sweeping a lock of it out of my eyes, when I heard Jack's voice.

"Jack's here?" I said, and I looked into the field, wiping the remaining tears from my eyes into my hair where it was wet. He walked slowly through the field toward us.

"Oh yeah, he's here," Roxy said.

"Yeah," Gail said, eyes rolling.

I was glad to see he was alive and well. But then *of course* he was alive and well; he'd left for the Rhine right after we left for the butcher's. Jack smiled, and his eyes were bright, no doubt he'd been fed by the winemaker and had rested too.

"Jack!" I lumbered toward him, smiling, and when he got an arm's reach away, I hauled off and popped him in the nose.

Roxy gasped behind me, followed by a giggle, while Gail bit her lip.

"Hey, why'd you gotta do that for?" he said, but I'd turned back around to hug the girls.

"Come on, Kit. Let's get you cleaned up," Roxy said, and we walked toward the farmhouse, arm in arm, leaving Jack in the meadow holding his nose. "The winemaker's wife made a pie," Roxy said. "Not like Nonna's, no way, but a sure better tart than I could have made…"

Roxy went on, trying to pretend that everything was all right, but there was no mistaking, or forgetting, that one of us was missing.

I slept restlessly but in clean sheets. And in a real bed. When I woke, I'd forgotten where I was and it was daylight. I sat bolt upright. The last moments of my dream played out in my mind, images of me and Red in the tent, tending to one of our boys. Her red hair tucked under her headscarf, asking me what new trouble I'd gotten myself into.

"Red?" I called out, and the image dissolved like baking soda in stirred water.

Roxy stared out the window. "I think our boys reached the Rhine. We'll be able to leave soon." She looked at me over her shoulder. "We're waiting for word about liberation from the village."

The winemaker's wife came into the room after a soft knock. "Mademoiselles?" She wiped her hands on her apron, smiling, her skin wrinkly as an overcooked baked potato left on the counter to cool. She dipped her hand into her apron pocket, pulling out what looked like a handful of jewelry tangled in her bony hand. "You pick…" she said. "You pick." She separated three lockets and said a bunch of words in French, pointing, before shoving a gold one at Gail, and I understood that these lockets were valuable, probably her most prized possessions.

We were used to the villagers giving us small gifts, but this was something else. She wouldn't take no for an answer.

She handed me and Roxy each a silver one. Mine was engraved with fancy writing that turned out to be a swirly design. I held it in my palm, and it felt heavier than I thought a locket should be. The winemaker's wife smiled, reaching for the locket and showing me how to break it apart into two lockets, twisting them in her hands like popping the lid off a jar. I gasped. "Two?"

Roxy smiled. "It's for Red," she said. "When she comes back."

The winemaker's wife turned to leave. "Wait," I said, and she stopped in the doorway.

"*Merci*," I said, and she shook her head this time.

"No, mademoiselles," she said, almost tearfully. "Thank you." Then she shut the door and left us with our lockets.

I closed my eyes briefly, vowing never to take it off, pressing the locket to the flat of my chest. Not until I found Red, or she found me. Never. And that little act made me feel like someday I really would be able to take it off, and give her the other half.

Roxy had gone back over to the window. "It can't be long now. Come see." She waved me over. Smoke billowed in the sky like a brush fire. "Bastard Germans, no good rotten piece of…"

"Roxy!" I said, because she didn't just say bastard. She said a lot more. Words I'd only thought of.

"Hell, Kit. They won't recognize us back home, ya know?" Roxy said. "I don't know how to talk like I used to. I'm… changed."

"I know, Rox," I said. "Me too. I'm going to hell for the hells and damns I say."

Gail got a clean dress for me from downstairs. Such a thin little thing, and tattered, but I'd slipped it over my head and when I felt it brush against my skin, the hairs on the back of my neck prickled from the memories of the last few days. "I never thought I'd long for my old fatigues," I said. "Olive drab and worn."

Gail locked the bedroom door, and she and Roxy sat on the bed. "Listen, Kit," Roxy said. "Not sure how to tell ya this but…" Roxy reached under the bed and pulled out the bag of jewels. "Jack, well… he…" She plopped the bag into the sagging mattress gap where my body had lain, and opened the flap.

I gasped. "You still have them?" I plunged my hand into the sparkling jewels, wiggling my fingers in them. Roxy and Gail looked at each other.

"Well ya," Roxy said. "See, that's the thing—"

"Kit?" Jack knocked on the door, and I pulled my hand out.

"In a minute!" Roxy yelled, before whispering. "We were waiting for Red to tell us what to do. Remember? Back in the cave, she said we should hold on to it."

"Hasn't he asked you about it?"

"Well of course he has," Roxy said. "He thinks this is my medical bag, retrieved from where I'd buried it. I swear I think he hit his head on a rock or somethin'. We told him you had the jewels."

Jack knocked again, and I was the one who shouted this time. "In a minute!" That got him to stop, but I felt him standing on the other side of the door, trying to listen.

"Well?" Roxy whispered. "What are we gonna do with it? Gail and I talked about it. This is Nazi money. Who knows where it came from—it's blood money. Every single person they've imprisoned. Get rid of the person, and keep their assets is what the newspapers reported back home."

"I know… I know…" I said. "We can't give it to Jack. Not after what we went through to get it, and especially how we were tricked by that sergeant of his, Meyer—that's the one I don't trust." I looked back at the door and then dropped my voice so low even I could barely hear myself. "I think *we* should decide who gets it. Where it goes. I definitely don't want it to wind up in our government's coffers."

Roxy blinked, her eyes big and round, waiting for me to tell her what we were going to do. Gail held her wounded arm, also looking at me.

Jack knocked a little more urgently this time, and I closed my eyes. If Red were here, she'd tell me to make up a story. I looked at the girls.

"It *is* your medical bag, all right? The only one we have left after that hell we went through," I said, and Roxy nodded. Jack knocked again, and I told Gail to open the door and for Roxy to hide the bag.

He stood in the doorway holding a rag to his nose. A bruise had started to purple between his eyes, and I knew I'd popped him pretty dang good, but he didn't say a word about the slug I gave him. "Can I come in?" he said, and I pointed to the bed where he could sit. "Now, can you tell me what happened?"

"What have you heard?" I said, and Roxy and Gail shifted their eyes from Jack to me.

"I heard their story," he said, pointing to the girls, "right up to where you drove over the mine."

I smiled, laughing a bit. "Oh, yes… the mine. Pity you missed that. Pity you missed all of it. The butcher… the poison bullet that Gail bought…" I rolled my eyes, taking a deep breath, not sure if I could recount our entire journey without slugging him again. "Perhaps you should tell me your story," I said, and his face scrunched the best it could with a sore nose.

"I talked to the pharmacist and his wife. You fed us to the butcher and then walked away…"

He shook his head, holding the rag to his nose. "I don't know what they told you, but the truth is they kicked me out moments after you guys left, saying I wasn't welcome anymore. I collapsed more times than I care to admit finding the river, and I barely made it across. If it wasn't for the winemaker's wife and her pies, I wouldn't have the strength to stand properly. I would have gone with you to the butcher's if I thought I was well enough," he said, and I unfolded my arms, which had been tightly crossed throughout his story. "Honest."

"Really?" I said, and he nodded. It was hard not to believe him after hearing him out, especially after the way the pharmacist had treated me last night. "Then I'm the one who's sorry," I said, pointing at his nose indiscriminately. "For the whack. You understand though, right?"

He waved me off. "Sure… sure…" And he acted like it was no big deal, but I think that was because he didn't want to talk about how a girl had hit him. "I understand."

"Good," I said, and we waited for him to ask about the diamonds, smiling, looking at each other, which gave me a few more seconds to think about my story.

"What happened with the package?" he said. "Did you hide it?"

I looked away before standing up, which was my way of buying even more time. "Sorry, Jack… and girls," I said, looking at Roxy and Gail, "but I lost it in the river. Gun is gone too. One of those things, ya know? The rain, and the current. The bag slipped through my fingers like Doctor Burk slipped through my fingers." I turned to Jack after taking a deliberately long pause. "And frankly I don't want to talk about it again. We lost a member of our team, two actually, and it seems inconsiderate to bring up the package after what we'd been through to finish the job you'd started. The fact is, the Germans will never find it, unless the Rhine dries up. And you know that won't happen in this century. All right?"

Jack's face was one of shock.

"Well," I said. "Are you going to say something—"

He bolted to his feet, walking to the door with an angry huff. I looked at the girls, who shrugged, and I started to think my story wasn't good enough, that he'd seen right through it and knew it was a lie. We watched him rub his face, then tilt his head back and stare at the ceiling.

"I know it's not what you wanted to hear," I said. "Sorry."

He turned around suddenly, and I lifted my chin, fully expecting him lash out.

"I'm not mad," he said. "Not at you guys."

I slumped forward. "You're not?" I almost couldn't believe my own ears.

"It's not what I wanted to hear, you're right, but the important thing is the werewolves don't have it." He sat back down and in a surprise twist, he placed his hand on mine momentarily, giving it a slight pat. "Sorry for erupting like that, and sorry for putting you all through this. You were incredibly brave, and I blame myself for getting shot in the first place and not being well enough to go with you."

I smiled. "You do?"

He nodded. "And you're right. You have been through enough. You all have. We don't have to mention it again if you don't want to."

Roxy's face was frozen as much as Gail's, the dim sunlight glimmering off bomb haze through the window made them look even more in awe of what I'd achieved. In one fell swoop, I got Jack to never ask me about the package again.

We couldn't leave the vineyard until we got word that the nearest village had been liberated, which had yet to come. Another night away from our hospital, but a night we were in France. I used the winemaker's old medical kit to redress Jack's wound, telling him it was part of the supplies Roxy had salvaged from the river. I made him sit in their library, which was cozy with plush chairs and lit up with candlelight.

I set the kit on the side table and picked through the few items she had left that were unused. "I have to take your shirt off," I said, and I helped him pull his shirt up over his head. He only moaned a little bit, but I think he was trying to act tough, and sat bare-chested in the chair with the candlelight flickering over his muscles.

"I've seen and heard a lot of wounded boys out here," I said. "You don't have to hold it in. If it hurts, tell me."

He nodded, and I unwrapped the bandage, but it wasn't the one I'd given him in the cellar. "Who dressed this for you?" I said.

"I did," he said. "Why? Didn't I do a good job?"

Surprisingly he did do a good job, and his wound was healing and the infection was almost gone. After cleaning him up a bit with the one alcohol swab left in the kit, I rewrapped his arm. His eyes flicked to me, and he caught me looking at his chest.

I turned away, blushing. "All done," I said, and I patted his back before helping him with his shirt. He stood up and watched me gather up what was left of the kit, and I had the feeling he wanted to keep talking to me. "Yes, Jack?" I said, and his eyes trailed to Roxy and Gail who'd walked into the library.

"Nothing," he said.

"Oh?" I said, and I held my breath. The girls hugged the wall.

"Well, I want to say thanks," he said, and after staring at me for a moment, he pointed to his arm. "For the bandage."

"Yeah, of course," I said, and he left, nodding once to Roxy and Gail on his way out.

Both girls gave me looks, but it was Roxy who looked like she wanted to whistle. "I punched his lights out, guys," I said. "He doesn't like me."

"Those eyes of his…" Roxy said. "He was looking at you, and not a casual glance, let me tell ya."

"Nah," I said, but I had started to believe her.

The bombing had stopped. And the one night there wasn't any rain, we weren't out in it. By morning, we were anxiously waiting in the upstairs bedroom for word to leave. Roxy paced the room, nearly pulling her hair out, when a motorcycle motored up to the house. "Someone's here," she said, and we ran to the window to see the winemaker and his wife talking to the driver in the grass. Moments later they all hugged, and the wife waved for us to come down.

Roxy gasped. "We can leave!"

We dashed out of the room and pounded down the stairs. The crack of unfiltered daylight beaming through a lift in the haze nearly blinded me, and I walked slowly into the field, shielding my eyes.

Jack squinted, pointing into the air, and a B-17 cut through the haze and flew right over us, metal rattling, engines thundering, sending a tingling shiver up my spine. The joy I felt at seeing our boys changed into a swirl of nerves, realizing they could be on their way to bomb a baited train car. It was too much to think about, and I instantly closed my eyes.

"We have to believe," Roxy said, wiggling my hand, and I nodded.

The winemaker and his wife drove us into the village in their field truck. I'd been at the front when our boys liberated villages, but our hospital never stayed long enough to see the people truly celebrate because we were always on the move, on to the next battle. There were cheers, and dancing, and people waving from open windows, but there was also something else, something very sinister happening in the square. We got out of the truck and stood on the sidewalk. Men rushed past with French flags draped over their shoulders, shouting for the traitors to show themselves. Three women were brought out of a building into the square near the dry fountain.

"What are they doing?" I said.

Roxy shook her head, holding on to Gail. "I don't know…"

I could only stand and gawk. The villagers taunted them, and when they stripped the women of their dresses and made them stand in their slips and bare feet, we gasped.

I reached out blindly for Jack. "What are they doing?"

"We can't intervene," Jack said, turning to us. "It's what they do to collaborators. We have no say."

Gail put her hand over her mouth when they brought out the scissors. But it was Roxy who hid her eyes when they sheared the women's hair from their heads. The crowds cheered, pointed, and jeered.

"It will be over soon," Jack said as if to make it better, "and they'll have to bear the cross they sewed for themselves— helping the Germans." He walked away, but we stood in the street, watching, unable to look away.

One woman looked at me through the crowd, her eyes locking with mine. Her hair was thin, brown, and wispy near her eyes. The baby in her arms cried, and she could do nothing to soothe him. She tipped her head back, and in a few short moments, she was crudely removed of her hair.

"Ah hell, Rox. I can't look anymore," I said, listening to them goad her.

"Come on," Roxy said, and we walked down the crowded street. Numb. I thought I'd seen it all. All the war had to offer. The liberation of this village was a clear reminder that not only was there much more to come, but also so much I didn't know.

"Where are our boys?" I said, and Jack told us they had moved out, heading north.

I looked at Roxy, a breath of air escaping from my mouth. They decided not to cross the Rhine after all. At first, I didn't know if I should laugh, cry, or be glad. But then I felt relieved, thinking Red's train car might be safe after all.

We followed Jack through the village. Wine shops

handed out bottles of wine, shoving them into people's hands. Troupes of dancers blocked us on the road, children jumping and skipping, women singing. And just beyond the excitement, through the many bodies that had crowded around us, two Sisters rang a bell near a tall stone building, dressed head to toe in dusty black and white habits. A bucket had been brought out with a sign to help the orphans of the war. Passers-by dropped coins into it and what trinkets they could part with.

I grabbed Roxy's arm, startling her. "Roxy!"

She clutched her chest from having been scared. "What?"

My heart thumped. "I know what to do!" I swallowed, gathering my words. "With the package." She tried to see what I was looking at, when I pointed. "Over there."

Her mouth fell open as did mine, and after a moment on the street, with us watching the Sisters, Gail locked arms with me. Roxy nodded. I nodded. And without words, we walked toward them down the cobblestone street and up to the sidewalk where the Sisters rang their bell. I slipped the bag of jewels into the bucket.

Thump.

Our backs were turned when they lifted the bag up and looked inside, but we heard one of them shriek with joy. "That's for you, Red," I said, and we kept on walking.

"I do kind of wish we'd kept a diamond or two, maybe even those four rubies," Roxy said. "You know... a souvenir, for everything."

I pressed my locket to my chest, feeling the metal close to my heart. "Yeah."

26

KIT

We got a ride to our field hospital, but it was Jack who drove us to the administration tent to meet with Sergeant Meyer. We stood like drowned rats that had been set out on the pavement to dry. He looked us up and down, removing his reading glasses and pushing away a map he'd been studying on his desk.

"Good Lord." He looked at Jack. "Is this all of you?"

"You tricked us," I said.

Meyer glanced at me before looking back at Jack, who didn't say a word.

A girl came into the tent with a tray and a steaming kettle of tea. "You dirty son-of-a-bitch," I said, and she turned right back around.

Meyer blinked a few times, looking caught off guard by my cursing, before standing up with a jolt, pointing a finger at me. "Listen here…"

"Don't, sir," Jack said, pushing his finger out of my face. "Don't. Not after what they've been through."

I was already feeling righteous when we walked in, but when Jack stood up for me, my spine hardened even more than it had. "We lost our doctor in the river. He's dead. And Red…" Roxy put her hand on my shoulder, and I swallowed dryly. "We may never see her again."

"Why didn't you tell us the truth?" Roxy said. "Why'd you have to lie?"

Her question hung in the air, and Meyer looked a little lost for words. Gail stepped forward.

"We had a right to be prepared," Gail said. "We would have gone anyway. But what you did wasn't right, sir. Wasn't right at all."

"Yeah," Roxy said.

"Yeah," I said. "We would have gone anyway. We're battle nurses, don't you know?" I folded my arms, waiting for him to respond, but he sat back down at his desk, rubbing his head.

"I'm… I'm sorry," he finally said.

"Yeah?" I said. "Is that all?"

"I didn't think you'd go. Especially you, Kit. Not after—" he looked at the others "—what happened the last time we'd met."

"Listen. I want Red listed as a POW. All right? And promoted to increase her pay." He nodded. "And I want Doctor Burk's family given a special medal. I don't care what it is, but they deserve something more than a telegram."

"Of course," he said, blubbering. "I'll do what I can."

"Yeah, well you'd better. We have a secret me and you, and don't think I won't use it."

He stood back up. "Is that a threat?"

I smiled. "No. It's a fact, sir."

Roxy pulled the soldiers' dog tags from her dress and placed them on the sergeant's desk with their wedding bands. "Come on, Kit. Let's get out of here." And all three of us turned on our heels, but before we could leave, Meyer spoke up.

"Did you get the package?"

I looked over my shoulder, pausing. "Yeah. We did." And we walked out of that tent, leaving Jack to explain how I'd lost it.

"Do you think he'll believe you really lost it?" Roxy asked once we were outside.

I shrugged one shoulder. "Doesn't matter." I looked at her. "Does it?"

Moments later Jack emerged from Meyer's tent to drive us around our field hospital to our nurses' tents, looking a little washed up and drained from what I was sure was a doozy of a conversation. I didn't ask how it went, because I didn't care.

He opened the jeep door for me, and I stopped, looking at him and then to the seat that awaited me.

"Thanks," I said, and I got into the jeep, making eyes at Roxy and Gail.

"Opening a door for a woman," Roxy said, climbing in the back. "Out here? In the war?" She whistled.

Jack pulled up near the mess tent and while the others got out, he walked around to open my door again. We stared at each other for a moment, with his hand still on the door. "Will you... ahh..." He looked at his feet when he talked.

"Oh, here it comes," Roxy said as she passed. "Spill it will ya, Jack? We have a war to get to."

He cleared his throat first. "Kit," he said, looking up.

"When this war is over, would you have dinner with me? At a real restaurant with forks and nice plates."

I laughed. "I socked you in the nose, Jack." He looked a little embarrassed, and that's when I realized he *really* did like me. "Yeah, Jack," I said. "I'll have dinner with you." I almost told him I thought about our time in the cellar while we were separated, and that it gave me hope when I was at my lowest, but then decided to keep that to myself.

I kissed his cheek.

"What'd I do to deserve that?" he said.

I smiled. "Maybe one day I'll tell you," I said, and I turned to walk away when he called out to me.

"Kit. Listen," he said, "I'll do everything I can to find Red."

"Thanks, Jack," I said, and Roxy hooked my arm, and together with Gail, we started the slow walk back to our tent and past nurses washing their hair.

Nosy Noreen lifted her head from her helmet, suds in her hair, one eye closed from the sting of the soap. "Where have you been?" she said, but we didn't answer.

"They're back," I heard, followed by, "They look awful!"

"Hey, where's Red?" one said, but we kept walking, not even a glance in their direction, when all of a sudden Benny the photographer snuck up behind us.

Flash!

I snatched the camera from his hands, gritting my teeth and squeezing the strap, thinking about chucking it over our tent. "Here!" I shoved it into his chest when he cowered. "Damn you, Benny. Can't you tell we're not in the mood for photographs?"

"Yeah, sure, all right, Kit," he said. "Whatever you say."

Noreen shook out her wet hair, standing next to Benny. "Why are you wearing dresses?" Her little nose turned up. "You girls are up to something."

"What did you say?" I said, and I took a pointed step toward her.

"Kit," Gail said. "She's not worth it."

"I know you've been in our tent," I said, "and if you ever come in here again, I'll... I'll—"

"You'll do what?" Nosy folded her arms. "You've been missing for days. And why are there only three of you?"

My heart raced at hearing her voice, having her question us. Roxy forcefully turned me around and pushed me to walk toward our tent. "Buzz off, Nosy!" Roxy said to her over her shoulder, before tuning to me. "You gonna be all right, doll?"

"I don't know, Rox," I said, and I felt a raindrop on my arm. "I'm feeling all sorts of things, and being back at our tent, it feels..." My hands shook out in front of me as more raindrops fell.

"You ready to go in?" Roxy said, and after staring at the closed tent flaps for a second, I nodded, but I still wasn't ready. I didn't think I'd ever be ready. She pulled the tent flaps back and I took a step inside with Gail.

Red's blanket was still folded where she'd left it on her cot, her ration packs still unopened, and mail from her mother bundled with brown string lay at the foot of her mattress.

"Don't touch anything," I said.

"But we'll be bivouacking soon," Roxy said.

"Just don't touch anything, all right?" I sat down on her cot, feeling her thin mattress under me.

"I can still smell her," Roxy said. "She's everywhere in this tent, Kit."

"I know," I said. "I smell her too." And I did, like a ghostly memory of what used to be, a nauseating reminder of the love we had for her.

Roxy found our dog tags where we'd left them. I picked up the box of letters I'd written to Nurse Blanchfield and flipped through the pages. So many complaints. So many stupid remarks. None of it mattered. None. I threw the box against the side of the tent and letters flew up into the air.

Roxy and Gail sat down, each slipping their tags over their heads.

"Kit…" Roxy said.

I walked around, one hand on my hip, closing my eyes and feeling the pounding throb of a migraine, seeing Red on the train, a darkened figure with the glow of the interior light casting on her hair. Her hand tapping her heart.

"She didn't use it," Roxy said, and I stopped pacing. "I feel it."

"We have to hope," Gail said. "It's all we have now."

"Yeah." I lowered myself onto Red's cot. "Hope." I slipped my dog tags over my head and held Red's tags in my hand. "What's that we always say?" I said, but I knew. "We have to believe?"

"Yeah, Kit," Roxy said. "We have to believe."

We hugged, all three of us, and wept. We wept for Red, what we'd been through, and because we were the lucky ones who narrowly survived. Our lockets dangled from our necks, clinking up against each other as we hugged. Three. When there should have been four.

And somewhere in between the sobs, we made a promise

to never talk about what happened during those five days in September.

We packed up that day and moved north to Nancy and then on into Luxembourg, picking up our lives in the field as if we'd never left. Meyer arranged for news to spread that Red and Doctor Burk had been transferred to explain their absences. That was the hardest part—acting like nothing had happened, as if those five days in September didn't exist. On the outside, I was the competent, calm nurse Red had taught me to be, but on the inside, I was plagued with the constant, nagging question of where she was, and what happened to her, steering my thoughts and haunting my days and nights.

In October, we'd stopped setting up Red's cot, and shared the responsibility of caring for the brown box that held the last of her things. Eventually, the Nurse Corps sent her belongings home to her mother along with her dog tags. By December, the Battle of the Bulge had sent us more wounded and casualties in a single day than I'd seen in all the days since landing on the beach. The rain still hadn't stopped; everything and everyone was wet. However, we were now very used to life on the battlefield, and did what any good nurse would do—what Red would do—and carried on.

A soldier with his arm blown to bits was brought into our clearing tent. "How old are you, soldier?" I asked, moving the examination light closer to his eyes, which were crystalline as glass, beautiful, yet forever tormented.

"Twenty-two, ma'am," he said. "Am I gonna live, ma'am?"

I took a good look at where a German bullet had punctured his flesh and ripped it open like an overcooked hotdog. "Absolutely," I said, rolling up my sleeves.

"Are you sure?" he said, still worried.

Roxy leaned in. "Ya, she's sure. Kit here, she never lies. She's from Washington." She handed me her forceps. "You'll be holding your sweetheart's hand in no time, let me tell ya."

The boy had gotten it with a wooden bullet, soaked in something pink. No doubt poisonous, but it hadn't split like it was intended. "How do you know?" he said. "The medic said it could be poison."

"It is poison." Gail was about to stick him with morphine, but held up her arm instead, showing him her pink scar. "But look," she said. "I bought one too once, and I survived. Now they call me Bullet."

The soldier smiled after Gail stuck him with some morphine. "Thank you, ma'am. Bastard Germans," he murmured, but then apologized for saying bastard in front of Gail.

Roxy leaned over and kissed his forehead as his eyes got droopy with morphine.

He would survive, but whether or not he could use that arm in the future we had no way of knowing. Gail had gotten lucky with only losing the movement of her pinkie, which she kept hidden from our new surgeon; otherwise, she'd be sent back to General.

A jeep pulled up outside in the mud and rain. I heard raised voices, someone asking for me, then Jack blew through our tent flaps, half smiling, half shocked. "Kit..." The surgeon barked at him to leave, and he did, but not without leaving me in a panicked state. I quickly sewed the boy up and sent him to evac.

I looked at Roxy, whose eyes had gotten big. "Do you think?" I said.

"I don't know," Roxy said.

I pulled my cap off and twisted it in my hands. "Could it be…" I swallowed. "Could it really be?" I watched the closed tent flap carefully, hearing Jack's footsteps sloshing around in the mud on the other side.

"You can come in now," Roxy said, throwing open the flaps, and I expected him to rush into the tent, but instead he walked in cautiously. He took off his dripping hat, and my stomach dropped. I felt behind me for the nearest cot to sit down and immediately began to sob, covering my face.

"Would you get a load of that," Roxy said, and I looked up.

A man. Heavily bruised, rough and haggard.

"Sam?" I think my heart stopped because I didn't feel it beating. I stood up, and he rushed over to me for an embrace. It took a few seconds to breathe, then I sobbed into his shoulder.

Sam pulled me back. "Hey ya, sis."

"Hey ya, back," I said, and we hugged again, knowing he'd never know how close he'd come to dying at the hands of the resistance. I looked over his shoulder as he hugged me, at the open tent flaps with the rain spitting in, and for the first time I stopped waiting for Red to walk through them, and looked toward the ceiling and the heavens, clutching the locket with her half, and thanked her for my brother's life, and mine.

27

EVELYN

I stood in front of the mirror in our hotel in Atlanta, feeling out the itchy skirt suit I'd bought for my interview. It was the perfect shade of pink, and something I imagined Gail wearing. Jack noticed how uncomfortable I was.

"I don't know why you packed a skirt," Jack said. "You hate skirts. In fact, I can't remember the last time I saw you in a skirt. Maybe at our wedding—wait, that was a dress. That probably doesn't count."

I sucked in my gut, twisting the skirt around, but I still didn't feel comfortable. I exhaled, my middle ballooning. "Ah hell, I should have brought pants."

"It's not too late," he said. "I can run down to the shop in the hotel lobby."

"No..." I said, still looking at myself in the mirror. I'd cut my hair into a nice bob, and dyed it dark brown, covering all my gray. At least I had that.

Jack pulled back the window curtains to look at the

parking lot below where guests had started to arrive for the reunion. "Too bad you didn't bring your uniform."

I laughed. "My fatigues?"

"I'm serious," he said, pointing out the window. "Look…"

Little old ladies walked across the parking lot in their white dresses and blue cape uniforms, arms hooked on young men, probably their sons, helping them inside the hotel, patriotic red, white, and blue corsages pinned to their lapels. My mouth hung open.

A knock at the door brought in Michelle and her husband. I had told her about the beach landing, how I met her dad during the war, and just before we left Washington for the reunion, I told her about those five days in September. Well, as much as I was willing to speak out loud before the interview. She was surprised, to say the least, and took it all in without saying a peep. When I was finished, she wrapped her arms around me and cried. But it was a good cry, saying she understood me more than she ever had before, and she welcomed me home, and it was the first time I'd heard those words—welcome home—and started to feel like I was.

"Your mom doesn't like her outfit," Jack said.

"Actually, I have something," Michelle said, wincing slightly, holding up a bag. "I hope you don't mind."

"What is it?" I said.

"I did some research and I heard some of the women were going to be wearing their old uniforms." Michelle set the bag on the bed and pulled out my old fatigues, olive drab button-fly pants and matching faded shirt.

My jaw dropped. "How did you find these?"

"Dad said you had a box in the cellar with some of your old things," she said.

I shook my head after staring at the button-fly pants. "I can't wear this."

Michelle held the shirt to my shoulders until I took hold of it myself. "Why not?"

I looked in the mirror, the olive drab color contrasting with the pink suit beneath it.

Michelle pulled a pair of shiny boots from the bag. "And I bought these. In case." She looked at my patent-leather heels but flicked her hand at my uniform. "Clicky shoes wouldn't go with this outfit."

I smiled. "Fatigues, dear. They're called fatigues." I closed my eyes briefly, still holding the shirt to my shoulders. "I can't believe I'm about to say this, but I think I will wear them." I slipped into the bathroom to change, tearing off my pink suit as quickly as an old lady could without pulling a muscle. One foot after the other I put my old fatigues on, a familiar feel of twill with a smidge of stiffness from age.

"God," I breathed. "They fit."

I fixed my collar and centered my locket, looking at myself in the floor-length bathroom mirror. I reached for my Max Factor face powder, dusting my nose. The others were quiet on the other side of the door, then I heard a knock.

"Yeah?" I said, closing my compact.

"Are you okay?" Michelle said, lips very close to the door.

I tossed my compact into my cosmetic case to run my palms down the front of my shirt, tucking the tails into my pants and then rolling up my sleeves where my nurse patch was still sewn. "I just need a minute."

My eyes welled with tears, but not for the usual reasons. I thought of the girl I once was. The lives I saved. The lives we all saved. It was a strange feeling to put something on after so many years, yet feel as if you'd recently worn it. I emerged from the bathroom only to see all three of them sitting on the bed, Jack with his hands folded and Michelle and her husband smiling.

"Mom, you look great!" she said, standing. "I can hold your locket for you since you're not wearing the suit."

"No," I said, looking in the mirror. "Today it stays." And while they talked about how we should get going, I suddenly found myself clutching at my locket and my chest. I turned toward the window, and Jack asked Michelle and her husband to wait for us outside. A gush of tears dripped off my cheeks onto the Berber carpet.

"Honey," he said, and I took his hands.

"I'm fine." I smiled through the tears, feeling my heart and my forehead, which surprisingly felt all right, considering. "It's just a lot all of a sudden." I'd asked Roxy and Gail to join me for the interview. They accepted for their own reasons, and I felt some relief that I wouldn't be alone, but that didn't change the fact that I'd be telling the world what happened those five days in September for the first time, and Jack, my dearest husband, he'd be hearing the truth about what we did with the giant, and how I didn't lose it in the Rhine.

"There's umm…" I gulped. "Jack, there's something I need to tell you, something that will come out in the interview."

"Oh?" he said. "Something I don't know?"

I squeezed his hands, then thought I should tell him now.

Break the dam, get it over with. "I want you to know…" I struggled, closing my eyes tightly. "God, this is hard."

I took in a big gulp of air.

"Evelyn, honey," he said. "Nothing you could say would change us. We do things in war… We all did things in that war. You don't need to make excuses."

I exhaled that gulp of air, nodding. "I didn't lose the diamonds in the Rhine," I said, pausing to gauge his reaction but he only stared. "We three decided to hold on to them, and then we…" I winced. "We dumped them in a nun's kettle in the village."

He laughed. "What?"

"We promised to keep it a secret between us three. After a while, it became one of those things that didn't need to be mentioned. I couldn't talk about the giant and not bring up everything about Red. It became a necessary evil."

He hugged me unexpectedly. "Evelyn Kit Jones," he said. "I love you. I only wish I knew so I could have seen those nuns' faces."

"You're not angry? For keeping this secret from you?" I said, and he shook his head. "All this time I felt guilty for not telling you."

"Don't feel guilty," he said. "Not anymore." We hugged again.

I looked at my watch. "We should go. I told Roxy and Gail we'd meet downstairs."

We took the elevator downstairs and waited in the lobby. Women walked in, some with canes, some in wheelchairs with hearing aids. Not all had worn their uniforms; some wore pink suits similar to the one I had up in my room. "Where is she?" I said, standing on my tiptoes, feeling the stiffness of the boots and looking over gray and silver bobs of hair, when suddenly Roxy appeared, like the parting of the Red Sea, walking toward me, smiling, and wearing her old fatigues. We instantly embraced, and the warm comfort of having her with me brought more tears to my eyes.

"Hey ya, doll face," Roxy said, and when we pulled away, she gave me a look-over. "Looks like we had the same idea with our old unis."

"The last time I wore this I was with you," I said, and we hugged again.

"Now, where's that reporter?" she said. "I need to thank ole Nosy's son for coming to your house that day. If he hadn't, you wouldn't have called me and maybe none of us would be here." She pulled back. "You gonna be all right?"

I nodded. "Yeah."

Roxy's husband walked up behind her. "Sam," I breathed, taking my brother's hand. "Boy, are you a sight. New Jersey is too far away." I took Roxy's hand next. She had found her dreamboat after all, marrying my brother a month after I married Jack.

"Are you ready for this?" Sam said, and I only slightly nodded.

"I don't know," I said. "I guess I'll never be truly ready, but it's something I need to do."

Roxy pulled me to the side to talk. "I'm nervous," she whispered. "You know your brother doesn't know all of what we did. I skipped over a lot. Another war story I wanted to forget." She paused. "But how could I forget?"

"Do you still get headaches?" I asked, and she nodded.

The din of noisy women reuniting after more than forty

years rose to a blaring level, people recognizing each other despite the decades that had passed and the wrinkles that had set into each and every one of our once plump faces. Displays had been set up, old tents complete with cots, and the old medical supplies we'd used—looked like the organizers stole it from the nearest museum. Hostesses and ushers passed out programs, all dressed in period costumes and uniforms.

Michelle stepped forward, and it had been several years since she'd seen her aunt and uncle. "Man, oh man..." Roxy's mouth hung open. "Where'd you dig this thing up?"

Michelle laughed. "Aunt Dorothea," she said, and Roxy shushed her.

"I'm known as Roxy here. I've got a reputation to maintain around these broads." She sucked in her gut, holding her breath, before letting all the air out like a deflated balloon. "It's good to see you." They hugged.

A producer led me and Roxy to a room not far from the ballroom, where a set had been erected for interviews. Robert walked up, clipboard in his hands, and introduced himself to Roxy, who looked at him strangely as they shook hands.

"Sorry for staring," Roxy said. "You're the spitting image of your father. And your mother. A clone of both of them!" She turned to Sam but hiked her thumb at Robert, mouthing her shock.

"And the others?" Robert said to me. "Red and Gail. When you telephoned, you said the girls would be joining you."

Roxy spun around; her eyes as wide as I'd ever seen them. "Red?"

"They're next," a producer said, pointing at us, and Robert rushed to sit down in his interviewing chair.

"You didn't tell him about Red?" Roxy whispered, and I shook my head. "I guess they really will get an earful today. Won't they, toots?"

"I'm Gail Barry!" I heard behind a curtain, and her voice was so loud, and still prissy, which made me chuckle.

Roxy smiled. "She's here!"

Gail walked in, brassy hair feathering around her face, throwing her blue cape over her shoulder. She smiled the instant she saw us, and we squealed like little girls before hugging, all three of us. Then we cried. Neither of us had seen Gail since we left the Corps, only kept in touch through our Christmas greetings and an odd letter here and there.

"You two are going to ruin my makeup," Gail said, wiping tears away, but still smiling.

"I can't believe you still had this cape," I said.

Gail laughed. "I thought it'd be cute," she said. "Looks like I should have worn my fatigues."

"Trust me, toots," Roxy said. "I almost busted my buttons getting into these pants. The cape is a better idea."

We were quiet for a moment after our private little reunion, looking at the set, and at the four chairs that had been brought over when there were only three of us.

"Are we really going to do this?" Gail said. "I never thought I'd see the day."

"I have to, Gail," I said, just as her husband Carl had come in and put his hands on her shoulders, giving her a quick kiss on the cheek before joining Sam and Jack. Gail and Carl married not long after the war, but she kept her maiden name. They met during the Battle of the Bulge; he was the new surgeon assigned to our unit.

"I know you do, Kit." Gail took a deep breath. "Truth is, so do I. Carl doesn't know the half of it. The war wasn't something we wanted to talk about." She rolled up her sleeve, showing us her jagged white scar on crepey skin. "But the truth is, I got a counselor not long ago and I noticed I started to feel better talking about it."

"Same," Roxy said, just as Robert called us over.

We sat down next to each other. The lighting technician repositioned a spotlight, centering it on us three, and I closed my eyes from the intense brightness of it. When the television camera zoomed in, my heart raced and my neck got warm. I felt the locket against my chest under my fatigues before reaching for Roxy's hand, and then Gail's with the other. All the tension, all the worry, all the fright I'd been carrying in my shoulders, in my head, in my mind, expelled from my body with one deep breath.

There was no going back now.

"It was a pleasure serving with you ladies," I said, turning to each of them. "I'd never said it before, and I want you to know."

They each nodded, pulling tissues from their pockets. Robert sat across from us, notes in hand, with a producer powdering his nose. He told us how portions of our interview would be played during the dinner program, and how the rest would be featured on television. I nodded, understanding that everything I said wouldn't be retractable.

"And Red?" he questioned, looking at the fourth, empty chair.

"Are we starting?" I said.

"Oh…" Robert shuffled through his notes. "Yes, I suppose so." He turned to the cameraman. "Are we ready?" he said, and the cameraman nodded. Robert smiled into the camera. "Here we are with Evelyn "Kit" Jones and Dorothea "Roxy" Anderson and Gail "The Bullet" Barry, battle nurses from the 45th…" He looked at us three. "There is another nurse, one who served with you. Can you tell me about her?"

And we told our story. For the first time ever, and in painstaking detail. By the end of it, every producer in the room was speechless, mouths drawn, some having to sit down. Robert never asked a second question. Didn't have to.

Some had applauded when Roxy talked about going back at night to retrieve the soldiers' dog tags in Lichtenau, then there were gasps when Gail told them about the tea. But there was stunned silence when I told them about Red, and what she'd done for me.

"Not a day goes by I'm not reminded that my life had been spared, and yet another was taken," I said. "She was my friend. Red was her nickname, but her real name was Grace Turnbow. And if you were to look up what "grace" meant in the dictionary you'd find her picture. Because I'd never known a greater woman, a greater person on this earth who would lay down their life for a feisty little pipsqueak from Washington State." I wiped my eyes of tears after looking at Michelle and Jack. "Because of her, I had a life."

Roxy nodded, and so did Gail, pressing tissues to their eyes.

"She saved us all in one way or the other," I said. "I tried finding her mother after the war, but I never could. I thought she must have succumbed to a broken heart after receiving Red's dog tags in the mail along with her belongings."

A producer walked up to Robert and whispered urgently into his ear, flipping through the notes on her clipboard before turning to me. "Mrs. Jones," the producer said, "what did you say her name was?"

I wiped my dribbling nose with a tissue. "Grace Turnbow, she was the greatest—"

"Are you sure?" the producer said. "From Oklahoma?"

I scooted up in my seat after a pause. "Yes." Roxy and Gail both squeezed my hands. "Why?"

She whispered again to Robert, pointing to something she had written down before Robert took the clipboard himself, looking a little lost for words, staring at me.

"Evelyn," he said, gulping. "Grace Turnbow—Red—she was rescued from a POW camp in 1945. In Germany."

"What? What are you saying?" I said.

"Evelyn," he said. "Red's alive."

Roxy stood up. "If this is some kind of cruel joke, I'll… I'll…"

Robert shook his head. "It's not a joke. In fact, she's not just alive. She's here!" he said, and I fainted into a wrinkled heap onto the floor.

I woke to Roxy fanning me with her folded program, and Gail checking my pulse. A small crowd gathered around. Jack and Michelle clutched each other, looking down at me.

"Kit," Roxy said, sniffing. "Did you hear that? Did you hear what he said?"

"She's alive, honey," Jack said, leaning down. "She's alive," he said, only this time his voice wavered, and I knew what I'd heard was for real.

"Where... where..." I said as Jack helped me up. My head was still light and my legs wobbly. Gail took my hand, and Roxy pointed toward the ballroom.

Robert waved for the camera crew to follow us as I stumbled off trying to find my friend.

"This way, this way," Roxy said, motioning, and my gait turned into a fast shuffle through the crowd, pushing people out of the way.

"Sorry... pardon me..." I walked out onto the stage, a blurry-eyed old woman in shiny black boots and faded olive drab fatigues. The crowd in the ballroom was a mixture of chit-chat and laughter and elevator music. I shielded my eyes from the overhead lights. "Red..." I scanned the crowd. "Red... Grace Turnbow..." People turned, looking up at me as if I was crazy. The chatting quieted as my voice rose. The music switched off.

"Who'd she say?" I heard.

"Red!" I yelled, looking into the crowd. "Grace Turnbow!" Roxy touched my shoulder, looking for her too.

Old nurse after old nurse turned to stare, the room turning deafeningly quiet. "Red—"

"Kit!" I heard from the middle of the room, and I gasped.

The crowd parted, and there she was. Dressed in a pink suit like the one I had upstairs. She walked slowly toward me. Still tall and shapely, ginger-red curls thinned with gray. I hurried down the platform stairs—*plunk, plunk, plunk*— in my heavy army boots, and into her arms in the middle of the ballroom. Roxy followed, and then Gail piled on, and we cried hysterically. People clapped for what seemed like many minutes, hands patting our backs. The music turned back on. And Robert, with his camera, was in our faces.

Red wiped tears from her eyes, touching my hair. "Jesus, Kit, you haven't aged." She looked at Gail and Roxy too. "None of you have!"

An ugly cry poured from my eyes, unable to control my emotions, and Jack ushered us into a conference room where a few of the mock nurses' tents had been erected for viewing, and where Robert couldn't get to us. Red never let go of me.

We sat down on two cots in one of the tents where the lighting wasn't as harsh, and our surroundings were quiet with the tent flaps closed.

"I thought..." My throat turned dry. "You were dead. This whole time."

"I tried to find you," Red said. "All of you. But the war was over and I went back home. Then we moved." She shrugged. "God, I missed you ladies. I didn't know what happened to you. I hoped you were all still alive." She wiped her tears with tissues Gail had given her. "I went to the library and looked through old phone books."

"Me too," I said. "I did that."

"We all did it," Gail said, sniffling into her tissue.

Red told us what happened to her, saying there was a fight between her and the conductor and she'd lost the morphine. They weren't bombed, but she was taken to a prison camp and nearly died of tuberculosis. "So, life's been hard since then." She coughed and her lungs wheezed. "I've never been the same."

"What about you?" Red held my hands. "You obviously made it through the river, back to the hospital."

And I told her what happened, how I'd gone back to the pharmacy and made the wife drive to the river, and how

I crawled through the night to the safe house. "And we told the OSS I lost the package crossing the Rhine," I said, "but that's not what happened."

Red looked pleasantly surprised. "Oh?"

"We gave it to some nuns on the street corner," I said.

Red's mouth fell open. "You did?"

"Yeah," Roxy said, followed by Gail.

"Well…" I said, smiling.

Roxy sat board straight. "Well, what?" Her eyes turned beady.

I reached for my locket, pulling it over my head. "Turns out not all of it went to the nuns." I twisted the locket in my hands, but instead of splitting into two lockets, it opened up to four little rubies shining up in the dim tent—the ones me and Roxy wanted to keep but Red wouldn't let us. "A souvenir," I said. "You know… for the trouble."

Red smiled. "You don't say?"

"Evelyn Kit Jones," Gail said, mouth hanging open.

I handed each girl a ruby.

"You've been saving them all this time, doll?" Roxy said. "All these years?"

I shrugged. "Yeah." I thought about all those visits to the library, looking through old phone books and cold calling every Turnbow in the state. "I guess deep down I never gave up hope. You know? I believed."

Red smiled. "Yeah."

And we spent the rest of the night in that tent together, but we didn't talk about the war like you'd think.

We talked about our lives.

Author's Note

This is a work of fiction, though the experiences the characters had in the Nurse Corps, starting with their arrival on the SS *Pendleton* four days after D-Day, was inspired by the numerous diaries and interviews I read from WWII nurses who served on the front lines. I took great care in the setting, trying to create a plausible nursing environment for Kit, Red, Roxy, and Gail, but of course took certain liberties when necessary to create a compelling story.

When I read a historical novel, I like to know what inspired the author. Here are a few tidbits I think you might find interesting. The idea for Evelyn's postwar story came to me after I read about a WWII nurse whose doctor called her a liar after she described symptoms of post-traumatic stress disorder. She was left feeling hopeless during a time when little was known about PTSD; I can only imagine how devastating that would have been.

The setting. The Battle of Arracourt ticked all the boxes, from the location, the timing, to the pause in fighting, which made it possible for my characters to disappear for a few days. What sealed the deal for me was when I read that an uncooperative high-ranking SS officer had been brought into one the clearing stations. My writer's mind went rampant with what-ifs, imagining all that could have happened when the army realized who they had in their hands.

The Nazi war chest. This was very interesting to learn about. One rumor I read was that it was quartered and split, loaded onto train cars, and sent into the Alps. Another rumor was that a portion of it was sent to Bavaria, thought to fund the postwar resistance army being trained in Aachen (Werewolves of Aachen). When I learned this, the pieces for my story started to fall into place.

This story is different than my other books, but also similar. Each woman had their own reasons for joining the Nurse Corps, and each woman had something to lose and something to gain by going on a dangerous mission across enemy lines. This is, as I said, a work of fiction, though I hope through this story, we can celebrate and recognize the bravery and heroism of the real nurses who served. They were the brave ones. They were the heroines.

I hope you enjoyed my story! Thanks for reading.

Acknowledgements

This novel would not have been possible without my husband and two kids, who are a constant source of love and support. Thank you to my agent, Kate Nash, who loved this book the moment I pitched it, and encouraged me to write it. Thank you to my editor Hannah Smith, and the wider team at Aria Fiction, for giving this novel a home. Hannah, editor extraordinaire, your feedback and advice has elevated my writing and made my novels shine; I'm forever grateful.

A writer needs a tribe to survive, and I have one of the best, most supportive tribes ever. After I completed the first draft of this book, I shared it with one person, which feels a little like walking outside with only your underwear on. That person was fellow writer Paula Butterfield. Thank you for always reading my work, sometimes at a moment's notice, even when you have your own pages to work on. I'd go crazy without my writers' group: Sandy Barker, Fiona Leitch and Nina Kaye. I talk to them daily, and I can't tell you how much a writer needs that. Writers Terry Lynn Thomas, Aimee Brown, Carmen Radtke and Marie O'Halloran are always there for writerly questions—and when I say always "there," I mean within seconds. Thank you to my friend Alisha who connected me with the most amazing sensitivity reader for this novel. Katrina, thank you so much! You took time to read my book during one of the busiest times of year, and you gave me valuable feedback. To the readers, thank you for buying my books and allowing me to call this my job.

Last but not least, thank you to my parents, my sister, my in-laws, and my extended family who are the first ones to pre-order my books and quite possibly own more physical copies than me. A special shout-out goes to my dad, who talked to me at length about the sounds of war and helped me perfect one sentence in particular that took over a half hour to write.

About the Author

ANDIE NEWTON is the USA Today bestselling author of *The Girl from Vichy*, and the author of *The Girl I Left Behind*. Andie holds a Bachelor degree in History and a Master in Teaching. She would love to say she spends her free time gardening and cooking, but she's killed everything she's ever planted and set off more fire alarms than she cares to admit. Andie does, however, love spending time with her family, trail running, and drinking copious amounts of coffee.

Facebook: fb.me/newtonauthor
Twitter: @andienewton
Instagram: @andienewtonauthor